LOST CITY

JEFFREY POOLE

Jeffrey Poole's Epic Fantasy Books
Bakkian Chronicles:
The Prophecy
Insurrection
Amulet of Aria
Disneyland Debacle (short story)
Winter Wonderland (short story)

Tales of Lentari
Lost City
Something Wyverian This Way Comes
A Portal for Your Thoughts
Thoughts for a Portal
Wizard in the Woods
Close Encounters of the Magical Kind
The Hunt for Red Oskorlisk (short story)
May the Fang be With You (Pirates trilogy #1)
The Hammer is Strong with This One (Pirates #2)
These are Not the Stones You're Looking For (Pirates #3)
Blast from the Past

Dragons of Andela
Harness the Fire
Strike the Spark
Clear the Water

Mysteries by J.M. Poole
The Corgi Case Files Series
18 delightful cozy mystery novels featuring corgi
sleuths, Sherlock and Watson

LOST CITY

Tales of Lentari, Book 1

JEFFREY POOLE

Secret Staircase Books

Lost City
Published by Secret Staircase Books, an imprint of
Columbine Publishing Group, LLC
PO Box 416, Angel Fire, NM 87710

Book layout and design by Secret Staircase Books
Interior illustrations created by Brett Gable, used with permission.
First Secret Staircase paperback edition: July, 2023

First Secret Staircase e-book edition: July, 2023

* * *

Publisher's Cataloging-in-Publication Data

Poole, Jeffrey
Lost City / by Jeffrey Poole.
p. cm.
ISBN 978-1649141323 (paperback)
ISBN 978-1649141330 (e-book)

1. Lentari (Fictitious location)—Fiction. 2. Epic fantasy fiction
3. Dragons and mythical creatures—Fiction. I. Title

Tales of Lentari : Book 1.
Lost City
Poole, Jeffrey, Bakkian Chronicles epic fantasy series.

BISAC : FICTION / Fantasy/Epic.

813/.54

For Giliane —

This story wouldn't be here without you. I absolutely LOVE it when you say,
"I've got a great idea for a book!"

What else you got lined up in there?

ACKNOWLEDGMENTS

I have a long list of people to thank for helping me with this book. First and foremost, I have to thank my wife. Not only does she suggest ideas for stories, she also proofreads my work, points out problems, and then helps me fix the problems! Nothing makes me smile more when she asks me if I have my notebook handy as she has a couple of ideas.

Second, I'd like to thank all my beta readers. You guys rock! Taking the time out of your busy schedules just to help an author with his book says volumes to me. Giliane, Jamie (Lia), Diane, Scott Poe, Raymond & Kristen Baker, Caroline Roberts, Caroline Craven, Derek Pritchard. And also, to Secret Staircase beta readers: Susan, Sandra, and Paula—Thank you all so much!

I'd also like to thank my illustrator. Mr. Brett Gable, a fan of the series, volunteered when I asked for help. He's responsible for the illustrations of the hammer and the QM. Don't know what the QM is yet? You will! You can find more of their work by checking out their websites, listed below.

Once more I also have to thank the loyal fans of the series. Without you guys this book would never have seen the light of day. Your kind words of encouragement, also known as a friendly nudge to get off my keester and write more, means everything to me! Thank you from the bottom of my heart!

J.

Table of Contents

Prologue

Chapter 1 — Burn Or Not A Burn   12

Chapter 2 — More Than Meets The Eye   31

Chapter 3 — Adventurers Assemble   49

Chapter 4 — Dwarves Hate Water!   79

Chapter 5 — Twice Is Not As Nice   100

Chapter 6 — What In The Whorl?   123

Chapter 7 — Not Fond Of Heights, Either   144

Chapter 8 — Needle In A Haystack   169

Chapter 9 — Two Trees or Not Two Trees   192

Chapter 10 — Armin' The Hammer   209

Chapter 11 — Lost City No More   227

Chapter 12 — Once Upon A Nar   251

Chapter 13 — Just Say No To Bullying   279

Chapter 14 — Joyful Homecomings   308

Author's Note   318

Fan Submissions   320

Tales of Lentari #2 sneak peek!   322

Hammers are never adorned with jewels. Repeated blows will loosen any adornments.
You saw something that shows otherwise?

A famous key maker. For a dwarf.

Prologue

Sticking close to his father's side, the young dwarf peered with undisguised wonder at the workshop before them. Row after row of sledge hammers, swages, fullers, chisels, punches, drifts, and tongs hung from hundreds of pegs. Work tables, shelves of tools, and stacks of molds were everywhere. Lined up against the far wall were four gigantic anvils.

Lukas swallowed nervously. This was nothing like his father's foundry. Whoever heard of a workshop having more than one anvil, let alone four? His father's was tiny compared to these. Then again, his father made axe handles. His area of expertise didn't require that large of an anvil. In fact, it didn't really require one at all, and that was the reason why they were here.

Intent on inspecting the huge anvils up close, the dwarf child broke away from the group and moved toward the back wall. A heavy callused hand suddenly dropped on his shoulder and spun him about until he was facing the rest of the group. Two black eyes peered suspiciously at him from behind a worn leather helmet.

"Master Maelnar will be teaching us the nuances of working with silver, gold, and other precious metals," his father quietly told him. "If I can see for myself what techniques he uses when working with silver, and what tools he uses, then I might one day be able to sell something besides axe handles. Do not even think about wandering off. If you cause me to miss the part on smithing silver you won't be able to sit for a month. Do you catch my meaning?"

"But you told me you know his son," Lukas accused. "You and Uncle fought side by side together with Breslin. Does that not mean they owe you a favor?"

His father sighed heavily. "I want no special recognition. This is a skill I will learn on my own."

"If you say so, Father."

"Roll your eyes at me again and I'll smack them right out of your head."

The boy cringed. His defiant expression quickly vanished.

After what felt like hours, the boy watched as the famous key maker finally reached under one of his tables and plunked down two metal bars; one was gold, the other silver. Maelnar then retrieved several sets of tongs, both large and small, from one of the shelves nearest to him and then unfurled a long strip of dark blue fabric across the table. Lined up in a row of pockets was a set of small hammers with heads of various shapes and sizes. He slowly walked the length of the table and pointed at various hammers, explaining that the plethora of sizes was for shaping the malleable and ductile metals into different contortions.

Disinterested, the boy again decided to inspect the far recesses of the workshop. As he slowly edged away from his father, he once again headed toward the row of anvils when a commotion drew everyone's attention. Two of the smaller underlings, also known as children to Lentarians, and evidently brothers, had started brawling. Over and over, they rolled around the floor, arms wrapped around the other, as each tried to pin his opponent to the ground.

The boy watched as his father and several adults tried to separate the two brothers. The distraction was all he needed to slip quietly away to admire the workshop's many features at his own leisure. While everyone focused on separating the two fighters, the child walked around the closest anvil and silently noted its dimensions.

He was aware of the quarrel behind him, but he continued to ignore it. The workshop and all its fascinating treasures were what demanded his attention. Someday he hoped to have a workshop as impressive as the one he was now in. Lukas tried to catalog the various tools on the walls, but there were just too many tongs and hammers. Wouldn't it be great if someday his own workshop had so many tools that even he didn't know how many…

Something slammed into him and threw him off balance. It was one of the brawlers, having been shoved across the room by his brother. Off balance, eyes open wide with fright, Lukas flailed his arms in an attempt to avoid tipping over backward. Directly behind him was the red hot furnace and there was nothing to arrest his fall.

Chapter 1 — A Burn or Not a Burn

Metallic clangs echoed noisily off the stone walls as an adult dwarf hammered mercilessly on a long thin strip of metal. Rotating the metal rod so that the flattened side was now facing up, the hammering began anew. On and on, the dwarf pounded away on the anvil. Hefting the heavy black hammer easily, the dwarf paused to wipe his forearm along his sweaty brow. Giving the strip of metal an angry scowl, and a rather fierce shake, the hammering began again.

Lukas appeared in the doorway, arms laden with scrolls and books. Depositing the load on a table already covered with metal shavings, small hammers, and several tiny files, the child quietly watched as his father continued to pound the same piece of metal over and over. After waiting a few moments, the boy cleared his throat. The relentless clanging finally ceased.

"Is it finished?"

Silence.

"How does it look?"

"Terrible."

"May I see it?"

"No. There's nothing worth looking at. I've already melted it back down."

"Didn't you say you'd get a second opinion before any drastic action was taken?"

"Trust me, it was terrible."

"Still having trouble with the hammers?"

"Really? What gave you that idea?"

The child stooped to pick up several small hammers that were on the floor.

"I doubt these fell off the table of their own accord," the boy observed, ignoring his father's sarcasm. "Only the hammers found their way to the floor. No tongs, no files, and no scraps. Therefore, I would deduce that you might be having difficulty with the —"

"I already know what I'm having difficulty with," Venk snapped. Twisting around to grab one of the diminutive hammers, he gestured angrily at his son. "Look at this thing! My hand is too big to wield this properly."

"What type of hammer is that?"

"Lukas, I know you know what type it is," Venk said in exasperation. "I do not need you to test me to see whether or not I know their nature."

"Father, is this hammer for planishing, embossing, raising, or riveting?"

Sighing, Venk took the tool and felt the hammer's head. The hammer was two-sided; one head was flat and the other was domed.

"Raising."

Lukas looked down at the hammers he was holding and selected one with two flat surfaces, one smaller than the other. He held it out to his father.

"*This* one is a raising hammer. *That* one is an embossing hammer."

Venk studied the two hammers. "The one with the rounded end is for embossing?"

"Aye. The raising hammer should be used first, to get the silver into the shape you want it to be. The embossing hammer is used to smooth the surface."

"That explains all the blemishes. Wizards be damned. When did you become an expert on silversmithing?"

"When I read the books that Master Maelnar recommended. All of them."

"Books are for scholars. You learn by getting your hands dirty."

Lukas smiled. "After six months one would think your hands would be dirty enough."

"Do not start sounding like Athos," his father ordered.

Changing the subject, Lukas gestured toward the table.

"I have the information you requested from the archives. Master Argon agreed to loan us everything you wanted, provided you show him how the axe turns out."

Venk turned toward the table and started rifling through the documents. "I cannot fathom who in their right mind would want a troll skull on an axe. Wait, what is all this? Lukas, what have you brought? I asked for pictures! There's nothing but writing here! How am I supposed to fashion a troll skull unless I have a picture?"

"Read the descriptions, Father. Everything you need to know is there."

"What I need to know is what a troll skull looks like."

Lukas raised his eyes off the document he was reading and settled them on his father.

"You said you fought dozens of trolls. With Uncle. How is it you do not know what their skulls look like?"

"A troll is not a creature that had to be cleaned like a fish," Venk argued, tucking a stray wisp of his beard back into his belt. "Those cursed fiends ambushed us while we were looking for the human prince. I had no time to inspect them up close when another troll was preparing to bite my face off."

"So you must have noticed how many teeth they had, how big their fangs were, how wide their mouths could —"

"Lukas." Venk sighed heavily. "I was too preoccupied to notice and even if I did, I certainly would not remember. *Help* me. Find a suitable description in that mess which tells me how to make this accursed skull."

"Yes, Father."

Five hours later Venk was painstakingly smoothing out the blemishes on an elongated object the size of his son's clenched fist. It was a silver troll skull, ready to be attached to the axe handle he had completed last month. Venk beamed. This was one of his better attempts. His customer should be pleased. The original order called for a dragon skull to be on the other side of the axe, but Venk had flatly refused. Due to recent events, his attitude toward dragons had completely changed. He had told the customer that he wouldn't dare dishonor a dragon by putting it and a troll on the same weapon. The client had finally relented, agreeing the axe would be just fine with only the troll skull on one side.

The dome of the skull shone with a mirrored finish. Two eye sockets gleamed evilly back at him. Four fangs, two upper and two lower, protruded from the closed jaws.

Grabbing the cloth he had been using to buff the silver, he applied another coat of rubbing compound to the skull and admired how the many blows from the tiny embossing hammer had practically disappeared. Perhaps Lukas was right and he should reconsider his decision to not read the books that Master Maelnar had suggested to him.

"What's that?"

His son's voice snapped him out of his reverie.

"Hmm?"

His son pointed at the silver object he was holding.

"What is *that*?" Lukas repeated, frowning at the object.

Venk proudly offered the silver skull to his son for his approval.

"That, m'boy, is a silver troll skull just like the customer wanted."

Confused, Lukas looked up at his father.

"What were you reading?"

"Eh? What do you mean?"

"Father, what were you reading?"

"What's the problem?" Venk gruffly asked, annoyed that his son wasn't beaming with pride.

"The troll skull is inaccurate, father."

"Next, you'll tell me dragons don't spit fire!"

Lukas ran his finger along the top of the troll's cranium.

"An adult troll has a bony ridge running the length of the skull, starting at the base of the neck and ending half-way down the forehead. This skull doesn't have that ridge. Unless the customer wants an infant troll skull, I would fix this."

"How do you know that?"

Lukas sighed and rolled his eyes. "I read it. From the same book I gave to you."

The child walked deliberately over to the table and reached for the open book.

"Now wait just a moment." Venk hurried over to the small work table and yanked the book out of his son's grasp. He gestured angrily at the page on the right. "Nowhere does it state that the skull has a ridge."

Lukas pulled the book down lower so that he could see the descriptions for himself. With his father still holding the book, Lukas glanced down at the aforementioned paragraph.

"There is no mention of a cranial ridge in that passage," Lukas admitted. "The problem is —"

Venk smiled. "Ha. Thought as much."

"The problem is," Lukas continued, ignoring his father's outburst, "this passage refers to an infant troll. The description of the adult skull is on the opposite page."

Venk's angry eyes jumped from the right page to the left.

"Well I'll be a son of a…"

Sure enough, the description of the adult's skull was there, along with mention of the infernal cranial ridge his son had reminded him about.

Lukas noticed his father's darkening mood and hastily pointed back at the small furnace.

"It shouldn't be too difficult to fashion a cranial ridge out of more silver if you have some left in the smelter."

With a scowl, Venk donned his thick leather gloves and pulled out the tiny pot of molten silver. His son was right, of course. It shouldn't be too difficult to add a line of silver to…

Turning too quickly, Venk stubbed his toe on the closest table leg and lurched forward, smashing his knee into a stool. Since working with molten metal would undoubtedly set any wood furniture ablaze, all of his shop's furniture was solid metal. His knee throbbed mercilessly. Venk hurriedly set the iron pot down on his workbench before any of the molten silver could spill out. Unfortunately, a tiny drop splashed out of the pot and arced gracefully through the air. It landed high on his son's right shoulder. He cried out in pain.

* * *

One week later, Venk and his son were standing patiently in the home of the clan's healer. Lukas' burn had refused to heal despite having numerous salves and bits of herbs applied to it. In fact, the wound had become infected in only a matter of days, forcing the desperate parents to seek out the services of the healer. The last thing either of the parents wanted was their son's secret "deformity" becoming known.

Venk twisted his beard so much that it began to resemble a knotted rope.

"Venk. Young master Lukas. What seems to be the problem today?"

Venk's head snapped up. Master Peridal had finally appeared. Tiny and withered, the gray bearded healer approached the two of them and eyed them speculatively, no doubt trying to determine why they required his services.

"He's got a burn on his shoulder."

"Does he now? Very well. Come with me."

Master Peridal turned to walk into his study. Father and son followed silently.

"Sit there," Peridal instructed Lukas. "Remove your shirt and we will have a look."

Lukas hopped up on the bare wood stool and pulled his tunic over his head. Peridal peeled back the bandage on the boy's right shoulder and gently prodded the wound, noting that the burn had indeed become infected. Catching sight of what appeared to be gray blobs on the young dwarf's back, Peridal slowly walked around the stool. The healer's eyes widened with surprise as he observed a large disfiguration on the boy's skin that looked as though a mass of tiny fluffy clouds had descended from Topside and taken up residence on Lukas' back. The large gray mark stretched from the base of Lukas' neck to just above his waist. Peridal turned to the boy's father.

"It's a burn he received months ago," Venk explained. "It never festered and from what my son tells me, he was never in any pain."

"Yet it failed to heal properly," Peridal observed.

"Aye."

The healer poked the boy's back in several random spots. "Do you feel any pain?"

Lukas shook his head. "No."

Peridal looked at the boy's father, surprise evident on his face. "It's a tattoo."

"My son does *not* have a tattoo. He was pushed into a furnace and the mark appeared as a result. End of story."

A corner of the boy's back caught the healer's eye. Peridal dropped down on one knee to inspect the lower left corner of the 'tattoo'. A section the size of a large pebble had caught his eye. It was darker than the rest of the mark and stood out vividly.

"This looks like a hammer."

Venk nodded. "I've seen it. It's not any style of hammer I'm familiar with. My son got the burn on Master Maelnar's forge. I figure the surface of the furnace must have had that hammer on it somewhere."

"I would argue that the mark has been tattooed on young Lukas' back," Peridal told Venk, running his fingertips along the surface of the 'hammer'. No scars, no damaged tissue, not even so much as a wrinkle could be detected. Very peculiar.

"Well, if we were to believe this is a burn, and not a tattoo, and since he is in no pain, there is not much I can do. Give it some time. I am certain it will fade away on its own."

Satisfied, Venk nodded. It was what he wanted to hear.

Peridal indicated the boy's infected shoulder.

"Now *that* is a burn. I have just the thing for it."

* * *

Several months later the neighboring city of Borahgg sent out a call for every available healer to help battle a pox that had rapidly spread throughout the population. Peridal and his apprentice were immediately dispatched to their southern neighbors. Together, they worked long hours treating case after case of sick people with symptoms ranging from simple blisters to dangerously high fevers and pustules covering their bodies. It was close to a full week before Borahgg's chief healer, Kovabel, was certain the epidemic had been neutralized. Finally able to relax, they all agreed to share a communal meal at the council chambers and compare notes before parting ways.

"It is without a doubt the fastest infection rate I have ever witnessed," one Chanusian healer noted, eliciting nods from the others. "Treat a family member in the morning and the rest of the family will become infected by midday. Simply incredible."

"At least there were no fatalities," Kovabel noted, taking a healthy swig of ale.

"There shouldn't be, not after we inoculated the entire populace," another scoffed.

Finished with his meal, Peridal pushed his plate away and pulled out his pipe. "I still find it alarming how quickly this virus spread amongst the people. I treated a young boy two days ago and within an hour the boy's sister was standing before me."

"Stranger things have happened," one of the apprentices piped up, eager to add something to the conversation.

Packing tobacco into his pipe, Peridal's brow furrowed as he tried to remember the name of Master Jocastin's apprentice.

"Indeed, young Creedyn," Kovabel said. "Just last week I treated an underling who had a small contusion on his upper arm which I thought was a tattoo of a guur. I accused the poor lad of falling in with the wrong crowds."

"I'll bet the boy's father loved that," one healer quipped, eliciting several chuckles from his colleagues.

"I think we can agree," Peridal began, slowly, "that we have all witnessed something during our careers that simply defies logic. I am no different. Earlier this year, I treated a boy for a burn on his shoulder."

"What's so remarkable about that?" Jocastin asked.

"His shoulder wasn't what had drawn my attention; it was his back. It was covered with what the father called a burn, but it wasn't a burn. I maintain it was a tattoo. It looked as though he had rolled in soot. He was —"

"Children often play in the dirt," Jocastin interrupted. "Soiled skin should not arouse suspicion."

Peridal rolled his eyes. "Care to let me finish?"

Jocastin impatiently waved him on.

"In the lower left corner of the mark there was a hammer. Not a style that is in use today, but still undeniably a hammer."

Curiosity piqued, Jocastin and several others leaned forward. "A hammer, eh?"

Peridal nodded. "Aye."

"Can you describe it?"

"It was upside-down and resting on its head. I remember seeing a jewel on the head, and a —"

A new voice interrupted their conversation.

"Unlikely. No one puts gems on axe heads."

Peridal, Jocastin, and several others turned to see an on-duty guard standing nearby.

"Too easy to be dislodged," the guard said.

"How would you know?" Jocastin asked. "Are you an expert in the creation of hammers? Have you made many?"

The guard shook his head. "I have not. But *he* has."

The group turned to see who the guard was pointing at.

All conversation died off and it became eerily quiet.

A dozen feet away, enjoying a meal, was perhaps the single most recognizable dwarf in Borahgg. Maelnar, the famous portal key maker, was staring pointedly at the group of healers.

"I have made a few hammers in my time," Maelnar began, rising from his table where he was having lunch with one of his many granddaughters. "He is quite right. Hammers are never adorned with jewels. Repeated blows will loosen any adornments on a hammer's head. That's why decorations are typically carved into the surface. You saw something that shows otherwise?"

Peridal nodded. "Aye. The hammer was resting upside down on its head. A jewel was visible on the large part of the head, while the other side of the hammer —"

"Tapered to a point," Maelnar finished for him. "An atypically small point."

Peridal nodded, unsurprised that a master blacksmith would know more about hammers than he.

"Are you familiar with that type of hammer, Master Maelnar? I have not seen the like before."

Maelnar sighed. "The description reminds me of —." One of his young granddaughters suddenly appeared and tugged on his sleeve, trying to pull him back toward their table.

"Come on, grandfather! You told me I could pick whatever dessert I wanted!"

Maelnar smiled at the young girl. "Aye, I did. I will be right there."

With a pout on her face, the girl returned to her table and crossed her thin arms over her chest.

Maelnar returned his attention to the healer. "Please forgive the intrusion. As I was saying, I remember seeing a hammer that fits the description you gave, but damned if I can remember where I saw it."

"A journal of metallurgy perhaps?" Peridal suggested.

Maelnar nodded. "Perhaps. It will come to me. Good day, sir."

Nodding politely, Peridal turned to the group of healers

as though there had been no interruption.

"As I was saying, the hammer on the —"

"Forget the hammer!" Jocastin remarked as he turned to watch Maelnar and his family disappear through the building's exit. "You spoke with Maelnar! That's remarkable!"

"So, I spoke with an affluent blacksmith," Peridal huffed out with annoyance. "Just because he is well known does not mean we should all act like fools. Are we done here? I am looking forward to returning home."

A chorus of agreement met his ears. The healers finished their meal and headed to their respective cities.

* * *

"What's the matter, grandfather?" a small voice suddenly asked him. "Are you well?"

Surprised, Maelnar glanced down at his granddaughter, the same one who celebrated her birthday earlier today. He smiled and knelt down beside the girl.

"All is well, Trindolyn. I was presented a puzzle earlier today and I am keen to solve it before it drives me insane."

The child's face lit up with wonder. "I love puzzles, grandfather! May I help?"

"I wish you could, lass."

"Maybe I can! Tell me about the puzzle. Oftentimes if you describe a problem to someone else then enlightenment is just around the corner. Do try, grandfather."

Maelnar stared at Trindolyn with a look of bemusement on his face. Since when had his seven-year-old granddaughter become so wise?

"Very well, princess. Do you remember at lunchtime when you interrupted me talking with the strangers?"

The child's face turned red. She had been thoroughly admonished by her parents for interrupting her grandfather when he had been discussing grownup matters.

"I am sorry, grandfather."

"Bah. Think nothing of it. Anyway, one of those healers mentioned seeing a strange mark on a boy's back. A boy close to your own age from the sounds of it. This mark is what intrigues me, Trindolyn. A hammer was visible."

"What is so important about a hammer?" Trindolyn asked thoughtfully.

"The hammer is a unique design. A jewel was on one side of the head and the other side tapered to a point. I have seen a hammer with a jewel on it before but I cannot remember where."

Trindolyn swelled with excitement. "I have seen it before, too, grandfather! It's a hammer from one of my storybooks."

Maelnar eyed his youngest granddaughter. "You think you recognize this hammer from one of your stories?"

Trindolyn again adopted her trademark stance by crossing her thin arms over her chest. "I don't think. I *know*."

"Enlighten me, lass."

"Grandfather, how is it you don't remember?"

Maelnar swallowed his impatience and pulled the girl up onto his lap.

"Help your grandfather out, will you? What story are you referring to?"

"The one you have read me many times."

Maelnar took several deep, calming breaths.

"Which one, princess?"

"The story of Nar, silly!"

Maelnar hesitated. He did remember that one of Trindolyn's favorite bedtime stories was about the fabled lost city of Nar.

"You think that hammer is Narian? Have you seen a picture of such a hammer?"

The child nodded. "Aye! It's in my book. The king carried one, and—"

"Where is this book now?" Maelnar wanted to know.

"My room, with all my other books."

"Would you kindly fetch it for me?"

"Of course, grandfather."

Eager to please, Trindolyn leapt off her grandfather's lap and darted away.

Maelnar leaned back in his chair behind his desk and stroked his beard. The hammer was Narian? Incredible. There had been no known hints or clues from Nar in many centuries. No supposed sightings and no new rumors had recently surfaced that he knew of. There were only a few known Narian documents in existence and all were accounted for. There was the military dispatch inquiring as to the combat readiness of the one of the two Narian armies. There was a sheet of parchment with a list of provisions. And finally, there was a map of the northwestern section of the Bohani Mountains. Thanks to that map, that particular area of the Bohanis had been searched incredibly well.

Maelnar glanced at the framed document next to a portrait of his father. That small map was perhaps the most valuable possession he owned. Everyone knew he had it, and practically everyone had at one time studied it. In the lower left corner of that document was another hammer. It, too, was upside-down.

So, what was the image of a Narian hammer doing on an unknown boy's back? He had never been a believer of coincidences. The mark had to mean something!

Maelnar tapped his fingers on his desk. First things first. Before he would let himself get excited, he had to inspect Trindolyn's book and see for himself what her hammer looked like. Wouldn't it be fascinating to discover another authentic reference to Nar and have it been under his roof all this time?

His granddaughter zipped back into his study several minutes later and proudly plopped her book down on his desk. A tattered, illustrated children's book he was very familiar with met his eyes. Trindolyn was right. He *had* seen this book many times, having read it to his own children and countless grandchildren over and over. He picked up the thin, dilapidated book entitled *The Legend of Nar* and began to flip through the crinkled pages.

> In the annals of history,
> Long has it been told:
> Lying deep beneath the mountains,
> Was a fabled city of old.

Located within its walls,
A dwarf clan held reign.
Unchallenged masters of metal,
Apprentices they did train.

Secrets of their armor,
Were sought year after year.
Impervious from attack,
From sword, bow, and spear.

As word of their skill,
Spread rapidly throughout the land,
Commissioned suits of armor,
Kings and warriors did demand.

At the height of their fame,
A catastrophe they did befall.
The city was abandoned,
By one and all.

Many have searched,
Explored realms afar.
Searching, always searching,
For the lost city of Nar.

Maelnar harrumphed to himself and closed the book. He gently turned it back over to study the cover. Nowhere could he see any hammers, just an artist's rendering of a generic city with hundreds of tiny figures outfitted in suits of armor. The city had been drawn from an aerial point of view and encompassed dozens of buildings. Also, the artist must have believed that every building in Nar had been made of solid gold as the city sparkled with radiance. Even the streets were paved with gold.

Maelnar flipped to the page with the passage about kings and warriors. The illustration depicted a king at the head of an army, presumably leading them into battle. Sure enough, the tiny king was clutching a hammer, but it was too small to show much detail.

He sighed. His granddaughter, not having much experience with hammers, understandably associated the description of the hammer he was looking for with the only picture of a hammer she had probably seen. The picture was much too small to show any—

Maelnar turned the page and hesitated. The catastrophe. This time the artist had drawn a close up of the king. The tiny figure was gesturing for his people to follow as the structure they were in went up in flames. Ignoring everything else in the busy scene, Maelnar singled out the king and stared at the tool in his right hand. It was a hammer, and damned if it didn't have a red gem on the head of it. His eye then caught sight of the king's shield.

Maelnar swept aside piles of papers and various small instruments on his desk as he searched for his reading glass. The tear-shaped paperweight served double duty as a magnifying lens as his eyes had trouble focusing on anything that tiny. Setting the glass down on the illustration, Maelnar leaned over his desk and stared intently at what he saw. The Narian crest was proudly displayed on the king's shield and was a match for the crest on his prized map. The shield contained a picture of a hammer, and it was upside-down. A large rectangular striking head, displaying a bright red jewel on its side, also met his eye. Didn't the healer say that the hammer on the boy's back was also upside down?

Maelnar tapped his fingers on the open page and thought about what he knew of Nar. Surprisingly, it wasn't very much. Everyone knew that Nar once existed but it had been abandoned by its people many centuries ago. Its location, however, was the mystery. It was said that the city lay somewhere beneath the heart of the Bohanis, but to this day no traces had ever been found. The general consensus was that the city had been constructed deep beneath a small valley nestled between three barren crags; unfortunately, no such valley could be found. The problem was the northern mountains practically stretched from coast to coast and remained largely unexplored. Besides, his people were known for burrowing through the hardest stone, so unfortunately that meant the city could be anywhere. Many a dwarf had willingly spent decades of their lives searching for, but never finding, Nar.

So, what was a Narian hammer doing tattooed on a young boy's back? There was only one way to find out.

Thanking Trindolyn, Maelnar set off to find Kovabel.

* * *

"What's this all about?" Athos demanded as soon as his brother opened the workshop door. "What's gotten you worked up so?"

"Maelnar has summoned me! He asked for me by name, dolt! Should that not be cause for concern?"

"We fought side by side with his son," Athos proudly reminded him. "Do you think it that improbable Breslin didn't mention us to his father?"

"He wants to see it."

"What? Your ax? Have you finished it?"

Venk turned and hit his brother on the arm hard enough to push him back a step or two. "Why would he give a ruddy hell about my ax? He wants to see Lukas' mark."

Athos cringed. He knew the mark on his nephew's back was something Venk was desperately trying to keep hidden. "How would he even know about that?"

"Peridal. The old fool must have told him. How or when he met Master Maelnar I cannot fathom."

Athos was silent as he considered the ramifications of his nephew's deformity becoming known.

"Do we know what was said?"

"No."

"Then there is nothing you can do. If you have been summoned to Borahgg, then you must go. I wish I could go, too."

"Then this is your lucky day."

"Eh? What's that?"

"*We* have been summoned, dear brother."

Turning away from Athos' thunderstruck expression, Venk called for his son.

* * *

"It's a burn, nothing more," Athos insisted. He was sitting with his brother and nephew in Maelnar's study while they all waited for the healer to arrive.

"If the boy did have a burn, do you not think it would have healed by now, lad?" Maelnar gently asked. "Did you ever wonder why the mark remained?"

"Father, I was never burned," Lukas insisted again. "I have been burned before and it hurts. Believe me, it hurts. This did not."

"Lukas, you are not helping the situation."

"If you are worried about what is discovered here," Maelnar told them, in a hushed tone, "then be assured nothing leaves this room."

A surprisingly young dwarf, for a healer, entered the room followed closely by two underlings.

"What seems to be the pro-"

"Master Kovabel," Maelnar interrupted. "There will be no need for apprentices today."

Kovabel shrugged and dismissed his assistants.

"You remember hearing about the boy with the mark on his back?" Maelnar asked the healer.

Kovabel nodded. "The boy from Master Peridal's story, I presume. Aye, I do remember."

"Here he is. I would like you to inspect his back and ascertain, if you can, the origin of the mark."

"Certainly." Kovabel turned to Lukas and patted the stool in front of him. "Young master, please have a seat and remove your tunic."

Lukas hopped up on the stool and pulled his shirt over his head. Maelnar got out of his seat for a better look. Both he and Kovabel crowded close to Lukas' back.

"That's no burn," Maelnar observed, gently touching the pebble-sized hammer on the boy's back. He pulled out Trindolyn's storybook and flipped to the page with the close up of the king's hammer. They were a match.

Maelnar turned to Athos and pointed back at his desk.

"I have a stack of blank parchment on my desk right over there. Could you hand me one? And the quill and ink next to it?"

Once Athos had handed the items over, Maelnar knelt down next to Lukas and tried to sketch what he saw. His hand refused to cooperate. Confused, Maelnar stared at his motionless hand and again tried to recreate what he was looking at on the boy's back. Again, his hand refused to move. Alarmed he had forgotten how to sketch, Maelnar thought back to the golden dragon sword his human friend Sir Steve possessed and tried to sketch the hilt. His hand instantly began to draw.

Certain there was nothing wrong with his hand, he flipped the sheet over and tried again to sketch the shape and design of the large mark. Again, his hand refused to comply. His eyes widened. This was no burn and this was certainly no tattoo.

"The mark is Narian. I'm certain of it."

Holding the open storybook close to Lukas' skin as he inspected the hammer, the book slipped out of his grasp and started to fall. Belying his age, Maelnar deftly caught the book before it could hit the ground, but not before it bounced off of Lukas' back. As soon as the book came into contact with the boy's skin, the outer edges of the mark suddenly sharpened, as if coming into focus. Once contact was broken, the mark lost focus and reverted back to its previous state.

Maelnar gasped with shock. He stretched out his arm toward the boy and gently touched the book to Lukas' back and held it in place. The outer edges focused again and became a braided decorative border. The elegant frame elongated as it approached the tiny upside-down hammer and flowed around it without breaking its pattern. Within moments the mark was contained within a delicate border that stretched completely around it. There, in the top center of the border, was a prominent sign that they were on the right track. A shield had also been incorporated into the woven border. It was the Narian crest: a larger upside-down hammer sitting on a field of purple velvet with silver scrollwork.

Having witnessed the appearance of the border, Venk and Athos stared at each other in shock. Maelnar clapped a hand on Venk's shoulder.

"There's no doubt about it, lad. The hammer is Narian

and has been placed on your son's back for a purpose!"

Chapter 2 — More Than Meets the Eye

Venk stared at Lukas' back and motioned for Athos to join him. The two brothers stared a few moments at the newly revealed border encircling Lukas' mark.

"So what does it mean?" Venk demanded, turning to Maelnar as if he believed the famous blacksmith was withholding information.

Maelnar held up a hand. "I hope to find out. A moment, if you please. Lukas, I need you to recall the day you received the mark."

"Burn," Venk hastily corrected.

"Mark," Maelnar insisted, fixing Venk with a steely glare.

Venk made several grumbling noises but otherwise didn't say anything.

"It happened the day we attended the training seminar," Lukas began.

"When was that?"

"About six or seven months ago."

Maelnar stroked his beard thoughtfully. "I hold seminars frequently, lad. I'm not sure that I —"

"There were two squabbling brats," Venk reminded him.

Maelnar nodded. "Ah, yes. The only seminar I gave where I decided to include children. I remember thinking then that I probably wouldn't include them again, seeing how of the three who did attend, two got into a fight. So, young Master Lukas, can you tell me what happened the day you got that mark?"

"I keep telling my father I wasn't burned," Lukas began. "I lost my balance and almost fell onto the forge. I was able to catch myself in time."

"Do you remember feeling anything?" Kovabel asked him. "Were you warm? Cold? Did you feel anything on your back?"

Lukas was silent as he thought about that fateful day. Had he felt anything out of the ordinary?

"Nothing unusual," Lukas reported, shaking his head. "It was warm. I wished I had brought lighter clothes."

"And your back?" Kovabel insisted. "Any prickling sensations, or pain, or perhaps just a sense that something was about to happen?"

Lukas shook his head. "No, nothing like that."

"Did you witness anything that you found peculiar?" Maelnar prompted.

Lukas hesitated. "Like what?"

"Strange smells, or noises that sounded out of place, or… what is it, lad?"

Lukas' brow furrowed. "I did hear something when I went to inspect the anvils, but I paid it no mind."

Maelnar, Kovabel, Athos, and Venk all crowded close.

"I heard someone singing."

Venk appeared as though he wanted to say something derogatory, but a stern look from Kovabel quelled any thoughts of sarcasm.

"Male or female?" Maelnar wanted to know.

"Male. It wasn't very loud. I remember thinking somebody must have really been bored if they were singing out loud."

Maelnar's face broke out into a grin after he caught sight of Venk's horrified expression. Lukas, however, had been staring straight at his father when he spoke. The boy's eyes opened wide as he realized his folly.

"No! That's not what I mean! The seminar wasn't boring! I thought it was very interesting!"

"So interesting that I caught you sneaking off," Venk reminded him.

Lukas' cheeks reddened.

"What about the singing?" Maelnar gently asked, hoping to steer the conversation back on track. "Could you identify the singer?"

Lukas shook his head. "The singing was soft enough that it had to be coming from right beside me, but when I turned to look, I was by myself."

"We must find out if anyone else heard this singing," Maelnar told Kovabel. "If so, we'll dismiss it. But if not, then it must be related."

An assistant was summoned and instructions were relayed.

"As soon as you have anything, report back here at once."

His assistant, an underling barely older than Lukas, bowed. "I understand."

Venk raised a hand.

Kovabel noticed instantly. "Aye, what is it?"

"Excuse me," Maelnar interrupted, scowling at the healer at the same time, "but in my study all questions are directed to me."

Kovabel bowed low. "My apologies."

"Master Venk, do you have a question?"

"Just for my own piece of mind, could I inspect your forge?"

"Whatever for?"

"I just want to see for myself whether or not there is a symbol of a hammer somewhere on the surface."

Maelnar shrugged. "I can save you the time and say there isn't, but feel free to examine it in person. In fact, while we are waiting, let's all head to my workshop. Master Venk, lead the way. It's through that door on the left."

"If there is nothing else," Kovabel interjected, "I will be on my way. This is clearly no burn, and as such there isn't anything I can do for the boy."

Maelnar bowed. "Agreed. Thanks for coming, my friend."

Thirty minutes later, after running his hands over every square inch of the unlit forge's surface, Venk was convinced. He couldn't find as much as a slight blemish anywhere on the furnace. The forge clearly hadn't been responsible for placing the mark on his son's back. So what had caused it? Who was responsible?

A different underling poked his head into the room and caught Maelnar's attention. After handing the key maker a note, he departed as quickly as he had arrived.

"This is interesting," Maelnar reported, after he had skimmed the contents of the paper. "No one heard any singing besides young Master Lukas. However, four trainees did report seeing a brief flash of light. All four believed it was what had set off the two brothers."

"I had been staring straight at the underlings," Venk recalled. "I could tell from the way they were glaring at one another that a brawl was about to happen. However, I didn't see any flash of light."

"Nor did I," Maelnar added.

"I think jhorun is at play here."

Everyone turned to stare at Athos.

"There is no other explanation for it," Athos insisted. "My nephew didn't get burned but he has a mark on his back. Part of the mark revealed itself when it came into contact with that Narian book. This is clearly an enchantment of some sort. We must consult a wizard. Do we know any who would be willing to help out?"

Maelnar sighed heavily and rolled his eyes. Of all the infernal luck.

"Aye, I know one."

"Do you think he'll help us?" Athos asked.

"Of course, he will," Maelnar grumbled. "It'd give him something to hold over me. Very well. I'll send word to

Shardwyn. Come with me back to my study."

Venk nodded. He and the others fell into step behind him. "The human wizard in R'Tal. Excellent choice. I hear he is very knowledgeable."

Maelnar continued to mutter under his breath all the way back to his office. Grumbling softly, he reached for a sheet of parchment on his desk. He handed the message to an underling with instructions to deliver it to his son, Breslin. His son was the owner of Mythryd, one of the famous Mythra weapons. Each weapon allowed mental contact with the other two holders provided they were in contact with their weapons. Rhenyon, Commander of the Royal Guards in Castle R'Tal, was another holder. Hopefully he would facilitate the delivery of Shardwyn's message.

Thirty minutes passed before the wizard's response arrived. From the way Maelnar scowled when he read the reply, Shardwyn must have been delighted to lend his expertise in the matter and did not hesitate to rub it in.

The air suddenly crackled with power. Those who didn't have their hair woven into braids or tied in place suddenly discovered their hair standing straight up. A tiny globe of light appeared ten feet away and rapidly expanded in size. A bright white light lit the entire room for a few seconds, causing everyone to cover their eyes or turn away. The light faded to reveal a tall figure wearing gleaming white robes decorated with mystical runes woven in gold thread and held together by a blue velvet belt. Maelnar was glad to see that the wizard had elected to shave off the beard he had been *attempting* to grow. Maelnar grunted. No one could grow a beard better than a dwarf.

The tall, thin man swaggered over to the group of dwarves and bowed low.

Maelnar shook his head. "Really? Do you think you could have planned a more extravagant entrance?"

A huge grin split Shardwyn's face. "Whatever do you mean?"

"In all the years I have known you," Maelnar stepped close to Shardwyn and pointed at one of the golden runes on his right sleeve, "never have you worn such a garish outfit as that. Do you even know what that symbol means?"

Shardwyn looked down at the rune woven on his sleeve and nodded. "It's an ancient symbol of power. That one is for courage, I believe. I can understand if you didn't know that."

Maelnar stifled a laugh. "That symbol is not as old as you might think. It's one of a special set of symbols dreamt up by a group of laborers. That one means 'wash with care'."

Venk and Athos snorted as they tried to contain their laughter. Enjoying this exchange between dwarf and human, both brothers looked at the wizard to see what his response would be. Would he be angry? Embarrassed?

Shardwyn threw his head back and howled with laughter.

"That explains so much! No wonder my tailor had such a twinkle in his eye!"

Shaking his head, Maelnar pointed at Lukas. "Would you be so kind as to tell us what you see on the boy's back?"

The wizard wiped the corners of his eyes with his sleeve and approached Lukas. Still chuckling over the thought of his tailor pulling one over on him, Shardwyn knelt down to inspect the boy's exposed back. What he saw silenced him instantly.

Immediately recognizable was the large hammer on the crest at the top of the mark. If not for the fact that he had devoted several months late last year tutoring young prince Mikal about Nar, then the importance of the upside-down hammer would have been lost to him. Now, however, having read everything in the castle's library that had anything to do with the fabled lost dwarf city, he fancied himself an expert on the subject.

Maelnar tapped him on the shoulder. "No doubt you have noticed the Narian hammer. See the scrollwork surrounding the rest of the mark? That appeared not long ago when another reference to Nar came into contact with it."

Forgetting he had shaved off his beard, Shardwyn stroked his chin thoughtfully.

"A symbiotic charm. Very peculiar. May I ask which document you were referring to? I believe I have read everything which references Nar."

Maelnar retrieved Trindolyn's storybook from his desk

and presented it to the wizard.

"This."

Shardwyn took the shabby little book and made a tsk-tsk noise.

"Really, dwarf, this is the best you can do? Perhaps you might be interested in touring a proper library, stocked with thousands of *real* books and scrolls."

Maelnar pressed his fingertips together and kept his expression neutral.

"That is my granddaughter's storybook. Ever see it before?"

"Of course. R'Tal's library has an extensive selection of children's literature. Our copy is in much better condition, I might add."

"Mm-hmm. I held the book to that mark and the border appeared."

"Have you tried holding a different Narian artifact to it to see if anything else happens?"

That brought the dwarf up short. "I haven't."

"Everyone knows you own the only Narian map in existence. In fact, I see it hanging right over there. Why don't you hold it up to the mark and see what happens?"

Maelnar bit his lip as he turned and walked to the wall behind his desk. He gingerly lifted the framed map down from its holder and reverently laid it on his desk. He carefully pried open the frame and gently pulled the small map out.

"Do be careful with that," Shardwyn scolded. "There aren't many genuine Narian documents left in existence. It'd be a shame if —"

"Would you kindly hold your tongue, wizard? I know what I'm doing."

Maelnar motioned for Lukas to join him. Stepping next to the large wooden desk, Lukas rose up on his toes to get a better look at the map. It wasn't anything spectacular. The map just showed a simple topographical view of an area east of Lake Raehón.

"Would you kindly turn around so that we may see your back?"

Lukas obediently spun and faced the wall.

Shardwyn cackled triumphantly. "See? See? I told you so!!"

"What is it? What's going on?" Lukas inquired.

Venk instantly appeared at his son's side and motioned for Athos to join him. A new section of Lukas' back, the lower left portion, had started to come into focus, but only marginally so.

Shardwyn began emptying his pockets. Spells, parchment, quills, two bottles of ink, no fewer than a dozen bottles filled with various powders and liquids, and several tiny mechanical devices were deposited on Maelnar's desk.

"Can I offer you a trash receptacle?" the dwarf wryly asked.

Shardwyn pushed aside several of the diminutive machines and selected one that had a tiny pendulum and several complicated knobs and dials.

"What is that?" Maelnar asked, standing up on his tiptoes to peer at the tiny golden device.

"I call it my FJT. Foolproof jhorun tester. It'll check to see if there is any jhorun present."

Shardwyn held the device next to Lukas. The pendulum instantly started swinging back and forth, chiming every time it did so.

"There you have it. Jhorun."

"I could have told you jhorun was present, you egotistical ninny," Maelnar muttered.

"But now we know for certain, don't we?"

"Does that thing say what type of enchantment it is?" Venk anxiously asked. "And what we have to do to break it?"

"It does not," Shardwyn sadly told him. "It only tells me that there is a high level of jhorun here. And it's Narian in nature. All kidding aside, may I make a recommendation?"

Surprised by the serious tone the wizard had adopted, Maelnar nodded.

"Last year when I was researching Nar, I —"

"Why were you performing research on Nar?" Maelnar interrupted, curious.

"Kre'Mikal's school lessons. He was asked to do a report on the subject and he enlisted my help. Anyway, we discovered there was a dwarf living amongst the Kla Rehn clan in the Selekai Mountains that claimed he was one of the last descendants of the Narian people. He claims he is the best Narian scholar in existence. Self-proclaimed, I might add. Ask him."

Maelnar was silent as he considered the wizard's proposal.

"Bet you didn't think I would find a descendent of Nar, eh?" Shardwyn gloated. "He is a learned dwarf with a very keen mind."

"I'll tell Tristofer you said so."

This time it was the wizard who was shocked.

"I never said his name!"

"You didn't need to say his name."

"You know him?"

"He is the *only* Narian scholar, wizard. Of course, I know him. As to whether or not he's a genuine Narian descendant, I wouldn't get too cocky."

"Eh? What's that?"

Ignoring Shardwyn, Maelnar continued. "When he arrived in person to request access to the archives, who was I to deny a scholar? I'll summon him to see what he thinks."

"It'll take a long time to get from the Selekais to here," Shardwyn observed.

"Perhaps. In this case, however, I'll give him about ten minutes."

"Unless you have Lady Sarah tucked away here somewhere, I'd say not, dwarf."

"That's how long it takes me to get here from the archives," Maelnar explained.

"He's here? *Now?*"

"Aye. He never left."

"What has he been doing all this time?"

"Research."

"For three years?"

Maelnar gave the wizard a smug smile. "We dwarves are very —"

"Stubborn?" Shardwyn guessed.

"No. We are very —"

"Obstinate?"

"I was going to say methodical."

"What are you standing there for? Send for him, dwarf! I'm just as keen as everyone else to see what this mark means!"

Giving Shardwyn a speculative glare, Maelnar sent word for the visiting scholar to join them. He had said it would take around ten minutes for someone to come all the way from the archives. Once the scholar learned about the nature of the request, he made it there in five.

A middle-aged dwarf wearing a dark brown tunic with matching trousers, complete with a floor length khaki jacket lined with numerous pockets filled with papers and scrolls, burst into the room. As soon as he skidded to a stop, his spectacles slid down the tip of his nose and became tangled in his gray-streaked beard. As expected, he was completely out of breath. There were at least five bags slung over his shoulders into which more scrolls and books had been jammed. Every one of the bags was threatening to spill its contents out onto the floor. More than likely a paper trail had been left all the way from the archives.

"Is it true? A new Narian clue has been unearthed? Where is it? Who has it? You must show it to me!"

Keeping his face expressionless, Maelnar handed the thin storybook to the wheezing scholar who was trying to extract his glasses from his beard.

"Very well. Here you go."

Confused, the scholar opened the book as he put on his glasses. He stared at the crinkled pages.

"Is this a joke, Master Maelnar? I know you think my work is laughable, but I swear to you it is no laughing matter. I cannot fathom why—"

The scholar trailed off as Maelnar handed him his glass paperweight.

"Now I'm really confused. What am I supposed to do with this?"

Maelnar gently pulled the book from Tristofer's hands and placed it on his desk. Selecting the illustration depicting the catastrophe, Maelnar set the glass down on the tiny figure of the king.

"Tell me what you see."

"This is a children's book," Tristofer complained. "You cannot possibly expect me to think that... Heavens above, is that a Narian power hammer? Who wrote this? Why do I not know anything about this book? Where did you get it? How long have you had it?"

Maelnar shrugged. "As to how long it has been in my possession, I cannot say for certain, only that I've had it for a very long time."

"Castle R'Tal has a copy as well," Shardwyn added, drawing the scholar's attention. "I cannot say for certain how long, either."

"Who is this human?" Tristofer asked, eliciting a squawk of outrage from the wizard.

Maelnar tried, but failed, to hide his smile.

"This is the wizard from R'Tal, Shardwyn. Shardwyn, allow me to introduce Tristofer of the Kla Rehn. He has been scouring the Archives in hopes of finding a piece of evidence that has thus far been overlooked and will, once deciphered, present him with the location of Nar's main entrance. Does that about sum it up, Master Tristofer?"

Shardwyn frowned at the scholar. "What makes you think you will be successful where others have tried and failed?"

"I am different," Tristofer declared. "Never will you find anyone with more dedication and perseverance than I."

Maelnar nodded. "Perseverance, aye. No arguments there. Now, I asked you here to get your professional opinion on *that*."

Tristofer turned and followed Maelnar's pointing finger. He saw Lukas, still facing the opposite wall. The scholar went very quiet. He slowly approached Lukas and leaned down to inspect his back.

"The decorative scroll of the Second Age! Where did you ... How did you ... Look! Another Narian power hammer! I think I need to sit down."

Athos slid a chair from across the room toward his brother, who deftly caught it and flipped it around to get the chair under Tristofer's rear before he could collapse to the floor.

"This is very important, Tristofer," Maelnar gently told

him. "What does this mark tell you?"

Ignoring the question, Tristofer pointed at the lower left section of Lukas' back. "Do you see that? Do you see the area that's trying to come into focus?"

Maelnar, along with Shardwyn and Venk, squatted down next to the scholar. Athos elected to remain standing.

"What is it?" Venk asked. "Do you know what this mark is?"

Tristofer nodded excitedly. "It's a Questor's Mark!"

Maelnar, Shardwyn, Venk, Athos, and Lukas responded identically: "A what?"

"It symbolizes a beginning of a quest!" Tristofer said excitedly. "In essence, what we're looking at is a complex, multi-layered spell which tells a person what to do! Do you have any idea how rare these are?"

Venk scowled. The last thing he needed to hear was the mark on his son's back was a Narian *To Do* list. "Are you certain of this?"

"Very. The Kla Rehn's Archives contain several volumes of books about the Narian culture."

"Allegedly contain," Shardwyn murmured.

"One of these volumes spoke in great length about the lost art of layered spells and how the Narian people were quite fond of them."

"Allegedly spoke of," Shardwyn again murmured.

Maelnar nudged the wizard with his right shoulder. The mutterings ceased. Maelnar tugged on Shardwyn's right sleeve and nodded toward the Questor's Mark.

"Shardwyn, have you heard of a multi-layered spell?"

Shardwyn nodded. "I have, aye."

"Perhaps you could explain how a layered spell works. Several of us here, myself included, are not familiar with the process."

Delighted to be of help, Shardwyn bowed. "Absolutely! My apologies for not suggesting it before. Now, where should I begin?"

"How about from the beginning?" Athos grumbled. Venk chuckled and received a wink from Maelnar.

"A layered spell is a combination of more than one spell,"

Shardwyn began. "The first spell is invoked by the caster. Its effectiveness dictates the behavior of the second. And if there's a third, it will base its own behaviors on the second, and so on. Let's say—"

Venk held up a hand and coughed loudly.

"May I ask a question before you get too much further?"

Shardwyn clasped his hands behind his back and smiled. "I would encourage you to ask as many questions as you can, dear boy. What do you wish to know?"

"First off, I am much older than you are, wizard," Venk began, "so stop calling me boy." Athos swallowed a laugh.

Shardwyn nodded.

"Second, we dwarves are known for not meddling with jhorun, yet several times now you have spoken of enchantments and casting spells. A dwarf wouldn't dare cast a spell and dishonor themselves."

"Ah! Not all dwarf clans think the same, do they Master Venk?" Shardwyn pointed out.

"No clan we're aware of will touch the stuff," Athos stated. "Unless you are unlucky enough to be born with it."

"Very true," Maelnar added. "Thankfully jhorun-wielding dwarves are very rare. The last one I knew about restored a fossilized egg, which hatched a female guur, and I can't begin to express my sadness at how unpopular he was with his fellows when everyone learned what his jhorun had done. If not for Sir Steve, and his fire throwing jhorun, we would have been driven from our home by now."

"Be that as it may," Venk argued, "why are we hearing about spell casting and jhorun being performed in Nar? Correct me if I'm wrong, but it's a dwarf city. No one should be practicing jhorun there."

Surprised, Shardwyn turned to Maelnar and raised an eyebrow. "He brings up a good point. What were the Narian people doing, practicing jhorun?"

The corners of Maelnar's mouth turned upward in the beginning of a smile. "Perhaps one day we will know. Now, what else were you saying about the mark? How difficult are these layered spells to cast? Have you ever tried?"

Shardwyn sighed. It was a fair question.

"I have tried only one. And I will say that I was successful, but it was probably one of the more difficult spells I have ever cast. The spell had two components. You see, I lost my hat once and I decided to cast a spell to search for it. Then I added in a conjuration spell to bring it to me."

"You cannot summon anything if you do not know where it originates from," Maelnar explained to the dwarf brothers.

"Imagine building a child's playhouse out of parchment," Shardwyn told them. "Whereas it can be done, it's difficult and prone to fail as the structure isn't sound. That's what this spell was like. I could have just as easily searched the entire castle in the time it took me to get the results of the first spell accepted by the second spell so that I could not only learn of my hat's location but to also get it to appear at my feet."

"So, it really isn't worth the trouble," Athos guessed.

Shardwyn nodded. "Correct."

"Can you determine how many layers are in this one?" Tristofer asked the wizard.

Shardwyn leaned close to Lukas' back and began mumbling to himself, at times selecting several of the tiny instruments from the table and holding them next to the mark.

After ten minutes, Shardwyn straightened and motioned for Tristofer to join him. Maelnar and the two brothers also joined them. Forgetting, or possibly ignoring, the fact that others were present, Shardwyn singled out the scholar and began reporting what he learned.

"I see evidence of locator spells. Since part of the mark revealed itself when it came into contact with another item suggests a symbiotic charm is in effect. The mark was clearly given to the boy, so there are traces of a messenger spell. Those are just the three I can see, and I'm certain there are many more layers involved. Remember the paper analogy from earlier? This … this would be the finest crystal. Only a wizard could have cast this."

"How do we get this part to reveal itself?" Maelnar asked Tristofer, pointing to the section of the mark that had started to come into focus. "If this is a Questor's Mark, as everyone believes it to be, then what is the next step?"

"We, or namely the holder of the mark, must accept the quest," Tristofer answered.

"And if he doesn't? What then?" Venk wanted to know.

Tristofer sighed and tugged on his beard, more to relieve an itch than to suggest any cognitive distress.

"These marks are rare. The only mention of them that I know about tells us what to do should one of these arrive. I do not know what would happen if the mark were refused. I would imagine it would simply stay there until either the quest was accepted or else death takes the holder of the mark."

Athos raised a hand. "If my nephew undergoes this quest and is successful, then the mark will vanish?"

The scholar nodded. "In theory, aye."

"In theory?" Venk repeated, frowning.

"This is a civilization that existed thousands of years ago," Tristofer cautioned. "Whether or not we're right could be anyone's guess."

"Can you determine when that spell was cast?" Venk asked. "Is this a remnant from ancient Nar or did someone actually cast the spell in recent times?"

Everyone turned to the wizard.

"The boy received the mark earlier this year, am I right?"

Venk and Athos both nodded.

"Then it was cast within the year."

"Are you aware of anyone that could have created the mark?" Maelnar asked.

Shardwyn shook his head. "I have no qualms in revealing that I could not have cast that spell. It is beyond me."

"Does that mean there's a more powerful wizard out there somewhere?"

Shardwyn shrugged helplessly. "I certainly hope not, master dwarf. Whether there is or isn't, I will need to inform the king."

"How do I accept the quest?" Lukas suddenly asked.

"You *don't*," Venk told him flatly.

"The mark is on me, Father. I was given it for a reason."

"You will let someone else determine that reason," his father told him.

"If you want the mark removed from his back, and I

know you do," Athos told his brother, "then we should see this through."

Venk rounded on his brother. "And are you prepared to … to … we don't even know what we would have to do!"

"Irrelevant. If this is what it'll take to remove that mark from my nephew's back, then so be it. I'm ready."

Venk sighed and turned back to Shardwyn.

"Very well. What do we have to do?"

Tristofer raised a hand. "I believe I can answer that question. The answer can be found in the history books. Those who were lucky enough to get a Questor's Mark would say, in a loud voice, 'challenge accepted'. Then it is said that the first leg of the journey would be revealed."

Lukas looked at his father, who nodded in return. The boy cleared his throat.

"Challenge accepted."

The lower left quadrant of the mark shimmered and suddenly leapt into focus. A series of wavy lines appeared. Centered in the midst of the lines was the outline of a humanoid head. Long, flowing hair was splayed out to the right.

Venk tapped the image of the head. "Is this supposed to be a human's head? In the water? How does that help us?"

Just as baffled as the rest of the group, Maelnar grunted. "I'm not sure. Does this mean anything to anyone? How's this supposed to —"

Maelnar trailed off as he caught sight of Shardwyn. The wizard was rocking back and forth on the balls of his feet, practically bursting.

"Alright Shardwyn, what is it? I can see you have something to add."

"It's a nixie!"

"A what?"

"A nixie!"

Maelnar shot a glance at Tristofer, who shrugged. "I'm not familiar with that word."

"A nixie is a water sprite, my dear fellow. How can you not know what a nixie is?"

"There aren't many subterranean lakes, wizard. Perhaps you have noticed? Besides, haven't the water sprites been extinct for centuries?"

Shardwyn nodded. "I'm aware. Terrible shame. They were a very friendly species. Too trusting, I'm afraid, which is what led to their downfall."

"I'd say this confirms the spell, which put that mark on my son, was cast many years ago," Venk decided.

A smug smile appeared on Maelnar's face. "The map depicts an extinct species. Methinks it was *not* cast earlier this year, wouldn't you agree, Shardwyn?"

The wizard crossed his arms over his chest and said nothing.

"Get back to me on that. Now, when these nixies were alive, what was their native habitat? And if you tell me 'water' I will personally dispose of everything presently cluttering up my desk."

"Only the purest freshwater lakes, like the ones you would find nestled in the thick of a forest."

"Which forest?" Athos asked.

Shardwyn shrugged. "Any forest."

"That's just great. Where do we start? What exactly are we looking for?"

"Do you have a map of Anakash Forest?" Shardwyn asked Maelnar.

Tristofer patted several of his pockets before he produced a rolled tube of paper from inside his jacket. He unfurled the map and placed Shardwyn's bottles on each corner to prevent the map from rolling back up.

"Been holding on to this for a while," the scholar admitted. "Not sure why."

Shardwyn tapped a small lake southwest of the river

village of Donlari. The lake was surrounded on all sides by leagues of forest.

"I would start here at Lake Alpin, master dwarf. This is the largest freshwater lake in the area and was their last known location."

"Last known location?" Athos sputtered. "Of the nixies? Why the ruddy hell did you not say so before?"

The wizard sniffed disdainfully. "No one asked."

"Do we even know what we are looking for?" Athos asked, annoyance written all over his face. "The last thing I want to do is trek halfway across the Kingdom of Lentari without any real indication of what we're supposed to be doing. Let's say we find this insignificant body of water. Then what?"

"Have no fear," Tristofer reassured him. "The mark is our guide."

Athos stared at the scholar. "Our? This is a family affair. *We* will deal with this."

Athos' resentment bounced harmlessly off the scholar's chest. "Aye. *Our.* Who better to interpret a Narian mark than a Narian scholar? Trust me, there are no better scholars suited for this journey. Besides, it'll be fun!"

Athos placed himself directly in the scholar's path and crossed his arms over his chest. "Fine. Tell me this, scholar. You said that mark is the start of a quest. A quest to find what?"

Tristofer regarded Athos with an expression he typically reserved for dealing with mentally challenged individuals.

"Why, the lost city of Nar, of course."

Chapter 3 — Adventurers Assemble!

Not again!" Maelnar snapped. "Do you know how many times I have heard you claim that definitive proof of Nar's location has been found? Twenty-six, Tristofer. Refresh my memory. How many times were you proved wrong?"

"Well, twenty-six, if you must know. This time is different!"

Maelnar crossed his arms over his chest. "If ever there were a time to convince me, lad, it would be now."

"Can you not see that this mark is a map?"

Maelnar held up the map he was still clutching in his right hand.

"*This* is a map. *That* is a mark. Map. Mark. See the difference?"

Tristofer was unfazed. "Look at the facts, Master Maelnar. The multi-layered spell that created the mark was cast recently."

"You don't know that for certain."

"Shardwyn has all but confirmed it. The mark reacts to —"

"I have not," Shardwyn contradicted.

"The mark also reacts to Narian artifacts," Tristofer continued, ignoring Shardwyn's objections. "It also—"

"I have a question," a small voice asked, and was promptly drowned out by the heated argument between Maelnar and Tristofer. Shardwyn was the one who noticed Lukas' raised hand.

"I believe the young master has a question."

Everyone turned to Lukas. Everyone but Tristofer, that is. Taking advantage of the sudden silence, the scholar tried yet again to convince everyone that the mark was indeed a map.

"If you will just listen a moment, you will see that —"

Shardwyn held up his right hand as a warning. White sparks erupted out of the tip of his index finger as he did so. Tristofer instantly fell silent.

Lukas was silent for a few moments as he thought about how to best phrase his question. "Do all Questor Marks have some type of reaction when brought into contact with other Narian objects?"

Tristofer waved his hand as though he was shooing away an irritating insect. "I'm sure they do. Now, obviously the —"

"Wait a moment," Venk interrupted. The gruffness of his voice managed to silence the scholar.

Tristofer glanced irritably at Venk to see why he had been interrupted.

"If jhorun is involved, how do we know the mark doesn't react to all maps? Or all books? Can we verify my son's mark only reacts to Narian items?"

Maelnar nodded. It was a valid question. And, he had just the thing to address Venk's query. In the top drawer of his desk was a dagger rumored to have been created in Nar. Unfortunately, no one could authenticate it. For over two centuries it had remained locked in his desk. Maelnar retrieved the dagger, but not before he wrote out another request and handed it to an underling.

"See to it that it arrives here with all the speed that can be afforded," he told the boy. The underling nodded and slipped away through the door.

"The owner of this dagger asserts it is a true Narian dirk. I disagree, as does most everyone else. Let's see what happens to the mark."

Unsheathing the small four-inch dagger and holding the curved blade close to the boy's back, Maelnar and Shardwyn both leaned over to inspect the mark. No changes.

"Do you have access to any other Narian artifacts that we can use to test this hypothesis?" Shardwyn asked him.

"The Archives has one other artifact, which I have just sent for," Maelnar told him. "It's an inventory list from a Narian merchant. It's one of the few Narian documents we know to be true. If young master Lukas' mark reacts to that list, we'll know."

"Hold that storybook next to him now," Athos instructed. "Now that the quest has been accepted, will the mark react again?"

Curious, Maelnar retrieved his granddaughter's book and held it out to Lukas' back. The tiny Narian hammer within the border darkened and became more pronounced. Pulling the book away from the mark resulted in the hammer becoming several shades lighter. Maelnar repeated the test with the map and then the dagger. Same results with the map, but the dagger failed to elicit a response from the mark. Tristofer was right. The mark was only reacting to authentic Narian artifacts. He was definitely going to have to research the book's author when he had some time.

Ten minutes later the inventory sheet arrived from the Archives. Keeping the document in the sealed frame, Maelnar held the scrap of paper to Lukas' mark. Sure enough, the hammer intensified in color one more time. It reverted back to the same shade as the rest of the mark once the paper had been pulled away.

"Very well," Maelnar conceded. "That's one point for Tristofer. However, this still doesn't convince me this is a map to Nar."

"Of course it's a map," Tristofer insisted. "Think about

the mark's origin. Only the strongest and most talented wizards could have cast the spell necessary to make that mark. And the very existence of that mark proves that a quest is waiting. How can we not see it through to the end? Especially when it will lead us to the lost city?"

"What if the person who cast the spell was Narian?" Lukas wondered aloud.

Everyone fell silent. Most everyone.

"Of course!" Tristofer exclaimed, drawing frowns from both Maelnar and Venk, with the latter directing his scowl at his son. "We have to ask ourselves if this might be a misfired spell cast by a Narian centuries ago. Or could it be that there are survivors still living in Nar that are trying to make contact? If so, why did they wait so long? Why choose to give the mark to a boy when it should have been given to someone more…"

Tristofer trailed off as both Venk and Athos focused their angry stares on him.

"Suitable. I was going to say suitable, not deserving."

"Wise choice, scholar," Athos mumbled under his breath.

Tristofer groaned aloud and ran his hands through his hair. "Why can you not see what needs to be done? What do I have to do? Present these clues to someone else to see what their opinion is? One clue by itself is enough to warrant an expedition. If you take into consideration the discovery of all the clues, in such a short amount of time, then you must see that an expedition is inevitable. There is only one question you must now consider: do we ignore or do we act?"

"Present the clues to whom?" Maelnar asked suspiciously. If the scholar was threatening to make his findings public, then he was in for a rude awakening.

Tristofer shrugged. "To anyone who will listen. This is too important to ignore. I'm sorry, Maelnar, but if you do not convince the Council to —"

Tristofer's threat came to an abrupt halt as Maelnar looked over at Shardwyn and then inclined his head toward the scholar. He whispered a few words to the wizard. Moments later a heavy piece of burlap appeared out of thin air and adhered itself to Tristofer's mouth, silencing him instantly. No amount of pulling would dislodge the piece of cloth and restore his speech. The scholar's surprised eyes locked on Shardwyn's. The wizard shrugged.

"Apologies. I was challenged to render someone mute from ten feet away. I told him I could do it from a hundred. Besides, I have always wanted to try that spell."

Tristofer turned to Maelnar, his eyes pleading for an explanation.

"Listen carefully," Maelnar began, in a much lower tone than was expected. The others inadvertently crowded a little closer so as to hear what was being said. "Several prominent families have spent countless fortunes on expeditions to find Nar. Powerful families. If this is as legitimate as you say it is, then this must be kept very quiet."

Tristofer squawked with outrage. He had a chance to be a part of the single most important archaeological discovery of his people in the last millennia and he had to keep quiet? Everyone knows scholars share their work!

Maelnar nodded at Shardwyn, who waved his arm dismissively. The seal over Tristofer's mouth disappeared.

"And I suppose if I were to announce my findings, I would find my mouth sealed shut again?" Tristofer asked, casting a condescending look at the wizard.

"Indubitably."

"Will I ever be allowed to share the discovery?"

"That remains to be seen."

Tristofer sighed. "But you will send an expedition, will you not?"

Maelnar was silent as he stared down at the map which had been in his family's possession for centuries. His eyes flicked to the merchant paper brought over from the Archives. Finally, his gaze settled on the young lad's back and the Questor's Mark it held.

"Let us adjourn until tomorrow. I will meet with the Council and see which course of action they wish to follow. I will send for everyone when a decision has been made. Shardwyn, before you return to R'Tal, may I have a word?"

Surprised, the wizard followed Maelnar out of the room.

* * *

It took the Council of Elders less than two hours of deliberation to determine an expedition to locate Nar was warranted. After all, if it was true, and the boy's back did contain a map to Nar, would Borahgg not benefit greatly from its discovery? The fabled armor alone would fetch kingly sums and sustain their economy for many centuries to come. What warrior wouldn't want a suit of impenetrable armor to protect them when they walked onto a field of battle? If they could unlock the secrets of Narian metallurgy, then their economic future was guaranteed.

As Maelnar had reminded them, armor wasn't Nar's only contribution to the people. Powerful tools, enhanced by unknown means, had the capability of outperforming any other tool in existence. The Narian power hammer, it was said, could pulverize any rock with a single blow. And the forges! Their forges could melt any metal with minimal effort, regardless of its composition. That was technology that Borahgg desperately wanted to get its hands on.

The problem was the Council was certain other clans would love to unlock the secrets of Nar, too. Maelnar's recommendation that no word of the expedition was to be mentioned, to anyone, was upheld. As it was Maelnar, the celebrated Strathos, or key maker, who had brought the discoveries to the attention of the Council, it was left to him to determine who would be allowed to go on the Nar expedition.

Later that day, Maelnar was back in his study and was again addressing the same faces from yesterday, with one addition: his only son, Breslin, was present.

"Venk! Athos! Nice to see you again, lads!"

The two dwarf brothers bowed. Venk thumped his son on the back of his head to get his attention and waited for him to follow suit.

Breslin approached father and son and returned their bow. "Ah! Would this be the collector of dragon scales?"

Lukas smiled at the boisterous newcomer. "Aye. Madisonia and I still fight over who has the better dragon scale. I do, of course."

Breslin grinned. He winked at Venk as he went down on one knee to regard the youngster at eye level.

"Word has it that Venk here went to great trouble to acquire those scales. Value them well. The dragon he stole them from was enormous!"

Lukas smiled. He already knew his father had been given those scales by Pryllan, a very friendly green dragon. She was mate to Kahvel, who was dragon liaison to the human king. Lukas knew that Pryllan and her mate had been involved in the huge human skirmish last year, the same skirmish his father and uncle had participated in. What their roles had been remained unclear to him, as fighting and killing monsters did not interest him in the slightest. Collecting fascinating souvenirs, such as dragon scales, did. Therefore, he elected to smile and nod his head as everyone expected him to.

"So, what's the word?" Athos asked. "Are we going on this expedition or not?"

Maelnar nodded. "The word is, it's a go."

Tristofer's eyes opened wide. He thought for sure Maelnar would be telling him that yet another hoped-for expedition had been abandoned. He could only hope his name was one of those who were allowed to go.

"I have been tasked with determining who will go. Since this expedition has been sanctioned by the Council, I have to wonder whether or not we should send an armed presence? Or is discretion better? In the end, we decided the expedition should remain small. Unnoticed."

Tristofer had started to twist his beard through his fingers.

"The members are … Lukas. Clearly the bearer of the mark must go. As such, his father and uncle will also go."

Venk and Athos both nodded.

"Since we are dealing with a time and place that hasn't existed for many years, a scholar would prove to be useful. Tristofer, you're invited to go, but I can't speak for your clan. I encourage you to contact the Kla Rehn as soon as possible, or if you tell me who you'd like me to contact on your behalf, I'd be more than happy to do so."

Tristofer formally bowed. "I'm sure the Kla Rehn

wouldn't have any objections. There's really no need for you to contact them. I know they'd want me to go."

Maelnar raised an eyebrow. "Indeed. Very well. The final member of the team will be Breslin. As my son, and the newest member of the Council, he will speak on its behalf should the situation call for it."

Breslin nodded his approval. Shardwyn gave a little cough and cleared his throat.

"Fear not, wizard. I have not forgotten. Last night Shardwyn and I touched upon the subject of extra precautions, in case any unpleasant situations are encountered. Shardwyn volunteered to provide several spells which can be invoked by anyone, regardless of their level of jhorun."

Confused, Athos turned to his brother and nudged him. "Did he just say that we have to use jhorun?"

Venk elbowed him back. "Were you not listening? He said that the wizard will give us some spells to use in case we encounter any difficulties. Even if we don't have any jhorun, which none of us do, we will still be able to use the spells."

"I don't want anything to do with it," Athos said, as he crossed his arms stubbornly over his chest. "Dwarves don't use jhorun."

Venk shoved his brother aside and faced Shardwyn. "Pay him no mind, wizard. Anything you can give me so that I may protect my son will be much appreciated."

Shardwyn nodded. He pulled a small white sack from within his robes. Opening the drawstring silk pouch, he withdrew a white sphere the size of large pebble. A symbol had been etched onto the surface with what looked like maroon ink. The symbol was a quill.

"There are five spells in the sack," Shardwyn began. "One for each of you. This one is for sending a message. Note the quill. All you have to do is to have a message planted firmly in your head, invoke the spell, and speak the name of the person you wish to give the message to. Somebody hurt? Need to call for help? Use this spell to send word."

"How many times can we use it?" Breslin asked, taking the small circular object from the wizard.

"Just once, good sir," Shardwyn told him. "Use it wisely."

"Are all of these only allowed to be used once?" Maelnar asked, frowning. This wasn't the type of help he had envisioned.

Shardwyn nodded. "Aye. Do not let that concern you. I have considered all possibilities and I do believe I have you covered in any type of emergency."

Bemused, Maelnar smiled. "Indeed. Very well, let's see what other spells you have to offer."

"Of course. As I said, this one is for sending a message." Shardwyn opened the pouch and placed the other four spells on the closest table. He selected a sphere with several wavy lines etched on the surface. "This one, when properly invoked, will bestow the powers of levitation upon its caster. If you find that you must scale a tremendous height, or descend a ravine or canyon, this spell will be invaluable."

"How long will the effects last?" Breslin asked.

"Enough to get the task done," Shardwyn answered as he turned to retrieve the next spell. He selected the one with a tear drop on its surface. "Ah. Here's one I'm very proud of. This will conjure water. Parched of thirst? Need to quickly douse a campfire? This will do it."

"How much water will it summon?"

Shardwyn smiled at Breslin and tapped his right ear. "When you ask a question, you really need to speak up. Lately I find that I'm becoming hard of hearing. Now, let's see what else we have."

The next spell to be selected had a picture of a shield.

"Protection," Shardwyn told them, smiling patronizingly as he did so. "Perfect for protecting campsites for the night."

"But for only one night!" Athos complained.

"You really need to speak up, Master Venk. I am having a terrible time hearing you."

"I am Athos. He's Venk."

"My sincerest apologies. Now, listen carefully. The last will probably be the most helpful."

Catching sight of the symbol, Maelnar nodded. "Fire."

"Aye. The holder of this spell can summon fire. It'll be perfect for lighting campfires to chase away the chill of the night air."

"But it can only be used one time!" Athos complained again. "What if we need to use it on more than one night?"

The wizard's condescending expression remained on his face. "Would you rather I just hand you a map and say here's where you need to go?"

Athos returned Shardwyn's frank stare. "That would be lovely."

"Balderdash. Those spells are meant to be used when all other avenues have been explored."

"We will use them only when we have no other recourse," Breslin assured him.

Satisfied, Shardwyn turned to Maelnar and shrugged, as if to say he had done all he could.

"Get some rest, lads," Maelnar told everyone. "Be ready to depart by sunrise."

* * *

By late morning the next day, the group of adventurers was topside and traveling south. Since virtually all dwarves were agoraphobic, all five members of the group remained huddled together as they walked. No dwarf wanted to be out under the open sky for too long. Topside simply had too many dangers lurking about, not the least of which was the unspoken fear of jumping too hard, or getting knocked up into the air and not having anything to prevent one from floating away. If anyone were to ask a dwarf if they would prefer to be subterranean or topside, then the questioner was obviously an imbecile.

At the moment, the five dwarves were traveling through the lush valley that lay south of Lake Raehón, Lentari's northernmost body of water. The lake was ringed by mountains on all sides except for a small valley that jutted up against the lake on the southeastern edge. Protected by the elements and its remoteness, the valley was home to a plethora of wildlife, most notable being the large, dimwitted bolgers. The slow-moving quadrupeds were shaggy brown beasts with large flat feet, a short squat neck, and a wedge-shaped head. Two spiraled horns curved upward and then down the back of its skull before flaring off to the sides, giving it the appearance of having two large spikes protruding from its sides when viewed from a distance. The creatures roamed the valley, always searching for the tastiest piece of grass.

Another notable inhabitant of the area was a species that fed on the bolgers: dragons. The bulk of the flying variant of wyverians called the northern Bohani Mountains home, with a high concentration of dragons living near Lake Raehón. Several dwarf clans chose the small valley as their "front doors" for that very reason. They couldn't have designed a more secure front entrance. Thankfully a truce existed between dragons and dwarves, so if one were to come into contact with the other, then pandemonium would not ensue. For the dwarf.

As the lake began to grow smaller behind the travelers, the grassland they were traversing seemed to stretch on for infinity. The dwarves knew the valley was small by most standards, but when one averaged four feet tall, even a small valley seemed endless. Thankfully, they could see the northern border of Anakash Forest, visible as a faint green line just below the horizon. Once they made it to the forest, it was a three-day trek through the trees to the mighty Zylan River. Once they crossed the river, Lake Alpin should only be a two or three hour walk southeast.

Venk grumbled softly to himself. How had he gotten himself into this predicament? Sure, he wanted what was best for Lukas, and he was more than willing to sacrifice everything to make that happen. Even now, as they marched through the waist level grass, he wished he was safely back at home under the ground. Heck, he would much rather read the books that Maelnar had recommended than go on another adventure. Anything but this.

The sun was high in a cloudless sky and beat down mercilessly on the fully armored, leather-clad dwarves. The only one who seemed to be enjoying himself was Lukas, who had been spared from having to wear the extra layers of protection as the leather armor didn't come in his size. Tristofer, while not outfitted in protective gear, had elected to wear a jacket that had even more pockets than his previous one and, as before, it was crammed full of various items—books, scrolls, bottles of ink, a fresh pack of new quills, and spare reading glasses—among other things. Thankfully, Venk noted, the scholar appeared as uncomfortable walking through the grass as he was.

"Never thought I'd be doing this again so soon," Venk grumbled as he followed his son up the next hill. They had already crossed a dozen of these grassy knolls and there were at least twice as many directly in their path.

Athos glanced behind him, not to check on his brother but to ascertain his nephew was managing to keep up with the group. Not only did Lukas not appear to be fatigued, but he was also inspecting various blades of grass; picking up every twig they stepped over, and even turning a few rocks over to see what kind of insects lived below. The boy's eyes were alive with wonder as he uncovered treasure after treasure.

Athos stopped walking to allow Venk to catch up. He slapped his brother on the back.

"We have made it, what, three leagues and you are complaining already?"

Venk caught his son's eyes and pointed off to the distance. When Lukas looked away, Venk made a rude gesture toward his brother. "If dwarves were meant for walking long distances, then we would have longer legs."

With as much stealth as a dragon, which was considerable, Breslin appeared behind the two of them and draped an arm over each of their shoulders.

"We are on the adventure of a lifetime, my friends! We are searching for Nar! How can you not be in a great mood?"

There was a clinking of metal as the axe strapped to Breslin's back shifted position and made contact with the simple black axe fastened to Venk's.

"Are the stories about that axe true?" Venk asked as he eyed the striking red weapon.

"What might those stories be?" Breslin wanted to know as he pulled Mythryd off his back. "What have you heard?"

"I have heard that your axe is lighter than any other and that no one can wield it but its rightful owner."

Breslin smiled. "Actually, it —"

"I heard," Athos interrupted, "that it can cut through any material, even metal. Is that true?"

"Well, I have never tried to —"

"I heard you could throw it and it will return to you, much like my orix."

Breslin looked at the brother in the jet black armor and raised an eyebrow. "An orix? That is an antiquated weapon, my friend. No one uses them anymore. Are you jesting?"

Athos ran a hand along one of the two belts crisscrossing his chest. Sliding something out of one of the belts, he flicked his wrist. Two extendable arms appeared and locked into place with a loud click. Athos held the orix up so that Breslin could see it.

The dwarf was holding a modified boomerang, one that had been crafted to resemble a dragon. Its front legs were curled slightly under it while its hind legs were bunched together as if rearing into the air. The tail and wings, which had been concealed under the rest of the dragon's long sinewy body, had snapped into place to complete the picture.

Breslin studied the rudimentary weapon and noted its coloring. The dragon's body had been painted an emerald green color, with the very tips of its wings and ears painted black. He had seen this dragon before.

"It's Pryllan, is it not? Kahvel's mate."

Athos nodded, pleased. There weren't many people who could correctly identify which dragon he had modeled his orix after.

"Aye. After last year I've had a change of heart about dragons and thought it would be a noble way to honor them."

"I'm surprised you didn't make it gold. Kahvel is much more intimidating than Pryllan."

Athos patted the sheath strapped to the other belt on his chest. "My spare orix is gold."

Breslin nodded. "Admirable. Can you hit anything with it?"

Venk rolled his eyes. "Here we go."

Athos puffed out his chest with pride. "I hit whatever I'm aiming at."

Breslin nodded. "So you say. Do you see that clump of

grass that's darker than the rest? The one that has a flower stalk in the middle of it? Can you hit it?"

Athos looked. About thirty feet away he saw the clump of grass that was darker than its neighbors. He targeted the bright yellow flower sitting on the lone stalk and flicked his orix into the air.

The green weapon spiraled neatly through the air as it curved to the left in an elliptical orbit. The yellow flower disappeared into a puff of petals as the orix hit the plant and kept going. The orix spun through the air for another few seconds before it smacked back into the hand of its thrower. Athos grinned at his brother before turning back to the Council's representative.

"That's not bad," Breslin admitted. "Although the target was fairly close, it was a good shot."

"Fairly close? *Fairly close?* Very well. Pick a target, Master Breslin."

Realizing what was coming, Venk sighed dramatically and sank down into the tall grass. Lukas followed suit a few moments later.

"What are you doing?" Tristofer asked as he stared at father and son. The scholar turned to Breslin and Athos, confusion evident on his face. "Is a cessation of our expedition really the best course of action at this time?"

Lukas stared at Tristofer with large, unblinking eyes. "What?"

"He wants to know why we've stopped," Venk translated. "You may as well make yourself comfortable, scholar. This might take a while."

Still unsure what was happening, Tristofer squatted down into the soft grass and stared in bewilderment at Breslin, who kept pointing out objects for Athos to hit. Thus far Athos was true to his word. His skill with the orix was not to be taken lightly.

"I will say that I have not seen anyone with a better cast," Breslin finally admitted after spending a quarter of an hour watching Athos hit various targets. Athos had even been able to shave a few inches of growth off a clump of grass fifty feet away. That was impressive! "What's the range?"

Athos raised his right arm and watched the orix spin in its elliptical orbit until it expertly returned to his hand.

"The farthest I've been able to cast with any amount of accuracy is about one hundred and fifty feet."

"Accuracy notwithstanding, what's the farthest you have ever thrown it?" Breslin inquired, curious. Athos' skill had impressed him greatly and he was considering whether or not he should approach the Council and suggest the guards take up the ancient weapon once more.

"Depending upon the design, and how it's thrown, I've been able to hurl an orix close to three hundred feet."

Breslin nodded his head. He was convinced. He was definitely going to reintroduce the archaic throwing weapon at the next Council meeting.

"I still prefer my crossbow," Venk called out to them. "Better range."

"You mean easier to use?" his brother teased him.

"You can take your beard and shove it up a …"

"At least I won't run out of ammunition," Athos continued, wiping the tears from his eyes.

Venk patted a pouch on his belt. "I have enough bolts, never you fear."

"Uncle!"

Athos glanced over at his nephew.

"Think fast!"

Lukas pulled up a small clump of grass, grasped it by the tips of the long blades, and swung it around his head. Gaining speed, he finally released the grass after the fourth swing. Lukas waited. His uncle had yet to miss a target, and provided everyone was out of harm's way, Athos would be unable to resist a chance to show his skill.

Athos was waiting. As soon as the clump had hit the apex of its upward climb, he flung the orix at the falling grass. The clump was instantly transformed into a cloud of falling blades. The orix, encountering barely any resistance from the grass, kept traveling ahead and disappeared around the next grassy knoll.

"I'll get it, uncle."

Lukas rose to his feet and started to climb the hill when

Athos told him to stop.

"It'll come back. This valley is perfect for throwing orixes; there are no trees. This hill isn't big enough to hide any obstructions, so it couldn't have hit anything. Just wait a moment. It'll be back."

Ten seconds passed. No orix. Everyone turned to look at Athos.

"It'll be back, I assure you."

"It wasn't thrown that hard," Venk pointed out. "It should have returned by now. You must have hit something."

"I'll look," Lukas told them again. The boy climbed thirty feet to the top of the grassy knoll and looked down at the other side of the hill.

"Father! Uncle! You might want to see this!"

Hurrying up the hill as fast as he could run, Venk arrived at his son's side, his crossbow cocked and loaded. He looked down and gaped at what he saw. Athos and Breslin arrived moments later, holding their axes. Wheezing and gasping for air, Tristofer followed.

"You really do need to get out more," Breslin told the scholar.

Sitting at the base of the hill, no more than fifty feet away, were two dragons. Two massive reptilian heads jerked in their direction as the dwarves appeared. Both dragons tracked the dwarves as they cautiously descended the hill. While there might be a truce in effect between wyverian and dwarf, neither truly trusted the other.

The closest dragon was a deep blood-red color, with a tinge of purple near the tips of its wings and tail. It sported two large, slightly curved horns that were jutting straight out of its skull and, at the moment, were trained on the group of dwarves. A row of spikes sprouted from the base of the dragon's skull and extended down the neck. Halfway down its back the spikes became plates which continued to run the length of its spine, giving it an appearance of being heavily armored. Giant leathery wings remained extended, ready to propel the dragon to safety if it thought the situation called for it.

The second dragon, ivory white in appearance, also

watched the dwarves. It was larger and older than the first and clearly believed it had nothing to fear from the dwarves as its wings were folded and remained that way. As the second dragon shifted the bulk of its weight onto its rear legs, its scales shimmered and the white coloring became a rich copper. Enjoying the show it knew it was putting on, the now-copper dragon shifted position again and regained its white coloring.

"Impressive," Breslin commented, as he approached the pair of dragons. "I am Breslin of the Kla Guur, son of Maelnar."

The red dragon bowed its head. "Greetings, Breslin of the Kla Guur. I am Rhamalli. This is Samara."

The white dragon nodded. It suddenly cocked its head, opened its jaws, and spat something small and green onto the ground before them.

"I give up. This is the toughest kyte I have ever tried to eat. I fear I may have cracked a fang."

It was Athos' orix, dripping with dragon drool.

"You tried to eat my orix?"

Twin pale eyes studied the dwarf. "What is an orix?"

"It's an ancient throwing weapon."

"Your ancient throwing weapon was going to hit me."

"So, you ate it instead?"

Samara's nose lifted. "I thought it was a kyte."

"A kyte is a small flying creature that loves to roost in trees," Tristofer helpfully informed Lukas.

"Everyone knows that," Lukas replied in an exasperated tone. "It's a feathered avian that comes in a variety of colors and can reside just about anywhere. Don't treat me like a child."

Tristofer closed his mouth and shoved his hands into his pockets.

Ignoring his nephew's outburst, Athos shook his head and looked up at the white dragon. "There are no kytes around here. If you want kytes, find some trees. You didn't break it, did you?"

Samara grunted with annoyance. "No. I should have known no kyte, or any other creature, would willingly fly into my open jaws. I tried to chew it. Got it lodged in my fangs. It came loose just now."

Athos looked down at his prized orix, covered in saliva, and grimaced. He gingerly retrieved it and tried to clean it on the grass, which only succeeded in getting both drool and grass stuck to his weapon.

Tristofer tossed over a small piece of cloth. "And people say I cram useless objects into my pockets. Hmph. You never know when you'll need to polish a weapon."

Athos rolled his eyes and dried off his orix. The pressure of the dragon's enormous jaws must have caused the extendable arms to collapse. He flicked open the arms and locked them back into place. He glanced up at Samara, who had been watching with rapt fascination.

"See? No kytes here, just my orix. I use it as a means of self-defense."

"Defense?" Samara's long neck snaked about as he inspected the local environment. "Against whom? Or what?"

"It was for practice."

"Ah. Why wouldn't it break?"

"It's made from an alloy I made myself. Lighter than wood but much stronger than iron."

"I'll bet I could crunch it," Samara declared, as if challenging himself to do just that at a future date. He watched the dwarf fold the weapon back into its inert form and slide it into the sheath on his chest. "I could…"

Rhamalli thumped his tail irritably onto the ground. "Another time, perhaps." He turned his attention back to the dwarves. "Where are you off to?"

"Why do you want to know?" Breslin inquired.

"Five dwarves marching under the open sky? You are up to something. Rinbok Intherer wants to know what."

"You can tell the Dragon Lord that it is our business," Breslin replied calmly. "Tell him that we are heading south and that's all he needs to know."

"How far south?" the red dragon asked.

"A fair distance."

Engrossed in the conversation between Breslin and the dragon, Venk didn't notice Lukas edging closer and closer to the large ivory dragon. For a creature so large, it could certainly move fast when it wanted to. Samara's huge horned skull was suddenly inches from Lukas' outstretched hand.

"Is there something I can help you with, young dwarf?"

Lukas leapt backward in alarm, tripping over his own feet and plopping down on his rear. Venk was at his side in a flash.

"Keep your distance, dragon."

"He approached me, dwarf."

"What's going on?" Breslin demanded, stepping between the dragon and the boy.

"That dragon just scared Lukas," Venk accused.

"He did not!" Lukas insisted, leaping to Samara's defense.

"I did not," Samara said, at the same time.

"What happened then? What were you…" Venk trailed off as he noticed several scales that were peeling off of Samara's body. "Really? Was one dragon scale not enough for you? Why do you need another?"

"Another what?" Samara asked. His gaze traveled down the front of his chest until it fell on his front left foreleg. Several scales left over from his last sloughing had yet to fall off. "The boy wants a scale?"

Lukas emphatically nodded his head yes while his father rubbed his temples.

Samara scratched his left leg with his right and kept at it until the remaining scales finally fell to the ground. All together, seven scales, each the size of a large stone, were now ripe for the picking.

Lukas beamed his appreciation up at the ivory dragon and knelt down onto the soft grass to select his prize. He then approached his father and spun him around until he had access to their pack of belongings. Lukas slipped the scale into one of the pockets. Venk pointed at another of the iridescent scales and told Lukas to pick it up as well.

"Think I can return home without one for Madisonia as well?"

After both scales were secured in the pack, the dwarves returned their attention to the dragons.

"As I was saying," Breslin started again, "what we do is our business. The Dragon Lord does not need to poke his nose into that which doesn't concern him."

Rhamalli shook his head. "The reason I ask, dwarf, is the time of the hunt is now. We could exchange favors."

Breslin risked a glance with the brothers. "A hunt? Favors? Explain."

"Every two years, a group of dragons are chosen to hunt the serpent," Rhamalli explained. "It and its offspring live in the waters humans call the Sea of Koralis."

"I know absolutely nothing of this," Breslin confessed. "I didn't know dragons participated in any type of hunt."

"Well, we do. Samara and I were two of the chosen. The others are on their way."

"What does that have to do with us?" Athos asked.

"If you are heading in that direction, we can take you along."

Lukas' face lit up again.

"Really? Riding on the back of a dragon?"

Both dragons growled and shook their heads.

"We could carry you," Rhamalli clarified, "but not on our backs. No one rides a dragon."

"Sir Steve rode Pryllan," Venk pointed out.

Rhamalli approximated a shrug. "With permission only. Be that as it may, no one rides on our backs. We can carry you, but only if we know if your destination lies east."

"Lake Alpin supposedly lies mostly south, I'm afraid," Tristofer helpfully supplied.

Breslin, Venk, and Athos groaned aloud. Athos cuffed the scholar on the back of his head.

"Do you not know the definition of discreet?"

"Lake Alpin?" Rhamalli shook his head. "I know not where that is."

"Nor do I," Samara admitted.

"What do you expect to find there?" Rhamalli wanted to know.

Athos went tight-lipped. "It is our own business, dragon."

Rhamalli was silent as he studied the dwarves for several moments.

Tristofer, mistaking the dragons' silence as a willingness to let the matter drop, smiled with relief. "See? You have nothing to worry about. They don't know where the lake is. Our secret is safe."

"So, they don't know where it is. Who's to say they couldn't find out?"

"Why would we find out?" Samara asked, confused. "The affairs of the dwarves interest us not."

Rhamalli closed his eyes and went still.

"What's he doing?" Breslin asked as he suspiciously eyed the motionless dragon.

Samara sighed. "He's poking his nose into the affairs of the dwarves. I believe he's asking where Lake Alpin can be found."

"Blast it! We don't want anyone to know where we're going!" Breslin cried out in frustration. "Why don't we just send out a broadcast of what we're doing instead?"

Rhamalli's eyes snapped open and he visibly straightened.

"Lake Alpin is a small freshwater lake located southeast of the point where a river the humans call Zylan splits in twain."

"So now you know where it is?" Breslin demanded. "Why did you not say so before?"

"I just asked. I was given an answer. Still your tongue, dwarf, and I'll explain."

Breslin's eyebrows shot up. Had he just been told off by a dragon?

"I consulted with Rinbok Intherer. He knew where to find your lake."

"How far away is it?"

"Five hours, as the dragon flies," Rhamalli answered. "Three months as the dwarf walks."

"Three months?"

The huge ivory dragon chuckled loudly. Breslin turned to Samara and glowered up at the mammoth creature.

"He's mocking me, isn't he?"

"Of course."

"How long will it truthfully take us to get there?"

Rhamalli shook his head. "Unknown. I know not how fast you travel."

"How far is the lake from Donlari?" Lukas asked.

Rhamalli's gaze shifted to the boy's.

"That's the first intelligent question I've heard, young dwarf. The answer is less than a day."

"So, what was going to take nearly four days will now take less than one. I think that's a good trade, Father."

Venk snapped his fingers. "That reminds me. Thanks, son. What favor do you require for transporting us to Donlari?"

"Rinbok Intherer has a large amethyst that he would like split into four gems of equal weight. Can you do this?"

Breslin suddenly smiled. "My father can and I'm sure he'd *love* to do that for the Dragon Lord."

Rhamalli nodded. "Excellent. The others have been summoned. They will be here in ten minutes. Once we arrive at the human village, then we will have fulfilled our obligation. Do we have an accord?"

Breslin drew Mythryd from his back and clanged it gently on the talons of Rhamalli's open claw.

"We have an accord."

* * *

Lukas had never been so excited in his young life. He and his father were each being gently, but firmly, gripped in a massive dragon claw. Every downward beat of Samara's wings propelled them higher into the sky, ever closer to the white puffy clouds Lukas had always admired whenever he had the chance to see them. That was hardly ever, as his father had adopted every other dwarf's trademark dislike of being Topside.

He was flying through the air! Well, Samara was flying through the air, but nevertheless, he wanted to see and experience everything! No one was going to believe he had ever flown with a dragon. Not only that, it was with a whole group of them!

Lukas looked to his left and saw Rhamalli flying a little lower than they were. Even though he couldn't see them, Lukas knew the red dragon held his uncle and the scholar. If he watched long enough, he could see several papers fly out from beneath the dragon and flutter away on the wind, destined to fall forgotten to some desolate section of the forest floor far below. As always, whenever that happened, Lukas could imagine hearing a squawk of outrage from Tristofer, as he no doubt pleaded with the dragon to decrease their speed and altitude.

To his right he could see the large black dragon holding Breslin. He had forgotten the name of that dragon as it had too many syllables to remember, let alone pronounce. Ahead of them, barely visible as specks in the sky, flew seven other dragons of various colors. Two were green. One was yellow. Another two were red. There was a white dragon with dark stripes, and way out ahead, leading the way, was a brilliant cobalt blue dragon. Lukas had overheard Rhamalli mention two of the dragons were female, but as to which ones they were, he had no way of telling, nor was he going to ask. That sort of question typically ended with the adults laughing at him.

Lukas fidgeted in the claw as he jostled about to find the prime vantage point for watching the passing countryside far below. Not having much luck leaning out over the dragon's claw, as he was too short, Lukas ducked down to peer through the gaps between the talons. There, far below them, were the tree tops of Anakash forest. His father had said that it was going to take three days just to reach Zylan River. At this rate, if the dragons would just fly them straight there, they could be there in only a matter of a few more hours. As it was, the dragons were flying predominantly east, not south. It was a blessing that they were altering course long enough to drop them off in Donlari.

Just then a swirl of mist obscured his vision. Tiny droplets of water coalesced on his face, chilling him instantly and taking his breath away. What had happened? Lukas ran a hand over his face and inhaled, testing the air. The unmistakable scent of water was everywhere. The clouds! The dragons were flying through the clouds!

"This is amazing!" Lukas shouted to his father.

When no response was forthcoming, Lukas glanced over at the Samara's other claw, which held his father. Venk had both eyes screwed shut and was gripping the dragon's talons so tightly his knuckles were turning as pale as the scales.

"Father! Open your eyes! We are flying through the clouds! You don't want to miss it!"

His father didn't respond. Lukas tried again, but realized that no matter how loudly he shouted, his words were lost to the rushing wind. The swirling mists cleared and Lukas gasped with surprise. Gone was the ground. The trees could no longer be seen. There were no visible mountains and no discernible landmarks anywhere. For all he knew they were no longer flying east but had instead doubled back and were headed home. There was simply no way to tell. Lukas' jaw started to ache as he was smiling so much. They were flying so high that the clouds he had seen from the ground were now those that he could see far below.

Huge billowy masses of white fluffy clouds were everywhere--directly to their right, to their left, and as far as the eye could see straight ahead. Up here, it was peaceful and serene. If he were a dragon, he would never touch back down on the ground. He would spend all his time up here.

"I wish I was a dragon," Lukas whispered, more to himself than to anyone. "I wish this journey would never end."

"All good things must come to an end, young Lukas."

Samara's voice was strong, powerful, and easily heard. Had the dragon really heard him whispering to himself?

"Can you really hear me?" Lukas asked again, in the softest whisper he could manage, unable to even hear himself.

"Of course."

"Wow."

"Dragons have far superior visual and aural abilities, surpassing every other creature that we're aware of."

"Amazing."

"You like flying?"

"I wish I could fly all the time," Lukas sighed wistfully.

"I was unaware dwarves cared this much for heights. Your father appears to wish he were back on the ground."

"I know you won't drop me," Lukas told the dragon. "Nothing bothers a dragon in the air. It's perfectly safe."

Samara grunted. "Up until last year I would have agreed.

Now we know otherwise."

"What happened last year?" Lukas asked, curious.

"We encountered a foe that attacked us from the air," Samara explained, banking slightly right as he followed Rhamalli around a huge pillar of clouds. "Luckily, we were also shown how to defeat the foe. Too many of us believed we were invincible in the air. It was a brutal reality check."

"Did any dragons die?" Lukas whispered in shock, hoping against hope that none did.

"No, although several were close to perishing."

Lukas breathed a sigh of relief.

Samara suddenly turned his massive head to the right and inhaled.

"We are approaching the human settlement."

Lukas stood up on his tip toes to peer over the dragon's claw. All he could see far below were the approaching tops of the clouds.

"How can you tell?"

"Two ways. First, I can see the village."

"Really?"

"Aye. But most of all, I can smell them."

Lukas laughed. "Humans smell bad?"

Samara nodded. "Aye. They are very easy to track. Humans have always wondered why they do not make great hunters. That's why."

"Will there be dragons around the lake we're going to?" Lukas asked hopefully.

"I cannot say," Samara's gentle voice answered. "Dragons live wherever they choose. What I will say is that a dragon will not choose to live in an area that has little game. There must be a plentiful supply of food or else the dragon would starve."

Lukas nodded. It made sense.

"If you do encounter one around these parts, be cautious. A dragon is highly territorial. If it feels threatened, it will eliminate the threat."

"How will I know if a dragon lives nearby?"

"Look for blackened trees, or dark scorches in the earth. Those are indicators a dragon is near."

Just when Lukas thought his clothes had completely dried out from his first encounter with the cloud bank, Samara dipped his wings and banked sharply to their right, angling them toward the heart of another enormous cloud. Lukas realized with a start that he was about to be soaked again. The young dwarf craned his head and held his breath. Great pillows of feathery mist towered thousands of feet above his head. Were they about to go through that? Lukas glanced up at the ivory dragon's enormous body and saw that Samara's wings had leveled off but were now partially folded against its back, causing them to tip downward and increase their speed. They were going to miss the large cloud after all. Barely. It was a shame dragon riding was forbidden as the views from the dragon's back would be much better than from beneath its belly.

Catching sight of the ground layer of clouds rushing up at them, Lukas' eyes widened. The downy white clouds were now racing toward them so fast that there was no time to brace for impact. Lukas gasped with shock as they blasted through the thick layer of clouds as though they had been shot out of a cannon. There, many hundreds of feet below them, Lukas finally caught sight of the ground once more.

The forest was gone. The trees, visible as a rapidly fading green line far behind them, had been replaced by open prairie, dotted with scraggly bushes and gentle rolling hills. A large, flat river bisected the land and stretched away to the east.

Samara's wings picked up the pace and began to beat faster as the dragon slowed their descent. Up ahead, or rather farther down, Lukas could see Rhamalli glide in and touch down next to the river. The black dragon followed suit moments later.

Puzzled, Lukas looked around the surrounding area. Where was the human village? Weren't the dragons supposed to be dropping them off there?

"Something the matter?" Samara inquired as he spiraled lower and lower. The ground was only a few hundred feet away now.

"Where's Donlari?"

"About a league to the east."

"Why didn't you land there?"

"What do you think would happen if the humans spotted ten dragons circling about overhead and then saw three land in their village?"

Lukas smiled. "That would be bad."

"Precisely."

As Samara came in for a landing, he beat his wings furiously in order to make the transition to the ground as smooth as possible. All the grass in the area was flattened by the blast of wind, appearing as though a giant had stepped on it and squished it flat.

The claw finally opened and the talons, which had held him in position for so long, finally separated. Lukas hopped down to the ground and then turned to face the dragon with a smile on his face.

"I would like to say thanks for the ride. I will never forget it."

Samara nodded his head. "Would you do me a favor, young dwarf?"

Lukas enthusiastically nodded his head. "Anything!"

"Would you kindly inform your father that the ground is once more beneath our feet?"

Lukas glanced over at his father. Venk was still clutching one of the talons and had a look of grim determination on his face as though he was being subjected to the most heinous of tortures.

"Father, what are you doing? Let go!"

"Absolutely not! The fiend wants me to let go so that I…"

Realizing it was not necessary to shout in order to be heard, Venk cracked an eye open. Samara had extended his foreleg and was holding his open claw over a patch of grass. Venk was dangling two feet off the ground, still clutching the talon.

"How about that. We've landed."

Samara snickered. "Your powers of observation astound me, master dwarf."

Venk dropped to the ground and glared at the dragon. "Ha ha. I am as ill in the air as any of your ilk would be under the ground."

"Not true," Samara disagreed. "Land dragons live in subterranean caverns."

"Perfect. I didn't need to know that."

They thanked the dragons and said their farewells. Moments later they watched as the graceful creatures rose into the air and disappeared into the clouds.

Breslin approached.

"I did not think I could ever find a more unpleasant method of travel than Lady Sarah's teleportations."

"When Lady Sarah teleported us from one place to the next, it was instantaneous," Athos argued. "However, I could never get over the sensation that my insides had been left behind."

"You prefer the dragon?"

Venk was silent as he considered which was the lesser of two evils. Close to a minute passed before Athos finally cleared his throat.

"While my brother figures out what he wants to say, I think it best if we head out."

Breslin nodded. "I agree. What do you think, lads? Do we make for Donlari or should we find this lake that everyone is making a fuss about?"

Unaccustomed to long bouts of travel, Tristofer meekly raised a hand and suggested they try to find lodging in the village.

Breslin turned east and saw the outskirts of the village at least a league away. He suddenly squatted down and motioned for Lukas to approach.

"What do you think, Master Lukas? Seek shelter in the human village or should we make for the lake?"

"Why are you asking me?"

"You bear the Questor's Mark. I will let you decide."

Lukas anxiously looked at his father, who shrugged and jammed his hands into his pockets.

"Let's find the lake."

"You heard him. We will find the lake and camp there."

Tristofer groaned in exasperation and began to grumble.

Several hours later Breslin and the rest of the group were crouching down low next to several squat shrubs. The area was thick with pine trees that were at least a hundred feet tall. So many trees dotted the landscape that the sun's welcoming rays could not break through to the forest floor. Most of the lowest branches on the trees hung well above their heads and the dwarves easily navigated their way through the forest.

Breslin carefully pulled a low-lying branch out of their line of sight and peered anxiously at the tiny lake before them.

"What do you think, lads? Is that it?"

Venk and Athos both shrugged, mimicking the other perfectly.

"I thought it'd be bigger," Tristofer commented. Frowning, he started searching his robes for the map Shardwyn had given him. "I do not see how a lake this size could have sustained an entire population of nixies. It's just not possible."

"Maybe these nixies are tiny beings no bigger than a bug," Venk suggested.

Breslin pointed to the map Tristofer was perusing. "What does the map say?"

The scholar didn't say anything as he held the map one way then completely reversed it and held it upside down. Venk and Athos shared a worried look with Breslin.

"It might be the next lake over."

Breslin held out a hand. "Give me the map."

"It's my map! Shardwyn gave it to me!"

"You can keep the map if you can tell me which direction north is."

Tristofer twisted to his right and peered through the trees. He then turned left and then finally leaned back to look up at the distant treetops.

"Umm… that way?"

Breslin and the two brothers turned to look right. All three shook their head. Venk sighed.

"Lukas, would you kindly point out which direction is north?"

Lukas turned a little to his right and silently hooked a thumb behind him.

"Excellent, son."

Tristofer reluctantly surrendered the map.

"Wizards be damned, Tristofer. The lake Shardwyn circled is two leagues to the east. I thought you knew what you were doing."

"I don't get outside much, alright?"

"Evidently. This way, follow me. We will have to hurry if we intend to make it before sunset."

A few hours later, as the sky began to darken, they finally broke free of the trees and approached the second lake. This one was much larger; it would take several hours to walk around the entire perimeter. Lukas suddenly gasped with surprise.

"What is it?" Venk asked as he rushed to his son's side. "Is something the matter?"

"It's my back! My back is tingling!"

Chapter 4 – Dwarves Hate Water!

So what does that tell us?" Venk asked, turning to look at the others. "It means we are on the right track, right? Lukas, let's see the mark."

"I'm willing to wager another clue has revealed itself," Tristofer guessed.

"Like before?" Athos inquired. "When the picture of the sprite didn't appear until contact with another Narian piece of junk was made?"

Tristofer bristled with annoyance. "They are called *nixies*, and they were *not* pieces of junk. They are treasured, *genuine* pieces of Narian culture, clearly unfit for a churlish brute such as yourself."

Athos stared incredulously at the scholar. Had his ears deceived him? Did the scholar really say what he thought he had? Athos turned to his brother to get his opinion. Venk, however, was trying to disguise his laughter as a series of coughs.

"No one calls me a girlish brute," Athos growled.

"The word was churlish, not girlish," Breslin added, doing a remarkable job of maintaining a neutral expression on his face.

"Oh. What does churlish mean?"

Venk hesitated as he tried to think of its definition.

"Uncivilized," Breslin supplied for him.

Athos marched over and crossed his arms over his chest. "You're calling me uncivilized, scholar?"

"Come on, Athos," Venk chided his brother. "He's not that far off the mark."

Athos considered and then shrugged. "I suppose I've been called worse."

Breslin approached Lukas and squatted down low. "Can we see the mark, young sir?"

Lukas pulled his jerkin up to his chin and faced the opposite direction. Tristofer rocked back on his heels and smiled.

"Hah! See? I told you so!"

Athos and Venk simultaneously pushed Tristofer aside and studied the Questor's Mark. Previously, the top left portion of the mark had been just as smudged and illegible as the rest, but as before, it was starting to come into focus. If they wanted the next part of the mark to be revealed they were going to have to find another Narian object. That had to mean there was something else in the area!

Venk glanced around the secluded glade. There was something hidden here? Where? How were they supposed to find it? Could the nixies, when they were alive, have hidden something in the forest? For all he knew whatever they were looking for was at the bottom of the lake.

"I'm getting a headache," Venk muttered, more to himself than to anyone.

Tristofer promptly produced several mint leaves from one of his many pockets and slapped them down into Venk's hand.

"Here, rub these into your hair. It'll help take care of that headache."

"Excuse me?"

"You most likely have a tension headache, caused by contracting muscles covering your skull. Mint leaves have long been known to be a remedy."

Venk sighed and removed his helmet. He ducked behind the closest tree, presumably to give Tristofer's remedy a try.

"What do we do now?" Athos asked. "Sounds like we're supposed to find these nixie creatures. How do we do that?"

"We don't," Tristofer told him. "Nixies are extinct."

"How certain are you of that?" Breslin asked. "Am I not addressing the person who tried to convince my father that the mark was a map? By that argument, are we not in the right place? Why would there be a reference to a creature that's extinct? Are you saying this isn't a map now?"

Tristofer crossed his arms. "It's a map, I assure you."

"Excellent. I believe we were led here. As you will see, another corner of Lukas' back has begun to come into focus, just like before. It must mean we're on the right track. Do you see where I'm going with this?"

Tristofer sighed. "All I'm saying is if nixies still exist, don't you think that someone would have seen them after all these years?"

"If the existence of a species depended upon the ability to conceal themselves, do you not think it's possible they would have learned to do just that?"

While Breslin and Tristofer debated, Athos stared out at the quiet lake and slowly scanned the area. Aside from a flock of bright red kytes chatting noisily nearby, there wasn't anything else noteworthy about this lake. Could there be beings hiding in the water? Athos shuddered. He couldn't think of a more horrid predicament. Water was meant for drinking and bathing. Immersing oneself? Absolutely not.

The incessant arguing suddenly ceased. Athos glanced over to check on his companions. The scholar was now checking various pockets, looking for who knew what. A quick glance at his brother confirmed his own suspicions that Tristofer's welcome in the group was dwindling rapidly. Venk was frowning at the small pile of junk that was growing steadily bigger as Tristofer emptied more and more pockets.

Venk cleared his throat. "Let's assume these nixie things

do exist and *are* hiding. What do we know about them? How do we find them? Can we set some sort of a trap?"

Breslin looked at Tristofer to answer, but the scholar was oblivious to all as he rifled through his jacket pockets.

"Tristofer, what are you looking for?"

"My map! I've lost Shardwyn's map! It's gone!"

Venk groaned aloud. Lukas, who had been staring up at the vivid red birds in the trees, dropped his gaze to the ground and started to search for the fallen piece of parchment.

"No, I don't think it'd be on the ground," Tristofer told the boy. "I must have lost it on that ghastly ride with the dragons. Confound it!"

Venk and Athos gave the scholar a pitiful look.

Tristofer was taken aback. "What?"

"You used it on the way here, remember? You held it upside down."

Tristofer paused in his search.

"That's right. I did."

Breslin sighed. Now he was starting to get a headache.

"I last saw you holding it at the wrong lake. You must have used it once I gave it back, right?"

Tristofer had resumed his search of his pockets. "Of course."

"You obviously didn't want to lose it, right?"

Tristofer nodded. "Absolutely."

"So knowing you might misplace it, you chose a special place to put it. Where?"

"Up my sleeve, of course."

Tristofer straightened. He gingerly prodded the left sleeve of his jacket and heard the crinkle of paper. He rolled up his sleeve and smiled sheepishly as the missing map fluttered to the ground. Surprised, Tristofer turned to Breslin.

"How did you do that? How were you able to make me remember?"

"Try having a famous father with a memory ten times worse than yours will ever be."

Taking another long look at the glade, Breslin came to a decision.

"We'll make camp here. Lukas, would you see if there's

anything we can use as firewood? Master Venk, would you help him?"

Venk nodded and tapped Lukas' shoulder to get his attention. Together the two of them disappeared into the woods.

Breslin lowered his voice to a whisper. "Athos, check the area and be certain nothing is lurking about."

"How far?"

"Half a league should be plenty. I want no surprises."

Athos nodded and pulled his black handled axe from its holder on his back. "Agreed."

* * *

The sun had set an hour ago and the stars had come out in droves. Hundreds of thousands of tiny pinpricks of light winked down at them from above. The buzzing drone of wood burrowing insects echoed noisily from all directions. The colorful kytes had finally stopped their incessant warbling and were now all asleep in their trees, beaks tucked under one of their wings.

"Did you know that Narian diggers had no fear of becoming trapped in the rock? Not as long as they were wearing their armor!"

Tristofer had been regaling them with stories the entire time they had been setting up their camp. It was as if he had never been given a chance to share his life's passion with someone who would listen, and now Lukas was sitting cross legged on the ground, staring at him with his large unblinking eyes. Tristofer told him of wonderful discoveries in metallurgy, amazing mechanical devices created to make day-to-day life easier, and weapons superior to all others; all were waiting for them once they discovered Nar's location.

With his duties complete, Venk selected a thick broken branch of firewood and sank down on the ground next to his son. He pulled out one of his daggers and began to carve several designs into the chunk of wood. While not really interested in what the scholar had to say, he wanted to make sure Tristofer didn't confuse his son with too much inaccurate information.

Thinking another willing member had joined his small audience, Tristofer told them both about the most highly sought after items to come from Nar: armor. Those who wore true Narian armor could rest easy, knowing no sword, nor spear, nor any type of projectile could penetrate their protective covering. It was said that kings and warriors from all across the land came to beseech the Narian blacksmiths for customized suits of armor. The secret of their armor's success was never discovered, making any surviving pieces worth their weight in gold.

"Many have tried to find Nar," Tristofer told them. "Fortunes were depleted as insistent families spent years searching with nothing to show for their efforts."

"How many times have you set out to find this city?" Venk mildly asked. He frowned at the wood he was holding. His attempts to carve a troll skull from the wood were not that successful.

"Six times," Tristofer told him with a smile.

"How far have you made it?" Small curls dropped onto his lap as he continued to whittle away at the chunk of wood.

"Not very far," Tristofer admitted. "I led several expeditions to the northeastern section of the Bohanis. I was convinced I had found the Valley of the Three Crags."

"I take it you were wrong?"

Tristofer grunted with annoyance. His most recent failed attempt was still a bitter point of contention between him and Maelnar.

"You said the Narians made good armor?"

"No," Tristofer corrected. "I said they made *great* armor."

"What about weapons?"

"It sounds strange," Tristofer admitted, "but they weren't known for their weapons. They focused more on tools than weapons."

Busy carving one of the two fangs on a troll's lower jaw, Venk paused.

"What can you tell us about that power hammer I heard you mention earlier?"

Tristofer nodded. "The Narian power hammer. What I can tell you is that it's an immensely powerful hammer that is rumored to be able to pulverize the hardest stones with a single blow."

"Do you think they used jhorun to make it work?"

The scholar shook his head. "I do not. In all my years of research, not once has there been any mention of jhorun when it came to Nar."

"How do you think the hammer works? You must have a theory."

Athos and Breslin appeared. Each claimed an open spot near the fire. Athos leaned up against a large boulder and pulled his pipe and tobacco out from a pouch on his belt. Breslin mumbled something and pulled his own pipe out, but then scowled as he realized he had forgotten his pouch of tobacco. After packing his pipe, Athos tossed the pouch to Breslin, who nodded appreciatively. Breslin packed his pipe full and tossed the pouch back.

"I personally think the gem is the key," Tristofer continued. "It somehow enhances the hammer. I see no other reason for it to be there."

Lukas nodded. "My friends all think the hammers are more dangerous than the swords."

Venk's hand paused as he worked to remove another sliver of wood. He regarded his son as though he were staring at a stranger.

"You've talked about Nar before?"

Lukas twisted around to look at his father. "Aye. With my friends. Sometimes we pretend we're Narian soldiers. We always carry hammers, never swords."

"The hammer was important to the Narians, obviously," Tristofer told Lukas, turning to face the young boy. "It's featured on their crest, and of course, it's featured on your back."

"Why is it upside down?" Lukas wanted to know.

Curious, all three adults looked at the scholar for an answer.

Tristofer was silent as he considered. "Presumably because it was heavy."

Lukas thought for a moment and then shook his head. "I don't think they'd make a hammer that they couldn't wield properly."

Venk noticed with keen interest that Tristofer had started to fidget uncomfortably. Enjoying this exchange between his son and the scholar, Venk let the half-carved skull drop into his lap, forgotten. He crossed his legs at his ankles and waited to see how Tristofer would respond. Chewing thoughtfully on a broken twig, Breslin looked over at the scholar and waited for a response, too. Bored, Athos pulled his pack over to himself, retrieved a small whetstone, and proceeded to sharpen his axe.

Tristofer shrugged. "Why they chose to depict the power hammer in such a manner is a mystery that will have to be solved once we find Nar."

Lukas nodded. "So you don't know. That's all you had to say."

Tristofer frowned as the child nonchalantly shifted his attention back to the twinkling stars. The last thing he needed on this expedition was another opportunity in which he could lose what little credence he had left. One couldn't project an aura of confidence when one became stymied by a simple boy.

The following morning began abruptly as Tristofer awoke with a start and let out a bellow of outrage.

"A pox on this accursed place!"

"What the deuce are you blathering about now?" Athos demanded grumpily from his hammock. He had draped his heavy parka across himself and sometime during the night he had completely covered his face. He was now propping a corner of his makeshift blanket up, peering at Tristofer from within the recesses of his warm cocoon. "Keep your voice down, will you? You've been hanging around the humans too long if you think a measly eight hours is enough sleep."

"My books! My things! They're gone!"

Breslin, forgetting he was sleeping several feet off the ground, made a move to stand and ended up tangled in his hammock. He crashed heavily to the ground. Moments later, his snores resumed.

Tristofer hurried over to his sleeping form and shook

him roughly to wake him up.

"We've been robbed! Everything I brought with me has vanished! This is a catastrophe!"

Breslin finally cracked an eye and glared at the scholar. A quick glance up confirmed the sun had not risen, although it was close. The sky was beginning to lighten as dawn approached. Breslin's brow furrowed.

"You wake me up to tell me you've misplaced something?"

"I didn't misplace anything. It was stolen! We've been robbed!"

Breslin gave a quick cursory check of himself by patting several of his pockets. He pulled his pack from where it was leaning up against a tree and rifled through it.

"Everything is here. Food, water, weapons. I haven't lost anything."

Venk checked his belongings, and his son's, and confirmed that they weren't missing anything, either. He looked over at the still form of his brother, swaying gently in the breeze.

"Athos? Are you missing anything?"

The parka covering Athos bulged slightly as he checked the contents of his pockets. An arm snaked out from under the warmth of the parka and checked the status of his pack, which was sitting on the ground directly beneath him. The thin leather cord he had used to tie his pack and his hammock together remained intact.

"My stuff is fine," Athos grumpily responded. He pulled his arm back in under the covers and tried to go back to sleep.

Tristofer started to whine. "So it's just me? Oh, that's just great. Why do these things always happen to me?"

"I'll help you look for your things."

Tristofer turned to see Venk's young son swing his legs out over his hammock and drop lightly to the ground.

"Your pockets were all full," Lukas remembered as he stared around at the forest floor. "It's too much stuff for one person to carry off. Let's look for clues!"

Tristofer crossed his arms over his chest and sulked. "It's *not* junk."

An entire hour was spent searching for some signs of what had happened to Tristofer's possessions. No signs, no footprints, not even a trace of any of Tristofer's numerous books could be found. He might as well have dug a hole, held his jacket upside down over it, and then filled the hole back up. The scholar was right. His things had vanished. Only when the group had officially given up the search did Lukas give Tristofer a glimmer of hope.

"I think I see something!"

Tristofer hurried eagerly to Lukas' side.

"What? What is it? Have you found something?"

"No, but I see something. Look, there in the water. There's something floating about twenty feet away."

Tristofer shaded his eyes from the overhead sun and squinted out at the water. There was something in the water, and it looked an awful lot like —

"It's one of my books! What is it doing in the water?"

"Isn't it obvious?" Venk asked as he joined his son at the water's edge. "I'd say your things were pilfered by a nixie."

"Where's your proof?" Tristofer sputtered. "You have none. Why? Because nixies are extinct."

Venk looked left, then right, and then behind them. "See anyone else around here? It's quiet enough where we would have heard the splash of your book being thrown. I think it was carried in."

"How did you know that nixies could leave the water?" Tristofer asked. His respect for Lukas' father rose by several levels. That fact wasn't commonly known.

"You aren't the only one who has heard stories."

"Who..."

"Our father regaled us with many a tale when we were young," Athos explained, finally extricating himself from his hammock. "Tobin used to tell stories of when he and my grandfather would sneak Topside and listen to the nixies sing."

"They sang?" Tristofer asked, astonished. "I have never heard any mention of singing."

"Exactly how often do you research anything besides Nar?" Breslin asked.

"My knowledge about occurrences that may or may not have happened Topside is severely limited as my area of expertise is focused on but one thing: Nar."

"Sounds like you have used that line before," Venk observed.

Tristofer smiled mischievously. "Once or twice."

Breslin rubbed his temples. His head was throbbing mercilessly. It was becoming uncomfortably common for him to get a headache in Tristofer's presence. He sighed.

"In case someone present," Breslin began, "happens to know a thing or two about these water sprites, perchance that person, or persons, will care to enlighten those who don't?"

Tristofer looked at Lukas' father and held out an arm in an open invitation to accept Breslin's request. Venk shook his head no. Tristofer turned to look back out over the water at his floating book.

"I'll tell you what I know about nixies but first we must get my book back. Who's the best swimmer?"

Three adult dwarves and one child all cringed.

"It's your book," Athos pointed out. "If anyone has to get wet, I'd say it should be its owner. That means you."

Tristofer gazed helplessly back out at the water. "But I can't swim! Surely one of you must know how to swim. Lukas, help an old man out and fetch me my book."

Lukas shook his head no and hid behind his father.

"Venk?"

Venk shook his head. "No."

"Breslin?"

"I've never waded in any farther than my knees. Not a chance."

Desperate, Tristofer turned to the last member of their group. "Athos, do you think that…"

"Never learned how, pal."

"Tristofer, you know we all avoid the water," Breslin patiently reminded him. "We don't swim for a reason. We sink."

"I know, I know," Tristofer snapped. He turned to look longingly at his floating book. As if on cue, the book slipped below the surface and didn't reappear.

"Someone must have taken your things," Breslin told him. "I want to know who, or what, is responsible."

"As I said before," Venk reminded everyone as he laid a hand on his son's shoulder, "I think this is a prank masterminded by the nixies."

"You don't know that," Athos scolded. His trademark frown had reappeared on his face.

"We've searched this entire area and have found no traces. The one thing that has been found was in the water. According to Shardwyn, this is the last known location of the nixies. I'd say this proves they're still alive."

"How long has it been since anyone has seen a nixie?" Lukas wanted to know.

"Oh, about a day ago," Athos muttered softly.

Breslin, standing nearby, snorted with laughter and expertly disguised it as a cough.

"At least five hundred years," Tristofer answered. Neither he nor Lukas had heard Athos' comment. "According to Shardwyn."

Lukas' naturally inquisitive nature took over.

"What'd they look like? You say there's a picture of a nixie on my back. Is it accurate?"

"Ordinarily I'd say that I wouldn't know," Tristofer answered with a smile, "but both Shardwyn's notes and the Questor's Mark are a match. The nixies are humanoid, about a quarter the size of a human, which makes them about half our size. They have long black hair usually tied so that it falls evenly down their back. Their skin is pale, almost to the point where it appears light green. Naturally, they have gills. Where the gills are located remains a mystery as no one has ever studied a nixie up close. There are reports of nixies venturing out onto dry land for a period of several minutes, which suggests they can hold their breath that long. They can't survive out of water; that much is certain. What's also certain, since they pilfered my belongings, is that they are a mischievous people. Whether they puncture the bottom of boats or pull them under, many people have reported mysterious accidents when trying to cross any body of water said to be inhabited by a tribe of nixies."

"So they're dangerous," Athos decided, absentmindedly resting his hand on the handle of his axe.

"They won't openly harm anyone," Tristofer countered. "Quite the opposite. If a boat sinks in their water, they'll make sure all occupants make it to shore, albeit typically the wrong shore."

"Then why bother sabotaging the blasted boat in the first place?" Breslin asked.

Tristofer shrugged. "Maybe they take offense to someone else using their waters? Perhaps they're offended by people who don't swim? No one can say."

"In that case, they're going to just love us," Athos grumbled. Breslin chuckled.

"How can we tell them we're friends?" Lukas suddenly asked, drawing everyone's attention. "We need to let them know we won't hurt them."

"There is a way, aye. The problem is," Tristofer scratched the back of his head, "it's more likely we could find the nixies on our own."

Breslin gave Lukas an approving smile and tousled his hair. He turned to face Tristofer.

"It seems to me that this quest is one huge challenge after another, so it fits that we have to accomplish some task to proceed. What do you need, Tristofer?"

"An orikai flower."

"A what?"

"It's a rare flower that I haven't seen in over a hundred years."

"Describe it. There's got to be one around here."

Tristofer shook his head. "I can tell you, but it won't do any good. It's probably the most rare and sought after flower known to exist."

"You've got to be kidding. We're looking for pontal now?" Athos threw his hands up in protest. "This is *not* the type of quest I signed up for!"

"Ignore him," Venk told Tristofer, glaring at his brother as he did so. "What are we looking for?"

"You're looking for a tri-petal flower that has purple elongated petals with white edges. The column and stamen are golden that will sparkle when exposed to the sunlight. It's presumed the nixies are attracted to the reflected light."

"Sounds like a very unique flower," Breslin admitted. "So once we find one of these flowers, then what do we do?"

"I doubt very much you'll find an orikai, but if you do, you'll know it. The flower lives on a distinctive blue stalk that looks a lot like a vine. If you find it, bring it back here as quickly as possible."

"Split up," Breslin told the group. "Find one of these flowers. Call out when you do."

"You're not going to find one," the scholar insisted. "There haven't been any sightings for a very long time."

Breslin grabbed Tristofer by his jacket collar and dragged him along. "Don't think you're getting out of searching. The more eyes, the better. Get moving."

Four hours later, after meticulously combing the area around the lake and then expanding the search for a full two leagues beyond, Breslin was forced to admit Tristofer had been right. There were no exotic purple flowers anywhere in the area. How were they supposed to summon the nixies now?

"Is there any other way to get their attention?" Venk asked.

The group was sitting around the fire ring, eating their midday meal, which consisted of cold mutton and hard crusty bread. Several fallen logs had been dragged over to serve as seats.

"There's no other way that I'm aware of," Tristofer admitted. He was hot, sore, and quite ready to take a nap. He hadn't had this much activity in the last five years combined.

"Then we must find one of these flowers," Breslin decided. "Who's got the spells Shardwyn gave us?"

"I do. I've got them in my pack," Venk answered.

"Get them, will you? I think it's time we use one of them."

Curious, Venk stood up and went to his pack. Retrieving the small silk bag, Venk handed it to Breslin. The bag was opened and upended on the ground in front of the fire. Selecting the white sphere with the symbol of the quill on it, Breslin gathered the other four spells and dropped them back into the bag and handed it back. Venk pointed at the sphere Breslin was still holding.

"That's the messenger spell. Who are you going to contact?"

"My father. He wants this quest to succeed just as much as we do. Therefore, we're going to make it his problem to find one of these blasted flowers."

Venk and Athos grinned at the same time in the same manner. Each caught sight of the other and the two brothers gently clinked their axes together.

Breslin closed his fist tightly around the spell and mentally instructed it to deliver the message to the correct recipient.

Father, we are at Lake Alpin. We have discovered that there's a strong chance nixies still exist, but we must summon them. We need an orikai flower. It's a purple flower with three petals. Gold stamen. We need this as soon as possible.

The sphere grew warm, surprising Breslin into opening his hand. The sphere flashed brightly and then vanished.

"That's just great. Now I'm seeing spots everywhere."

"We all are," Venk complained.

"Now what?" Athos wanted to know. "How long do we have to wait?"

"As long as it takes," his brother told him. "We have no idea how long it'll take for Maelnar to find one of these accursed flowers. If he isn't familiar with local pontal in this region then it might take him a while."

An hour and a half later, there was another flash of light, but this time a small wooden box had appeared and was sitting on the ground in front of the group. Breslin knelt down to retrieve the box. Standing slowly, he opened the tiny chest to reveal a striking purple flower with three elongated petals ringed with white. And a note.

Be sure you know what you're doing, son. You have only one shot at this as this is the only known orikai flower in existence in all of Lentari. The owner was very reluctant to part with it. On a side note, Shardwyn had to promise all kinds of favors in order to obtain it, so for that, I'm in your eternal debt!

"Now that we have it, what do we do with it?" Athos asked.

Tristofer was at a loss. "I'm not sure. If I were to offer an educated guess, I would say that since nixies are water sprites, we should place the flower on the water."

Athos reached for the wood chest, intent on throwing it and the flower out into the lake when Breslin suddenly twisted to his right and blocked the outstretched hand.

"Let's have Lukas do it. He's the one with the mark."

Breslin held the chest down low so that Lukas could reach in and extract the flower. Holding the delicate purple flower by its blue stem, Lukas walked to the water's edge and gently placed the offering on the water's surface.

Pulled by an unknown current, the flower floated out about fifteen feet. It rotated lazily as it floated away from the shore, as if guided by an unknown hand beneath the surface. After spinning about for a few more rotations, the flower silently slipped beneath the surface and disappeared from sight.

"Now what?" Athos demanded. He had expected something to happen, whether an immediate reaction from the nixies, an appearance, anything! But alas, the water was as still as a windless sea.

"That was a complete waste of —"

Athos trailed off as ripples formed in the water. Beginning at the point where the flower had sunk, tiny waves radiated outwards, and eventually caused the water to lap against the shore's edge.

"Look!" Lukas was pointing out at the water.

A tiny head appeared at the center of the ripples and was staring directly at them, unblinking. It had jet black hair, pale skin, and striking blue eyes.

"We mean you no harm," Breslin began diplomatically, taking a step toward the lake.

The head vanished beneath the waves.

"Nice going," Athos remarked as he gave Breslin a light punch on the arm. Breslin punched him back.

"Like you could have done any better," Breslin angrily retorted, retreating backward a few steps.

"Quiet!" Venk snapped. "It's back!"

Sure enough, the nixie's head had broken the surface of the water and was again staring at them. Going on a hunch, Lukas gently approached the water's edge and lifted his jerkin to expose his back. He carefully turned around so that the creature in the water could see the reason why they were there.

The nixie moved closer to shore and gripped a partially submerged broken tree. It pulled itself up so that it was mostly out of the water and stared at the boy's back.

"Well, there's no doubt about it. That one is a female," Athos told his brother.

The nixie had glossy green scales covering its torso but even though the scales sparkled iridescently, it couldn't disguise the womanly curves of its gender. Athos was right. This nixie was female.

Tristofer, who remained mired in place, pointed an arm at the nixie and whispered excitedly to Breslin.

"Look! There at the base of her neck. Do you see her gills? She has six gills total, three on each side. This is remarkable!"

Breslin, determined to make a good first impression for all dwarf kind, stepped forward again, arms open in what he hoped was a welcoming gesture. The nixie bolted from her perch on the sunken tree and dove back into the water.

Venk turned to Breslin and angrily smacked his right shoulder, spinning him around until the two were face to face.

"Stop doing that! We're here to establish contact, not to frighten it away! Get back over here and let's see if she comes back."

As soon as Breslin and Venk moved away from the water, the ripples appeared again and once more the female nixie was eyeing them from the safety of the water.

After giving the adult dwarves a speculative look, the nixie turned her attention back to Lukas. He pulled his tunic up and squatted down near the water's edge.

"Can you help me?" Lukas asked the water sprite. "Does this mean anything to you?"

The nixie's head dipped below the water's surface only to reappear moments later right beside him. Venk flinched as the nixie raised herself out of the water and approached his son. Breslin put a restraining hand on Venk's left shoulder while Athos put a hand on the other.

Delicate webbed fingers gently touched the hammer in the crest on Lukas' back. After a moment's hesitation, a string of chirps and clicks erupted from the nixie's mouth.

Lukas smiled at his father. "She sounds just like a kyte, doesn't she?"

More ripples appeared in the lake as first one, then two, and then many more nixies surfaced. Several dozen sets of blue eyes all focused on the small group of dwarves.

"This is starting to resemble a very bad idea," Athos grumbled to himself. He had set his axe up against his pack which was, unfortunately, at least twenty feet away from him.

The first nixie turned to look behind her and made another series of clicking noises. One male nixie, with just a few streaks of black through his otherwise gray hair, swam steadily closer. The old nixie joined his much younger counterpart near the shore and gazed with rapt fascination at the mark on Lukas' back. The male was motionless for a few moments as it studied the mark.

"What do you seek?"

The voice was high and shrill, barely resembling anything more than a squeak. The voice could have been made by either the male or female, it was so high. However, the dwarves knew from the way the older male was regarding Lukas that he was the one who had spoken.

"I'm so very pleased to meet you!" Tristofer began. "I'd like to —"

"I'll handle this," Breslin gruffly interrupted. He faced the nixie and tried to soften his expression so that he didn't appear threatening. "We are on a quest. As you can see from the boy's back, we are searching for —"

"You seek the object," the male interrupted, still addressing Lukas.

Breslin shrugged. "I was going to say answers, but let's go with that. What object are you talking about?"

The nixie didn't say anything but instead waited for Lukas to respond.

"Ask him what object he's talking about," Breslin whispered to Lukas.

"What object?" Lukas asked as he dropped his jerkin back down and turned around so that he was facing the water. He sank down and sat cross legged on the ground.

The old nixie pointed at Lukas' back.

"You want to see the mark?" Lukas asked, reaching for the hem of his shirt. "I can show it to you again if you'd like."

"The mark of Nar is upon you."

The four adult dwarves looked excitedly at one another.

Lukas nodded at the nixie. "Can you tell me anything about it?"

The water sprite gazed with fascination at the boy's back. "It's Narian."

"Thanks for letting us know. Er, will you tell us more about the object you were talking about?"

The old male turned to look back at several of his followers and uttered a string of nonsensical chirps and clicks. Half a dozen of the closest nixies vanished beneath the surface.

"We will give you the object in exchange for your offering. We knew one flower remained, but had no idea where it was or how to bring it here. You have done this for us. We are grateful."

"What's so special about that flower?" Breslin wanted to know. The old nixie continued to ignore him.

Figuring he should ask any question that Breslin voiced, Lukas repeated the question to the nixie.

"We cannot stay on dry land. If we are caught outside the water for too long, we become a flower. An orikai flower. The only way to restore a nixie to its former self is to submerge the flower back into its native waters. You have done this for us. There are no more orikai, no more trapped nixies. You have freed the last. It is for this reason we are in your debt."

"Did you know that?" Breslin whispered to Tristofer. "About the flowers?"

"As I said before," Tristofer whispered back, "pontal are not my specialty. So no, I didn't know that."

"What can you tell us about the object you're giving us?" Breslin gently asked from his position away from the water.

The male nixie finally turned his head and made eye contact with him.

"It is an object that has been resting in our lake for many centuries. It has a Narian symbol on it. The boy's back shares this symbol."

There were several congratulatory arm shakes as Venk, Athos, and even Tristofer, all gave each other friendly pats on the back.

The six nixies that had departed resurfaced, struggling to lift an object between them. More nixies swarmed to their aid, as collectively they lifted a surprisingly small four inch by four inch square metal plate that was no more than an inch thick. The metal object was plunked down into the soft mud at the water's edge before all the nixies save the old male disappeared back into the water.

Lukas reached into the water to retrieve the metal plate but was surprised at how heavy it was. He ended up using both hands to pry it off the ground and then struggled to stand up. His father and uncle were next to him in a flash. Venk took the piece of metal from his son while Athos managed to snag Lukas' belt to keep him from tipping over into the water once he became off balance.

Venk reached back into the water and swished the metal plate back and forth a few times so that the muck and grime from the lake bed were washed away. Curious, he stared down at the object in his hands.

The metal was the color of tarnished bronze and was far denser than anything he had ever encountered. Something this size should have been lighter and much easier to handle. It was perfectly smooth on all surfaces except for one corner, the lower left, depending on how you held it. That corner depicted the Narian crest. The all too familiar upside-down hammer met his eyes.

Venk squinted at the metal. What was it made of? This one piece alone was actually heavier than his largest hammer, but nowhere near the size of it. What was it used for?

"What do you have there?" his brother asked him, coming to stand beside him.

"Do your eyes not work? It's just a square piece of metal."

Breslin and Tristofer joined him moments later and together they inspected the object.

"Thank you very much," Lukas told the male nixie, who was still watching from the safety of the water.

Surprised, the adults turned back to the lake and watched as the nixie gave them all an impish smile. Moments later the old male returned to his watery realm below.

As soon as Lukas joined his father and saw the crest, his back began to tingle. He giggled as the sensations traveling up and down his spine tickled him mercilessly.

"What's the matter with you?" Athos asked his nephew. "What's so funny?"

"Something is tickling my back!"

"Pull up your shirt," Tristofer ordered. "We must see the mark!"

Lukas pulled up his jerkin once more and rotated until he was facing away from the adults. Venk leaned close and held the metal plate next to his son's back. The top left section of the Questor's Mark, the part that had started to come into focus earlier in the day, rippled outward and became legible. What they saw drew gasps of alarm and a few curses.

A two-headed dragon, with its long leathery wings partially spread, was clearly visible. In its front left claw, it clutched a gem.

"*Wizards be damned!*"

Chapter 5 — Twice Is Not As Nice

Since when does a dragon have two heads?" Athos wanted to know. "They're bad enough with one. Most dragons have fangs that are longer than my arms. The last thing we need right now is to deal with a dragon with twice as many fangs. It must be a mistake."

Breslin looked at Tristofer. "You're the scholar. I know you told us your field of study focused primarily on Nar, but you must have at least heard of a two headed dragon, right?"

Tristofer sadly shook his head. "Not once in all of my studies, readings, or teachings have I ever heard of a dragon with two heads. I'm sorry, my friends. I cannot help you there."

"What do we do?" Venk asked. "We've come this far. We can't give up now."

"Our next course of action is simple," Breslin informed everyone. "We must find ourselves a dragon and ask them about this. If this unique dragon does exist then I would think another dragon would have heard of it, or perhaps even tell us where we can find it."

"How do you propose we do that?" Venk asked.

"Do what? Find a dragon? That's easy. We return home. You can't walk ten paces in our valley without seeing signs of a dragon."

Lukas was crestfallen. They had to walk all the way back home before they could start the next leg of the journey. That would take days!

"Don't look so glum," Athos told his nephew. "We know what we need to find. We just need to know where to look."

"But the two-headed dragon could be right around here!" Lukas complained. "It'll take days to make it all the way home!"

"True. We are a patient people, nephew. We'll get there, just give it some time."

Just as they were about to depart from Lake Alpin, now known to be the *confirmed* home of the last band of nixies, Breslin stopped and turned back toward the water.

"What is it?" Venk asked, automatically walking around Lukas to put himself in front of his son.

"I thought I heard something. Splashing water. Anyone else hear that?"

Athos nodded as he appeared at Breslin's side. "More nixies?"

Suddenly a small object floated to the surface. Did the nixies have something else to tell them?

Tristofer was delighted.

"It's a book! It's one of my books! How wonderful!"

More objects surfaced. Whatever force the nixies had been using to hold Tristofer's pilfered possessions underwater had now decided to let go. All of his items bobbed to the surface.

"I'd get them now, while you can," Breslin told the scholar. "Wait too long and they all may sink."

"But that means I'll have to get… to get…"

"Wet," Breslin finished for him. He clapped a friendly hand on the scholar's shoulder and tried to conceal his smile.

"Better hurry."

With a muted curse, Tristofer stripped off his jacket and hurried into the water. He made it about five paces when the ground disappeared and he plopped straight down into the lake. Sputtering, cursing, and floundering as much as a recently caught fish that had been dropped on the ground, Tristofer managed to collect his belongings and dump them on the shore.

"What now?" the sodden scholar asked. "It'll be hours before everything is dry."

"We don't have time for that," Breslin informed him. "Just stow everything back in that jacket of yours and let's continue."

* * *

For several hours they tromped through the forest, heading north. Lukas, steadfastly against returning home, hadn't uttered a word as he followed his uncle and the rest of the group. Hands shoved deep in his pockets, he deliberately walked slower than his father, causing Venk to constantly check behind him to verify that his son was keeping up. Lukas fumed. There had to be something they were missing, something that would help them find this special dragon. Was the jewel it was holding the same type of gem that was on the surface of the hammer? If so, that would suggest that maybe they were looking for pieces of some type of mechanical device. Maybe Tristofer was right and the gem acted like a power source. Maybe if they returned to the glade and searched a little harder, they could find some type of clue.

WHAM!

Lukas, with his head up and his eyes lost in the clouds high overhead, walked right into his stationary father. The impact was so strong that he had knocked himself dizzy and ended up collapsing to the ground.

"You really concern me sometimes, boy," Venk quietly told his son as he lifted Lukas back to his feet. "Were you daydreaming? Watching the clouds? What was it this time?"

"Nothing."

"Clearly, or else you could have seen that we have all stopped."

"Why *are* we stopped?"

"Because we want to ask you something."

"Really? Now? What do you want to know?"

"Do you feel that we're missing something?"

Lukas stared at his father in shock. Had his father been reading his thoughts?

"W-what? Why do you say that? Do you think we're missing something, too?"

Surprisingly, Venk nodded, along with the other three adults. Shocked, amazed, and quite confused, Lukas stared at the faces gawking back at him.

"What's going on? Why are you all -watching me?"

Breslin approached and knelt down on one knee.

"Tell me, young master, what are we looking for?"

"A two-headed dragon," Lukas hesitantly answered, unsure where this was going.

"Right, I know that. But what are we off to do right now? What are we looking for?"

"A dragon, so that we can ask if it knows anything about the creature that showed up on my back."

Breslin nodded and smiled. If only all children were as bright and intelligent as this one.

"Exactly. Now, what would you say if I told you that a dragon just sought us out?"

"What? There's a dragon here? Where? How did they know to come?"

"Let's go find out, shall we?"

"Where is it? How do you know where it is?"

Venk sighed. "You really need to pay more attention to what is going on around you. We heard the dragon fly by just moments ago, which is why we've stopped. Dragons can move in stealth when they want to, which means this one wanted us to know it was here. So, I say we should go make contact."

"And if it's a dragon that wants to make us its lunch?"

Tristofer asked. "What then?"

"Then you'd better hope you can outrun the person you're standing next to."

The dwarves peered cautiously from the safety of the trees toward the open grassland that edged Zylan River. This particular river, the dwarves knew, stretched all the way to the great Sea of Koralis from the furthest western shores. Wide, flat, and very slow moving, the river was just over a mile wide at its broadest and narrowed to a few hundred feet at its slimmest. Unfortunately, this area was where the river forked off and the second branch angled southwest. As such, it would be a mighty long swim if they were to attempt to cross it. Fortunately, the creature sitting on the southern riverbank directly between the dwarves and the river caused them to dismiss any thoughts of a crossing.

"We meet again."

The group of dwarves edged from behind the trees and ventured into the open. A large, familiar blood-red dragon with purple flanged wings met their eyes. Breslin approached the dragon and bowed.

"Greetings, Rhamalli. To what do we owe this pleasure?"

The dragon lowered his head down to ground level so that he could converse with the dwarf, eye to eye. Unfortunately, this put the dragon's enormous horns less than twenty feet away from the dwarf.

"You're the one who wanted to speak with a dragon, land dweller. Here I stand before you. What do you wish to know?"

Surprised, Breslin looked back at his companions. How had the dragon known that they needed its help? Athos returned his gaze and shrugged. Venk held up both hands as if to say that he had nothing to do with the dragon's presence. Tristofer was cowering behind Athos.

"How did you know we needed to consult a dragon?" Breslin asked. "Have you been spying on us?"

Every Lentarian knew, including the dwarves, that a dragon's aural capabilities were only exceeded by its impressive visual abilities. A dragon could not only spot prey from great heights, but it could hear everything in the surrounding environment, too. Rhamalli could have been several miles away and would have still been able to watch and listen in on their conversation with the nixies.

The great red dragon went silent. Whether it was an indication it had been caught eavesdropping, or the dragon thought it beneath it to have even tried, no one could say.

"Aren't you supposed to be somewhere else?" Venk asked, curiously. Didn't the dragon tell them that they were on their way to hunt the great serpent in the eastern sea? What would make a dragon abandon its brethren and instead spy on a small group of dwarves?

"I never made it to the hunt," Rhamalli admitted, correctly guessing what the dwarf was thinking. "I turned back before the sea was in sight."

"Why?" Lukas wanted to know.

Two slitted reptilian eyes focused on him.

"Because of you, young dwarf."

Venk automatically grabbed Lukas' shirt and tugged him backward a few feet while he and his brother stepped around the boy to shield him from the dragon's gaze.

"Fear not," Rhamalli told them. "I am here at the request of the Dragon Lord."

"What's the Dragon Lord's interest in our quest?" Breslin asked suspiciously. "We aren't doing anything that should have attracted his attention."

"Think of it as a favor," Rhamalli explained.

"A favor to whom?" Breslin wanted to know.

The dragon went silent again.

"My father asked him to keep an eye on us, didn't he?"

Rhamalli came very close to smiling.

"That's just great," Breslin grumped. "Over nine hundred years old I am and yet he still treats me like a child who's unable to fend for himself."

The rest of the group managed to keep their smiles concealed.

"Show him the mark, Lukas," Venk instructed.

Lukas hoisted up his jerkin and presented his back to the dragon. Rhamalli lowered his thick long neck and gazed at the Questor's Mark. His two massive horns, protruding out the top of his cranial ridge, came disconcertingly close to Lukas' skin. As soon as Rhamalli's eyes saw the newly revealed illustration of the two-headed dragon, it jerked his head up and regarded the band of dwarves.

"It's a zweigelan."

"A what?"

"A zweigelan. You have no doubt noticed the two heads," Rhamalli explained. Everyone, including Tristofer, crowded close to Lukas so they could all hear Rhamalli's explanation of the unique dragon. "They are independent and allegiant to no one. Highly territorial, they are known to accost travelers entering their domain and make their victims solve puzzles or riddles. A successful answer results in the traveler going about their business. An incorrect answer results in the forfeiture of all their belongings."

"What would a dragon need with various items folk typically carry around with them?" Venk wondered aloud.

The dragon shook its great red head. "Unknown. They collect any number of things. Because of this, their nests tend to be massive."

"So this Zwei... zwei... Two Heads collects things," Athos observed. "One of these beasties must have the gem we need in its nest, only we don't know which one."

"Do you know where we can find one?" Venk asked, hopeful. "Is there a zweigelan nearby?"

"I know not."

Breslin sighed. "That's not very encouraging."

"Yes, it is," Tristofer countered. The scholar took a moment to collect himself. He finally turned to face the dragon. "How many zweigelans are there?"

Rhamalli was silent as he relayed the question to the wyverian collective chattering away in his mind. After a few moments he had an answer.

"Three."

"Where?"

Another silence.

"Two reside in Ylani."

"We have no time to search Lentari's northern neighbor," Breslin told the dragon. "What about the third?"

"The third lives here, in Lentari."

The group looked excitedly amongst themselves.

"Where, exactly?" Breslin wanted to know.

"Unknown."

"Can you find out?"

"A moment, if you please."

Rhamalli fell silent as he yet again conversed with the other members of his species. His large, silver eyes eventually closed and he became as still as a statue. After a few minutes of motionless silence, Breslin gently cleared his throat.

"Ahem-ahem."

Rhamalli cracked an eye and regarded the dwarf.

"What's going on?" Breslin asked. "Do they not know?"

"Not only do they not know," Rhamalli told them, "but it seems we have created a massive debate. Everyone is arguing. Some feel the zweigelan is hiding in the northern mountains. Others feel that perhaps it calls the Selekais home, here in the south. I personally feel that Rinbok Intherer views this as his opportunity to locate the zweigelan once and for all and see to it that it knows *every* dragon answers to him."

"How does this help us?" Venk asked.

Rhamalli smirked. "There are now dozens of dragons in the air, all searching."

"For ol' Two Heads?" Athos whistled appreciatively. "Nice."

"While they are searching, what can you tell us about the gem it's holding?" Venk asked as he pointed to his son's back.

Rhamalli returned his attention to the boy's back and noticed the jewel clutched tightly in the dragon's left front claw.

"Either that's an enormous jewel or else the gem has a unique shape."

"What?"

"Observe the bottom of the claw. You can see the tiniest bit of a sharp point just below the lowest claw. Either it's holding the largest jewel known to exist or else it was drawn that way to emphasize the unique shape of the gem."

The four adults stared intently at the gem. Rhamalli was right. Visible as a tiny point on the underside of the claw was the bottom of the jewel. Was the gem that large or was there something else they were missing?

Becoming more and more comfortable with the friendly dragon, Tristofer approached and knocked his knuckles on Rhamalli's front foreleg. Once he was sure he had the dragon's attention, he pointed back at the Questor's Mark.

"I have a theory. Dragons like treasure and jewels, right?"

Rhamalli was silent as he studied the scholar.

"Right?"

The great horned head slowly nodded.

"Excellent. Stay with me now."

Rhamalli snorted derisively. "Twists and turns abound, but I'm managing to follow along."

"Uh huh. Anyway, with regards to that gem, if it was shaped normally, we wouldn't be seeing the bottom of it, right?"

Rhamalli nodded.

"Are there gems so large a dragon could hold it like that?"

Rhamalli held out his front foreleg and opened his claw. Three dwarves could have easily sat on his open palm.

Tristofer nodded. "I'll take that as a no. Therefore, it must be as you said: a jewel with a unique shape. Of all the gems you've ever encountered, have you seen any with really unusual shapes?"

"I have not, but I will ask the others." Rhamalli's eyes closed as he relayed the question.

Breslin turned to the scholar. "Where are you going with this?"

"I think we may be looking for pieces of some type of Narian device."

Lukas let his shirt fall back into place and smiled up at Tristofer. "That's what I think, too!"

Tristofer grinned affectionately down at the youngster and nodded.

"A device to do what?" Athos wondered.

"We won't know that until we have all the pieces."

Breslin nodded. "It's a plausible theory."

"A jewel can come in other shapes and sizes," Rhamalli's deep voice informed, startling them. "However, they are exceedingly rare and therefore highly coveted. History, hues, and shapes all contribute to their desirability."

"Do you know anything about Nar?" Tristofer asked the dragon. Fifteen minutes ago he would never have believed he would be having a discussion with a dragon, let alone about Nar. "Have you ever seen a Narian gem?"

"I do not know much about Nar other than it was a city populated by dwarves. I have seen many jewels, dwarf, but whether or not any of them were Narian remains unknown."

Rhamalli's neck snapped up and quickly turned east. Athos was on his feet in a flash, gripping his black axe tightly in both hands. Venk also leapt to his feet, pushing Lukas down with one hand while reaching for his crossbow with the other. Tristofer let out a cry of alarm and knelt down on the ground beside the cowering boy.

"What is it?" Athos whispered to the dragon. "What do you smell?"

"I smell nothing," Rhamalli answered, still staring off to the east. "They think they found traces of the zweigelan."

"You're kidding!" Venk exclaimed. "That was quick!"

Rhamalli finally turned his head to stare down at Venk.

"I don't think you realize how many dragons are searching for the outcast. It was only a matter of time. I personally thought it would have been located much sooner."

"Remind me to never make the Dragon Lord angry," Tristofer whispered to Lukas.

Lukas looked way up at Rhamalli's distant head and coughed to get his attention.

"Is the two-headed dragon nearby?"

Rhamalli turned to look down at the dwarf child. "As a dragon flies, aye. As a dwarf walks, no. Several leagues from the northern edge of the Selekai Mountains one of my brethren spotted a few burnt trees and several scorch marks on the ground."

"Couldn't have been caused by a renegade campfire?" Venk asked.

"Only if those responsible had a bite radius large enough to fell a tree."

"Can you take us to it?"

"I can lead you to the place I was shown," Rhamalli told them. "I have been instructed not to engage the zweigelan. I am only to identify its lair. How the five of you plan to acquire this gem is beyond me. However, speaking on behalf of the Dragon Lord, we are intrigued."

"Wonderful," Athos grumbled.

It took the better part of a day and a half of solid traveling, over some of the hardest terrain any of the dwarves had ever encountered, before they came across a small glade with several blackened trees. Also immediately apparent were the two large sections of earth devoid of any grass, plants, or vegetation other than a few traces of burnt grass around the edges of the scorch marks. The dwarves all squatted down next to one of the bare patches and compared notes.

"Two marks, both of which are roughly the same size," Breslin noted.

"Two heads, two blasts," Athos remarked. "Makes sense."

Venk turned to regard the trees. "Burnt trees to the south. I can see the beginnings of the mountains back there as well. I also see the downed trees Rhamalli mentioned. What do you think? Are we in the right area?"

Just then, Rhamalli flew over them, temporarily casting a huge shadow. The dwarves looked up in unison.

"Without a doubt," the dragon's voice said as it floated down to them.

"Can you see anything else up there?" Breslin called out in a loud voice.

"Aye. I can see the human village of Donlari, off to the northeast."

"Really? I didn't know we were that close. How far away is it?"

"As the dragon flies, it's about…"

"We aren't dragons!" Tristofer yelled up as Rhamalli flew over them again. "Stop telling us how long it'd take you and instead tell us how long it'd take us from the ground!"

They all heard the dragon's laughter.

"The distance to the human village is equivalent to

the amount of ground already covered after our meeting yesterday."

Exasperated, Athos turned to his brother. "What'd he say?"

Venk shrugged. He didn't know, either. Tristofer chuckled.

"He means it's as far away as what we've already traveled. About a day and a half."

"Why didn't you just say so?" Athos shouted at the open sky. "Why make it so difficult?"

"Where's the fun in that?" Rhamalli asked as he circled lazily in the sky.

Breslin turned to Tristofer and held out a hand.

"Can I see that map Shardwyn gave you?"

"As long as you promise to give it back."

Unfurling the map on the ground, Breslin studied the forests south of Zylan River. He tapped the northern border of the Selekai Mountains and slowly traced his finger along an imaginary line until he stopped at a point still within the boundary of the forest but southwest of Donlari.

"I figure we are right about here. Rhamalli told us the zweigelan likes to accost travelers. It wouldn't be able to do that unless it had a supply of victims. In order to do that, it'd have to situate itself next to some type of road or path. Now, I think we can rule out this road that runs along Zylan River. If too many people were attacked then the human king would have noticed and would have done something about it. Besides, I heard somewhere that the main roads between villages are enchanted against harm. No, my friends, I think what we're looking for is something smaller. Something that could barely be perceived as a path, yet obviously someone uses it from time to time."

"A path between what?" Venk wondered aloud as he stared down at the topological map of Lentari.

"Avin lies to the west, here," Breslin said, indicating a spot on the map west from their location. "And Donlari is here. The road connecting the two villages is a far cry from being a direct route. There must be other unsanctioned routes folk can use if they so choose."

"Your premise is Two Heads is preying on anyone who

uses one of these paths?" Athos asked.

Breslin nodded. "Aye. Look around, my friends. There must be a path nearby or else why wouldn't the zweigelan have attacked someone here?"

Try as they might, they could find no traces of any type of trail, not even after they split up and spent three more hours searching. Only when it became too dark to see did they give up their search and make camp for the night. They could only hope that luck would favor them the next day.

It did.

Breslin awoke the following morning to the sounds of kytes chirping, insects buzzing, and several unknown animals scurrying about high above their heads in the trees. Swaying gently in his hammock, he finally opened his eyes. Staring straight down at him was the massive horned head of the dragon.

Breslin jerked so violently that his hammock spun him around and deposited him on the ground with a thud.

"What the blazes are you doing? You just scared ten years off my life!"

Rhamalli turned his great head to look back at the two dwarf brothers. Breslin followed his gaze. He narrowed his eyes as he saw several pieces of gold exchange hands.

"Told you he wouldn't wake," Athos chided his brother as he pocketed his earnings.

Breslin finally rose from his position on the ground and stalked over to Athos, who had enough sense to put his face back into neutral.

"You wagered against me?"

Athos sheepishly nodded.

Breslin held out a hand. "I want a cut."

Athos hesitated for a few seconds before handing him a piece of gold.

Rhamalli shook his head. "Dwarves and their gold."

Breslin cast a disdainful look up at the dragon. "You're a dragon. You are in no position to heckle me about possessing gold, wouldn't you agree?"

The dragon harrumphed, but didn't say anything.

"What are you doing down here, anyway? Aren't you

supposed to be looking for a path?"

The dragon nodded. "Aye. I found it."

"You did? When? How? Where?"

Rhamalli turned and looked toward the distant mountains. "Half a league south there is a path with a faint scent of human about it. I believe that is what you're looking for. Can I ask what your intentions are? How do you plan on proceeding?"

Breslin smiled mischievously. He indicated the others should huddle close.

"I have a plan. Lukas, stay close. I must talk with you as well."

Limbs cracked and twigs snapped noisily, breaking the eerie calm of the forest. Flocks of brightly colored kytes retreated to the safety of the air, all the while voicing their displeasure about being disturbed from their perches amongst the trees. A child's wail sounded, startling the kytes into silence.

"Father! We're lost! We are never going to find our way out of here! We're doomed!"

"Be silent, boy! Just as soon as we can return to the safety of our tunnels, all will be well. You'll see. Now stop that caterwauling and help me figure out which way is north. Do you really want to be stuck out here at night? I don't. Now *move*!"

"But you don't know which way we're going! I'm tired of walking. Can't we just sit for a moment?"

Venk grabbed Lucas by the scruff of his shirt and physically pulled him along the ground. Lukas, in a scripted act of defiance, crossed his arms over his chest and went perfectly still. Unfazed by his son's act of defiance, Venk simply dragged Lukas along after him.

"You're doing great," Venk told him in the softest whisper he could manage.

Lukas smiled. "This is fun! I hope it works!"

For thirty minutes father and son argued with each other, all the while creating the loudest ruckus they could, figuring they were probably being heard all the way to Donlari. Lukas had thrown a temper tantrum every ten minutes, as he was instructed. Venk would curse loudly and throw about rocks and tree limbs in a fit of anger. They were close to giving up when a large shadow fell over them.

"Have we another visitor?" a strange voice hissed.

Venk, already gripping Lukas by his shirt collar, spun in place while reaching for his crossbow. Lukas was flung like a discus. The boy was due for a rough landing but Athos popped up over the bush he was hiding behind and snagged his nephew out of the air. Slapping a hand over Lukas' mouth, Athos shoved the boy down to the ground.

"Stay here and stay hidden."

Venk placed his right boot into his crossbow's stirrup and pulled the string back, locking it into firing position, all without breaking eye contact with the creature standing before him. It was the zweigelan, but it wasn't what he was expecting. This dragon was small, much smaller than any other he had ever seen. Its coloring was a mottled green with flecks of brown scattered unevenly all over its body. Its long sinewy body resembled a giant serpent with legs, only it had two heads. Gaunt, leathery wings were folded flat against its back while its long tail had hooked itself around the closest tree. However small this dragon was, it still towered over them.

"It's been way too long since we've had another visitor," the second head purred, eliciting a nod from the first.

The zweigelan's tail released the tree and it started to move. Not toward the bushes, where his friends were, but right toward Venk. Either it hadn't detected the presence of the others or else it didn't care. Both heads were fixated on the dwarf and peered silently at him, as though they were capable of reading his innermost thoughts. After a few moments of silence, both sets of jaws opened, revealing several rows of razor-sharp teeth. Each head was large enough to easily swallow a dwarf whole.

Venk loaded a bolt and took aim. "Keep your distance, dragon."

The zweigelan paused in its advance and eyed the dwarf.

The left head blinked its bulbous green eyes at him.

"Dragon? We are no dragon. We are zweigelan!"

"Indeed, we are," the second head agreed.

Venk scratched his head. "That's your name?"

"It's what we are," Right Head told him.

"So, what's your name then?"

"We are zweigelan!" Left Head and Right Head answered in unison.

"You don't have a name, then? That's sad."

Left Head growled ominously while Right Head gazed impassively at him.

"What should we do with it?" Left Head asked. "Does it taste good?"

Venk swallowed nervously. The dragon was supposed to ask a riddle or present him with a puzzle! It was considering eating him? That couldn't be good. Suddenly, inspiration struck. Smiling, Venk faced the two-headed dragon.

"Sorry about the misunderstanding. You looked like a dragon to me."

"We are more than a dragon! We are better!"

"Allow me to venture a guess. Because two heads are better than one?"

A snort of laughter was heard from one of the nearby bushes.

"Do not try and insult us, biped," Left Head hissed down at him. "We are far superior, in every fashion."

"Yes, we are," Right Head agreed.

"Prove it," Venk challenged.

Left Head nodded. "Very well. A riddle. We have a riddle for you. If you —"

"You'll never solve it," Right Head informed him.

"If you solve it," Left Head continued, casting a glare at its other head, "you may leave. Alive."

"And if I cannot?"

"Then you forfeit all that you carry."

"If I refuse to answer?"

Both heads grinned maliciously. "Then we *eat* you."

Venk pretended to think for a moment. "Agreed. Actually, you know what? I have a proposition for you."

Taken aback, the zweigelan stared incredulously at the dwarf.

"Intrigued, we are," Left Head said.

"Very intrigued," Right Head agreed.

Venk turned to the bushes and motioned for his companions to join him.

"Ask your riddle. If we are unable to answer, then not only do you get all my possessions, but you get all of theirs as well. See the one wearing the long jacket? Trust me, he has a lot of junk I'm sure you'd love."

Tristofer's cry of outrage was cut off as Breslin stuffed a wad of grass in the scholar's mouth.

"And what is it you seek, should you answer correctly?"

"You won't," Right Head added.

"You take us to your nest and we can select one item from anything you have."

Right Head looked at Left Head.

"Is it a trap? Can they solve the riddle?"

"How could they?" Left Head argued. "We haven't told them yet."

"The biped is confident. Too confident."

"What have we to worry about?" Right Head insisted. "We are much smarter than they are!"

Left Head nodded. "Very well. We will make the deal."

"But what will they want in return?" Right Head asked, showing signs of concern.

"It matters not. They will not be successful."

Venk coughed loudly. "You guys know that you're speaking loud enough for everyone to hear you, right?"

Ignoring Venk's question, the zweigelan advanced on the small group.

"We have an accord. Here is your riddle."

Both serpentine necks began to sway from left to right.

"*Never resting, never still,*" Right Head intoned.

"*Moving silently from hill to hill,*" Left Head continued.

"*It does not walk, run, or trot.*"

"*All is cool where it is not.*"

"What is it?" both heads asked together.

Baffled, Venk turned to look at Tristofer and noticed

his blank expression. He didn't know. Venk glanced at his brother and then at Breslin. All had the same crestfallen look on their faces. No one knew the answer.

"Oh, that's just perfect."

* * *

"Might I remind you, again, that this was your bright idea?"

"Tristofer, if you don't stop whining, I'll personally shove another handful of grass in your mouth."

"But all my things are gone! Again!"

"You may have noticed this, but I feel I should point it out anyway. All of our stuff is gone, too. Stop complaining."

"What are we going to do now?"

"Simple," Athos told the scholar. "We find Two Heads and take the gem. After we take back our things. I will not lose my axe to that conceited excuse of a dragon."

"Rhamalli?" Breslin called up to the empty sky. "Can you tell where it went?"

"No," Rhamalli's voice said as it floated down from above. "It noticed me following and dipped below the tree tops, squeezing itself into spaces where it knew I could not follow. It knew how to elude me, which suggests it has eluded many other dragons before me. Rinbok Intherer is angry. He wants this dragon found."

Athos cursed with disgust. "So there's no way to track it? Of all the blasted luck!"

Venk nudged his brother on the arm. "Quiet."

Athos' eyebrows shot up.

"Excuse me? You want me to be quiet? I am the elder brother. I say when to be quiet."

"Athos, shut up!"

Surprised at the commanding tone his younger brother had used, Athos fell silent. Venk was looking pointedly at Lukas. The child's eyes were closed.

"What's going on? Son, are you okay?"

The boy turned to his right and pointed off to the distant mountains. He looked up at Breslin. "It's that way."

"What? What's that way?" Tristofer wanted to know, turning to look south.

"That metal plate given to us by the nixies."

"You can sense its presence?"

Lukas nodded.

"Ever since it was given to us, I've felt it pulling, like its calling to me. Right now, I feel it again, only this time it's calling from that way."

Athos turned to Breslin and gave him an appraising stare. "You knew?"

Breslin nodded. "I suspected. I knew there was a good chance we'd be unable to solve any riddle presented to us from that infernal dragon, so I thought we'd better have a backup plan. I talked to Lukas after I outlined our plan. I had to know if he could sense that metal plate. He told me he could. Therefore, I knew tracking this dragon wouldn't be difficult."

Venk and Athos both nodded, impressed. Tristofer beamed.

"Well done, Master Breslin. Well done!"

* * *

"Oh, sure. We can track this dragon, you said. Shouldn't be difficult, you said." Tristofer gave Breslin his best attempt at a scowl. "What do you have to say for yourself now?"

The band of dwarves was standing before a sheer cliff rising several thousand feet into the air. Its bare rock beckoned menacingly, indicating there would be no scaling this behemoth. Athos and Breslin both felt the cliff's surface. It was smooth, as smooth as if the rock had been burnished several times by hundreds of their finest stone grinders.

In response, Breslin turned to look at Lukas.

"Is it nearby?"

Lukas nodded. He pointed up.

"I'm being pulled up. It's up there somewhere."

"Of course it is," Athos grumbled.

They all took several steps back and stared up at the sheer expanse of stone above them. The cliff's surface may have been perfectly smooth, but the wall was not entirely solid. Dark nooks and sunken caves were scattered all across the cliff as far as the eye could see. The dwarves stared up at the imposing cliff for so long that they all developed kinks in their necks at about the same time. Rubbing his, Athos turned to look at his companions.

"Anyone have any ideas?"

Breslin held out a hand to Venk.

"Spells."

"What?"

"Shardwyn's spells. One of them is levitation. Would you hand it to me, please?"

Venk pointed up at the wall. "It's up there, remember? My pack was taken."

"Wizards be damned."

"We climb."

"How? Our tools were taken, too."

Breslin let out an irritated sigh.

"Better give me a minute."

"You'll find the nest three quarters of the way up the mountain," Rhamalli's voice informed them.

"How did you find it?" Breslin asked, impressed.

"By smell. Humans and dwarves don't smell very good. There are many caves scattered across the cliff's face, but only one that reeks of man. I'm watching that cave now."

"Is Two Heads home?" Athos asked.

"No."

"Are you sure?"

"There are no signs of movement

"Then take us up there. Hurry!"

A distant wyverian form appeared high in the sky and came rapidly closer. Beating his enormous wings to remain aloft, Rhamalli extended his forelegs down onto the ground and waited for the dwarves to jump on. Once all five were sitting in his talons the dragon pumped his wings harder to gain altitude. Rising steadily upward, the dwarves marveled at the sheer size of the cliff with its many possible hiding places. Countless small, and some large, caves flashed by at an amazing rate.

Slowing their ascent so that he remained level with a particularly large cave, Rhamalli deposited the dwarves into the zweigelan's nest then retreated into the sky. He had already informed the Dragon Lord of the nest's location. In return, Rhamalli had learned that a formal invitation to join the wyverian ranks had been issued for the zweigelan. While unclear what that meant, Rhamalli was certain the renegade was not going to like it.

"I'm going on a hunch here, but I'd say this is Two Head's cave, no doubt about it," Athos observed, whistling as he looked around.

Piles upon piles of loot were scattered everywhere. Sunlight glinted off several chests full of gold coins and various pieces of jewelry. Another chest was open nearby and contained pieces of chainmail. A large bundle of spears was propped up in the far corner of the cave. Several open-ended barrels contained swords, axes, and various other hand-held weapons.

"Lukas, can you feel anything?" Venk whispered. While still daylight outside, the cave remained mostly in shadow and what he couldn't see made him nervous.

"Father, it's really close! It's somewhere over to the left!"

"What about the gem?" Breslin asked. "Can you feel that, too?"

"No, only the plate."

"Are we in the wrong blasted place again?" Athos hissed out, clearly frustrated.

"I don't think so," Tristofer told them. "Lukas, when could you feel that plate pulling you toward it? After you touched it, right?"

Surprised, Lukas nodded.

"Then it stands to reason he won't be able to feel the gem's pull until he touches it, too."

"Find our belongings first," Breslin instructed. "Then we'll find that gem and get out of here."

"Do you realize that until we find our things we won't be able to leave?" Tristofer pointed out.

"I do. Stop wasting time and start looking."

They split up and began sifting through the vast piles of

items. Athos located a stack of weapons that were relatively dust free. Mixed in amongst several short swords and a mace were his axe and Venk's crossbow. Mythryd, Breslin's red hued axe, was also there. As the rightful owners reclaimed their weapons, Tristofer gave a triumphant shout. He had found a stash of scrolls and books with his belongings mixed in. Figuring he didn't have the time to sort everything, he scooped up what he could see and dumped them into his pockets.

"Lukas found our packs," Venk called out. He pulled his own out from under what looked like a ship's folded sail and verified the white silk pouch containing the spells was there. He retrieved the levitation spell and slipped it into his front pocket.

Tristofer ran up to him, clutching an armful of books and scrolls.

"Do you have room for these? I can't fit them all in my pockets."

"What the blazes are you doing with all of that? Don't even think about putting that stuff in here. Carry your own junk."

"Please? I'll sort it out later. I just don't want to leave anything behind and I don't have time to check to see if I've missed anything."

Venk jerked his pack open and began jamming in dusty scrolls, moldy books, and decaying scraps of paper.

"When we get out of this, you are personally going to scrub my pack inside and out. Is that clear?"

Tristofer nodded enthusiastically. "Of course, of course!"

Venk grunted as he slung the ridiculously heavy pack over his shoulder.

"Wizards be damned, Tristofer. You better hope there isn't a weight limit on Shardwyn's spell."

"Stop dallying!" Breslin snapped out. "Help me find this blasted gem so we can get out of here before the zweigelan returns."

The group parted ways once more as they searched for the special jewel. What it would look like no one knew, but they did figure they'd know it once they saw it.

Venk pushed aside a heap of fabric, wondering belatedly if some traveler had lost the clothes off their back, when he saw a wooden chest. It was lying concealed beneath the fabric.

"What do you have?"

Venk looked up to see his brother approach.

"Just found a chest. I was going to see what was in it."

Together they pried the chest open. Both gawked in amazement. They had found the zweigelan's stash of jewels.

"Wonder how many of these once belonged to dwarves?"

Venk reached into the chest to pull out a sapphire the size of his clenched fist. He moved into one of the last beams of sunlight and held the jewel out. It sparkled radiantly, casting bits of light all about the cave.

"Is that the one we're looking for?" Athos asked.

"Give it to Lukas and see what he says."

Athos grunted and took the jewel, disappearing behind a pile of armor. He reappeared moments later and shook his head.

"Nope."

With a sigh, Venk dropped the gem on the ground and began digging through the chest of jewels, as if he were searching for a specific tool in his tool chest.

There it was! Without a doubt he knew he had found what they were searching for. It was a ruby a little smaller than his fist, but unlike any ruby he had ever seen before. It was a spiraled jewel! The helix shape was cool to the touch and caused the hairs on his arm to stand up. Venk excitedly turned to his brother.

"Look at this! This has *got* to be it. Now let's get out of ..."

Venk trailed off as he suddenly got the impression he was being watched. He and his brother nervously eyed each other. Then they both noted that the nest had gone eerily quiet.

Clutching the spiral gem tightly in his hand, Venk swallowed nervously.

"It's behind us, isn't it?"

Chapter 6 — What in the Whorl?

They had been caught. Somehow, and they didn't know how, the zweigelan had snuck back into its nest and ambushed them from behind. How was it possible that no one had seen it arrive? Why hadn't Rhamalli warned them?

Both brothers slowly turned to face the nest's owner. Not only had the zweigelan managed to get the drop on them, but it had found a way to slip by them and flank them from the rear of the cave. If the dragon continued its approach, and it gave every indication it was going to do just that, then the dwarves would be forced off the ledge and end up plummeting to their deaths.

Venk dropped the jewel into his pocket and pulled out his crossbow. He quickly cocked his weapon and loaded a bolt, clenching several more of the mini arrows in his left hand. Just in case. Athos had not only pulled out his own axe but had also grabbed a second axe from a nearby stash of weapons. The zweigelan sneered at them.

"What have we here?" Left Head ran a forked tongue

over its many teeth. "I do believe lunch has arrived!"

"We've never had a meal delivered to us before," Right Head observed. A glob of drool spilled out its gaping jaws and trickled to the ground. "We are grateful."

"We are not lunch," Athos said through gritted teeth.

"How did you slip by us?" Venk asked, hoping to stall the dragon. For what, he didn't know, only he had to try. If he and Athos could keep the dragon distracted long enough, perhaps Lukas would be able to slip away. Somehow.

"Never left, did we?" Left Head grinned. It clacked its teeth a few times, as if in anticipation of its upcoming meal.

"You were here the whole time?" Venk asked, not bothering to hide the exasperation in his voice. "Where? We didn't see you."

"We were disguised," Left Head gloated. "No one could see us."

"On the ceiling, we were," Right Head added.

"Be silent," Left Head snapped. "Our lunch does not need to know how we are able to camouflage ourselves."

Irritated, Right Head took a deep breath and prepared to let loose an enormous jet of flames. Left Head instantly ducked down low and came up rather abruptly under Right Head's open jaws, snapping its mouth closed in the process.

"Still your flames! You'll damage the nest, just like last time."

Disgruntled, Right Head looked down at the two dwarves and licked its chops. If it couldn't enjoy its lunch cooked then at least it could enjoy it raw. Right Head's jaws opened and it readied itself to lunge forward.

A spinning red axe suddenly swooshed by the two brothers and collided with a row of shields resting on the ground. Mythryd cut through two of the shields as though they were made of paper; the rest of the shields skidded across the floor and crashed noisily into a pile of plumed helmets, which tipped over several in the process. The zweigelan screeched with rage.

Venk looked down at a helmet that had come to rest against his foot. Inspiration struck. He gave the helmet a swift kick and watched it fly out over the edge of the cave and drop out of sight.

"What are you doing?" Left Head cried out, as if enmeshed in the throes of sheer agony. "You mustn't disrupt the nest! It took us years to organize our collection!"

"Years!" Right Head echoed.

Venk smiled maliciously. "Indeed? So, you probably would prefer if I didn't do this?"

He gave the signal to Athos, who turned to the nearest pile and gave it a swift kick. A stack of gauntlets were sent tumbling across the cavern floor. Several fell off the edge.

The zweigelan roared in anger. It rushed toward the closest intruder, who happened to be Breslin. Intent on ripping him to shreds, it reared both heads and prepared to strike. Breslin ducked behind one of the many piles of debris in the cave and vanished. Left Head stretched its neck up and over the pile, expecting to find the dwarf crouching on the other side. It ground its teeth in frustration. No dwarves were hiding there. Both heads quickly scanned the nest as it searched for other potential targets. Left Head spotted Venk at about the same time Right Head located Athos. Athos brandished an axe in each hand while Venk took aim at Left Head. Much to the dragon's chagrin, both dwarves stood next to several piles at the edge of its nest, closest to the drop off. Athos swung his axe like a club, using the flat of his axe head to smash through a huge stack of books, quills, and parchment.

The stack virtually exploded. Sheets of paper and books went flying everywhere. Since Athos deliberately aimed for the nest's entrance, most of the contents of the pile went sailing over the edge of the nest.

The zweigelan roared in agony. Defilers had entered the nest and were destroying years upon years of hard work. The dragon singled out one of the invaders, the smallest, which was hiding near the entrance, and advanced. Deftly maneuvering its sinewy body amongst its collection, the zweigelan approached the tiny biped.

Detecting movement in its peripheral vision, Left Head swung to its right and stared at the rapidly moving object. Confused, Left Head tracked a yellow object as it flew around the perimeter of its cave before it curved inward and glanced off its nose, leaving a stinging welt in the process. Left Head roared with frustration and watched the spinning object disappear behind a pile of armor. It didn't reappear.

The zweigelan took several threatening steps toward its collection of armor when two more tiny flying creatures appeared, taking off in opposite directions. The yellow creature spun as it flew, circling around from the left while its green counterpart spun through the air as it approached from the right. Too surprised to move, Left Head watched as both creatures curved again and once more leapt in to attack. The zweigelan finally regained its senses and ducked low. It watched with a satisfied smirk as the yellow object passed harmlessly over its head. Its green twin, however, flew directly into Right Head's left eye.

Right Head roared in pain. It glanced down to see that the green object had dropped to the ground, apparently lifeless. The zweigelan retrieved it from the floor. It was a piece of metal! One of the nest's desecrators must have thrown it. It must be a weapon!

Too angry to realize it didn't have a weapon as unique as the one it was holding in its collection, the zweigelan flung the curved green piece of metal out of its nest.

Watching from his hiding place, Athos scowled. "Blast it, Two Heads just tossed my green orix over the edge!"

"I'm sure we can get it back," Venk whispered back to him.

The zweigelan located the tiniest biped once more and lunged forward.

Venk saw what was happening and dove over the large stack separating him from his son. Pushing Lukas back toward his brother, he turned to face the dragon. This was the final straw. Venk was tired of all this junk. He was tired of this smelly cave. And more importantly, he was tired of the zweigelan threatening his son's life.

"One more step, dragon," Venk warned, "and so help me I'll smash through every pile in here and send everything over the edge. Do you hear me?"

The two headed dragon paused as it stared at the larger of the intruders.

"Back away from my son. Right now."

To make certain the dragon understood he was serious, Venk smashed his crossbow through a pile of leather armor. Gauntlets, greaves, and cuirasses tumbled out into the nothingness beyond the nest's border.

"I have three other piles within range," Venk calmly told the dragon, shifting his body slightly to his left so that he could easily reach a nearby pile of shields. "Look over there. Athos is ready to send your collection of swords over. See Breslin there? He has your chest of jewels. He's ready to throw the whole thing over the edge. You have five seconds to move to the back of the cave. Now."

The zweigelan's twin necks began swaying back and forth. Was it ready to strike or was it contemplating whether or not it should comply with Venk's order? The dragon shifted its weight forward, as if ready to take another step.

"Last chance. Take another step. *I dare you.*"

The seriousness of Venk's voice, along with his rigid body language, finally brought the dragon to a halt. With extreme reluctance, the zweigelan took a step backward.

"That's right. Keep moving."

The twin-headed dragon took another step back.

"Better move faster than that," Breslin snarled. He had dragged the chest of jewels out from under the piles of fabric and was now resting a foot on it as the chest teetered over the edge. "If you ever want to see these gems again, you'll do as we say."

Both heads growled angrily at Breslin as the creature continued to retreat farther into its cave.

"We are leaving," Venk informed the dragon, still using an eerily calm tone. "And we are taking our things with us."

"Your days are numbered," Left Head hissed angrily at them. "We'll find you, that we promise. You failed to solve the riddle. Your things belong to us."

"Thieves!" Right head screeched at them. "Insolent thieves deserve to die!"

Nodding, Venk pulled the spiral gem out of his pocket.

"I am sorry, but we need this more than you do. This will be coming with us, too."

"If it makes you feel any better," Breslin added, "we really didn't lose the bet. We know the answer to your riddle."

"We do?" Venk asked, turning to Breslin.

"I highly doubt that," Tristofer scoffed, appearing next to Lukas. "I didn't know the answer and I'm the scholar."

"Liar!" Left Head exclaimed, jerking upwards.

Right Head was twisting and turning as it tried to locate all five of the intruders. At that moment, it was directly over its twin. Left Head collided with Right Head, giving a hollow popping noise.

"No one has ever correctly answered the riddle!"

Breslin looked at the two headed dragon in pity. "Then find some smarter victims. The answer is 'sunshine'. My father taught that to me when I was a boy. He told me that my grandfather told it to him many years ago."

The zweigelan was speechless as it stared at the dwarves.

"I had a feeling you wouldn't hold up your end of the bargain," Breslin casually explained, "so we came up with a backup plan. Just in case."

Pleased, Venk turned back to the dragon and started ticking off points on his fingers.

"Alright, let's see. Riddle answered. Possessions reclaimed. Jewel found. I do believe it's time to depart."

"NEVER!" both heads screeched in unison. The zweigelan lunged forward, closing the space rapidly.

With their weapons at the ready, both Breslin and Athos plowed through several stacks of shields and swords. The dragon was horrified that even more of its collection had been lost. Spying a golden shield that was just starting to tip over the edge, Right Head darted out to snatch the object in its jaws before it was lost.

Not one to waste an opportunity to create a distraction, Breslin rotated Mythryd so that the dual cutting blades were facing away from him. He scrambled up several stacks of books and leapt toward Right Head, swinging his axe like a war club.

Mythryd connected with the gold shield in Right Head's fangs and generated an impressive clang which caused the entire dragon to vibrate uncontrollably for several seconds.

"Now's our chance!" Breslin told his companions. "Venk, you'd better be ready. Jump!"

"Excuse me?" Tristofer sputtered in shock.

The scholar began backing away from the cave's edge, but before he could take more than a few steps Athos and Breslin each hooked an arm and pulled him over the edge. At the same time, Venk looped his arm through his son's and leapt out of the nest, following the others.

Venk didn't know which noise was louder: the howling wind or Tristofer's screams. Retrieving Shardwyn's spell from his pocket, he invoked the levitation spell and fervently hoped it was strong enough to protect all five of them.

Venk squeezed the sphere as hard as he could as they fell. How was the blasted thing supposed to work?

"What are you waiting for? Slow us down!" Breslin hollered.

"You tell me how to get us to stop falling and I will!"

Everyone slammed to a stop. Venk and Lukas crashed into Athos and Tristofer. Venk covered Lukas' ears against the numerous curses.

"It worked!" Tristofer exclaimed, his aches and pains forgotten. "I didn't think that … you do realize we're still hundreds of feet from the ground, right?"

Everyone turned to look down. Sure enough, the distant treetops were visible at least five hundred feet away. They were floating, motionless, in mid-air. Breslin suddenly cursed again.

"Venk, get us on the ground. Hurry!"

Alarmed, Venk looked up. The zweigelan's twin heads had appeared over the rim of the cave and were staring down at them. A split second later it launched itself, plummeting straight toward them. Wings partially extended, it rapidly closed the distance. It would be over in just a few seconds.

"Nothing is happening!" Venk angrily told Breslin. "Damn all the wizards and their blasted spells! Why won't it take us down?"

The white sphere grew warm in his hand. Whatever force that was holding them suspended in the air disappeared, dropping the dwarves like stones from the sky.

"Don't drop us!" Breslin bellowed. "Just take us down gently!"

"There are no blasted instructions for this thing or I'd be more than happy to stop us!"

Once more the falling dwarves slammed to a halt. Everyone braced for the inevitable, as the dragon had been so close that they could smell its rancid breath. Incredulously, the zweigelan veered to the left and sped by them a split second later. It crashed through the green canopy far below and disappeared.

"What is it?" Lukas asked as he peered around his father's body and watched the tree tops shake and sway uncontrollably.

"Sounds like the dragon is fighting something," Venk answered. "What it is, I don't know."

"Will you please take us down?" Breslin asked. "Slowly this time. I don't think I can take any more sudden falls."

Venk glared at the spell in his hand. What was the trick to making it work? Didn't Shardwyn say it could be used to raise or lower something should the need arise? Why would he make it difficult to use?

"We want to go down. Slowly."

They all dropped another hundred feet before Venk managed to stop their progress.

"The next time I see that wizard I'm personally going to break his kneecaps," Breslin grumbled.

"It's a good thing we don't need to go the other direction," Tristofer said, glancing nervously at the sky.

"Which direction?" Venk asked, turning to face the scholar. "Up?"

The band of dwarves rocketed skyward as though they had been shot out of a trebuchet.

Athos hauled off and smacked his brother on the arm. Hard.

"Tell it to stop, you fool!"

"Stop!" Venk yelled.

Their brief ascent was abruptly cut off. Once more they hung motionless in the air.

"Do you not see what's going on?" Athos angrily asked his brother. "Every time you say *up*, or *down*, or *stop*, it responds to you. Be careful what you say!"

"Why wouldn't Shardwyn have told us that? I think the old fool needs to retire."

"You think?" Athos tugged his beard, hoping the pain would help clear his head. "Now tell it to lower us to the ground. Slowly."

Venk eyed his brother and then glared at his closed fist. "How am I supposed to do that? It's clearly worked so well before. Now, take us gently down, you lousy excuse of a spell."

A few seconds passed while the dwarves anxiously looked at each other.

"What's happening?" Breslin asked, twisting in midair to study their location. "Are we going down?"

Venk looked closely at the wall of stone next to them. "I don't think we... wait! Aye, we are. Look down there. Two Head's cave is getting closer."

"This is ridiculous," Athos spat in disgust. "The sun will set before we reach the ground. Can we not move things along?"

"Er, Venk, can I ask how much longer this spell will hold out?" Tristofer warily asked.

"Not much longer by my reckoning," Venk told him. He addressed his left hand again. "We need to get down faster than this."

The rate they were descending doubled, which wasn't saying much.

"Faster than that."

Their velocity doubled again.

"Getting closer. Keep going."

Their speed increased until they were being lowered to the ground at a much more comfortable rate. They had already passed the dragon's cave and were nearing the treetops when bad luck graced them once more. Shardwyn's spell gave out.

One moment Venk was clutching the small warm sphere and the next his hand was empty. As soon as the spell vanished, Venk knew with absolute certainty that they were in serious trouble.

"I'm really starting to dislike that wizard."

Venk and his companions screamed as they plummeted toward the trees. They punched through the forest canopy, snapping off twigs and getting mouthfuls of leaves and pine needles for their troubles. They dropped another fifty feet and hit something soft and springy. The surface stretched and recoiled bouncing them back into the air. The next landing was much harder—on a surface resembling a pile of shields all overlapping one another. The ground shifted, tilting steeply sending the five tumbling and sliding. They rolled along the ground, coming to a stop in a tangled heap of arms and legs.

Breslin was the first to crack an eye open. He was flat on his back, looking up, way up, at their savior: a dragon. Or more specifically, the owner of the wing they had landed on. The wing must have bounced them over to its leg where they slid down the heavily scaled foreleg to the ground. Confused, the dragon stared at the distant treetops, wondering what else was planning on falling from the sky.

"What do we do now?" Athos whispered to Breslin.

"Start smiling," Breslin whispered back. He cautiously regained his feet and cleared his throat as he did so. "Good day to you, my fine scaly friend. You have our thanks for breaking our fall."

The black dragon jerked its head down. Its eyes narrowed.

"You landed on her wing," a familiar voice told them. "She's not exactly happy to see you."

Rhamalli had appeared. The dark red dragon with the purple edged wings angled his head and indicated the dwarves should back away from the unknown dragon.

"They soiled my scales, Rhamalli!"

Rhamalli turned to look back at the black dragon that was now holding up her left foreleg.

"Kem, don't be melodramatic."

"Is there or is there not something dripping off my scales?"

Sure enough, liquid could be seen trickling off the glossy black scales, coalescing onto the ground. Rhamalli turned back to stare at the dwarves with a shocked expression on his face.

"You urinated on her?"

Breslin's mouth dropped open, aghast. His expression quickly turned to anger as he looked at Athos, who angrily looked at his brother. Horrified, Venk looked down at his son.

"Boy, you'd better tell me you didn't do that."

Lukas shook his head. "I didn't."

Everyone slowly turned to Tristofer.

"Don't look at me. I didn't pee on the dragon."

Breslin gave Tristofer's clothes a quick once over.

"Why are your clothes wet?"

"My clothes aren't wet! What in the world gave you … wait. What's this? They *are* wet. Was it really me?"

Breslin sighed and closed his eyes. Shaking his head, he turned to face the black dragon.

"Please accept my humblest of apologies. I didn't know my companion would do that."

"It's water! I didn't pee on the dragon. Look, see? It's just water!" Tristofer held up his punctured water bag. "It must have ripped during the slide down. That's all, it's only water. Er, please don't eat us, Mister Kem."

"Kemxandra is a female," Rhamalli informed the scholar, albeit a little coldly. "I wouldn't think you'd want to insult the same dragon twice on the same day."

"Stop talking," Breslin told Tristofer. "Close your mouth. All the way. There you go. Keep it that way until we're safely away from here."

Tristofer nodded glumly and jammed his hands into his pockets. Meanwhile, Kemxandra had bent her long black neck down so that she could take a few cautious sniffs of her leg. Satisfied that it was only water, the female dragon resumed ignoring the dwarves.

Breslin shook his head as he scowled at Tristofer. He turned to look up at Rhamalli. "So what are you doing here? What happened to Two Heads?"

Rhamalli moved his vast bulk to the side so that the dwarves could see what was happening behind him. The zweigelan was struggling to escape, but it was a lost battle. A full-size green dragon was holding each of the two necks tightly against the ground while another green dragon had pinned its wings behind it. A third dragon, this one as white as snow, was leaning its enormous body against the zweigelan's, preventing any chance of an escape.

"You captured it?" Breslin asked. "Whatever for?"

"The rebel must be taken to Rinbok Intherer. There will be no renegades in his domain. This zweigelan has been a thorn in his side long enough."

"That's why it dove past us and disappeared into the trees," Tristofer mused. "It sensed the presence of the others and it was trying to escape."

Rhamalli nodded. "Aye. We knew it would flee once we had been detected. That's why more of us were hiding on the ground."

"Well played," Venk nodded, impressed.

"Rinbok Intherer is indebted to you for discovering the renegade's lair," Rhamalli told them. "He has authorized the five of you to be carried back to your valley if you so choose."

All five dwarves vehemently shook their heads no.

"Thanks, but I think we'll walk," Breslin told the dragon. "I think I can speak for all of us when I say that we're done with flying. Besides, we have to figure out what the next move is."

"Did you find what you were searching for?"

Venk held up the spiraled ruby.

"What's that?" Rhamalli wanted to know.

"It's a gem," Venk answered, using a tone typically reserved for Lukas whenever he asked a silly question.

"Your powers of observation do you credit, master dwarf. I have not seen a jeweled whorl before. Have you fathomed its part in your quest?"

Venk shook his head. "Not yet."

Athos located his fallen orix in a clump of prickly bushes. Cursing loudly, he retrieved his weapon and inspected it closely for damage. Not a scratch could be found. Smiling, he snapped it closed and returned it to its holder on his chest plate.

Several hours later, the dwarves were all sitting around the fire pit at their hastily constructed camp. Packs were stowed, hammocks were strung, and once everyone had finished their evening meal, only then did Breslin ask Venk to produce the unique jewel. Tristofer leaned forward and plucked the jewel out of Venk's hands just as soon as he laid eyes on it.

"It's almost cold to the touch. Anyone else notice that?"

Venk nodded. "Aye. Just as soon as I touched it. It made the hairs on my arm stand up."

"Are you thinking what I think you're thinking?"

With his water bag raised high in the air, Venk briefly glanced over at the scholar before taking several large swallows of the cool mountain water they had found earlier.

"I highly doubt it."

"It's synthetic. It has to be. Look how perfect the spiral is. Look how each cut is precisely aligned with the next. These gems don't occur naturally. The Narians *engineered* them."

Breslin grunted. "Balderdash. You have no proof."

"The dragons said they've never seen a jewel like this," Tristofer continued, anxious to prove his point. "We certainly haven't. What does that tell you?"

"It tells me that you still haven't cleaned the grime out of my pack like you promised you would."

Chagrined, Tristofer glanced at the grubby mess Venk's pack had become after he had stuffed it full of books and scrolls back at the zweigelan's lair.

"That's right, I did say that."

"I know you did," Venk agreed. "Get that moldy mess out of my pack and start cleaning."

"What about the gem? When are we going to see what happens to Lukas' back when we touch the gem to the map?"

"Soon. As for you, get busy. I'd like to be able to pick my pack up again without thinking about tossing it into the fire."

Resigned, Tristofer turned to the task at hand. The sooner he had Venk's pack clean, the sooner he could study whatever changes the jewel brought to the map. Regardless of what Venk had said, he was going to keep a close eye on the proceedings from his vantage point. However, the scholar in him had other ideas in mind. Noticing that he had acquired quite a few new books and pieces of literature from the zweigelan's cave, he decided to catalog the newest additions to his traveling collection of books and scrolls. The items that were originally his went into one pile while those that were new went into another. Not until they had been closely examined, of course.

Lukas and the gem were quickly forgotten.

As he dropped a moldy book about trade routes down onto the new pile, a piece of paper partially slipped from within its pages. Curiosity piqued, Tristofer pulled the yellowing parchment out and carefully unfolded it. It was a request from the human king to add an additional shipment of par bark to his order. Apparently, the king enjoyed the earthy taste of the spice and wanted to increase his supply. Tristofer tossed the paper onto the discard pile and returned his attention to the next book.

"What was that?" Breslin asked as he walked by with an armful of firewood.

"It's just a request from the human king to bring back more spice than he had originally ordered. Mundane stuff."

Breslin glanced back at the sheet of paper and noticed its condition.

"Which king? Kri'Entu?"

Tristofer leaned over to pick up the discarded paper. He shook his head.

"No. This king's name is Kre'Jurin."

"Kre'Jurin?" Breslin deposited his load of wood next to the campfire. "Kre'Jurin was king of the humans when my father was my age, and I won't even begin to tell you how many hundreds of years ago that was."

Tristofer shrugged. Whether it was two hundred years ago or two thousand, he didn't care.

"It goes to show you how long Two Heads had been terrorizing the area," Breslin explained.

"You'd think the Dragon Lord would have dealt with it long before we came along," Venk idly mused.

"Maybe he couldn't find him?" Breslin guessed. "Or maybe he had, and Two Heads had been given warnings, but elected not to pay heed? We may never know. What else do you have in there?"

Tristofer picked a few of the discarded books up and showed them to his companions.

"Nothing of interest, I'm afraid. We have titles on trade routes, horticulture, and even a book on bow making. Over there are a few children's books that I haven't checked yet."

Breslin looked down at the half dozen badly damaged books and shook his head. He looked at Lukas and motioned him over.

"See anything down there that you'd like?"

"No. They're all dirty."

"They may be able to be cleaned."

About to shake his head no, Lukas hesitated. A thin book barely thicker than a leaflet caught his eye. The cover, torn in several areas and missing the lower left portion, looked familiar. He stooped to pick the thin book up. Giving it a shake to dislodge years of dust, Lukas peered at the cover. It was a picture of a city. A golden city.

Lukas wiped the cover on the grass next to him and looked again. A badly tattered copy of *The Legend of Nar* looked back at him, only this copy had been illustrated by a different artist.

"Father, come see! It's a copy of *The Legend of Nar*, like that which Master Maelnar showed us, only this one looks older."

Venk abandoned watching Tristofer's attempt at cleaning his pack and joined his son. He frowned as Lukas handed him the dilapidated book.

"You have that book. You've read that book. I've read you that book. Besides, yours is in much better condition."

Lukas nodded. "Aye! But see here? The pictures are different!"

Venk brought the book up closer to his eyes. He squinted. The cover showed a picture of an aerial view of a city. The golden buildings sparkled radiantly while the tiny specs that were supposed to be Nar's inhabitants went about their business. Opening the first page, Venk began to read aloud:

In the annals of history,
Long has it been told:
Lying deep beneath the mountains,
Was a fabled city of old.

"I may not be a scholar, son, but I can tell you that this is the same book."

"It is not! The pictures are different!"

Lukas looked wildly around until he spotted Tristofer on his hands and knees scrubbing his father's pack. He ran over to him and dropped down on his knees as well.

"Tristofer, look! It's a copy of *The Legend of Nar*, but the pictures are different."

Tristofer, who had his head jammed up inside the freshly scrubbed pack to make certain he had extricated all traces of grime, pulled his head out and focused on the young dwarf.

"What was that?"

Lukas held out the frayed book. About to ask the boy what he was supposed to do with that, Tristofer noticed the different illustrations, too.

"Where did you get this?"

"From you. It was one of the books you brought back from the zweigelan's cave."

Tristofer sank back on his knees and slowly, reverently, read the book while he simultaneously inspected the illustrations. Right away Tristofer knew that the drawings were different from the one belonging to Maelnar's granddaughter. These pictures were dark; foreboding. It was as if the pictures had been commissioned for something else and as an afterthought had been assembled into a collection to be passed off as a piece of children's literature.

Tristofer turned to the page depicting the catastrophe and held his breath. The king! The king was shown holding his hammer and it was a much better close-up than in little Trindolyn's book. There, clutched tightly in the king's hand, was the power hammer with the red jewel clearly visible on the tool's head. Also visible was the small sharp point that comprised the other side of the hammer head. Next to the point was...

"Who has that metal thing from the lake?" Tristofer excitedly asked.

Athos and Venk both shrugged and held up their hands, palms up. They didn't have it.

"Breslin?"

Maelnar's son pulled his pack over to him and began rifling through its contents.

"Here it is. What's the problem?"

"No problem. None whatsoever. In fact, I think we just had several questions answered. Look. Look here!"

Everyone crowded around the book and looked at what Tristofer was pointing at.

"It's the king's hammer," Venk told him. "I remember looking at this when Maelnar showed all of us his granddaughter's book. So what?"

"But it's not the same picture, is it?"

Venk stared at the book with a blank expression. Athos merely shrugged.

"Trust me, it isn't. Look at the hammer. You can see much more detail in this illustration!"

Venk raised his eyes and met Tristofer's. "Fine. It isn't quite the same. What's your point?"

"Look at the hammer! Or more specifically, look at the hammer's head! See this right here? It's the object we were given by the nixies! It's the hammer's counterweight!"

Tristofer placed the square metal disk and the ruby whorl down on the book next to the hammer's pictograph.

Intrigued, Breslin stared at the hammer. The flat square block adjacent to the tapered point did resemble the gift from the nixies. And, if the ruby whorl was viewed straight down from the top, it did resemble a normal gem. It could be a match for the gem depicted on the power hammer, but if so, why the curlicue shape? Was the gem supposed to be embedded inside the hammer somehow?

Breslin scowled. Was that what they were doing? Tracking down pieces of an ancient hammer?

"After all this time, there's the proof," Tristofer proudly declared. "We have the weight and we have the gem. Each piece is leading us to the next. This is remarkable!"

Breslin wasn't convinced.

"Remarkable my arse. The purpose of this whole expedition is just to find pieces of a hammer? What about Nar? I don't care about some ruddy hammer."

"I think it's remarkable all right," Athos grumbled.

Tristofer beamed with pleasure.

"Thank you."

"It's a remarkable waste of time."

"Excuse me," Venk interjected. "The reason we're here is to get that blasted mark off my son's back. If we find pieces to some hammer, fine. If we find Nar, so what? I'm only interested in helping Lukas."

Tristofer's smile vanished.

"What is wrong with you people? This is a Narian power hammer! Think of all the advances in metallurgy we could learn if we could produce an actual, honest to goodness power hammer from Nar? Why, it would be worth more than its weight in gold! We'd be famous! Songs would be sung about us!"

Athos shook his head. "Not the songs I'd want to hear about."

"What I'm saying is, this is an important discovery! We cannot turn back now. We are so close!"

Breslin approached the scholar and gave him a condescending pat on his shoulder.

"Let me see if I have this straight. A Questor's Mark appears on a boy's back. It turns out to be a map leading us all across the countryside. We think we're being led to Nar but it turns out we're on a scavenger hunt for pieces of an ancient tool. Did I leave anything out?"

"Umm, er, you forgot to mention that we were carried across most of the kingdom by dragons. That must count for something!"

Breslin's face actually turned a few shades of green.

"That's an experience I do not ever want to be reminded about. Ever."

Tristofer sighed and sank down onto the closest log. He rubbed his temples. "Fair enough, fair enough. Before you come to any decisions, think of how much we all can benefit from studying the hammer! It could pulverize the hardest stone with one blow! How? Because of the metal the Narians used? Maybe it has something to do with the jewel? Or perhaps something else we aren't even aware of yet. Any way you look at it, this is an adventure we should see through, regardless of whether or not the prize at the end is a hammer or Nar itself."

Breslin sat down next to the scholar and began twirling the tip of his beard around a finger.

"Tell me this. Honestly. Do you now feel like we're still searching for Nar or are we now searching for this hammer of yours?"

Tristofer's eyes dropped to the flickering flames.

"I believe we're looking for pieces to the hammer. As much as I'd like to think it'll lead us to Nar, clearly our goal is to find all the pieces and re-assemble the hammer. Deep down, I still think that there might be some other purpose to this. I mean, why else would the Questor's Mark appear? Why now? But until we can find evidence that suggests otherwise, I'll settle for finding the hammer. If we're allowed to continue, that is."

Breslin nodded, pleased. It was what he now believed, too, and judging by the looks of the others, it was what everyone now believed. However, he didn't think the scholar would have admitted to him that he had felt the same way. The fact that Tristofer did confirm his own suspicions made him respect the absent-minded book lover a little more. Just a little.

"We continue on," Breslin decided.

"Whatever for?" Athos demanded, crossing his arms over his chest.

"For the reason Master Venk has said. The primary reason for this excursion is to rid young Lukas of his disfiguring mark. Besides, we cannot ignore the secondary purpose: from a metallurgical standpoint, this hammer comes from a more advanced culture than our own. My father will want to study it. Everyone will want to study it. Who knows? It may someday lead us to Nar itself, but until that day comes, we will not turn our backs. We continue on."

"You're just as nuts as he is," Athos observed, hooking a thumb back at Tristofer. "Very well. We keep going. This had better be one spectacular hammer."

"Oh, it's so much more than that," Tristofer began. "It can…"

"Not now," Breslin interrupted.

Tristofer bowed. "Right. Sorry."

Breslin clapped his hands together and vigorously rubbed them back and forth. "Shall we see where we're heading next? Master Lukas, if you please."

Lukas pulled his jerkin up to his chin and faced the other direction.

"I'll bet the top right is the next section to appear," Tristofer guessed.

"Lower right," Athos disagreed.

"I'll take center," Venk added.

"What's the wager?" Athos wanted to know.

"Wager?" Tristofer sputtered. "I'm not wagering."

Unfazed by Tristofer's reluctance to play, Athos pushed him out of their circle. Breslin took his place.

"I want in on this." Breslin tapped the top right. "I think Tristofer is right. For once," he added under his breath. "I think the right side of the map is next."

Venk held out a hand. "May I?"

Breslin nodded. He plucked the gem out of Tristofer's hands and gave the whorl to Venk, who gently touched the jewel to his son's bare back. Surprising them all, the far right section of the map, stretching from top to bottom, intensified and came into focus. A line of gray smudges still separated the different sections of the mark. Ignoring what that could possibly mean, Breslin turned his attention to the newest section of the map that had been revealed.

It was a waterfall.

Majestic cascading water appeared running alongside the right vertical border of the Questor's Mark. At the top of the waterfall, they could see tiny trees on either side. Judging by the size of them, it had to be at least two hundred feet high.

"Does anyone know how many waterfalls there are in Lentari?" Athos asked, turning to face his companions.

"Any idea which one that is?" Breslin asked.

"I'd like to take an educated guess and say Drammli Falls," Tristofer said.

"On Lentari's eastern coast?" Breslin asked. "The Great Sea of Koralis is a long way away. What makes you say that?"

"The cliffs give it away. Look at it. See those crags and indentations? The cliffs bordering the eastern sea are like that. I saw it for myself a number of years ago."

Breslin nodded. He sat down and pulled out his pipe. "Then it's settled. We leave for Drammli Falls at first light."

He lit the tip of a twig and held it out to his pipe, inhaling as he did so. In just a few moments his tobacco was lit.

"Rhamalli, if you're listening, and I know you are, we'll see you there."

Venk and Athos both stifled a laugh.

Chapter 7 — Not Fond of Heights, Either

"How do we even know we're heading toward the correct waterfall?" Athos complained. "Do you really want to take his word for it?"

Tristofer turned to look at Athos with undisguised hurt on his face.

"That was uncalled for."

Athos shook his head. "No, it's not. I seem to recall being guided to the wrong lake."

"It was an honest mistake."

"I seem to recall you lost the map."

"Misplaced," Tristofer hastily corrected. "I *misplaced* the map."

"You couldn't answer Two Head's riddle."

"Well, neither could you!"

"I'm not the scholar, you are."

"Your point is taken, Master Athos," Tristofer sniffed,

raising his nose in the air. "Trust me, the waterfall we want is the one we are heading toward now."

Athos mumbled something under his breath. Wisely deciding he didn't want it to be repeated, Tristofer kept silent.

Breslin held up an arm, signaling the group to halt. They came to a stop near the trunk of an enormous evergreen, which wasn't surprising as the trees were growing so thick that barely any sunlight found its way to the forest floor. Lukas craned his neck to look up at the distant treetops, wondering why they had stopped. Had Breslin heard something? Had the zweigelan escaped and was now pursuing them?

The boy shuddered. The last thing he wanted to see was the mean two-headed dragon again.

"Why have we stopped?" Venk whispered, unsure if he needed to lower his voice but thought it couldn't hurt to be safe.

"The trees are beginning to thin," Breslin explained. He pointed north. "Behold! There's a pathway through those trees ahead. See it?"

Venk nodded. He could see a small, but well-worn, trail snaking amongst the trees as it angled northeast. They had finally caught some good luck!

"I hope it's one of those enchanted paths," Tristofer remarked.

Breslin shook his head. "I doubt it. This one is way too small. As long as it leads out of the forest we'll be fine. Let's move."

The five of them stepped out onto the dirt track and wordlessly headed northeast. They wove tightly around the trees, oftentimes circling the massive trunks instead of just veering off in another direction. Clearly the pathway's creator wanted to proceed in a direct line and wouldn't tolerate any deviations whatsoever.

"That's the fourth tree we've walked around," Breslin remarked. "If they would have just angled the trail ten degrees north, they could have completely bypassed the last two trees."

Athos snorted. "Humans. How are we to know what goes on in their tiny little brains?"

"Not all humans are like that," Breslin returned, frowning at Athos.

"No dwarf would ever disgrace themselves by creating such an appalling track," Athos carried on. "Look at it. It was hugging that last tree so tightly that I could smell the bark."

"Be glad you're not a human then," Venk pointed out as he nudged his brother in his ribs.

"Absolutely," Athos agreed. "I'd never be able to live with myself."

"Just what the ruddy hell is wrong with my path, you snot-nosed bearded excuse of a fool?"

The dwarves came to an abrupt halt. Standing before them was a scrawny human armed with a bow much too large for him to effectively handle. Nevertheless, an arrow had been nocked and was ready to shoot.

Breslin studied the gaunt human. He was middle aged, scraggly, looked malnourished, and was dressed in rags. Hooked to his belt was a quiver full of crooked, homemade arrows. Joining him were half a dozen more humans all in the same condition as their leader. Four had bows and two carried crossbows. All were aimed at their party.

"Drop your packs, your weapons, axes, and anything else of value you may be carrying," the first thief instructed. "Be quick about it."

Breslin gripped Mythryd tightly, having pulled his beloved red axe the moment they had been accosted. Venk and Athos had also drawn their weapons. Tristofer, as was the norm, was cowering beside Lukas.

"We don't want any trouble," Breslin cautioned. He glared at the thieves' leader. "However, we will not be surrendering any of our weapons. Go about your business before someone gets hurt."

Those who weren't ready to fire their arrows became so. Bowstrings were pulled back and the dwarves were targeted. Smiling profusely, the leader strode forward and sneered at them.

"You're about to become a pincushion, dwarf. You have one minute to decide."

Venk nervously eyed the ruffians. Every one of them

was ready to fire and their proximity to the shooters was too close; if the arrows were loosed there'd only be one outcome. The dwarves huddled together to consider their options.

"They have the upper hand," Venk whispered to Breslin.

"*We* have the upper hand," Breslin whispered back. "I think now would be a good time to use another of Shardwyn's spells."

"Which one?" Venk wanted to know.

"Do you think it matters? Any one of them will do. Just get one and be ready! Follow my lead."

Breslin slowly straightened and then pretended to be angry. He slipped his pack from his shoulder and let it fall to the ground. The others mimicked him. While the thieves chortled gleefully amongst themselves, Venk nudged his pack open and slipped a hand inside, hoping he would be able to quickly locate the silk bag containing the spells. As luck would have it, the bag was sitting just inside the opening. Venk shoved his hand in and grabbed one of the spheres. He glanced down at it as he nodded to Breslin. It was the fire spell. Perfect! Hesitating a few moments longer, Breslin knelt to retrieve his pack from the ground.

"I do believe I've changed my mind."

On cue, Venk threw the sphere at their attackers and mentally invoked the spell, hoping they'd be able to get to safety before the expected wall of flames appeared. He grabbed Lukas and dove to the ground, followed by Athos, Tristofer, and Breslin.

The muggers roared with laughter.

Confused, Breslin looked up at their attackers. His face reddened as he saw what had happened. Shardwyn's fire spell had only generated a single flame, enough to light a candle. Or, in this case, the tip of the arrow closest to them.

"Wizards be damned," Breslin muttered.

"He will be once I'm done with him," Athos grumbled.

"Ooo, I'm scared, dwarf," the leader sneered. "For a moment there I actually thought things were about to turn ugly, like an unfortunate incident that happened to me years ago. But this?" A quick puff extinguished his burning arrow. "This I can deal with. That little act of insolence is going to cost you."

The ground suddenly lurched so violently that everyone was thrown off their feet. Two massive claws broke through the wall of trees and parted them, as though a giant's hands were opening a really large set of drapes.

Trees were uprooted, some snapped in half as a large opening appeared. Rhamalli thrust his head into the opening and growled at the humans.

Breslin held up a hand and indicated the dragon. "Ah! I see introductions are in order. Rhamalli, lunch. Lunch, meet Rhamalli."

The group of thieves broke rank and fled. Way out ahead, and already disappearing into the forest, was the group's fearless leader. The dwarves heard someone shout something about giving up this line of work for good, and then the humans were gone.

"We had them right where we wanted them," Athos told the dragon.

Rhamalli nodded his massive head. "Of course, you did. Why aren't you out on the enchanted path? It's just over there, past the edge of the forest." Luckily, he had been nearby and was alerted by the wizard's spell in time to intimidate the band of cowardly humans.

The dwarves peered sheepishly through the trees and out onto the open grassland. They had only been about thirty feet from exiting the forest.

"We were following this one," Breslin explained, looking down at the tiny trail. He blinked. It was gone!

"We were duped," Athos told him. "I'm not happy about it either. We should have been able to tell. We were led right into an ambush."

"There's the path," he told the dwarves, indicating a well maintained, cobbled path heading east. "The human king had it enchanted against harm. Stay on it and you'll be safe."

"We are not a lost group of school boys," Athos retorted. "Try not to treat us like such."

"Forgive me. That was not my intent. Follow the road and it'll lead you to the human village of Donlari."

"Great," Athos muttered, "that's just what we need right

now: an entire village of humans. No thank you."

"I think I'd have to agree," Breslin began. "Perhaps we should—"

"Look to the underling," Rhamalli scolded them. "He needs sustenance and rest."

"Are you trying to tell me how to take care of my own son?" Venk demanded. He glanced at Lukas standing quietly behind him and nudged his shoulder.

"Are you able to keep going?"

Lukas shrugged. "Of course."

"Rhamalli is right," Tristofer told them. "We need to rest. Donlari should be an acceptable resting point."

* * *

"It's an insult. Just because humans are bigger than us doesn't mean we can't have our own rooms."

"Athos, for the last time, they only had one room left. It's fine. Relax."

Athos glared at his brother then eyed the lone bed in the room.

"Who gets the bed?"

"Lukas and I do," Venk calmly told him.

"And the rest of us?"

A knock came from the door. Venk opened it to reveal a rolled-up mattress standing on two legs.

"Don't just stand there," Breslin told him from the other side of the mattress. "Get out of the way!"

Venk stepped aside in time to avoid getting hit by the unfurling mattress. The straw pad was only four inches thick, but it was certainly better than sleeping on the hard floor. Tristofer appeared next, dragging a second mattress along the ground behind him.

"I'm a scholar, not a laborer," he wheezed as he took off his spectacles and wiped his brow with his sleeve. "The least that Thacken fellow could have done is brought this up here for us."

"At least the proprietor let us use them," Breslin told him. "No charge. Now stop complaining."

Athos reached behind the scholar and easily pulled the mattress into the room. Setting the two pads next to each other pretty much took up the entire floor space, but no one complained. Within minutes everyone was sound asleep.

The next morning the dwarves awoke well past sunrise. Thacken, the owner of the inn, almost summoned the village constable due to the lack of activity from that room for such a long period of time. Thanks to the loud snores coming from the dwarves, the cleaning girls all believed there was a deadly animal in the room and refused to enter it.

Once the dwarves finally descended the stairs and had a meal, they dropped several pieces of silver on the large wooden counter and bowed to the owner, thanking Thacken for his hospitality, and left.

"Sleep well, did you?"

The dwarves all paused as they looked up. They expected to see the dragon's large form overhead or circling high in the sky.

"Where are you?" Athos demanded as he cast his eyes about. "How is it we can hear you but not see you?"

"When a dragon so chooses it can accelerate to a speed usually undetected by most eyes."

"You're telling me you're flying faster than we can see?"

"Aye. From the time we started this conversation I have passed you three times."

Dumbfounded, Venk stared at the sky and waited. Where was the blast of air, the beat of wings? Something! Venk felt somewhat foolish.

"Until I decelerate, you won't see me, Master Venk," Rhamalli's voice floated down from above. "I can see that you're trying."

"Just when you thought you knew everything about dragons," Athos muttered.

"We really don't know anything about dragons," Tristofer protested.

Breslin approached the scholar and slapped him on the back.

"Ever hear of sarcasm, Tristofer?"

"Of course, I have. Oh." Tristofer turned to stare up at

the sky. "Do dragons sleep?"

"Not in the fashion you are accustomed to," came the dragon's reply.

"What do you mean?"

"We enter into a state of consciousness where we shut off our senses and rest."

"That's like sleeping, isn't it?" Lukas asked.

"No, young Master."

"What's the difference?" Venk wanted to know.

"The difference, Master Venk, is that my senses will resume at a moment's notice. I'm aware of everything around me. I just choose to ignore it."

"I get it," Tristofer said, smiling. "You meditate."

"I am unfamiliar with that word."

"To meditate is to engage in contemplation or reflection."

There were a few moments of silence as Rhamalli considered.

"I accept your definition. Aye, we meditate."

The dwarves followed the road, which hugged the river, for two days before they finally arrived at Lentari's eastern coast. There, stretching farther than the eye could see, was the great Sea of Koralis. Looking north they could see that the land curved gently northeast, while looking south showed the land continuing the curve southeast. However, there were no signs of a waterfall because they were at sea level. Unfortunately, it meant they still weren't anywhere close to their destination.

"Do we camp for the night or should we keep going?" Athos wanted to know.

"Tristofer, check your map," Breslin instructed. "How much farther is the waterfall?"

Careful not to have misplaced the map this time, Tristofer retrieved it and studied it.

"I'd say about two more hours northeast as we follow the coast. However, I have to point out we won't be on the road as it veers west. We have to follow the coast, not the road."

"How close is R'Tal?" Breslin inquired.

"From Drammli Falls? About an hour north."

Breslin nodded. "Not far then. That means we should be safe when we leave the path."

Venk nodded, encouraged. He didn't want any other surprises when it came to the safety of his son.

"I say we continue," Breslin decided. "Besides, there aren't any rocks or trees here for us to string our hammocks."

"And there will be when we get to the waterfall?" Tristofer asked. "How can you be so certain?"

"What's the matter? Tired?"

"Utterly exhausted," Tristofer admitted.

Breslin smiled. "Acknowledged. Be patient. I know there are trees because the Questor's Mark shows them."

Surprised, Tristofer glanced over at the boy who was busy chatting with his father.

"I forgot. You're right of course. I think I can make it."

"Excellent. Let's go."

Two and a half hours later they found the waterfall. The ground had risen steadily ever since they turned north, so by the time they encountered the waterfall they were well over three hundred feet above sea level. Lukas' mark indicated there'd be trees about and it didn't disappoint. There were plenty of pine trees available that would be perfect for stringing hammocks.

The sun had just set, so as darkness was settling in, the dwarves constructed their camp. Venk and his son searched for firewood while Breslin and Athos strung hammocks. In the meantime, Tristofer fetched rocks to be used as their fire ring.

"Think we're in the right place?" Athos murmured to Breslin as he tied one end of a hammock to a tree.

"You don't?" Breslin shook his head. "Lukas' mark has been incredibly accurate in every way thus far. We won't know we're in the right place until Lukas tells us if he feels anything."

"Where would you hide something in a waterfall?" Athos wondered aloud.

"Probably in a cave behind the falls."

Tristofer approached them.

"Assuming you're right," the scholar began, "how exactly do you propose we verify that? Did you see how high up we are?"

"I say we string him up and lower him down the cliff," Athos thoughtfully suggested, glancing briefly at Tristofer before returning his gaze to Breslin. "That way we could let him investigate all he wants."

All the color drained from Tristofer's face. "You wouldn't dare."

Breslin laughed. "He's joking. Pay him no attention."

Tristofer breathed a sigh of relief. "Thank goodness."

"I wasn't joking," Athos muttered under his breath.

Tristofer gasped with alarm. "That's not funny."

Breslin turned away before Tristofer could see him smile.

The following morning found everyone standing at the edge of the cliff staring down at the water far below.

"Are you sure, son?" Venk asked. "You can't sense anything?"

Lukas shook his head. "I can't feel a thing. I'm sorry, but until I touch whatever it is, I won't be able to sense it."

Tristofer looked over at Athos and frowned. Athos was staring straight at him and smiling. Tristofer surreptitiously moved away from the ill-tempered brother.

"Is your back tingling at all?" Tristofer asked the boy.

Lukas paused as he tried to sense whether his back was reacting to the area or not.

"No."

Venk frowned. How were they supposed to know where to look if they didn't know where to start? Drammli Falls was huge!

Lukas shrugged and moved off south, farther away from the river and waterfall. They all watched him turn and move back toward them. As he neared, he veered west and walked along the river for just a bit. He turned again and returned to their side.

"Nope, I still can't feel anything. My back usually tingles a little to let us know we're in the right area, but so far, I haven't felt anything."

"What does that tell us?" Athos asked. He turned to

Tristofer, expecting an answer.

"It tells us that our destination is still far away," Tristofer answered. "Either we're in the wrong spot or else the object we're looking for is at the other end of the waterfall."

"The other end?" Breslin repeated. "Does that mean we have to go…"

"Down?" Venk finished for him. "Figures. So, how are we supposed to do this?"

Breslin turned to Tristofer. "Got any ideas?"

"Well, I'd suggest we send the one member of this party who can fly down to investigate. Perhaps Rhamalli can see something we can't."

"I can see plenty," Rhamalli's voice rumbled, startling all of them.

They turned to see the giant dragon sitting on the edge of the cliff, leaning his long red neck out over the precipice. How long Rhamalli had been sitting there was unclear. The fact that this was the second time in as many days that they had been surprised by his appearance did not go unnoticed by Breslin.

"What is it with you dragons? How is it you can move with such stealth that no one can see or hear you?"

Rhamalli said nothing.

"Fine. Be cryptic. We don't care. What can you see?"

"Rocks."

"Aren't you a barrel of laughs? Anything else?"

"Water."

Breslin sighed while Lukas tittered quietly.

"Would you like me to inspect it closer?"

Breslin rubbed his temples. The dragon was starting to give him more headaches than the scholar.

"Aye, I would."

Rhamalli launched himself off the cliff and fell like a stone toward the surface of the sea. When it looked as if he was going to splash down, his great red wings unfolded and he arced gracefully above the water. He even dropped a foreleg down to lazily skim the surface of the sea.

As Rhamalli beat his wings to rise back into the air, he circled back toward the base of the waterfall. He circled a second and then a third time before he steadily rose back to the top and alighted on the ground next to them.

"There's nothing out of the ordinary I could see," the dragon reported. "No marks, no runes, no foreign objects of any type were observed."

Athos looked back at his nephew. Lukas was wandering slowly around the area, hoping to get his back to react to something.

"We're going to need to get Lukas down there to see if he can determine whether or not we're in the right area," Breslin announced. "Who wants to go with him?"

"That's not even a valid question," Venk told him. "Of course, I'll go. Do we know what we're looking for?"

"One of two possibilities," Tristofer told them. "After studying the picture of the power hammer closely, based on what we already possess, we are either looking for the handle or the hammer head."

Athos raised an arm. "I'll go, too."

Breslin nodded. "Good. Tristofer and I will remain topside."

"Thank goodness," Tristofer exclaimed.

Breslin looked at their wyverian friend.

"Will you carry the three of them down there?"

Rhamalli nodded. "There is a large slab of stone that looks as though it cleaved off from the cliff face. It appears stable. I can deposit them there."

"Sounds good. Venk and Athos, get your gear. Tools, hammers, chisels; take whatever you might need in case you find something."

Venk grunted in way of acknowledgement. He and his brother went for their tools.

Half an hour later, both brothers were standing on the slab of rock just north of the waterfall, staring up at the cliffs far above them.

"Where do we even start?" Athos shouted over the noise of the waterfall.

"Lukas said his back tingled the moment Rhamalli first landed on this rock. We flew all around the area. This was the only place where Lukas could feel anything. Therefore, it must be around here somewhere. Split up and look for anything out of the ordinary."

"Rhamalli said he didn't see anything unusual."

"Stop complaining and start looking!"

Venk and his brother quickly covered the entire surface of the roughly thousand square foot slab of rock. Rhamalli was right. The stone had broken off from the cliff due to natural erosion. Judging by the size of the slab, Venk figured it must have made a tremendous splash when it fell into the sea. Venk's eyes traveled up the cliff face and hovered over the large indentation from where the slab must have been originally sitting. Rhamalli had indicated that he hadn't seen anything, and Lukas had also indicated his back hadn't started tingling until they were as low as they could possibly be without landing on the actual fallen chunk of stone. That could only mean that the object they were looking for was either hidden somewhere underneath the stone, or else possibly within it.

"Rhamalli, can you hear me?"

The dragon's huge head swung out over the edge of the cliff far above and gazed down at them.

"Is there any way to tell what's below this slab? It isn't that thick. See the cliff there? Where the stone broke off? It's fairly shallow, maybe ten to twelve feet thick. We're farther away from the water than that. I'm thinking this stone must have landed on something. I'm wondering what that might be."

Rhamalli jumped off the cliff and was quickly circling about overhead as he studied the slab of stone.

"You're right. It's not as thick as I thought. I cannot tell what lies beneath. At a minimum, the water lies five feet beneath the bottom of the slab. It appears to be a rock formation of some sort. You're dwarves. Can you not tunnel through?"

"Of course, we can. Given enough time, we could. The problem is we need a faster resolution than that."

Athos knelt down and studied the stone's surface. He leaned out over the slab's edge and tried to see for himself what the slab was resting on.

"Take us back up."

Once the three of them were back at the top of the waterfall they compared notes.

"We have no way of knowing how long that slab has been there," Breslin told them. "I think it's safe to say that what we're looking for lies beneath. The question we must now ask ourselves is how do we inspect the other side? How do we move it? We need ideas. Let's hear them, no matter how preposterous."

Surprising them all, Lukas was the first to offer a suggestion.

"Shardwyn is a powerful wizard. He could pulverize that stone with a simple spell!"

"Even if he could," Venk patiently told his son, "there's no way to contact him. We've already used the messenger spell. Besides, I think this might be over his head. It's a very good idea, though."

Lukas beamed.

"Who else has an idea. Tristofer, what say you?"

"How long would it take our fastest diggers to tunnel through it?"

Breslin thought a moment. "It's hard to say without knowing what type of stone it is. It looks sedimentary. If I were to venture a guess, I would say two weeks. And that's creating a standard five-foot diameter tunnel. What if what we're looking for lies beneath a different part of the stone? They'd have to keep digging until they found it."

Rhamalli's deep voice drew everyone's attention. "What if the stone were broken in twain?"

"How?"

"Repeated strikes. Dragon fire is very destructive."

"You're telling us that you could break it?"

"Not without help," Rhamalli admitted. "I would seek assistance."

"From other dragons?"

"Aye."

"How long would it take?"

"Unknown. I have never tried to split a stone before."

Breslin bowed. "If you're offering, my friend, I'm asking. If you can, break that thing in two."

"Very well. I have just asked for help. Kemxandra and Cantreya are en route. They will be here soon."

Fifteen minutes later the large black female dragon was back, along with the white male dragon that had helped pin the zweigelan. Both were staring at Rhamalli as though he had just suggested all dragons should swear off flying.

"Would you please repeat that?" Kemxandra asked incredulously. "You want us to do *what*?"

Rhamalli extended his neck out over the cliff and looked down. The other two dragons followed suit.

"Do you see the slab of stone that has broken off the cliff and lies just above the water?"

They nodded.

"It is believed the stone slab conceals what the dwarves are seeking. The stone shelf must be broken. We are to render aid in accomplishing this task."

"How do you propose we do that?" Cantreya's gravelly voice asked.

"Repeated blasts by the three of us should accomplish the task."

Kem shook her black head. "I cannot believe Rinbok Intherer would want us to—"

"I've already informed him. He has no objections."

Kem's large black eyes narrowed as she stared at the slab hundreds of feet below.

"Think of it as a chance to practice your aim," Rhamalli suggested.

Kem's head swung around until she was facing Rhamalli. "Would you be insinuating your aim is better than mine?"

Cantreya chuckled; the deep rumblings were felt by dwarf and dragon alike.

Rhamalli gave the best approximation of a shrug that any of the dwarves had ever seen. "Your aim could benefit from repeated practice, Kem."

The black dragon sniffed disdainfully. "Perhaps my aim is not as accurate as yours. At least my shots do damage."

Cantreya's laughter grew louder. This time Rhamalli growled. "Do not even think of suggesting your shots are more powerful than mine."

"I destroyed three of the metal creatures last year. How did you fare?"

Rhamalli said nothing.

"What creatures?" Tristofer timidly asked.

Kemxandra glanced down at the spectacled dwarf. "Last year, during the battle with the human sorceress Celestia, we faced a mechanical foe that was extremely difficult to vanquish. I managed to dispatch three."

"Once you were told how," Rhamalli pointed out.

"Regardless," Kem continued, "I destroyed them. Refresh my memory. How many did you destroy?"

Rhamalli went silent again.

Nodding her head, Kemxandra smiled. "That's what I thought."

"Neither of you can match the power behind my blasts," Cantreya rumbled as he stirred. He unfolded his massive wings and stretched.

"I'd say we have the makings of a wonderful competition!" Breslin chortled while he rubbed his hands together. "The dragon that makes the final blast which splits the stone will forever after be known to be the strongest amongst the three of you. Agreed?"

As if sensing that something drastic was about to happen, the surrounding countryside fell silent. Insects scurried back to their lairs. Kytes anxiously retreated to their nests to verify their young were unharmed. For several seconds the dragons looked at one another as if mentally daring each other to make the first move.

"Two pieces of silver says the white one breaks it first," Athos whispered.

"Make it a gold piece," Breslin whispered back. "And I say Rhamalli will do it."

The ground lurched as the three dragons leapt off the cliff in a mad flapping of leathery wings. Cantreya immediately dove straight toward the slab and fired two quick blasts at the stone, expecting it to be reduced to rubble.

It wasn't.

Kemxandra and Rhamalli flew east over the sea before circling back and targeting the stone slab. Rhamalli fired off five shots, all of which bounced harmlessly off the stone's surface. Kemxandra elected to fire just one shot, but gave her shot as much power as she could muster. Inhaling sharply, she spat out an enormous fireball and watched it speed toward the slab. It impacted the stone with the force of a trebuchet. The large block creaked ominously but remained intact.

Three hundred feet away, from the safety of their camp, the dwarves listened to the relentless pounding the rock slab was taking. For close to an hour, the dragons blasted jets of fire at the stone shelf. The slab began to show signs of damage; jagged cracks had formed on the surface.

"What goes on here?" an authoritative voice suddenly demanded, startling the dwarves.

Jumping to their feet, the dwarves turned to see a dozen human soldiers approaching on horseback. At the front of the procession was a human Breslin was quite familiar with. He bowed to the human who was now holding up a hand, signaling his battalion to stop.

"Commander Rhenyon. It's an honor to see you again, lad."

Rhenyon dismounted and approached the dwarf. He clasped Breslin's forearm and gave it a mighty shake.

"Master Breslin! What the blazes are you doing out here? I've always heard its damn near impossible to get a dwarf out of a mountain, let alone five!"

Breslin grinned. He motioned for the others to approach.

"I believe you have already met Masters Venk and Athos last year. Over there is Tristofer. He's a scholar from the Kla Rehn."

Rhenyon nodded. He locked forearms with each of the brothers and then the bespectacled scholar.

"I remember you two," Rhenyon said as he turned back to the brothers. "You aided the Nohrin last year during the battle with Celestia, am I right?"

Both brothers nodded. Venk pulled Lukas to his side.

"This is my son, Lukas. Son, this is Commander Rhenyon. He is friend to the Nohrin and holder of another of the Mythra weapons."

Lukas' eyes went wide as they immediately settled on Rhenyon's sword.

"That's Mythron! He has the blue-bladed sword!"

Rhenyon briefly unsheathed his striking dark blue weapon and presented it to the boy.

Smiling, Lukas turned to his father to show him the fabled sword. "Father, can you make me one of these?"

Venk rolled his eyes. "Do you know how difficult it is to make a blue sword blade? Especially a dark blue one? I don't know what trick Master Kharus used when he made it, but I sure would like to learn it."

Rhenyon indicated the cliff's edge and began moving toward it. "Tell me, my friends, what's going on here? What are the dragons battling?"

Breslin smiled as he walked back to the edge of the cliff and looked down. Kemxandra and Rhamalli were still circling about as they blasted their fireballs at the stationary stone. Cantreya had located several outcroppings and was clinging to the rock face. He was blasting the stone relentlessly from his position, not that it did any good. More cracks had appeared in the stone shelf but it was still, unfortunately, in one piece.

Rhenyon looked down at the cliff face and watched the wyverian activity.

"Is this some type of dragon target practice?"

"We need to see what's beneath that stone slab," Breslin explained. "The dragons are kindly helping us save some time by breaking that giant piece of rock for us."

"That stone has been there as long as I can remember," Rhenyon remarked as he watched Rhamalli fly out to sea to circle about. "What do you think is under it?"

"I'm not really sure," Breslin admitted with a shrug. "It's something that will hopefully point us in the right direction for the next task."

"You're on some type of mission?"

Breslin nodded. "In a matter of speaking, aye. My father was presented a puzzle and he wants to solve it. I think he believes it could be beneficial to our people."

"Do you require assistance?"

Breslin looked at his human friend. The desire to tell the truth was strong, and he didn't like concealing anything. However, if there was still a chance that Nar could be waiting for them, he'd never hear the end of it if he let it slip now.

"I do not believe so, my friend."

Satisfied, Rhenyon nodded. The commander turned to study the circling dragons for another minute or two. Breslin watched the human from the corner of his eye. Did he suspect something?

"Tell me, why are you here?"

Rhenyon smiled. "Do you have any idea how far sound travels?"

Breslin let out a short bark of laughter.

"Heard them, didn't you?"

"The king thought we were under attack. When we couldn't find the source of the explosions I was sent to investigate."

"Sorry. It's just us."

"How do the two of you know each other?" Tristofer asked, sinking back down to sit cross legged on the ground.

"We met when we fought with Sir Steve and Lady Sarah during the battle of the guur."

Athos' eyes widened in disbelief. He turned incredulously to Breslin.

"You fought the guur during the battle in which those infernal bugs were eradicated?"

Breslin nodded. "Aye. It was one of the few times I was damn glad we were fighting side by side with humans, and one of them was a fire thrower."

Venk sank down onto the grass next to his son.

"Was fighting the guur as bad as the stories lead us to believe?"

"Worse," Breslin and Rhenyon said together.

"They're just bugs," Tristofer exclaimed as he polished his glasses. "How bad could they be?"

"Just bugs, Master Tristofer?" Breslin squatted down next to the scholar and thought how best to describe the terror that used to haunt his clan. "Imagine a ten-legged bug the size of Lukas. Imagine it is fully armored so that it's immune to arrows. Imagine it can move so fast that swords and axes are virtually useless. With me so far?"

Tristofer wordlessly nodded.

"Good. Now take that horror and multiply it by a thousand. That's what we faced when we fought them."

"How in the world did you vanquish them?"

"We killed their female. No female, no young. We did dispatch many of them, but with the female gone the colony couldn't replenish its numbers."

Tristofer was amazed, and his expression showed it. He sat there quietly in the grass as he tried to envision what weapons would possibly be effective against that type of adversary.

"As I said," Breslin reminded him, "one of the humans with us was Sir Steve. The Nohrin. He was, and still is, a fire thrower, and the most powerful one that has ever been recorded. He did most of the work."

"Impressive," Tristofer admitted. "Where is this fire thrower now?"

"Back in his world," Rhenyon told him. "He and Lady Sarah visit frequently. I just saw them last month when they came for the prince's fifteenth birthday."

An ear-splitting crack rent the air. Everyone jumped. Several of the horses reared up in fright. Breslin rushed to the cliff's edge, followed closely by the others.

"What was that?" Tristofer asked as he swallowed his fear of heights and joined them at the edge.

The three dragons soared by them and circled high in the sky. Cantreya and Kemxandra flew off moments later. Rhamalli circled around a few more times before coming down for a graceful landing.

"It is done," Rhamalli told the dwarves. The red dragon spied Rhenyon and his men. He lowered his head for a cursory sniff. "I do not believe we have met before, human."

"We haven't. I am Rhenyon, Commander of the Royal Guards in R'Tal."

"Rhamalli."

Rhenyon waited to see if any other titles were forthcoming. There wasn't.

"Pleased to make your acquaintance. Breslin, you appear to have everything under control. We'll be off. Good journey to you."

Breslin and the other dwarves bowed. After receiving a quick cuff on the back of his neck from his father, Lukas followed suit.

"And you. Give my regards to Kri'Entu."

Rhenyon nodded. He mounted his horse and galloped back the way he had come.

Breslin looked up at Rhamalli, clapped his hands together, and vigorously rubbed. "So! I had wagered on you. Athos and Venk bet on Cantreya. Who finally broke the stone?"

Rhamalli shook his head in disgust. "Kemxandra. Lucky shot."

"Indeed? Blast. I just lost three pieces of silver to Lukas. Was there anything below it?"

"Nothing significant that I could see. The stone was broken into three pieces. At the point of impact there does appear to be what could be a cavity of some sort directly below. I could not tell if it was natural or if it was artificial."

"Can you take Venk and Athos down to investigate?" Breslin asked the dragon.

Rhamalli nodded. "Of course."

Tristofer raised a hand. "Wouldn't young Lukas have to accompany them as well? So we can determine if we're in the right place?"

Venk frowned. He didn't relish the idea of putting his son in harm's way.

"Just until we can determine if something is down there. Once we do, *if* we do, then he goes back. Is that agreed, son?"

Lukas nodded emphatically, thrilled to be included.

Minutes later the three of them were staring at the broken slab. Lukas hadn't taken three steps before announcing his back started tingling. Venk nodded and signaled for his son to be returned to the others. As soon as Lukas departed, Venk pivoted in place. He wordlessly eyed the numerous scorch marks blackening the area. The giant slab of stone lay in three pieces. The section they were on, roughly half the size of the original, had jagged cracks running all across the surface. The smaller two pieces were about the same size and were now tilting haphazardly down, their far corners resting in the water.

"Has this stone always sloped down to the water?" Athos asked as he stared down at his feet.

"Looks like it slid toward the sea when it broke loose," Venk observed.

Athos approached the recently broken edge, and squatted down. He motioned for his brother to join him. He pointed at a gap of about four feet. The three pieces, sloping in opposite directions, revealed an opening just large enough for a dwarf to slip through.

"Give me some rope," Athos told his brother. "I'm going down."

Once Athos had been lowered into the hollow, he untied the rope and looked around the tiny cavity. This part of the stone, namely the undersides of the broken slab, had once been exposed to the elements. If something had been attached to the rock face, this was the correct side of the stone to be looking at.

Athos smiled. There was just enough light to look for irregularities. Catching sight of a discolored section of rock down near the narrowest part of the hollow, Athos dropped to his belly and inched forward for a better look. It was slightly yellow, standing out amongst a backdrop of solid gray stone.

He painstakingly checked the rest of the surface. The discoloration only existed in the one place. That had to be it!

"Did you get stuck down there?"

Athos looked back up through the narrow crack at his brother's concerned face.

"I'm fine. I found something. Hand me my tools."

"What did you find?"

Athos took his hammer and chisel and dropped back down to his stomach.

"I think there's something embedded in the stone. I'm going to find out."

A loud grating sound split the air and the slab lurched forward.

"Athos, get out of there! Hurry!"

Athos began chipping away at the slab's undersides. "Not until I get whatever this thing is."

Not bothering to keep his work neat, Athos sunk his

chisel as deep into the rock as he could, gouging out huge chunks of yellow stone in the process. After twelve inches he still hadn't found anything. The yellow stone had reverted to its natural gray color. What had happened? Was the colored stone just a natural occurrence?

"Think, Athos, think."

He recalled the long geological lectures he had attended back when he was an apprentice. Hadn't one of his masters said that pyroclastic deposits could permeate the surrounding rock, over long periods of time and therefore change its nature? While he doubted they were looking for anything volcanic in nature, it was possible that whatever they were looking for might have leeched, or tainted, the surrounding rock. If that were the case, the object they were looking for might not necessarily be directly beneath the discoloration. It could be off to the side.

Athos eagerly gripped his tools. He had to trace the yellowed rock back to its source!

The slab groaned and slid another foot or so toward the sea.

Venk's urgent voice called out to him.

"Athos, get your butt out of there! This whole damn slab is sliding into the sea!"

"It hasn't budged an inch in centuries. I think it'll be fine for another five more minutes."

The slab slid another foot.

"Any other bright ideas? You don't have five more minutes. Get out of there! If I get wet because of you I'll never let you hear the end of it!"

Athos ignored his brother and began frantically chipping away at the stone undersides. Where had the blasted yellow stone gone? He expanded his search, moving a few feet to his left, but came up empty. He could find nothing but gray stone.

The slab moved again. Cursing, Athos slid forward with the slab and continued chipping. There! There was more yellow stone! He doubled his efforts. A large heavy piece of yellow stone plunked painfully down on his chest. He angrily tossed it aside. Athos frowned. The yellow stone was gone!

The trail had ended there. The slab started moving again and this time it felt like it wasn't going to stop.

Athos snatched up the stone that had smacked him on the chest and scrambled up, toward his brother. Venk grabbed his outstretched hand and yanked. At the same time Rhamalli descended from the sky and plucked them both from the rock slab before it finished its noisy slide into the sea.

Once they were back on top of the cliff, Venk angrily turned to his brother.

"Cut it a little close, don't you think?"

Athos held up the yellow stone. "True, but I got it. I think."

Breslin looked at the yellow stone and then at the brothers as though they were mad. He was surprised to learn that the rock was easily twice as heavy as it should have been. "Why would a sedimentary stone be this heavy? This doesn't make sense."

Athos nodded. "Right. I think what we're looking for is buried in that stone."

Breslin pulled a small set of tools off his belt and sat down on a flat rock. Slowly and carefully, he started chipping away at the stone. Tiny flakes of yellow rock began to accumulate at his feet.

Venk cleared his throat. "Er, aren't there any larger hammers you can use?"

"And risk damaging whatever is in here? I wish I had my miniature tool kit. This chisel is way too big for this type of work. But I guess I'll just have to make do."

"Better make yourself comfortable," Athos told Tristofer while simultaneously winking at his nephew. "It looks as though we're going to be here a while."

"It must be the hammer head," Tristofer whispered excitedly. "It *must* be!"

After a while the stone Breslin was holding cracked open, much like an egg. Breslin caught a flash of metal before something heavy plopped onto his lap. Dropping his tools on the ground Breslin picked up the object and studied it.

Tristofer was right. It was a hammer head, and a unique one at that.

"There's going to be no living with him now," Breslin muttered.

Chapter 8 — Needle in a Haystack

Here he comes again." Venk sighed loudly. "How many more times must we endure this? He's a scholar. Surely, he must have been proven right before?"

"Would you like me to answer that?" Athos asked dryly.

Tristofer approached the spread-out pieces of the power hammer and gazed wistfully down at them. Again.

"After so long," the scholar whispered to himself, "we've finally got proof. We were right. *I* was right!"

Athos plucked the hammer head off the grass.

"So, you say the gem is supposed to be affixed somewhere on here? Where?"

Tristofer shrugged. "I'm not sure. I had hoped that there'd be an indentation, or a hole, or something to indicate where the gem was supposed to be inserted. I didn't know hammers came apart."

"They don't," Breslin assured him. "Once you assemble

the hammer you see to it they don't come apart."

"Where's that old copy of Legend of Nar?" Athos asked. "All right, look. This is obviously the head. See how the square striking surface is on one side and this metal dowel has been attached on the other? It's flattened there, in the middle. There's a hole in it. That's where the handle should attach. Now look, see here? This is the counter weight. It should slide on here."

"How does it stay together?" Tristofer asked. "What's to keep the counterweight from sliding off?"

"Er…" Venk stared blankly at the incomplete hammer. If all they were missing was the handle, how *would* it stay together?

"Maybe there's something we're missing," Athos suggested. "Where's Lukas? I want to know where we're headed next."

Breslin nodded. "Agreed."

Venk turned to see his that his son was sitting by the fire and quietly watching the proceedings. Venk pointed at Breslin and motioned for his son to join him.

"You're up, son."

Lukas nodded and pulled his jerkin up to his chin, hoping this would be the last time he'd have to expose his back.

Figuring the boy's father should be the one to hold the piece of tool up to the underling's back, Breslin looked at the prize they had found at the waterfall and silently handed it to Venk, who wordlessly accepted it. Venk gently lowered it until it touched the Questor's Mark.

The final section, which lay directly in the center of the mark, rippled outward and came into focus. Everyone leaned over Lukas' back to get a good look at their next clue.

It was a tree, a very unusual one.

Two different colored cedar-like trees, displaying separate root systems, appeared almost dead center in the mark. The two trees looked as though they had leaned toward one another or had merged together. Growing simultaneously, the enormous tree continued to thrive as it sprouted upwards as one combined tree. The roots to the left stretched out toward the nixie's pool and the right-side roots extended toward the edge of the water fall. The foliage of the combined tree branched in all directions, coming to rest next to the zweigelan on the top left-hand portion of the map and stretching right to the top of the falls.

"That must be one mother of a tree," Athos observed. The others nodded in agreement.

"Has anyone ever seen such an unusual looking tree?" Breslin asked.

Tristofer shook his head. "If that tree is drawn to scale, then we have a major problem."

Breslin groaned. "What now? Out with it, scholar."

Tristofer pointed at Lukas' back.

"Everything that mark has depicted thus far has been very specific. Look at that tree. Clearly, such a tree exists. However, you know, as well as I do, just how difficult it'll be to locate it. I think … I think we are going to have a very difficult time locating this tree."

"So, what do we do?" Breslin wanted to know. "Anyone have any ideas?"

"Who is the foremost expert on trees?" Venk asked as he looked over his shoulder at the scholar. "Who do you recommend, Tristofer?"

The scholar was silent as he considered.

"Logically, I would suggest that we visit a library and look it up. However, how do we do something like that without arousing suspicion? Besides, I don't think consulting one of our libraries is the wisest move we could make."

"Why not?" Athos demanded.

"Do the Kla Guur have many trees in their city?" Tristofer asked, with a wry smile.

Athos' mouth closed with a snap.

"Judging from your expression," the scholar continued, "I will assume Borahgg has just as many trees as Bykram, which is precisely *none*."

"You're right. Dwarf libraries are out. What now? We find a human one?"

Tristofer shook his head. "Of course not. To utilize a human library would create an open invitation for the humans to ask questions about the nature of our mission. So the answer there is a resounding 'no'."

"Do you have any idea how many trees must be in Lentari?" Venk asked, frowning. "How are we supposed to find this one? It's like looking for a needle in a giant haystack. If it was as large as the picture depicts, then we might have a chance in finding it. As much as it pains me to say it, we need help.

"I don't know about the rest of you," Athos suddenly interrupted, "but I am damn tired of walking. We need to know exactly where we're going so we're not traipsing around Lentari looking for this blasted tree. Know what I mean, Tristofer?"

The scholar's smile vanished instantly.

"It was one time. One time! Are you ever going to forget that I led you to the wrong lake?"

Athos, Venk, and Breslin all shook their heads no.

"I think what Athos is trying to delicately say," Venk translated, "is to be as certain of the destination as you can be because it wouldn't be good for you to guide us to someplace like Capily over on the west coast and then have it revealed we are nowhere close to where we should be."

Tristofer nodded. "I agree. Thankfully in this case, I don't have enough data to offer a valid destination."

"What do you suggest?" Breslin asked him. "Who do we turn to for help? Who can we trust?"

"What about Rhamalli?" Lukas asked as he dropped his shirt back into place and turned around. "He has really good eyesight. He flies really fast. Do you think he'd look for us?"

The adults hesitated. Should they ask the dragon for help yet again? How would it appear to the others if it became common knowledge that they couldn't successfully complete their mission without constant wyverian help?

Venk looked at Breslin.

"Your call."

Breslin tugged on his beard as he considered Lukas' suggestion. With a resounding shrug, he turned to the underling.

"This is your quest, Master Lukas. It's your idea. I leave the final decision in your hands."

Unaccustomed to having an adult ask for his opinion, Lukas glanced at his companions who gazed back at him, awaiting his decision.

"The more eyes we have searching, the better," Lukas slowly said, remembering all the times his father had him and his sister searching for mislaid tools in his workshop. "I say we ask Rhamalli for help."

Breslin nodded. "Very well. We ask for help. Hopefully the dragon is still in the area."

"Suggesting I have something better to do?" came the dragon's dry response.

Breslin laughed. "Well, do you?"

"Clearly not."

"Have you seen the tree on Lukas' back?"

"I have not."

"Come down here then so we can show you. We need to find this tree."

"Trying to find a single tree out of so many is akin to locating a specific blade of grass in a meadow."

"Are you saying you can't find it?"

Rhamalli's deep voice sounded from behind them, startling them all.

"If given enough time, and enough perseverance, anything can be found."

"One of these times, I'm going to find out how dragons can move with such stealth," Athos grumped.

"Lukas, show him your back."

Lukas sighed, faced away from the dragon, and lifted his tunic. Rhamalli glanced at the now complete mark covering Lukas' back and shook his head.

"I have not seen a tree like that before."

"Think you could locate it if you flew over it?" Tristofer asked.

Rhamalli shook his massive head. "At the speed I fly, I could pass right over that tree and not know whether or not it was the right one. Based on the illustration, that tree will be identifiable by looking at its trunk. I can only see the treetop as I pass overhead. My gaze can penetrate the treetops if I stare at the same area long enough. However, in order to do that I would have to fly too slow to be useful. I do not think I would be able to render much assistance here."

Breslin nodded. "I understand. We'll have to figure out something else."

"Like what?" Venk wanted to know.

"As my father always told me when I was little," Breslin said, "we'll have to look it up. Tristofer is right. We need a library."

A lengthy discussion followed, but the consensus was that wherever they went, the library must contain a dendrology section—the study of trees. For various reasons, a human library was not an option, nor were most dwarf libraries. Tristofer's clan was closest.

"Where can we find them?" Breslin asked.

Tristofer hedged. "They are at the southeastern tip of Lentari. The terrain from here to there is very rugged. No paths, no roads, and certainly no help if we need it. Perhaps we should…"

"No," Breslin interrupted. "We're going. Everyone pack your gear. I want to be at least five leagues from here before the sun sets."

In truth, they only made it three leagues, but it was still an adequate start. They had passed the western road leading to Donlari just under two hours ago, and the snow-covered peaks of the Selekais were visible on the southern horizon. Also visible was the beginnings of the forest, unfortunately, another three leagues away.

Breslin looked at the open prairie with disgust. If they were going to make camp here, they'd do so knowing they were completely out in the open and exposed to anyone who might be passing by. Either they were going to have to post a guard or else…

"Didn't the sack of spells Shardwyn gave us have one that was for protection?"

Venk, who had been sitting on his pack while the group decided what to do, stood up and retrieved the spell bag. Pulling out the two remaining spheres, he studied the symbols etched onto the surface of each spell. One had a tiny shield, the other a rain drop.

"I think so. This one has a shield on it." He handed the spell to Breslin. "Are you going to use it?"

"Wonderful," Athos mumbled. "Who knows what that crackpot wizard is going to do to us this time?"

"We're out in the open," Breslin snapped. "Unless you want to take the first watch, I suggest you keep quiet."

Athos shrugged.

"Sorry. I didn't mean that the way it sounded. I'm exhausted. You're beat. Everyone is. We could all use a good twelve hours of rest. Everyone ready?"

Venk and Lukas blearily nodded their heads. Tristofer snapped awake and nodded his agreement, too, even though he didn't know what he was agreeing to.

Breslin invoked the spell and waited with bated breath to see what would happen. A few moments passed. Nothing. He stared at his hand. The sphere was gone. Something must have happened!

"What are we waiting for?" Athos asked tiredly.

"I'm not sure. The spell is gone. It did something, but I just can't tell what. That scares me more than the guur ever could."

Athos grunted. After nothing else happened in the next ten seconds, he decided to pull his ground cover from his pack and began scouting for the best location to set up his bed roll.

A flash of blue light temporarily blinded everyone as Athos was thrown violently backward. The blue light flashed again and he was then thrown forward, landing heavily on the grass.

Pushing fatigue aside, Venk quickly rolled to his feet. He had pulled his crossbow and Breslin had pulled out his axe.

"Wizards be damned! What was that? Is Athos alright?"

Breslin hurried over to the still form of Athos and chuckled.

"He's snoring."

"What hit him?"

Breslin shook his head. "Unknown. Wait. Let me try something."

He selected a small nearby rock and tossed it. The rock sailed about fifteen feet before the blue light flashed and flung the rock back. Breslin neatly snatched the rock out of the air before it could hit the other wall as had happened to Athos.

"I'm beginning to see the nature of Shardwyn's spell," Breslin told Venk. "Let me see how large an area we have here."

Breslin tossed the stone at random spots around their camp. He managed to catch the rock most of the times it bounced back.

"The shield is about thirty feet in diameter," he reported. "Let's hope no one sleepwalks."

Tristofer grunted sleepily. He collapsed onto his bed roll and was snoring within seconds.

Venk approached Breslin and looked anxiously back at his son, who was already asleep. "Any idea how long the spell will last?"

Breslin shrugged. "Your guess is as good as mine. Let's hope until morning at least."

"What if it doesn't wear off by then?"

"We'll worry about that if it comes to it."

Morning came. And went.

Lukas awoke to find himself in the middle of a musical concert of trills, chirps, and whistles. Everywhere he looked he could see little purple birds searching for tasty morsels. They were hopping all over their campsite, rooting around in their packs, scrambling over their weapons, even perching on those that were still asleep; a fluffy kyte was sitting precariously on his uncle's nose.

Lukas nudged his father awake.

"Look! There are kytes everywhere!"

Venk blinked a few times and rubbed the sleep out of his eyes. He smirked as he watched his brother absentmindedly swat at his face. Evidently the kyte perched on Athos' nose was tickling him with its feathers. Every time Athos swiped his arm the kyte would take to the air, only to return moments later when the sleeper went still again.

"I would say that the protection spell has definitely worn off," Breslin said as he noticed the antics between Athos and the kyte. He stretched his stiff back and glanced around their camp at the flurry of avian activity. "Did someone sprinkle some seed? Where did all these kytes come from?"

Venk shrugged. He and Lukas began stowing their gear.

"You have precisely five seconds to get off my nose unless you want to become breakfast," a gravelly voice suddenly barked out.

The purple kyte tweeted in alarm, rose into the air, and deposited a telltale symbol of its displeasure. Unfortunately for Athos, it landed in his open mouth.

"Gah! You wretched, disgusting, vile tuft of feathers!"

Grinning from ear to ear, Venk tossed his water bag to his brother.

The rest of the tiny birds rose into the air and circled high in the sky. The purple flock coalesced into a writhing mass as it circled. When it became clear the section of ground was not going to return to its docile state any time soon, the flock moved off.

Athos gargled another mouthful of water and spat it out. "That… that…"

"Was a crappy way to start the day?" Venk wryly asked, raising an eyebrow.

"Ha ha. Missed your calling. Should've been a jester."

Venk smiled again. He pointed at Athos' beard. "Might want to wash your beard."

"What? You've *got* to be kidding!"

As Athos upended the water bag over his beard, Venk helped Breslin and Tristofer stow their gear back into their packs. After a quick meal of dried meat they resumed their trek south.

"It sure is a nice day, isn't it?" Tristofer commented.

"If I hear you say how wonderful this day is one more time, scholar," Athos growled, "I'll personally make you eat that book you're holding."

Tristofer hurriedly put away his copy of his favorite book, *Klondaeg—The Monster Hunter*, a story about a fearless dwarf monster killer. While certain Athos would never make him actually eat the book, he wasn't about to press his luck with the irritable brother, either.

"What did I tell you?" Breslin's voice was heard saying. "We made the forest before midday. I told you we could do it."

"Only because we had you nagging us the entire time," Athos grumped.

"We finally get to put this infernal sea behind us," Breslin pointed out. "Doesn't that make you happy?"

"I don't think anything you say would please him right now," a deep familiar voice said.

Breslin shook his head. He looked up. As expected, the dragon was nowhere in sight. "How long have you been following us this time, Rhamalli?"

"I never left."

"You mean you could have carried us here the first time? Why didn't you?" Athos demanded.

"You never asked."

"I can't believe I'm going to say this, but could you carry us all there? As much as I don't want to fly again, I really don't want to spend the next several days walking, either."

"Carry five dwarves? Easily."

"*Will* you carry us the rest of the way?"

"Not without running the risk of dropping one of you. Look at my claws. You dwarves are small. For such a long flight, I might grip too tightly, or else forget I'm holding you. Or perhaps you might slip through my claws so I might unconsciously clasp my talons together more tightly than I should. I'd feel terrible if I knew that I had squished you all to jelly. Therefore, I'd prefer not to do that."

"Appreciated by all," Athos murmured, impressed that Rhamalli had clearly given some thought to trying to carry them all to the Kla Rehn's city.

"Do you have any idea how revolting that'd be?" Rhamalli continued. He glided in from the east and touched down gently next to the walking dwarves. His long serpentine tail twitched. "I'd have to clean dwarf goo off my scales. How disgusting."

Venk clapped his hands over his son's ears.

"Would you stop talking about turning us into goo?"

Rhamalli fell silent.

"Thank you. I'm with Breslin when it comes to flying, but I'm also in agreement about not walking all the way to Bykram. So, let me ask you something. What if we could guarantee that you wouldn't drop any of us? Then would you carry us to Bykram and save us from another several days of walking?"

Two wyverian eyes fell upon the dwarf wearing the red leather armor.

"I'm listening."

"What if we were to build something that all of us could fit in? We wouldn't be riding on your back and all you'd have to do is carry it."

Rhamalli considered. "Like a cage?"

"You're not getting me in any cage," Athos stated flatly.

Venk shook his head. "I'm thinking more along the lines of a basket."

Athos thoughtfully nodded. "I see where you're going with this. A large basket that we could all sit in, with a handle. The dragon could carry us without fear of injury to us."

"That sounds like an awful lot of work," Breslin observed. "Is it worth it? Bykram isn't that much farther away, is it?"

Tristofer shook his head no. "Not only is it nowhere close to here, there aren't any roads leading directly there. I may not be a carpenter, but I'll help build this device in whatever fashion, if it will prevent us from taking another step."

An hour later Venk handed the scholar a small ax and pointed to the growing pile of branches.

"Strip these of all smaller branches. Make them as clean as possible. We'll be sitting on these and I'm sure you don't want any broken branches poking us in the butt."

Tristofer hefted the ax and eyed the large pile of branches. He nodded. "I think I can handle that."

"Good. Breslin and I will start building the frame of the basket while Athos continues to gather wood."

"What can I do?" Lukas asked.

Venk pulled one of his daggers off his belt and handed it hilt first to his son. "Help Tristofer. The sooner these branches are stripped, the sooner we get the basket built."

Working together the basket was constructed in just under two hours. Once the large, tightly woven container had been completed, the five dwarves broke for lunch while Rhamalli continued to circle lazily in the sky.

"We should have thought of this sooner," Breslin exclaimed once he was seated in the basket and clutching his pack tightly on his lap.

Venk and Athos joined him moments later. Athos leaned over the lip of the basket and pulled his nephew in. Tristofer extended his arm and waited for someone to give him a hand as well. Breslin sighed inwardly and then grasped the scholar's hand. He was surprised to learn that he could barely pull Tristofer up the side of the basket.

"What the blazes are you holding?" Breslin puffed out. "A bag of rocks?"

"It's just my pack. There might be one or two books in there."

"Did you keep all those books you stole from the zweigelan?"

"I didn't steal them. I borrowed them. I didn't want to leave them behind. I still don't."

"If Rhamalli says there's too much weight in here, and something has to go, then I'm personally tossing it over the side whether or not you're holding on."

Once they had given Rhamalli the signal that the basket was loaded, and they were ready to depart, the dragon swooped in to snatch them off the ground, all while refusing to decrease the speed at which he was flying. All the dwarves were slammed against the basket floor. Higher and higher they rose into the air as Rhamalli hefted the unwieldy basket clutched tightly in his front left claw. Once the dragon had reached a comfortable altitude for flying, he banked right and headed south.

Lukas made a move to stand in the swaying basket but was violently yanked back down by his father.

"Not on your life, boy," Venk warned. "Stay down."

"But I want to see what's below! Join me! We're safe in here. What do you have to lose?"

"My lunch."

Lukas smiled down at his father and his uncle, who were both gripping the sides of the basket so tightly that their knuckles had gone white. He glanced at the other two adults and noticed they, too, did not appear to be enjoying the trip. Breslin's eyes were screwed shut, and his face looked a little green.

Lukas dropped to his knees and sat companionably next to Breslin.

"Are you alright?"

"Incredible. I miss Lady Sarah."

"You do? I thought you didn't like to be teleported?" Athos reminded him. His stomach, already questionable, clenched tighter at the thought of the female Nohrin's sudden teleportation jumps.

"I don't. But I'm willing to risk it if we could avoid the prolonged hell we're in now. I don't know how much more my stomach can take."

"Who is Lady Sarah?" Rhamalli's deep voice cut in.

"You should know her," Breslin scolded. "She's the human woman from another world who healed all you dragons that were hurt by those mechanical monsters."

Rhamalli nodded. "Of course. I should have known. What don't you like about teleporting?"

"It's a terrible jolt to the system. It's the same problem I have with flying: queasiness."

"So, are you saying you probably wouldn't like it if I did this?"

Rhamalli suddenly lurched to the left and then quickly to the right before righting himself and leveling off.

Athos, Breslin, and Tristofer all slapped hands over their mouths. Lukas stared intently at his uncle and then Breslin.

"You look as though you're about to be sick," Lukas pointed out. "Don't worry. We're making great progress. Do you see how fast the trees are moving by underneath us? From up here it looks as though the forest is alive. Look! It's like the treetops have become rippling waves! Up, down, up, down, and now left to right."

Breslin leapt to his feet and was barely able to get his head over the side of the basket before he sent his lunch down to the forest floor.

Tristofer clapped a hand over his mouth and looked away.

"What?" Breslin demanded, as he wiped his mouth with the back of a sleeve. "Haven't you ever seen someone get sick before?"

Tristofer hastily nodded. He had closed his eyes and was humming loudly to himself.

Venk smiled.

"Fighting the urge to taste your lunch for a second time?"

Tristofer nodded again.

"Get your mind off of it," Venk told him. "Think about something else."

"Like what?" Tristofer whispered between huge gasps of air.

"Like what is the plan once we reach Bykram. This is your home city. How are you going to handle it?"

"As discreetly as possible," Tristofer answered, still breathing heavily. "A former teacher of mine is our best bet. We didn't always see eye to eye but at least we respected one another."

"I assume he's still alive?" Athos asked, looking rather pale himself.

Tristofer shrugged. "I hope so."

The basket shook violently for a few seconds as Rhamalli was buffeted by strong air currents. Ten seconds later they were peacefully gliding south once more.

"When's the last time you were home?" Breslin asked, desperate to keep his mind off of what the dragon was doing and the fact that he knew just how far off the ground they presently were.

Tristofer twirled the tip of his beard around his finger.

"Let's see. I'd say it's been at least a hundred years."

"Since you've returned to your home city?"

Tristofer shook his head. "No, since I left the city."

"And you haven't returned home since? Why?"

"We didn't always see eye to eye."

"Who's the 'we' you're talking about?" Venk inquired.

Tristofer shrugged. "The Council."

"What didn't they see eye to eye with you about?" Breslin asked.

"Oh, it's nothing, really."

"More like it's nothing you'd like to talk about, is that it?"

Tristofer shrugged again. "It wasn't important. I left and haven't regretted my decision."

"Except for now," Venk reminded him.

The scholar ignored him.

Several hours later Rhamalli informed them that they were approaching a small valley in which several dwarves had previously been seen. Breslin, Venk, and Athos actually observed two dwarves dive into nearby bushes as Rhamalli deposited the basket near the northern edge of the valley. The dragon verified the basket and its cargo were unharmed before retreating back into the sky. The great red dragon turned to look back at the small group of dwarves as he strove to put as much distance between himself and the ground as possible.

"I trust you'll signal if you need my assistance."

Breslin gave the dragon a look of disgust before Rhamalli disappeared into the clouds. He shook his head as he glanced angrily at the two brothers.

"What was that supposed to mean? That we can't look out for ourselves? We don't need a wyverian protector, thank you very much."

"Speak for yourself," Tristofer argued. "I'm actually glad he's looking out for us. He's gotten us out of several predicaments already."

Breslin sighed and gave the valley a quick, cursory glance. "Where now, Tristofer? This is your home city. Where's the door? Better yet, where'd those two we saw disappear to?"

Tristofer pointed to the right. "See that large broken

stump there to the west? That's the main entrance."

Athos looked at the huge jagged stump and strode toward it, motioning for the others to follow.

"You'd think they would try and conceal their door a bit better than that."

Tristofer looked up at him with a blank expression on his face.

"Why do you say that? What's wrong with the door?"

"Look at the size of the trunk. There are no other trees around here even close to that size. The fact that the trunk hides a door is blatantly obvious."

Tristofer crossed his arms over his chest. "Well, it's not like we were … watch out!"

Athos had pulled an orix free from his chest bandolier and hurled it off. It zipped perilously close to the scholar. The green weapon spun away from them on its elliptical orbit, disappearing into the dense foliage southeast of the broken stump. They all heard a distinct metallic clang followed shortly thereafter by a cry of pain.

"It's considered rude to eavesdrop on someone," Athos called loudly to the bushes. "Even more so when you're spying on guests."

Two dwarves emerged from the thicket, one holding a metal helmet with a fresh dent in it. He was rubbing his ears, still hearing the clang of the orix. Both dwarves were dressed in black tunics and khaki trousers. Neither was armed, but had tools hanging on their belts, including a large hammer swinging on their hips.

"We weren't spying," the first dwarf said crossly as he inspected his damaged helmet. He pulled his hammer from his belt, flipped the helmet over, and gave it several whacks. Satisfied that the dent had been removed, the hammer was returned to his belt and the helmet was placed back on his head.

"Sneaking around while avoiding detection is generally considered spying," Breslin told them while Athos retrieved his orix.

"You arrived with a dragon!" the closest dwarf exclaimed. "How were we supposed to know you were friendly?"

"You automatically assume all dragons are evil?" Venk snapped.

Breslin stepped in front of Venk and held up his hands in a sign of peace.

"You'll have to forgive us. We generally do not hitch rides with dragons. The wyverians are allies and as such, we do not take kindly to anyone disrespecting them."

The second dwarf finally spoke.

"Allies? With dragons?? Where are you from, friend?"

"I am Breslin, son of Maelnar, son of Kasnar, of the Kla Guur. We come in peace."

"I am Timeki and this is Plukren, of the Kla Rehn."

After everyone had introduced themselves, Timeki looked hard at Tristofer.

"Don't I know you?"

Tristofer paled. "I doubt it. I would have remembered you."

Timeki's brow furrowed. He grunted. He looked first at Breslin and then looked suspiciously over at Tristofer, who avoided eye contact. "What is your business here?"

Breslin turned to Tristofer and slapped him on the back, startling the scholar into taking several steps forward. Tristofer nervously cleared his throat.

"I was hoping to speak with Master Rohath."

Timeki and Plukren exchanged glances.

"Sure. Right this way."

Timeki turned on his heel and led them toward the jagged stump. He pressed several knots on the stump's surface while Plukren did the same on the other side. The western face of the stump, the side facing away from the valley, swung outward revealing a steep staircase leading down.

The two members of the Kla Rehn descended a dark staircase without waiting to see if they were being followed. Shrugging, Breslin entered next, followed closely by Venk and Lukas. Athos pushed a reluctant Tristofer through the doorway while pulling the facade of the fake stump closed behind him, as he was the last to enter.

Fifteen minutes later they were standing in a well-illuminated cavern facing an intricately carved archway.

Dwarven runes had been carved into every square inch of the arch, starting at floor level and extending all the way up and over the arch until it touched the floor on the other side. A massive wooden door, replete with runes and symbols, was securely closed. As Timeki approached the large door, it noiselessly swung open as if it rested on well-oiled hinges. Another staircase was visible, leading down. Lit torches blazed merrily every ten feet.

"That's a neat trick," Athos admitted.

Plukren turned to look back at Athos.

"The entrance will only permit those from the city. The only way to visit Bykram is to be accompanied by one of its denizens."

"Then I'm glad we found you," Breslin commented.

Timeki absentmindedly rubbed the welt on his forehead. "Right, I'm sure you are."

Half an hour later they were met by a contingent of armed guards as they emerged into the great cavern Bykram called home.

"State your business," one guard gruffly asked them.

Timeki stepped forward. "They seek Master Rohath."

"Who?"

"That's not encouraging," Athos mumbled softly.

"Master Rohath," Timeki repeated. "I believe he was the former Master of Paleography."

"The former master of *what*?" Venk whispered to Tristofer.

"Ancient writing," Tristofer whispered back.

The lead guard thought for a moment and turned to point off toward a row of domed buildings.

"Take them to the great hall. The Council will decide what should be done with them."

"Pardon me," Tristofer meekly interrupted, "but we really don't need to speak with the Council. If you could just inform Master Rohath that one of his former pupils would like a word, I'm sure he would grant us an audience."

The guard shook his head no and again pointed toward the distant buildings.

Breslin cursed softly. "That's just splendid. Remember,

everyone, we cannot disclose the true nature of our quest. Therefore, I suggest you all let me do the talking."

Lukas fidgeted uncomfortably as he and his father, along with his uncle and the scholar, listened to Breslin talk with the ten adults seated in front of them. All of them had their arms crossed over their chests and every single one was frowning. The peculiar thing, Lukas noted, was that they were frowning at only one person: Tristofer.

They had been told that the Council was already engaged in its weekly session and that they would be seen almost immediately. Breslin had cursed quietly to himself as he had informed the other adults that he hadn't a chance to prepare himself for this upcoming confrontation. Yet again Lukas wished he had never been cursed with the large mark on his back. All this trouble and it seemed they were just being led on an extravagant scavenger hunt to find some old hammer. He had silently hoped they would find the fabled city of Nar, but no, it looked like they were only going to find a tool. Even that seemed unlikely since the Council had become very tight-lipped and was only giving one word responses to Breslin's friendly questions.

One member of the council, more heavily decorated with robes, necklaces, and ceremonial pins than the others, leaned forward to pick up his goblet of ale and, after draining the contents in a single swallow, thumped the metal chalice back onto the table. The loud noise startled everyone into silence.

"I've heard enough, Master Breslin," the decorated dwarf began, rising to his feet as he did so.

Breslin bowed toward the speaker.

"We all know that you're here looking for Nar."

Surprise registered on the newcomers' faces. Breslin recovered first, plastering a neutral expression on his face.

"Nar, Master Prixus?" Breslin repeated. "I do not know what you're referring to."

"The reason I know you're lying, Master Breslin," Prixus continued, "is because of *him*." Prixus raised an arm and pointed at Tristofer. "It's Tristofer, isn't it? What nonsense have you concocted this time, Tristofer, to dupe our brothers from the north into coming here?" Prixus turned to Breslin. "He must have been persuasive if your clan enlisted the help of dragons. I'm sorry to say you've come all this way for naught. You will not find Nar here."

Breslin turned to stare at Tristofer. "You've led expeditions to locate Nar from here, too?"

Prixus let out a short bark of laughter. "Didn't he tell you? That's why he was banished."

Athos, Venk, and Breslin turned incredulously to Tristofer. Athos burst out laughing.

"No wonder you didn't want to come here! You're banished? You left out that little part, didn't you?"

Breslin smiled as inspiration struck. He jammed his elbow into Athos' gut, cutting him off in mid guffaw. Returning his attention to Prixus, Breslin nodded.

Enjoying himself, Prixus returned to his seat. "So what does he have you searching for now? A rock? Perchance you're looking for a rare beetle? Trust me, you won't find anything."

Tristofer's cheeks were flaming red. "As a matter of fact, we have! We have —"

Breslin stomped on the scholar's foot. Hard.

Prixus leaned forward and rested both elbows on the granite table.

"Eh? Found what?"

"That he's a certifiable lunatic," Breslin answered, giving a resounding sigh. He scowled at Tristofer before he faced the table full of elders. He was pleased to see that all had lost their frowns and now had condescending smiles on their faces. "You're right. We were looking for something. But no longer. Do you know what he's had us looking for so far?"

Prixus smiled jovially. "Indulge me."

"Flowers, trinkets, rocks, books. Do you know he led us to the wrong location? I even caught him holding a map upside down!'"

"If ever there was someone who could sympathize, friend Breslin, it'd be us. Only one wrong location? The last expedition Tristofer led us on he took us to four wrong locales before finally giving up."

"Why was he banished?" Breslin inquired.

"For reasons I just explained. He had become a public nuisance. He wouldn't let the notion of finding the lost city rest, so it was decided he should be banished. I'm truly sorry he ended up with the Kla Guur. If you don't mind me asking, what were you looking for here?"

Breslin shook his head. "It doesn't matter. We're tired. We've traversed so many leagues that we called in favors from our wyverian friends to arrange transport."

Prixus' eyebrows shot up. "You rode a dragon?"

Breslin laughed and shook his head. "While that would have been easier, no. We were forced to construct a container to be carried in."

Prixus nodded. "That explains the reports I heard of a large basket. So you consented to be carted around like a basket of berries?"

Breslin rolled his eyes. "That was the final indignity. I was ready to call off the expedition right then and there, but Tristofer assured me that which we sought was nearby. It wasn't."

"What did he tell you was nearby?"

"A tree. A blasted tree! See any trees around here? Of course you do! Trees everywhere. Tristofer said this one looked as though two individual cedar trees had merged together and were thriving as a single tree."

Breslin stopped his narrative and held up all ten fingers. "We've found ten thus far, and none of them were the right one. He pleaded with me…"

"I did no such thing," Tristofer murmured softly.

"He pleaded with me," Breslin continued, growing angry, "to not give up. That *this* is his life's work. Whatever. I'm done. We're all done. We have inconvenienced our honorable brothers of the Kla Rehn long enough. By your leave, we'll return home."

Prixus sat back in his chair and tapped his fingers on his armrest.

"Two cedars growing together as one? Aye. I believe I have seen a tree such as the one you describe."

Breslin irritably waved off the comment.

"You're more than welcome to investigate," Prixus continued. "I'll have a map drawn up for you. The terrain isn't favorable as the tree I'm thinking of lies halfway up a mountain in the heart of the Selekais. There are no paths and no roads, only leagues and leagues of wilderness and forest. Obviously the existence of two trees growing together isn't as much of an anomaly as I had thought, since there are so many, but I thought I should mention it."

"How is it you remember this one?" Breslin asked, genuinely curious.

"In my youth I used to watch the dragons hunt the great serpent out at sea. When someone makes the same trip over the same land repeatedly, the traveler's mind tends to wander, and when it wanders it has a tendency to notice anything out of the ordinary. I must have passed that tree several dozen times."

Breslin shrugged. "The tree is probably gone now, but if it lies between us and the sea then perhaps we can get the dragon to fly by the area so we can see for ourselves. If the dragon refuses, then I won't lose any sleep over it."

Prixus nodded. "I'll inform my staff about the map in case you go."

Meeting adjourned, the Kla Guur visitors were shown to a large chamber where they were allowed to stow their gear and rest. As soon as the door closed, Venk grinned broadly and clapped Breslin on the shoulder.

"Never have I witnessed a more superb example of manipulation! Master Breslin, you have my admiration."

Athos also nodded. "Is it safe to say we finally caught some good luck?"

Breslin beamed, his smile infectious. "I would say so, lads. Now all we have to do is —"

"What?" Tristofer interrupted. "We're still going to search for the tree? But I thought… I thought…"

"That's why I told you to let me do the talking," Breslin reminded him. "I learned from my father long ago that practically any situation can be turned in your favor provided you know how to handle the participants. It was just a matter of convincing them that we weren't interested."

Tristofer sniffed. "You inferred I was a charlatan."

Breslin surprisingly pulled Tristofer into a one-armed hug. "You, my friend, have been right at every turn. Well, almost every turn." Breslin's voice dropped to a whisper. "Look what we have so far! We only need the handle to complete our Narian power hammer and now even that is within our grasp. Forget your old Master, my friend. We leave at first light!"

Tristofer was nonplussed. Slowly he nodded and his smile returned.

"Good. I really didn't want to see him anyway."

Chapter 9 — Two Trees or Not Two Trees

We've been at it for hours," Tristofer complained. "All these mountains look the same. How are we supposed to find a single tree amidst so many?"

"Have you decided where you want to look next?" Rhamalli's voice called down to them. "I have not seen any trees that match the picture on the boy's back."

"Neither have we," Breslin admitted. He frowned at the map he was holding. "Can anyone follow this? Does anyone recognize any of these landmarks?"

"No one can," Venk told him. "We've all tried. No one can make heads or tails of it. Look at this. What is this supposed to depict? Either a group of five enormous trees growing in a circle or else it could be a family of trolls relieving themselves."

"And for the record, we haven't seen either," Breslin added.

"Why would Prixus give us a difficult map to follow?" Athos gripped the walls of the basket tightly as Rhamalli banked right. "To purposely keep us aloft in this infernal basket?"

Venk twirled the tip of his beard around his finger before poking it back into his belt. "That's an interesting idea."

Tristofer looked up. "What is? That they purposely gave us an incorrect map?"

Breslin shook his head no. "I didn't sense any malicious intentions coming from Prixus."

"Maybe you weren't as convincing as you thought you were?" Athos suggested.

"Who do you think made the map?" Venk wondered aloud. "We know it wasn't Prixus. He said he'd have his staff take care of it. What if someone is trying to lead us astray? What if … what if this is just a prank?"

"It's not very funny," Tristofer grumbled. He, too, didn't care for flying and would just as soon be back on the ground.

"So what do we do now?" Venk wanted to know. "If this map is inaccurate, we should pay it no heed. Do we explore on our own?"

"Then my original argument comes back into play," Rhamalli's voice reminded them. "I do not think I would be of much help without knowing where to focus our attention."

"Don't fly over the mountains," a soft, quiet voice said. "Fly next to them instead."

Rhamalli's long neck stretched down so that he could peer under his own belly at the basket he was holding.

"What did you say, young Master Lukas?"

Lukas flushed. He had directed his comment to his father but apparently the dragon had taken it to be directed toward him. Lukas looked up at his father for guidance but Venk was curious as well.

"Speak up, boy," his father gently prodded. "What did you say?"

Lukas cleared his throat and found his mouth completely dry. "Rhamalli, you've said you can't see the tree as you pass overhead, right? Not unless you slow down,"

Rhamalli's great head nodded.

"Then don't," Lukas told him. "Fly next to the mountains, but not over them. That way we can look for the tree from the sides. It'll be easier to see."

Surprised, Breslin glanced at the dragon. Rhamalli cocked his head as if surprised he hadn't thought of that simple idea.

"Nice," Venk told his son.

"Prixus told us the tree was on a mountainside," Tristofer reminded him. "Think he was telling the truth?"

Breslin nodded. "Aye. We just have to find the right mountain."

"If we are to assume what Prixus told us about his youth is correct," Tristofer began, "and we are to assume this map is wrong, then all we need to know is what's the most direct route from Bykram to the sea? Rhamalli, do you think you can spot the route a dwarf would travel starting back at Bykram?"

Rhamalli angled his head down to study the passing landscape.

"I believe so."

"How many mountains do you think might contain the tree?"

The dragon's enhanced vision located the stump that was Bykram's main entrance and followed it northeast toward the sea.

"At least a dozen."

"Circle around," Breslin told him. "Start at the stump that serves as their main entrance and head toward the sea. We'll have to inspect each mountain from here to there."

Hour after hour they searched, endlessly circling the numerous mountains and hills that lay toward the sea from Bykram's location in the southern Selekai mountains. On numerous occasions they did spot trees with the potential to be what they were searching for, but upon closer inspection, every tree they encountered had only a single trunk. Nowhere could they find a tree comprised of two smaller trees merged together.

With sunset only an hour or two away, and after circling around the first six mountains which lay in their path, Rhamalli spotted a tree high up a steep rocky mountainside on the seventh that showed the most promise yet. Vigorously beating his wings to gain more altitude, Rhamalli flew as close as he dared to the mountainside so that everyone could see what he had noticed—a tree with two distinct root systems perched precariously on the tiniest of ledges. Three other straggly trees were situated nearby, also clinging unsteadily to the rocky cliff.

"That's it!" Breslin said excitedly. "Look! That's clearly two trees! You can see two separate root systems!"

Rhamalli circled around for another pass.

"Are you sure?" Venk asked as he squinted at the distant tree. "Looks like just one to me."

"It's the right one," Breslin assured them. "You can see the roots of each stretching off in opposite directions."

"The tree does match the illustration on young Lukas' back," Rhamalli agreed. "Note the foliage. The northern half of the tree has leaves that have turned bright red while the southern half has leaves that remain brown."

"We need to get down there!" Tristofer said excitedly. "That tree should be the resting place of the hammer's last piece! It must be there. We have to find it!"

Breslin and Venk observed the steep slope, the tiny outcropping of rock the tree was clinging to, and the overall lack of ground on which a person could stand upright. They exchanged a glance.

"How exactly do you propose to do that?" Venk asked as he and his brother turned to stare at the scholar. He hooked a thumb back toward the tree and frowned. "There's no place to stand. How are we going to inspect the tree when we can't even move around?"

"Take us back to the ground," Breslin told the dragon. "We need to figure this out."

The long scaly neck slowly bent down until the dragon's enormous head was looking straight at the basket. Two slitted eyes focused on the dwarf.

"Please."

Satisfied that the dwarf had turned the sharply worded command into a request, Rhamalli gently glided to the base of the mountain and set the basket down upon a small grassy knoll.

"Now what?" Athos inquired as he craned his head to look back up at the distant tree. The tree had to be at least a thousand feet above their heads.

"We brainstorm," Breslin answered. "We need some ideas. Let's hear it. Anything, no matter how preposterous. How do we scale a mountain without tools or rope?"

"Get what we need from Bykram," Venk suggested.

Tristofer automatically shook his head no. Breslin agreed.

"We can't return to Bykram for supplies without making it blatantly obvious that we found something. The Kla Rehn are out. No offense, Tristofer."

"None taken, I assure you."

Lukas turned to look up at the dragon's towering form before facing the mountain and slowly raised his gaze until it fell upon the distant tree.

"It's just a tree up on a mountain. I say we climb it."

Venk shook his head. "Without a safety harness? Without rope? I think not."

"We used to climb all the time when we were younger," Athos told his brother. "Over much worse terrain than that, I might add. Climbing a tree shouldn't be a bother. I'll do it."

"We're not talking about a simple tree," Venk pointed out. "Don't forget about the mountain that the tree is growing on. I don't want to climb that far up without the proper gear."

"How do we even know the handle is up there?" Breslin wanted to know. He turned to Lukas. "Could you sense its presence when we flew by it?"

Lukas shook his head. "I forgot to try. I'm sorry."

Venk studied the distant tree for a few moments longer before steering his son back toward the basket.

"Only one way to find out. Rhamalli, if you'd be so kind as to take us back up to the tree. Son, just like you did at the waterfall, see if your back starts to tingle. We'll figure out what to do next only if we know we're at the right tree."

Athos hopped into the basket and then leaned over to pull his nephew in. Venk climbed in moments later.

"Wait here," he told Breslin and Tristofer. "We'll be right back."

Ten minutes later they were back on the ground.

"Well?" Breslin demanded. "Is it there?"

Venk turned to look down at his son. He gently prodded his shoulder. Lukas smiled at Breslin and nodded his head.

"Aye. My back began to tingle the moment we got close to that tree!"

Breslin nodded. "Very well, the handle's presence is confirmed. Master Athos, are you still willing to risk exploring the tree?"

Athos nodded. "I am."

Venk raised an arm. "I'm going, too. My brother will not go alone."

Athos nodded in appreciation.

"I'm going too, father!"

One look from his father had Lukas wordlessly dropping his arm back onto his lap. The boy sighed. It wasn't fair! This was his quest! He should be the one allowed to go!

"Don't argue with me, boy," Venk warned, sensing his son was preparing to resist. "Trust me, if it's up there, we'll find it."

Strapping daggers, chisels, hammers, and various other tools to their belts and their baldrics, the two brothers retrieved the final addition to their gear: their primary battle axes. With a gentle clink as the brothers knocked their blades together, they strapped their axes to their baldrics so that the axe was fastened securely across their backs. Venk elected to leave his crossbow behind as he didn't think he'd need it. Together they turned to face the prone form of the dragon.

Athos approached the basket and made to jump in. Rhamalli finally stirred. A dark red foreleg snatched the basket off the ground just before Athos could hoist himself up.

"May I make a suggestion, master dwarf?"

Thrown off balance by the sudden disappearance of the basket, Athos spun around and stumbled to the ground, plopping unceremoniously down on his butt. A small hammer and a chisel went flying off his belt in the process.

"What the ruddy hell did you do that for?" Athos demanded as he rose to his feet amongst a series of clinks and clangs his gear made when he rocked to his feet.

"You won't be needing the basket," Rhamalli told him.

"Why not?"

"Did you see anywhere the basket could be set down?"

Surprised, Athos shook his head as he realized he hadn't.

"Er, no. What are you going to do? Let us ride on your back?"

Rhamalli's neck jerked straight up and his nose lifted.

"Absolutely not. I will carry the two of you in my right claw."

"Carry us?" Venk asked, hoping the queasiness he was feeling didn't come through with the tone of his voice. "I don't know if my stomach can handle that again."

"Lukas handled it perfectly," Rhamalli reminded him.

Venk scowled. "Great. Let's get this over with before I lose my nerve."

Bidding the others farewell, Venk and Athos climbed into Rhamalli's open right claw. Cringing nervously as the massive fingers began to close, both dwarves eyed the two-foot-long talons as they edged ever nearer. Fortunately, with his claw partially closed, the brothers felt fairly secure as they were carried up the mountain.

"If a month ago you would have told me that I'd be willingly riding in the claws of a dragon up a mountain," Athos mumbled uneasily, "I'd have labeled you insane. What the blazes are we doing up in the air like this?"

Venk smiled amidst his own queasiness.

"You're a good uncle. I appreciate what you're doing for Lukas."

"Don't you ever forget it."

"This isn't going to be easy," Venk warned, as they both eyed the tree looming closer with every passing second.

"If it was, then I'd say we have the wrong tree," Athos replied. "Nothing about this quest has been easy so far."

"Be ready," Rhamalli told them as the wind from his flapping wings bent several of the double tree's branches back to almost the breaking point. "I cannot approach any closer. I'll put you down on the ledge on the northern side of the trunk."

Venk eyed the tiny ledge from the safety of Rhamalli's claw.

"Ledge? You call that a ledge? That's no wider than a stair!"

Athos slid one of his hammers across his belt so that it was within easy reach for his right hand. If he had to make a quick handhold on the mountain's rocky surface, he'd need easy access to his best rock cutter.

Rhamalli deposited the two of them upon the tiny ledge then retreated to a safe distance about twenty feet away. He had located a suitable place to wait--clinging precariously, gripping a circular ridge resembling a large ring around the mountain.

Both dwarves lunged forward the moment their feet hit the ledge. They leapt for the low-lying branches and wrapped their arms around sections of the trunk, holding on as though their life depended on it, which in this case, it did.

"How long can you hold on like that?" Venk called out to the dragon.

"As long as is needed," Rhamalli answered. "The rock is bearing my weight. I'm not fatigued. And you?"

"We just have to get up the nerve to move," Venk told him, "which is easier said than done at the moment."

"Several feet to your left and just over your shoulder is another branch similar in girth to the one you're holding. Once there, you'll be within reach of a branch just off your left shoulder and slightly above your head. Make your way there. Then, more will be easily within reach."

Without releasing his death grip on the branch he and his brother were clinging to, Venk angled his head up and turned to look to his left. Sure enough, there was the branch the dragon wanted him to take. Inching forward at a pace slower than his beard growth, Venk finally convinced his left hand to unclasp the branch it was holding and reach for the one just above his head.

"I've seen grandfathers centuries older than you move faster," Athos told him. "Get a move on!"

Scowling at his brother, Venk pulled himself to the higher branch and waited for his brother to follow suit. Under Rhamalli's careful instructions, the two dwarves slowly explored the left-hand side of the Dual Tree, as they had started referring to it. They crawled as high as they could go without finding anything remarkable.

After an hour of climbing all over the Dual Tree, both brothers decided to take a moment or two for themselves to rest. Sitting in the fork of several large branches a fair distance from the tree's base, Venk leaned forward to inspect the trunk up close.

Reddish-brown and fibrous, the northern half of Dual Tree was at least seventy feet tall. It had thick, sharp, spreading, needle-like leaves that varied from two to three inches long. Venk gently sniffed. He detected a light, fragrant smell emanating from the wood.

"What are you doing?" Athos asked him from his perch several feet away. "Would you like a moment alone?"

Venk scowled at his brother. "I'm trying to learn as much as I can about this tree, alright?"

"And what have you learned so far?"

"Well, that this is no different than any other cedar that I have ever encountered. Do you know how many times I've seen groups of cedars growing together? Many times. Have I ever seen two growing like this? No. I've seen two trees sprouting from the same hole, but each grew in the opposite direction. What's so special about these two? Why are they growing together?"

"No clue," Athos told him.

"We've checked both the red half and the brown half. The only area we really haven't checked that well is Dual Tree's canopy," Venk told him, glancing up at the gently swaying treetops.

Athos shook his head. If he hadn't been tightly clutching the branch he was sitting on, he would have crossed his arms over his chest. "You want to check that up there, you go right ahead."

"Is there a problem?"

"Look how small those branches are. They won't hold our weight." Athos slowly shook his head. "Besides, if there was something up there, we would have seen it. I'm more inclined to think if there is an axe handle hidden in this tree, then it'd be somewhere around the trunk."

"How do we know that the handle wasn't hidden here when the tree was much smaller?" Venk argued. "I would think that it would have been carried upwards as the tree grew taller."

"Possible, but unlikely."

Venk studied his brother. "Alright, if you're so smart, where would you have hidden it?"

"Let's work this out. We know these trees don't grow together naturally, even when given the perfect opportunity to do so. You've said so yourself, am I right?"

Venk shrugged and nodded.

"Here we have two trees growing in close proximity, almost as if they were pushed together and forced to grow that way. Why would someone do that? Perhaps to conceal something?"

Venk froze. "You're telling me you think these trees were made to grow together in order to hide something?"

Athos nodded. "It's a hunch. I'll bet if we check the point in which the two trees come together, we'll find what we're looking for."

"Couldn't hurt to try. I thought I saw a small opening at the junction of the trees when we first arrived but figured it was just a trick my eyes were playing on me."

Athos swung his leg over and started sliding down the branch he had been sitting on, intent on bringing himself to a stop just before reaching the main trunk. However, a gust of wind suddenly appeared and blew him off balance. Flailing his arms, Athos toppled backward and, with a terrified look on his face, fell toward the ground hundreds of feet below. Venk lunged forward to try and grab his brother's hand as he fell past, but he wasn't fast enough.

"Athos!"

Before the dwarf could fall more than twenty feet, a red leathery surface suddenly snapped out beneath him and caught him, a safety net. Athos bounced on the wing much like a child would bounce on his bed at bedtime. The dragon stretched his wing out and then up to the tree. Rhamalli held it there while Athos clambered back into the safety of the tree's branches. Athos turned to stare at the giant red dragon still clinging precariously to the rocky wall.

"I will forever be in your debt. Never will I speak ill of a wyverian again. *Any* wyverian."

Rhamalli folded his wing back against his side and re-hooked his wing talon to the lip of the rock outcropping he had been gripping. He nodded solemnly to the dwarf, as if rescuing falling dwarves were a daily occurrence. Narrowing his eyes until they were mere slits, Rhamalli returned to his meditation, although this time he devoted a little more of his attention to the dwarves. The last thing he wanted to do was send a report back to the dragon lord that one of the dwarves had been lost under his care.

"Well, I'm awake now," Athos told his brother.

"I'll bet." Venk punched his brother hard on the arm. "Don't do that again. You scared me."

Athos hooked his right arm behind his brother's neck and pulled him close until they were practically nose to nose. He cocked his head back and butted Venk's head with his own, creating a loud clunk as their two helmets collided.

"Sorry. You are right, though."

"About what?"

"About seeing something under the base of the trunk. I saw it as Rhamalli raised me back up."

Venk turned to look down at the ground nearly thirty feet below them. Carefully, and making sure his handholds were firm, Venk lowered himself down to the tiny ledge. There! He had been right! The small rocky ledge the tree was growing on looked as though it had been methodically chipped away so someone could get under the tree. How long it had been there they didn't know, but one thing was for sure: someone had made the tiny hole. Luckily the small hole was just barely large enough for a dwarf to pass through.

Tucking most of their gear safely into a hollow formed by three massive branches forking off in different directions, Venk dropped to his belly and wriggled his way into the small opening. Athos was right on his heels.

The cave was much larger than either of them would have thought possible. Both were able to stand and their heads were still nowhere close to hitting the top of the merging trunks. Both dwarves craned their necks to look up; the roof of the cave was at least another four feet higher.

"Did you suspect this was here?" Athos asked as he glanced at the natural cavern formed by the intersection of the two trunks.

"Nope."

"What are we looking for?"

"You're seriously asking me that? A handle."

"You know what I mean," Athos replied crossly. "They wouldn't have left it out in the open. Someone else might have come in here at some point."

Venk pointed south. "You check that half and I'll check this one. Meet back here in an hour."

After crawling about on the floor for close to a half hour, both dwarves rose painfully to their feet. Venk silently studied the chisel marks near the entrance to the cave while Athos pulled his small hammer from his belt and began to tap various discolored spots on the inside of the trunk. Both trunks.

"Any luck?" Rhamalli's strong deep voice asked from outside.

"Nothing yet," Venk called back. "We're still looking. How's it hanging out there?"

They heard Rhamalli give an indifferent grunt.

"We're going as fast as we can," Venk assured the dragon. "Hang in there!"

They heard Rhamalli let out a "Hmmph." Had the dwarves been closer they would have felt the deep rumblings of the dragon's laughter.

"What's that?" Athos asked, pointing up at the tree's junction above their heads.

"What's what?" Venk inquired, looking up.

"I see several frayed pieces of string."

"String? What the blazes is string doing in a tree?"

Athos climbed on Venk's shoulders swaying left and right as he stared at the junction of the trees. A second string caught his eye. Then a third. They varied in length, from a fraction of an inch to no more than two. Athos counted seven frayed pieces of string poking out of the wood.

"There must be something embedded in the wood," Athos decided, eliciting a grunt from his brother. "If it's the handle, maybe it was wrapped in something?"

"How do you embed something in a tree?" Venk huffed out. His shoulders were throbbing and it was becoming increasingly difficult to stand motionless.

"Could a tree be made to grow around an object?"

Beads of perspiration trickled down Venk's back.

"Theorize later. What are you going to do about that string?"

Athos pulled the only other tool he had left on his belt: a small axe. However, even standing on his brother's shoulders, along with his foot-long axe handle, he still wasn't tall enough to reach the Dual Tree's junction point. Just then, the unique tree rocked.

"What was that?" Venk asked, momentarily forgetting the pain radiating down his shoulders and back.

Athos lowered his axe and looked around.

"I'm not sure. Maybe it's getting windy outside."

The sounds of creaking wood ceased.

Satisfied the tree had returned to its normal quiescent state, Athos let his axe slide through his fingers until he was only gripping the very tip of the handle, giving his range an extra three inches. He cocked his arm and prepared to swing.

The tree groaned again. Once more it felt like strong winds were trying to push the tree off the ledge.

"Hold up," Venk called up to his brother. "Get off my shoulders."

"Why? We won't be able to reach it if I get down, and even then, I can't quite reach."

Venk's voice turned sharp and authoritative.

"Athos, lower your axe and get on the ground. Now."

Surprised, and a little annoyed, Athos hopped down from Venk's shoulders and speculatively eyed his brother.

"What's the problem?"

"Every time you raised your axe, the tree groaned."

"Trees don't react to people," Athos argued. "Just a coincidence."

"I was watching you. Trust me. You prepared to swing

and the tree made noise."

Athos sighed. "You're suggesting this tree is self-aware. Prove it."

Venk nodded. "Very well. Have you noticed the Dual Tree has fallen quiet since you got down?"

"Coincidental."

Venk squinted up at the dangling frayed ends of the strings.

"How many strings did you see before?"

"Seven."

"Now there are four."

"What?!"

"The tree must have pulled the object farther in to get it away from you."

"Impossible."

"If you don't believe me, trust your own eyes. Look!"

Athos looked up at the dangling strings and cursed silently. Venk was right. Had the tree really pulled the object farther up itself? Was it really reacting to them?

Thinking along the same lines, Venk nodded toward Athos' axe. "Pretend you're going to hack into the tree. Let's see what it does."

"Gladly."

Athos pulled his axe back from his belt, strode over to the nearest wall, and made a few practice swings.

It felt as though the strongest hurricane imaginable just attacked the tree. The Dual Tree was shaking itself, as if an irksome insect had landed and it wished to rid itself of the pest. Mollified, Athos lowered his axe. Within moments, the tree had quieted down.

"Satisfied?" Venk whispered. "Dual Tree is already on shaky ground, as far as I can tell. We don't need it to jar itself loose from the mountain and end up destroying itself—and us. Keep your axe sheathed."

Ashen, Athos nodded. He slipped his axe back into its sheath and buckled it closed.

"I think you should apologize to the tree," Venk told him while managing to keep the smile from appearing on his face.

"Apologize? To a tree? That's not going to happen."

They both heard the rustling of leaves high up in the tree branches. Was it a coincidence?

"Fine. Tree, I'm sorry."

The rustlings continued.

"Now say it like you mean it," Venk told him.

Athos shot his brother a dirty look and tried again.

"Tree, I'm *very* sorry. Can we let this go now?"

The rustlings stopped.

"Now aren't you glad you listened to me?" Venk asked, unable to hide the huge grin on his face.

Athos ignored him.

Venk paused. An idea had occurred.

"Tree, there's something up your trunk, and it —"

Athos snickered.

"There's something embedded in your trunk," Venk hastily amended. "I don't think it's supposed to be there. If you'll permit me, I'll remove it and then we can be on our merry way and leave you in peace. What say you?"

Dual Tree gently swayed back and forth. Venk eyed his brother. Was the tree considering? It stopped rocking and fell silent.

"What happened?" Athos demanded. "Will it give us the handle?"

Venk looked up at the strings. He still counted only four. Apparently, the tree wasn't ready to part with its treasure.

"What about wyverian immunity?" Venk suggested. "We'll see if we can get the dragons to consider this mountain off limits to any type of wyverian activity. How's that?"

"You cannot guarantee that," Rhamalli informed them from outside. "You cannot speak for Rinbok Intherer."

"I know!" Venk hissed at the hole leading outside. "But I'm sure you could persuade him."

"Unlikely," Rhamalli muttered.

The tree continued to remain motionless and quiet.

"Ah! I have it! Athos here will personally plant a dozen saplings in our valley in your honor. He'll personally water them every day until they've grown strong."

Shocked, Athos smacked his brother on the arm. "What are you doing? I don't want to plant and water any trees. If you want trees to be planted, why don't you agree to do it?"

The telltale creak of wood assailed their ears. The tree was swaying again, only this time it was barely perceptible. Did it find the agreement acceptable?

"Give us that thing you've probably been holding onto for a very long time and Athos will uphold his end of the agreement. Do we have an accord?"

"No, we sure as hell don't!" Athos hissed with frustration. "Me? Planting trees? It'll be a cold day in…"

Venk elbowed his ranting brother in the gut. "Agree to the damn accord, you fool!"

Athos glared at the tree and was silent.

Venk elbowed him again. "Agree to it!"

"You'd better be willing to help me plant these trees. If I have to suffer through this, so should you."

"Fine, I will. Lukas, too. Now agree to the accord!"

"Harrumph. Very well. Tree, if you give us whatever it is you're holding there, I will agree to plant a dozen trees in Raehón valley. I'll also make sure the saplings receive all the water they need to reach maturity."

Athos turned to his brother and held up his hands, as if to say *satisfied*?

Apparently, Dual Tree was. They both heard a series of tremendous creaks and snapping wood as the tree shifted its position. Slowly, ever so slowly, the two trunks parted, revealing more of the strings. As the trunks slowly peeled away from each other, it was revealed that the strings were actually the fraying ends of what was once a burlap sack. Whatever it was concealing started to become visible as the trunks slowly inched apart. After about five minutes of painstakingly slow progress on the tree's part, a foot and a half long bundle, wrapped in a decaying sack, fell into Athos' hands.

Dual Tree's creaking and rustling abruptly stopped. After a few moments of silence, the trunks began to press themselves back together as they slowly reversed the separation.

Athos wordlessly unwrapped the burlap coverings, allowing the torn pieces to fall to the ground. After the last piece of cloth had fallen away, the two brothers stared at the object before them. Twenty inches long and covered with carvings, runes, and unknown symbols, the dark oak handle gleamed as though it had been polished the day before.

Athos looked down at the carved piece of wood and nodded.

"Think that's what we're looking for?"

"Without a doubt," Venk agreed.

"Want to get off this infernal mountain?"

"Like you wouldn't believe."

Chapter 10 — Armin' the Hammer!

I can't believe it. I just can't believe it! Look! We've recovered all the pieces! Hammer head, counter weight, handle, and spiral gem. Do you have any idea what historical significance these four objects hold? Hmm? Do you?"

"No clue," Athos mumbled. "And I suppose you're going to tell us?"

"Never since the time of the dragon riders has one of the famed Narian tools ever been recovered. If it proves to be authentic, think what benefits we'll learn from the metallurgical analysis!"

"If it proves to be authentic?" Breslin repeated. "Don't make me recant my earlier praise. You know just as well as I do that all four pieces are authentic. The only thing left to do now is to assemble the hammer. It should be simple."

"Who gets the honor?" Athos asked, hopeful that he might be selected to piece together the tool created so many centuries ago.

"I'd say the honor should go to Master Venk," Breslin answered. "We're all here because of his son."

Nodding appreciatively, Venk took the carved handle and examined the ends, searching for some indication of which way was up. Shrugging, he picked up the misshapen head and threaded the handle through hole to the right of the striking head. What was to prevent the head from sliding down the handle?

Venk picked up the spiraled gem and noted that the natural shape of the ruby whorl suggested it had to be inserted into the hammer. Maybe it could be forced in? However, there was nowhere to insert the gem.

The brainstorming session lasted another thirty minutes before the dwarves finally noticed it was getting late in the day and a suitable place to camp needed to be found.

"I want to be as far away from the Kla Rehn as possible," Breslin informed his companions. "They steered us away from the tree on purpose. I don't know who conspires against us, and until I do, I won't trust any of them."

"Is it any wonder why I didn't stay?" Tristofer muttered sarcastically under his breath.

Athos snorted with laughter and slapped the scholar on the back. Surprised by the sudden show of camaraderie, Tristofer chuckled as he scooped up the pieces of the hammer and safely stowed them in his pack.

An hour later, they were back on the ground, searching fruitlessly for a suitable campsite. Athos volunteered to scout the surrounding countryside. Thankfully, it was perfect. There was plenty of game in the forest and plenty of trees for stringing their hammocks, but they were startled to discover they couldn't find a single spring of fresh water with which to quench their thirst.

"How does this ruddy forest stay so blasted green without a river or a stream to sustain it?" Breslin grumbled loudly.

He, like the others, was tired of wandering aimlessly through the trees over uneven ground and was about ready to swallow his pride to call Rhamalli when Venk let out an exclamation of surprise.

Snatching his axe off his back, Breslin whirled around to see Athos similarly armed and glaring at his brother.

"What is it?" Breslin asked. He glanced all around before he faced his companion.

"I almost forgot. We don't need to look for water. We have Shardwyn's final spell, the one with the drop of water on it. I believe Shardwyn said it'd summon water."

Athos crossed his arms over his chest.

"How much water?"

Venk shrugged. "I don't know."

"Pah. I'd rather keep searching for water myself than rely on that imbecilic human and his spells."

Venk reached into his pack and pulled out the white silk bag. He fished out the remaining sphere with the drop of water etched onto its surface and eyed his companions.

"What could it hurt? Besides, we've got it, haven't we? Might as well use it."

Breslin yawned and stretched his back. He dropped his pack to the ground and inclined his head at Venk.

"Very well. We make camp here. Once we've settled, then we'll see what Shardwyn has in store for us."

"Shouldn't we try the spell before we make camp?" Athos asked. "What if the spell doesn't work and we still don't have any water?"

"Then we'll make do until tomorrow."

Grateful for the reprieve in walking, Tristofer allowed his heavy pack to slide off his shoulder and fall to the ground.

Within the hour hammocks had been strung, a fire started, and several fallen logs pulled in to serve as benches. Empty water bags were produced and held uncertainly as they each nervously eyed Venk. Gritting his teeth, Venk looked at the white sphere in his hand and thought back to the fire spell they were given. That spell had only produced a tiny flame, enough to light a candle. Surely this spell would summon enough water to satisfy five dwarves.

"Here we go. Brace yourselves."

Venk silently invoked the spell. It disappeared in a bright burst of light and was gone.

Athos angled his water bag back so that he could look

down its neck and see for himself how much water it contained. He scowled. It was the same as before. Shardwyn's spell hadn't worked.

Athos sighed loudly. "That fool has duped us again."

It was as if the skies had split open. It wasn't rain that assaulted them. Rainfall was comprised of drops of water that fell in various quantities. This was thousands of gallons of water falling out of the sky. Their campfire disappeared in the blink of an eye. Their firepit became a pool. Everyone was drenched in a split second's time. Branches were snapped off trees. Shrubs were ripped out of the ground. To add further insult to their injury, their hammocks were ripped off the trees, some still tied to their branches.

It all happened so fast that the dwarves didn't have a chance to duck for cover. Several seconds later it was over. The remnants of the flood followed the gently sloping land and had completely drained away by the time Breslin, Athos, Tristofer, and even Lukas turned to stare at Venk.

"I really hate that wizard."

Breslin looked down at the water bag still clutched tightly against his sopping chest. He wrung out his beard.

"Well, it worked. My bag is full."

Venk awoke early the following morning. Early for a dwarf, that is. The sun had risen high enough to permeate the dense foliage in the forest, scattering sunbeams all across the camp. One, unfortunately, hit Venk square in the eye.

Venk grumbled and rolled to his side, pulling down his helmet even further. Another beam blinded him. Blinking away the spots dancing before his vision, Venk saw that an errant beam of light had hit his brother's axe and bounced it his direction. Naturally the beam hit him right in the eyes again.

Softly cursing to himself, Venk swung his legs over his hammock and pulled his boots on. Grabbing a dried strip of meat, he wandered over to the bag that held the pieces of the hammer. He quietly pulled them out and assembled the Narian tool once more.

As before, the pieces fit together nicely, but it was still unclear how the gem fit into the puzzle.

"Perhaps young Lukas should give it a try," a voice softly suggested.

Venk looked up and saw that he wasn't the only one starting the day early. He bowed.

"Master Breslin. You're up early."

"As are you, Master Venk."

"Couldn't sleep. The damn sun thought it funny to see how many different ways it could get into my eyes."

Breslin grunted. Venk looked over at the still form of Lukas, asleep in his hammock. He looked back at Breslin and raised an eyebrow.

"You think my son should put the hammer together?"

"He is the bearer of the Questor's Mark," Breslin reminded him. "Perhaps this task should be his."

Venk's gaze returned to his son, who was now stirring. Once the boy's tousled head appeared and searched him out, Venk waved him over.

"What is it, Father?"

Venk deliberately disassembled the hammer pieces, making sure each piece was not in contact with the others.

"Care to give it a try?"

Pleased to be given such an important task, Lukas nodded. He eagerly gripped the handle and lifted the head into position. As had happened with everyone else, the head slid unencumbered down the handle. It would have smashed into Lukas' hand had his father not caught the head before it made contact.

"Assemble it down on the ground," he told his son. "That way you don't have to worry about anything sliding or falling off."

Lukas added the counter weight then picked up the gem. He looked at his father and then back at the hammer.

"I don't know where this goes."

"That makes two of us, boy."

Catching sight of the intricate symbols and runes carved into the hammer's handle, Lukas removed the head and counterweight, giving them to his father. Noticing that he still had the spiral gem in his left hand, he handed that to Breslin.

"Maybe the handle tells us what we need to do," Lukas suggested. He peered closer at a carving of a rudimentary kyte.

Venk caught sight of Breslin, who had been staring at his hand ever since Lukas handed him the jewel.

"What's the matter?" Venk asked in a whisper, intent on not disturbing Lukas during his examination of the handle.

Breslin had a look of surprise on his face. He glanced upward to note the sun's position.

"What is it?" Venk repeated.

"This thing is warm," Breslin whispered back. "Feels like it has been in the sun all day, but sunrise was less than an hour ago. Have you ever noticed it being warm?"

Breslin passed the gem to Venk who closed his fingers around it. Venk waited a few moments before looking back at his friend.

"It's not warm. It's cold."

Breslin snatched it back. "No it's not. It's warm. You can't feel that?"

They repeated the experiment, and Venk turned to Lukas.

"Son, when you held the gem, did it feel warm to you?"

Without looking up, Lukas shook his head no.

Venk looked back at the gem, then down at the rest of the hammer pieces.

"New plan. Master Breslin, you put that thing together."

Lukas handed the handle over to Breslin, who shrugged. Setting the jewel down on the grass, Breslin picked up the head and counterweight and slid them on. He picked up the gem, and the moment he came into direct physical contact with both the head and the gem at the same time, the ruby whorl began to glow. Venk hastily squatted to retrieve the fallen handle. He handed it to Breslin who gripped the head and weight tightly then slid the handle back into position. With a firm grip of the jewel, he gently lowered the hammer to the ground.

Breslin rotated the hammer, looking at the side of the head and let out an exclamation of surprise. There was now a tiny divot marring the once blemish-free surface of the axe head. Curious, he touched the tip of the jewel to the indentation.

The whorl spun in place, screwing itself into the head of the hammer. Instantly, it became lightweight, almost as though it had lost its mass. He gazed with rapt fascination at the piece. They had done it!

He was holding an honest-to-goodness power hammer from Nar!

The hammer vibrated with power, electrifying his arm, sending jolts of energy into his chest. His heart rate accelerated and his breathing increased. This was the *only* hammer a smith would ever want. The desire to smash something overwhelmed him and he looked around the glade.

Breslin strode to the nearest boulder and delivered a swift blow. Lacking the momentum of a full swing, any normal hammer would have bounced harmlessly off the huge stone. The horse-sized boulder shattered into several thousand pieces of gravel. Breslin was grinning like an underling with a new toy.

"I need to get one of these!"

He eagerly scanned the vicinity, looking for more potential targets he could reduce to rubble.

Athos suddenly appeared, axe in hand. He glanced suspiciously at his brother before noticing Breslin.

"What's going on?"

Breslin held up the hammer and showed Athos the sparkling jewel attached to the head. Recognizing the tool for what it was, Athos' mouth fell open.

"What the … How did you do it? What … what holds it together?"

Breslin tapped the jewel. "Tristofer was right. The gem was the key."

"Did someone say my name?" Tristofer mumbled as he appeared next to Athos. "What about me?"

Athos pointed at the hammer. "Look what Breslin is holding."

Tristofer stared so long at the assembled hammer that Athos had to poke him in the ribs to see if he had fallen asleep. After a few minutes of awkward silence, the scholar finally approached Breslin and held out both hands.

"May I?"

Breslin nodded. Gripping the hammer by its head, he held out the handle and waited for Tristofer to take it. As soon as it passed to Tristofer, the jewel faded and the hammer became inert. Tristofer dropped it on the ground.

Venk, who hadn't seen the tool go inactive, looked at Tristofer as though he had just dropped it off a cliff.

"What are you doing? Pick that back up!"

Clasping both hands on the handle, Tristofer heaved the tool off the ground, but only managed a few feet before it slid through his fingers and thumped back onto the ground.

"It's so heavy! I never dreamed it'd be so difficult to wield!"

Confused, Breslin strode three steps toward the hammer and plucked it off the ground as though it weighed no more than a feather.

"It's not heavy," Breslin told Tristofer. "At least, it isn't for me."

Venk held out a hand. "Let me try it."

He also struggled to keep the hammer off the ground. He grunted with surprise.

"It's not just Tristofer," Venk reported. "I've lifted anvils that are lighter than this."

Lukas pointed at the hammer's head. "The gem! Father, the gem is no longer glowing!"

"Really? It was glowing just a few moments ago." Venk leaned to the left and saw for himself that the ruby was now dark. His arms were aching, his grip tiring. He decided to let the hammer slide through his fingers and fall to the ground. He turned to Tristofer.

"Why'd it go dark for me?"

"When's the last time you washed your hands?" Athos joked as he stepped forward to try his luck. "Was it lit when you first picked it up?"

Venk thought for a moment. "I don't think so. Once Breslin let go, it went dark."

After a few minutes of struggle Athos also let the priceless Narian keepsake fall to the ground. He looked over his shoulder at Breslin.

"I can't say that I care for it that much."

Breslin picked the hammer up and watched the gem start to glow once more. As before, it was incredibly lightweight in his hand. He could wield it for hours without feeling any fatigue. Then, he saw Athos looking at Lukas and knew what he was about to be asked.

"Give that to him, would you?" Athos inquired. "I'm curious to see if my nephew would be able to lift it."

Breslin placed the hammer on the grass, head first, and took a few steps back. At the encouragement from his father, Lukas approached the tool, grasped the handle, and lifted.

The hammer didn't budge.

"Why does it work for you and no one else?" Venk asked.

Breslin considered the question.

"When I was a boy, my father used to tell me that I had Narian blood running through my veins. I always thought that all fathers must tell their sons that as a way to get them to behave. 'Do not disgrace your Narian ancestors,' my father would tell me."

"How many times did you get into trouble when you were a lad?" Venk asked, curious. Try as he might, he just couldn't picture the always reserved Breslin as a child, let alone one that got into trouble.

"I was an ill-tempered brat in my youth," Breslin added with a grin. "I guess it was my own way to get my father to pay attention to me as he never seemed to have time for anything else but his beloved workshop."

Athos glanced at the hammer and then back at Breslin. "So you're part Narian, is that it? That's why that thing works for you?"

"If that is so," Venk argued, "then why didn't it work for Tristofer? Isn't he a descendant? I do recall someone mentioning that at some point."

Everyone looked at the scholar, who was otherwise preoccupied by checking his leather boots for scuff marks.

"That must explain why my father was insistent that I join this expedition," Breslin exclaimed. "It wasn't to speak for the Council but rather, in case the mission was successful."

Venk nodded thoughtfully. "That means your father knew about your heritage. Did he know we were looking for a hammer?"

"I don't think so," Breslin answered. "There would have been no way for him to know. I can only guess that all other Narian tools and weapons would behave the same way. The wielder must be Narian."

Athos frowned. "So the hammer was intended for Breslin all along? Why not just send the Questor's Mark to him instead of Lukas?"

Athos suddenly straightened and a look of enlightenment crossed his surly features.

"I'll wager I know what happened. The mark wasn't meant for Lukas."

"You don't know that for certain," Venk began.

"Let me finish. The mark wasn't meant for Lukas, nor was it meant for Breslin. I'd say it was meant for Maelnar."

Breslin nodded. "I see your point. I'm part Narian and therefore so is my father. Lukas received the mark in my father's workshop, and I'm willing to bet that of all the people attending his seminar that day, he alone was the one who could lay claim to the Narian line."

Tristofer finally pulled his gaze up off the ground and joined the conversation.

"Why would someone want to give the Questor's Mark to Maelnar? No offense to your father, Master Breslin, but he's too old to go on an adventure such as this."

Breslin shrugged. "I don't know why my father was singled out, other than someone clearly knew he was of Narian descent. Who would know that?"

Athos crossed his arms over his chest while Venk jammed his hands in his pockets. Tristofer clasped his hands behind his back and waited for someone else to proffer an answer. Venk looked up.

"Does it matter, now that you have it? Whether it's you or your father, the hammer pieces have been found and have been assembled. What's more, the hammer actually works! My question is, what do we do now?"

"You feel like we're missing something?" Breslin asked

him. "Again?"

Venk nodded. "Don't you? This feels rather anti-climactic if you ask me. Tristofer, why are you acting so smug? What do you know that we don't?"

Tristofer had started smiling just a few moments ago. He was eagerly looking at each member of their party, as if trying to mentally share a secret with his companions.

Breslin sat down on the nearest stump and set the hammer head first on the ground.

"Out with it. Are we missing something?"

Tristofer nodded, much like an underling would if asked if they'd like a sugary sweet.

"Well?"

"I should say so! Our quest isn't over!"

"What? Yes, it is. We have overcome all the obstacles and found the pieces of the hammer." Venk pointed. "There it sits. What more is there to do?"

"Find Nar."

Venk groaned, Athos snorted, and Breslin sighed. Only Lukas seemed eager to hear what the scholar had to say.

"How?" Breslin wanted to know.

"By using the hammer, of course."

The two brothers sank down upon the closest stump and started whispering to each other as they wagered on the outcome of this confrontation.

"Use the hammer?" Breslin shook his head. "We're no closer now to figuring out where Nar is than when we first set out. The Questor's Mark was a map, all right, only it led us to the hammer and not to Nar."

Tristofer smiled. "Are you sure about that?"

"About the mark leading us to the hammer?" Breslin looked down and inclined his head toward the tool. "Pretty sure. As for the mark somehow leading us to Nar? Look around. There are no lost cities around here."

Tristofer squatted next to Breslin so he could speak with him eye-to-eye.

"The Questor's Mark guided us to the hammer. What if the Questor's Mark also leads the way to Nar? We just have to figure it out."

"Look, Tristofer." Breslin sounded tired as he removed his helmet and wiped a sleeve along his brow. "I know you want to believe that somehow we're missing something, but there's no proof that anything is amiss on the Questor's Mark. No one will ever be able to doubt you anymore. You've helped recover a Narian tool! That, by itself, is a remarkable feat. That hammer will be able to unlock some of the greatest metallurgical mysteries that have ever existed. Don't be too hard on yourself. I think you've done great work here. We all do, don't we?"

Venk and Athos both nodded. Athos wordlessly tossed a small pouch to his brother, figuring Breslin would have degraded the scholar for even suggesting that they were missing something. A quest was a quest. They came, they searched, and they found. Mission accomplished, as far as he was concerned.

Looking around the group, Tristofer smiled enigmatically. "We're not done yet, my friends."

Growing angry, Breslin stood.

"You had better base this on solid, tangible evidence," he warned. "No more guessing."

Tristofer didn't appear unsettled at all. In fact, he couldn't be more pleased with Breslin's choice of words.

"Master Lukas, could you come here a moment? Can you show us the Questor's Mark again?"

Lukas' smile vanished as soon as the scholar's intentions became clear. He had hoped that once the handle was found he wouldn't have to worry about exposing his back ever again.

Careful to face away from his father, Lukas rolled his eyes. He hitched his jerkin up to his chin and waited for the adults to finish commenting.

"You're only proving my point," Breslin was saying as he looked upon the Questor's Mark. "There are no more hidden areas. All sections have been revealed. There's nothing left to do."

"On the contrary," Tristofer began, still wearing his smug smile, "you couldn't be more wrong."

"Where's your proof?" Athos demanded.

Tristofer pointed at the Questor's Mark.

"Right there."

"You're looking at the same thing we're looking at," Venk pointed out. He was rapidly losing patience with the scholar, too. "Just get to the point, please."

Breslin's eyes widened. "Wizards be damned. Tristofer, you're right!"

"The Questor's Mark is still there. It was supposed to disappear once the quest was over. Remember?"

Athos slowly nodded. "Aye, I do remember that now. The mark is still there. Which means…"

"That we're missing something," Breslin and Venk said together.

Athos looked at the scholar and finally smiled. "You're enjoying this, aren't you?"

"Like you wouldn't believe," Tristofer assured him.

"So what *are* we missing?" Breslin asked. He hooked a thumb in Lukas' direction. "What does *that* tell you we need to do next?"

"Find Nar."

"You still think my son's back will lead us to Nar?" Venk asked incredulously. "There's nothing left to reveal. You're looking at the entire mark!"

Mumbling softly to himself, Tristofer squatted down next to Lukas and studied the mark. For nearly five minutes the scholar mumbled incoherently as his eyes skimmed over the Questor's Mark.

"Talk it out," Breslin encouraged, giving Tristofer a friendly pat on his shoulder. "If ever there was a person who could figure this out, it'd be you."

Tristofer's cheeks flushed.

"Let's review the facts," he quietly said to himself, but loud enough for everyone to hear. "The mark turned out to be a map and it led us to the power hammer, which is consequently working. The mark was probably intended for someone else, presumably Master Maelnar as it happened in his workshop. However, for unknown reasons, the mark was bestowed upon an underling.

"We have since learned that in order to operate the hammer, the one who wields it must have Narian ancestry or else the hammer remains inert and practically unusable. Master Maelnar knew this and therefore insisted his son, who is also of Narian descent, join the group. I believe someone purposely wanted to give Maelnar, or in this case, Breslin that hammer. That begs the question—who? Who would do that? *Why* would they do that?"

Breslin joined Venk and Athos on the log bench and watched with rapt fascination as Tristofer continued to recap all that they had learned thus far.

"One theory would be that there's someone out there who knows where Nar is and is trying to lead us there. However, if that were the case, why send us all over Lentari on a scavenger hunt looking for pieces of a power hammer? That theory generates more questions than it answers. That couldn't be right. Forget it."

Tristofer started to pace as his brain cells warmed up. Lukas dropped his shirt back down and joined his father on the bench. All four watched the scholar pace back and forth.

"I'm forgetting what Shardwyn said. The spell necessary to create the Questor's Mark is a very complex one, which suggests that whoever created it had plenty of time to do it. Taking that into consideration, what if that person knows the location of Nar and knows that the only way the city will be found is if the searcher also wields a power hammer?"

"Wouldn't that suggest that whoever created the Questor's Mark is being held prisoner?" Breslin gently asked.

Tristofer's head snapped toward Breslin. "Prisoner? Who said anything about a prisoner?"

"It's just a suggestion."

Venk rose to his feet. He pulled his son up with him and made a circular motion with a finger, indicating Lukas needed to turn around. The boy sighed again and pulled his shirt up.

"Let's assume you're right," Venk began, "and say this is not only a guide to help us find the hammer but also to Nar itself. How do we find it? Is there something we need to do in order to reveal the next step?"

Tristofer shook his head. "I don't think so. Let's look at this logically. If we are to believe that we've been following a map, picking up pieces to a hammer along the way, then I would say that the very last location to be revealed should be where we start our search."

Venk groaned. "You mean…"

Tristofer turned to look up at Dual Tree, visible as nothing more than a speck from this distance.

"Right. I think there might be more in that hollow between the trunks."

"It figures," Venk muttered darkly.

"So who goes?" Athos asked, still craning his neck to look up at the distant tree.

"As much as I don't want to," Breslin stated, leaning down to pick up the hammer, "none of you can wield this thing but me. That forces me to go. I'm hoping I can get a volunteer to accompany me."

Venk and Athos eyed each other. Neither wanted to go, but neither would refuse if asked. Athos caught sight of Lukas and sighed again. Slowly, he raised a hand.

Rhamalli deposited the two dwarves again on the narrow ledge. The huge red dragon took up his post, hanging from the nearby ridge, and kept an eye on the dwarves.

As soon as Athos' feet touched back down on the tiny ledge he lunged forward to wrap his arms around the closest branch. Breslin followed suit moments later. Athos grunted and shook his head.

"The last time I was up here I vowed I would never be this far off the ground again."

"And here you are," Breslin commented as he carefully tilted his head from side to side to take in his surroundings. "So how do we do this? Care to lead the way?"

Athos nodded and began picking his way down the tree trunk until he came to the opening at the base of Dual Tree. Casting a furtive glance behind him to make sure Breslin followed, he wiggled through the tight hole and helped pull Breslin in.

Climbing slowly to his feet, Breslin looked around at the inside of the hollow. Athos pointed up at the junction where the two trunks came together.

"That's where we found the handle."

Breslin nodded. He pulled an axe from his belt and moved toward one of the many branches running through the cave.

"Maybe there's something hiding behind one of these roots."

Breslin readied a swing when Athos caught his arm and held it firm.

The tree began swaying.

"Trust me, you don't want to do that."

"Don't mind him," Athos called out in a loud voice. "He didn't know. We won't bother you. We're just looking for clues. It's been suggested that we're missing something in here. I promise, no axes will be used."

Breslin gave Athos a speculative stare. "You talk to trees?"

The tree stopped swaying.

Athos gave Breslin a smug smile. "Only when it works. Now put that axe away."

One of the roots twitched.

After crawling about on their hands and knees for the better part of an hour, Athos finally sat back on his haunches and looked at his companion.

"There's nothing here. Tristofer may very well believe we are missing something, and he's probably right, but I don't think it's in here. Maybe we should check back at the waterfall?"

Breslin painfully rose to his feet and leaned against the closest wall.

"I'd have to agree. Roots and rock are the only things in here."

They both heard the creaking and groaning of twisting wood. Athos nudged Breslin in the ribs and pointed at one of the smaller roots. It was lurching back and forth as though the tree attempted to pull the root out of the rocky soil. Now free of its stony confines, the root swiped across the floor in a back-and-forth motion. Several times it collided with the far cavern wall, knocking a few small pieces of stone loose in the process.

"What's it doing?" Breslin anxiously asked Athos. "Did it do this to you last time?"

"It moved before, but not this much. This can't be good. I think we need to get going. We'll have to search the—"

The tree lurched violently, knocking the dwarves off their feet. One of the larger roots lifted up and extricated itself from the mountainside. Acting as a feeler, the root began questing about the room. The thick green tentacle bumped into Breslin and hesitated. The root retreated a few feet before it coiled back and snapped forward, thumping Breslin squarely in the chest, knocking him backward a few feet.

The root snaked out again as it searched about the hollow for the intruders. Breslin and Athos cautiously backed away from the tree's root.

"Rhamalli, we're getting ready to come out," Breslin shouted toward the tiny entrance. "Although I have no intention of leaping outside, would you please be ready to catch us in case we fall?"

The ground trembled as the dragon inched closer to the tree. "Is everything alright in there?"

"For the time being. That could change at any moment, though."

"Understood. I am ready."

A third root, larger and thicker than the rest, silently extricated itself from the ground and lunged forward. Once more, contact was made and Breslin found himself flying through the air. He impacted the far wall and slid down into a heap.

"Breslin! Hold on, I'll be right there!" Athos angrily looked up and scowled at the tree. "We didn't do anything to you! Stop this nonsense immediately!"

Surprisingly, the tree complied. The roots settled down onto the floor and became quiescent. Athos hurried over to Breslin and helped him to his feet.

"Are you alright? I think it's time to go while the tree is preoccupied. What are you waiting for? What are you doing?"

Breslin turned and placed a hand up against the wall. Leaning left and right, Breslin turned back to Athos, smiling profusely.

"What?" Athos snapped. "What are you smiling at me for? Did you hit your head? Maybe you should stay sitting down for a while."

Athos reached for his friend but Breslin batted away his hand.

"Come, come, look here. What do you see?"

Athos peered at the impassable wall before them and shrugged. "Stone. Lots of it."

"Stay right there but angle your head about twenty degrees west. Now tell me what you see."

Athos did as he was told and shrugged again.

"More rock. What are you going on about? There's nothing but…"

Breslin suddenly thrust his hand forward, appearing as though he was giving the mountain a violent shove. His hand, inexplicably, seemed to sink into the rocky wall.

Athos stared, open-mouthed.

Breslin beamed. "We have ourselves an entrance. A dwarven entrance!"

Chapter 11 – Lost City No More

How did you know that was there? I didn't see anything. I still don't." Athos leaned toward the mountain then farther away, to the left and the right.

"This one is harder to see, that I'll give you," Breslin admitted. "You'd have to be very familiar with igneous rock, which I am."

Breslin tapped an unremarkable spot on the wall and gestured for Athos to join him.

"Do you see this? The wall is granite, which I presume is what this entire mountain is made of. Here, though, it changes to basalt. Basalt is formed after magma cools, once it makes it topside. Granite forms as magma cools underground."

"So…"

"So this section of basalt," Breslin patiently explained, "has been blended with this granite to make it look seamless. Only a dwarf could pull that off as skillfully as this."

Holding his hands out in front of him, Athos gently felt around the mountain's wall until he recognized the cleverly disguised entrance. No wonder no one had ever found Nar, Athos thought with growing excitement. Not only was Dual Tree blocking access from outside intruders, only the most gifted geologist would discover the disguised entrance.

"What now?" Athos asked. "Should we bring the others up here?"

"Absolutely. Notify Rhamalli."

"I'm already on my way to retrieve them," Rhamalli's voice told them.

"Can we not have a private conversation?" Breslin demanded, addressing the empty air besides Athos.

They both heard Rhamalli's deep chuckle.

Moments later they were pulling Lukas, Venk, and Tristofer through the small entrance under the tree. Once their party was together again, Tristofer turned excitedly to Breslin.

"You found something! What is it? Tell me!"

"We *may* have found something," Breslin informed him. "We found a hidden entrance leading inside the mountain."

Tristofer let out a loud whoop and rushed forward to embrace Breslin.

"It's Nar! I just know it!"

"Unhand me. Don't get ahead of yourself, Tristofer. We must investigate. We'll need torches. See if you can find anything we can use."

Athos's hand shot up. "May I suggest another course of action?"

Dual Tree began swaying once more and several of its larger roots began pulling themselves out of the ground.

Remembering that the tree was sentient, although how a tree could develop the ability to listen and respond to regular speech eluded him, Breslin held up both hands.

"My apologies. We'll find something else. No burning wood, I assure you."

The tree settled down.

"Athos, go inside there and see if there might be a torch nearby. They frequently are."

Athos nodded. Losing sight of the opening yet again, he felt along the surface of the wall until he was sure he could duck through the small hidden door without smashing his head against solid granite. Athos slipped inside the mountain and disappeared. The group waited with bated breath. How long would it take?

Athos reappeared almost instantly, holding a footlong torch, replete with dust and cobwebs.

"There's one more torch on the other side of the door, but I figured one should do for now."

"What else did you see?" Tristofer eagerly asked.

Athos held up the unlit torch.

"Nothing. Couldn't see anything."

"Right. Sorry."

"Who's got a tinder kit?" Breslin asked.

"I do," Venk answered. "But it's back at the camp. Didn't think I'd need it."

Everyone turned to Tristofer, who began patting down his pockets once more. With an exclamation of triumph, the scholar pulled a small leather-wrapped bundle from within his jacket and held it up.

"I knew I had a tinder kit on me somewhere. Let's get a —"

Athos slapped a hand over Tristofer's mouth.

"Don't even *think* about saying that word. Call it, I don't know, call it 'supper'. Let's make supper once we're all through the doorway, alright?"

Tristofer nodded.

"Can you make, er, supper in the dark?" Breslin asked.

Tristofer shook his head affirmatively. "I believe so."

Breslin took his arm and shoved him through the hidden opening. "Excellent. Let's go. Rhamalli, I trust you can hear me, we're all going inside now."

"I'll be in the area," the dragon assured them.

They felt the ground shudder as the huge dragon released his grip from the mountain and pushed off.

Once the two torches were lit, the dwarves took stock of their situation. The tunnel they were standing in was not that large, maybe five feet tall with enough room for two dwarves to walk side by side. With Breslin in the lead, followed by Venk and Lukas, then Tristofer, and finally Athos, they made their way down the dusty tunnel, heading away from the entrance and the outside world.

"This is so exciting!" Tristofer exclaimed, pulling the torch from wall to wall, and down to the floor. "It would appear that no one has used this tunnel in centuries! Maybe the last people who used it were the Narians themselves!"

"We should properly excavate this whole area," Tristofer said happily. "Who knows what treasure might lie beneath the ground?"

Athos stomped his foot on the ground. A dull, muffled thud met their ears.

"It's solid stone. You won't find anything buried down there."

"A very good point, Master Athos. Come! Hurry! Let's see what else there is to offer!"

Breslin held up an arm and signaled the group to halt, pointing at a metal object on the left tunnel wall. He gently reached up and brushed away caked dirt, dust, and cobwebs. A closer examination revealed an oval plaque covered in runes and symbols. And there was the tiny upside-down hammer on the lower left of the plaque.

"What's it say?" Breslin asked, pulling Tristofer to the front of the line. He held up his torch so that the scholar could properly see the symbols on the elliptical metal surface.

Tristofer pushed his spectacles farther up the bridge of his nose.

"Well, let's see. I can't read the runes, but there's an axe, and it's leaning up against that kyte."

"Looks like the axe is sticking out of the kyte," Athos chuckled.

"Nonsense. A weapon next to an animal could mean, well, it might mean… Er… I'm sorry, I really have no idea."

"Our Narian scholar really isn't proving too useful in Nar, is he?" Breslin joked.

In the dark confines of the tunnel, Tristofer blushed.

"Let me try again. It says, 'This way to Nar'!"

Lukas looked up at him. "Really?"

"Perhaps. Sure, why not? Let's assume it does!"

They made it another hundred feet when they discovered

why the tunnel had so little use. It was sealed. A heavy stone door blocked the way. Athos took one look at the door and then looked back at Breslin.

"I'd say it's time to use that hammer, eh?"

Breslin looked down at the power hammer on his belt and grinned. This day couldn't get any better. He was going to be able to smash something with his new toy! How fun!

Pulling the hammer from his belt and relishing the electrified feelings traveling up his arm, he approached the door and readied his swing. But he caught sight of a familiar item embedded into the stone: a glittering red jewel. He squatted down and traced the outline of the gem with his finger, clearing away a coating of dust.

"There's a gem here," he called back to the others. "Looks just like the one on the hammer."

"What happens if you touch it?" Tristofer wanted to know.

"Nothing. I'm touching it now."

"Hold your hammer next to it," Tristofer suggested.

Breslin brought the hammer around and held the tool in front of the gem. A swirl of red light appeared deep within the jewel, perhaps a reflection of the hammer's gem.

The door creaked noisily and swung inward. Athos stared incredulously at the scholar.

"How'd you know to do that?"

"I didn't," Tristofer confessed. "I was just curious to see what would happen."

Pushing the stone door forward enough so that they could all squeeze through, Breslin again took the lead and led them farther into the mountain. Several times the tunnel they were following deposited them into another larger tunnel. Following the tunnels as they all sloped downward, they came across another sealed checkpoint. Breslin waved the power hammer in front of the gem, once he cleaned it off with the back of his hand, and the door creaked open.

As they passed through the second checkpoint, Athos turned to look back at the door that was still ajar.

"Should we be closing these things? I have no desire to give away our presence if there is someone hiding in here."

Breslin paused.

"Good point. Is there a gem on this side so that we won't be trapped inside?"

Athos searched the door and found the dusty red jewel. He cleaned it off.

"It's here."

"Excellent. In that case, seal the door back up, please."

Athos leaned his shoulder against the door and pushed it closed.

"There. No one will ever know we were here."

"Sure, they will," Lukas countered. "They can see our footprints."

Feeling a little foolish, the four adults looked down at the ground. Their footprints showed clearly in the heavy dust.

Breslin laughed out loud. "Ah. Well, that's that. Since it looks like no one else has been this way, I'm hoping it'll stay that way until we leave."

Sounds of their footsteps echoed loudly as the five of them exited the previous tunnel and emerged into an even larger one. Breslin silently looked around.

"Which way? I can't tell which way leads down."

"Which way is east?" Venk asked.

Lukas walked over to his father.

"Do you have the spell bag that Shardwyn gave you? It's silk, isn't it? I need that, a sliver of metal, and a small bowl with some water."

Tristofer began pulling things from his pockets. "Let's see. Miniature tools? No, we don't need that. Spectacle cleaner, emergency herb garden … ah! Here's a needle, Master Lukas, and a bowl."

"Father, can you take the needle and rub it along the silk for me?"

Venk grunted and took the needle. He pretended he was polishing the needle as he rubbed the tiny bit of metal against the silk.

Lukas selected a leaf from the pile of items pulled from Tristofer's pockets. He poured water from his father's bag into the bowl until it was about an inch deep. He gently set the leaf into the bowl. Then he pulled a string from the silk bag, threaded it through the needle, and gently placed the needle on the leaf. Lukas watched as the leaf slowly rotated until the needle was pointing back the way they had come.

"Left," Lukas promptly told them. "East is to the left."

"Well done," Venk said with a smile. Now he remembered the two and a half weeks he and his wife, Elva, had experienced when both of their children had been whisked away to learn how to survive on their own. For over two weeks their household was blissfully quiet.

"Left it is," Breslin said, leading the way.

As soon as they entered the larger tunnel, everyone noticed that the sounds of their footfalls changed pitch. Out in front, Breslin glanced down, sweeping the torch low to reveal large, flat flagstones, which deftly lined the tunnel floor, extending all the way to the curve of the tunnel walls.

The tunnel hadn't been used for centuries, and every thirty feet or so they'd find pavers jutting up off the floor, as if an unknown force had pushed them from below. Venk steered Lukas well away from the unwelcome tripping hazards.

Half an hour later the party came to a halt at a new obstacle. Another door, only this one was the size of a castle drawbridge. The massive arched door was made of stone and intricately carved with various scenes. Also woven around the perimeter of the door was a thin, delicate gold border that was no more than an inch wide. A closer examination revealed it to be interlocking gold rings. The intricate golden chain ran along the bottom of the door, up both sides, across the arch, and then ran down the front of the door to create four large interlocking circles.

Tristofer pulled out a stiff-bristled brush and began jumping in place and sweeping the brush in wide arcs, determined to clean as much of the door as possible. Leaving the scholar to hop about, Breslin and the others studied the sealed door before them.

"It's a security door," Breslin thoughtfully mused. "It has to be. Look at the size of that thing!"

Venk touched his shoulder and pointed at the direct center of the four interlocking circles. A dusty gem winked back at them.

"There's your way inside. It's another gem!"

Overhearing the news about the existence of the jewel, Tristofer abandoned his attempts to clean the door. Leaning up on his tiptoes to better reach the large ruby set in the stone, he pulled out a rag from somewhere within his jacket and polished the jewel until it sparkled. He looked up at Breslin.

"Would you do the honors?"

Breslin nodded. He presented his hammer to the door. For several tense seconds nothing happened.

"I don't think this door likes you," Athos commented with a chuckle.

Breslin lowered the hammer uncertainly. Now what were they supposed to do? Bash their way in? He hefted the hammer and readied a swing. Tristofer grabbed his arm.

"Wait! Put the hammer back. The gem started to glow just before you lowered the hammer. Give it a little more time."

Breslin presented the hammer to the door a second time, holding it directly in front of the door's jewel. Ten seconds later, the gem began to glow. Two minutes later the gem was still glowing, but the door remained closed.

"What do I do now?" Breslin asked, looking at Tristofer as he did so. "Keep waiting?"

Tristofer nodded. "Let's give it a few minutes. This could be some form of Narian security, or perhaps it could be that centuries of disuse have rusted the mechanics of the door and it's unable to open? Either way, we should wait a little longer."

Breslin shrugged and held his position.

Nearly ten minutes later they heard several loud metallic clicks, followed by a horrible grating sound as one piece of metal scraped over another. The giant door inched forward. The dwarves waited with bated breaths. Was that as far as it would open? Breslin leaned into the door and shoved.

The door didn't move, although it did rock forward a millimeter or two before settling back. Breslin nodded. It was up to them to push the door open far enough to gain entry. With the collective effort of all five in the group, the enormous door was shoved forward a few feet. Not enough for a human to squeeze through, but more than adequate for a dwarf.

"Is this the main gate?" Venk asked Tristofer as he pulled himself through. His gut had almost denied him entry into the city. He silently vowed to exercise more and eat less once he and Lukas were safely home.

"I believe so," Tristofer answered. "The size of the door alone suggests that this has to be it."

"Think it's been opened since their departure?" Venk wondered.

The scholar shook his head no.

"Look how long it took for us to get in. Did you hear that awful racket the door made when it opened? No, that's the sound of a mechanical apparatus that needs to be serviced. Quite frankly I'm surprised it opened enough for all of us to pass."

"It didn't," Athos reminded him. "We had to force it open, remember?"

Tristofer had already disregarded Athos' remark as he stared in awe at the abandoned city.

As the children's book had depicted, the city was situated in a huge, domed cavern. Large stalactites had once been removed from the roof of the space, but over time, had started to reclaim the cavern's domed ceiling. Soft golden light illuminated street after street of vacant, deteriorating buildings. Streets of flagstone, just like the main tunnel entering the city, ran everywhere, but unfortunately, the conditions were far worse.

Pavers had been pried loose and cast aside. Several streets had buckled, suggesting some type of seismic event had befallen them. Wherever they looked they could see damaged buildings, from huge gathering places to the smallest of residences.

"Something bad has happened here," Breslin remarked, looking around. His voice had dropped to a whisper. "If I were to venture a guess, I'd say a massive terra tremor is to blame for their downfall."

"Agreed," Tristofer whispered.

Venk nudged Tristofer in his ribs. Once the scholar turned around, Venk pointed at the farthest buildings.

"What's the source of the yellow light? It's not very

bright, but enough to see where we're going."

"Do you remember that decorative golden border on the main door?" Tristofer asked him. "I think that's their light source. It's probably part of their technology. Look around! That gold chain is everywhere. That's how we can see the buildings; they are all laced with that border. Quite ingenious, if you ask me."

"Is it me or is it getting brighter in here?" Athos asked, looking up at the ceiling then back at the city. He had only been able to make out a few of the streets when they first beheld the city, but now he was easily able to see three or four dozen streets with several dozen buildings per street. Had it always been like that?

"It's your imagination," his brother told him as he steered Lukas around another broken paver.

"No, he's right," Breslin announced. "Look. I can see the extent of the damage Nar has undergone. Looks like the eastern part of the city was hit hardest. Tristofer, any idea what's going on with the light?"

Tristofer shook his head and shrugged.

Lukas tugged on his father's sleeve and pointed at the ground. "Father, look! More footprints!"

Venk, Athos, and Breslin all squatted down to inspect the damaged street. Several sets of tracks were visible in the heavy dust, heading in every direction, approaching every structure. The closest was a large two-story building, which had housed two different tenants. None of the footsteps entered either shop.

Breslin walked up to the larger shop's open door and leaned in. He waved his torch around the room.

"I see at least three circular ovens. Broken crockery is everywhere." Breslin bent to retrieve a palm-sized piece of pottery. "This has a gold pattern running through it, too. What it's trying to depict, I cannot say. Any ideas what this shop might have been used for?"

"A bakery?" Venk suggested as he looked into the adjoining second shop. This one was much smaller than its neighbor, having a simple corner work table and a few shelves.

Venk knelt on the hard stone floor and picked up a tiny

chisel. A closer examination revealed a hammer, a second chisel, a pair of tweezers, and something that had a hook on one end and a pick on the other.

Brushing aside some of the dust on the floor revealed a glint of color coming from under the primary workspace. It was a tiny curl of gold, generating the tiniest bit of light. With his back protesting loudly, Venk straightened and inspected the tiny shaving. Where had it come from? How long had it been on the floor? Why was it … the curl stopped glowing. Venk's eyes narrowed. Why had the gold shaving gone dark?

Ignoring the stab of pain his back was sending him, Venk knelt back on the ground and held the curl down low. It began to glow again. Eagerly brushing aside several inches of dirt and dust revealed a number of other pieces of gold, all discarded as though they were wood shavings. All the gold pieces glowed until Venk straightened up.

Athos poked his head in the room. "What do you have there?" He leaned over Venk's hand and eyed the gold shavings. "Not much there, if you ask me. Still, it's a good start."

"Forget the gold for a moment," Venk told his brother. "It'll glow if I hold it down to the floor. It stops once I move it away. Bizarre, huh?"

"It must be part of the gold border found on all the buildings."

Venk nodded in agreement. "Exactly what I was thinking."

He gave the shavings to Tristofer and explained what he had learned about its behavior. The scholar nodded in appreciation and dropped the gold shavings into a vial which promptly disappeared into his jacket.

"From the looks of this one," Venk told the others as he came out of the smaller shop, "I'd say that they vacated the premises very quickly. I found tools and several gold ingots sitting in a small room at the back of the building. I doubt they would have left the gold willingly."

"Correlates with the first," Breslin reported. "Broken pottery everywhere. There were a few intact pots sitting on shelves and even a large ceramic bin in the back which I presume held flour. Wait. You found gold? I wouldn't think they'd leave that behind."

Venk grunted. "Right. I just said that. Why would they leave the gold?"

Breslin shook his head. He pointed at the ground. "No, I mean, why would *these* people have left the gold? According to the tracks, they didn't even bother going in to this building. What were they searching for?"

"Let's find a building they did go into," Athos suggested. "Maybe then we'll figure out what they were doing."

Venk held up a hand.

"Wait a moment. Son, come here. Let me see the mark."

Lukas approached and lifted his shirt. The mark was still there.

"Our quest isn't done," Venk said.

"Over here!" Breslin called out from up front. He was pointing to a large, single story structure. "I found a building the footprints have entered."

Tristofer nodded. "Let me guess. You're going to find a forge in there."

Breslin ducked through the open door and then reappeared moments later. He nodded.

"Aye, there is. How'd you know that?"

"Isn't it obvious?" the scholar asked. "It's a blacksmith shop. I'm willing to wager every blacksmith's shop here in Nar has been thoroughly searched."

Understanding, Breslin tapped his cuirass.

"Armor."

Tristofer nodded. "Exactly. Nar is known for armor. It's coveted by everyone and fetches a high price whenever a piece is put up for sale. The intruders, as I'll start calling them, obviously value armor more than gold. Why else would they leave those ingots behind?"

"They left them behind because they didn't know they were there," Athos argued. "I think if they had found them they would have taken them."

Tristofer shrugged. "Possibly. But the fact that they didn't even bother suggests they thought it wasn't worth their time and effort."

Unwilling to argue the point any further, Athos grunted

and returned to his examination of the neighboring buildings. Catching sight of a structure across the street that had a set of tracks leading into it, Athos nudged Breslin and pointed it out. A quick glance at the surrounding shops revealed one other structure visited by the intruders.

Splitting into two teams, as they had two torches between them, Athos and Breslin explored the second shop while Venk, Lukas, and Tristofer took the third. Both teams reported the same thing: a blacksmith had set up their foundry there. As with the first, the two blacksmith shops had been picked clean.

Breslin's eyes were drawn to the ground. Athos approached on his right while Venk approached on his left. They, too, noticed. Several fresh sets of tracks, as though they had been made just yesterday, led deeper into the city.

Breslin felt a shiver. They were clearly not alone. The dwarf party had left their own footprints everywhere and had made no small amount of noise in their approach. He turned to warn the group, but Tristofer was speaking.

"The city is becoming brighter by the hour. Look around! Give it an hour or so more, and we won't need the torches."

"I've noticed that." Breslin turned to face the scholar.

"I believe the city is reacting to our presence," Tristofer hypothesized. "How remarkable!"

Breslin got everyone's attention. "There is a chance that someone else may be lurking about. However, we're here for a reason and we need to find out what that reason is. For now, we investigate. Everyone ready? Move cautiously and let's see where these tracks lead."

Breslin pulled Mythryd from his back and silently followed the fresh footprints, ignoring the numerous older ones, through the city. Twisting and turning, the prints led them down wide, worn, paved streets as well as narrow, dark alleys running between large buildings. Moving farther west through the city, they noticed that the damage to the buildings here was much less severe. A few streets showed some slight damage, but otherwise the western section of the city was damage-free.

"How could an earthquake destroy one half of a city

without harming the other?" Breslin wondered aloud as they stopped and stared.

They were standing in a small plaza with vacant shops all around them. Doors hung open. Counters were strewn with various items necessary for that shop's business. Tracks had approached these shops, too, but hadn't entered any.

Resuming their trek through the somber city, the newer footprints finally dead-ended at another of the city's doors, only this one wasn't sealed shut. The stone door was barely ajar and moments later they saw why: an old, dented shield had been jammed between the door and its frame.

"Get a load of that," Athos commented as he squatted next to the shield. He looked at the others. "I could pull it out and let the door close. Then they'll never make it back in here."

Breslin was silent as he considered. "Better not. To do so would announce our presence."

"You don't think the rising levels of light in there have done that for us?"

"Alright, point taken," Breslin grumbled. He nodded toward the door. "Where do you think that goes?"

"To another hidden entrance," Tristofer answered. "Whether on the same mountain or a different one remains to be seen. But I'll bet Bykram lies in that direction."

"So we found where the intruder has been entering the city. Let's find out where he went on his last trip here."

Retracing their steps through the city, they kept a close eye on the fresh tracks in the thick dust. Breslin glanced back and could only hope that the intruders wouldn't be back for a while. The last thing he needed to worry about was someone getting the drop on them, someone who may or may not possess Narian tools and weapons.

Backtracking beyond their original entry point, they discovered several more workshops that obviously had been searched.

"Do you get the impression that this person is getting desperate?" Breslin asked, breaking the monotony of the stifling silence.

"I do," Venk agreed. "Think he's running out of armor?"

"The thought had crossed my mind," Breslin admitted.

"Tristofer, how does someone go about selling a piece of Narian armor?" He looked over his shoulder at the scholar, who was walking side-by-side with his brother.

"I'd contact someone who is familiar with marketing, uh, such goods without attracting attention."

"Have you ever heard of someone selling Narian armor?"

Tristofer nodded. "Every so often a piece changes ownership. Nothing to warrant any attention."

"Have you heard of a single person selling multiple pieces of armor at different times?" Venk asked.

Tristofer turned to regard his companion outfitted in red leather armor. He pulled out a rag, polished his spectacles, and put his glasses back on his nose while simultaneously stuffing the rag back into a pocket.

"An interesting question. I am reminded of a time, a number of years ago, when I still lived in Bykram. Master Rohath, knowing my area of study, contacted me nearly a decade after I had last seen him and said that one of his students had come to class wearing a set of Narian gauntlets. Ordinarily I wouldn't have thought much of this, and Master Rohath agreed, but the following year a different student came with a different piece of armor. A single greave, if memory serves, worn on his left leg. Just the one, mind you.

"Master Rohath's curiosity had been piqued, so when the next year a third student had appeared, wearing a guard brace over his right shoulder, he finally pulled the pupil aside and asked him about the armor, as clearly it was being worn as a symbol of status. 'My father bought it for me' the underling had told him. He looked up the two former pupils of his and was given the same answer. Knowing my penchant for any information on Nar, no matter how obscure, he tracked down one of the pupil's fathers and asked where he had purchased it, saying he knew of one other pupil, me, who would love to have a piece. 'A friend of a friend' is what he was told. When he contacted me and told me this, I dismissed it as fanciful coincidence. Now, I'm not so sure."

"How long ago was that?" Venk asked.

Tristofer thought back to the days after he had been

exiled from his home city.

"At least fifty years, maybe sixty."

Athos looked down at a set of prints that had almost been covered back up by more dust.

"Those tracks could be fifty years old."

Venk held up a hand.

"I'm curious. Your field of study is Nar, right?"

Tristofer nodded.

"An old master of yours contacts you out of the blue and informs you that he had come across three different pieces of Narian armor in as many years. This doesn't spark your interest?"

"It did," Tristofer admitted, "but I had just been banished, and contact with one in exile was forbidden. Master Rohath risked his career and reputation just to contact me. Even so, I felt betrayed, and I had no desire to return to the city, not that I could."

"Knowing now that Nar lies so close to Bykram, do you think the events are related?" Without waiting for the scholar's response, Breslin continued. "I think it's perfectly clear. Someone has been selling armor at Bykram and has been doing it for quite some time."

"And they've managed to avoid suspicion," Athos added.

"Why the fresh tracks then?" Venk wondered.

He looked back at the recently ransacked foundry and was silent for a few minutes. Athos approached and elbowed his brother in the ribs.

"What's bothering you?"

"I can understand why the intruders were searching for armor," Venk slowly began as he continued to work out the answer, "but that forge had been thoroughly searched, from top to bottom. Armor isn't small. A cursory glance should be all that's needed to determine if any pieces are present."

Intrigued, Breslin looked back at the foundry, too.

"What are you thinking, Master Venk? They were looking for something else?"

"Aye. And clearly, they thought it could only be found where there are forges. I think they were looking for clues."

Understanding, Breslin nodded, followed closely by

Athos. Bewildered, Tristofer looked at the other three adults before snapping his fingers in front of their faces.

"Pretend I don't know much about metallurgy, or common blacksmithing practices. Clues to what?"

"They want to know how the Narians made their armor. Think about it! If the secrets the Narians employed were ever discovered then other pieces of armor could be replicated and then passed off as authentic Narian artifacts. They'd make a fortune!"

Tristofer puffed out his chest and crossed his arms in a rare act of defiance. "Not in my lifetime."

"Nor in mine," Breslin agreed. "We must learn the identities of the intruders and put a stop to this scheme. I think that's what the Questor's Mark wants us to do. It wants us to save Nar!" Breslin thrust out his right hand. "Are you with me?"

Tristofer didn't hesitate and laid his hand over Breslin's. "Absolutely."

Athos laid his hand over Tristofer's. "I'm in."

Father and son added their hands to the others. "Us, too."

Breslin eyed the boy. "This has the potential of getting dangerous, Master Lukas. You must stick close to your father's side at all times, is that understood?"

Wide eyed, Lukas nodded.

"Tristofer," Breslin continued, "you will become Athos' shadow. Do not leave his side for anything, no matter what you see. That reminds me, do you have a weapon?"

Tristofer shook his head. Breslin pulled his small hand axe from his belt and held it out, handle first, to the scholar, who gingerly accepted.

"Where do we go?" Venk inquired. "Which way?"

Breslin held the torch down low once more and indicated the ground. "We follow the footprints. A great number of them head this way, to the east."

Athos shoved his torch into the ground and twisted until it was out. Breslin glanced up. He noticed that the light had continued to increase; the torches had become unnecessary. Both torches, once extinguished, were cast aside.

"Can you tell if the most recent tracks also head east?"

Venk asked.

Breslin and Athos squatted low and peered at the many sets of footprints scattered throughout the dust. Both dwarves nodded. Athos wordlessly pointed east.

Gripping his crossbow tightly, while Athos brandished his axe, the two brothers took the lead while Tristofer and Lukas followed close behind. Bringing up the rear was Breslin, who constantly turned to check behind them to verify they weren't being followed. The number of tracks began dwindling, the farther east they progressed. As they moved away from the heart of the city, and presumably from the mass of blacksmiths, the number of tracks also declined, as clearly the focus of the massive city-wide search existed elsewhere. The tracks they were following were joined by others coming in from other parts of the city. All were headed east, the same direction they were traveling now. So many tracks converged that they were now following a trail through the heavy blanket of dust.

Approaching the far eastern wall of the cavern, the group stopped and stared with amazement. The trail dead-ended right at the wall, but the wall itself caught their attention. Carved into the granite were ten columns forty feet high. Directly in the center, with five columns on either side, was a huge arched doorway, complete with a thirty-foot-high door. As before with the partially closed security gate, this door was also ajar. A single chair, stripped of all adornments and jewels, was jammed between the door and the frame.

The wall glowed brightly at their approach. The same golden chain was present throughout the columns and wall, but the light from the columns paled in comparison with that of the door.

The illuminated golden chain had been expertly attached to quartz crystals embedded within the granite door. Grand sweeping arches, interlocking circles, and jagged patterns covered the exquisite door, giving at first the appearance of a vast conglomerated mess of swirled lines and shapes. However, the more the dwarves stared at the door, with its brightly glowing decorations, the more the many patterns and shapes seemed to blend in flawlessly with one another. The more they looked, the more they were convinced that they were looking at a masterful piece of art and that this door was the entrance to Nar's imperial palace.

Tristofer moaned quietly as he noticed the exquisite chair jammed into the palace door. He quietly ran his hands along the dented tarnished metal, sensing that the chair was of the finest silver ever smithed. He peered anxiously into the dark recesses behind the door and immediately noticed that the open space was just enough to allow a dwarf to pass.

Without waiting for the others, Tristofer hopped onto the chair and boldly jumped into the darkness. The scholar watched with satisfaction as the great vaulted room began to lighten when the chamber detected movement. Moments later the rest of his group was standing next to him. Athos smacked the scholar on the back of his head, sending his spectacles flying off his nose.

"Don't do that again, you fool," Athos growled ominously at him. "We stick together. You will allow one of us to go first in the future, agreed?"

Hastily retrieving his glasses, Tristofer faced Athos' angry glare and meekly nodded. "Sorry. I couldn't help myself. I had to see what was in here!"

"Try harder next time," Athos told him. "There's a chance someone could still be here."

"I don't think so," Tristofer countered. He pointed at the closest wall. Several of the golden patterns had started to glow and were becoming steadily brighter. "Had someone else passed through here, this room would already be lit. Look how it illuminated itself once we arrived. We are alone, my friends."

Comforted by that thought, Breslin returned Mythryd to its holder on his back. A moment later he pulled the activated power hammer from his belt. Holding the unique hammer tightly in his right hand, Breslin beckoned for the others to follow.

The room they were in must have been a dignitary receiving room as it was large enough to accommodate several hundred people. Broken tables, chairs with missing legs, and damaged walls met their eyes. They noted with dismay that many of the chairs were similar to the one holding open the palace door. Just like the one outside, these had been picked clean of all their jewels and other valuable accoutrements. Even the nearby walls, once festooned with gold and jewels, lay stripped clean.

"Never have I been so ashamed to call myself a member of the Kla Rehn," Tristofer whispered in shock.

"Do not hold all the Kla Rehn accountable," Breslin softly told him. "I believe this is the work of one person, or perhaps by one family over a long period of time. But, by thunder, that ends now. Whatever remains will be preserved, no matter the cost."

Tristofer murmured his thanks. Athos and Venk each gave the scholar a friendly slap on the back to show their friendship and support.

"Prints are everywhere," Breslin reported as he squatted to inspect the floor. "I would imagine this was the first location that was pillaged, followed closely by the surrounding blacksmiths. We need to investigate."

"Master Tristofer, you wanted to find Nar. Congratulations. We're here. Where would you like to search first?"

"Well, perhaps we should search for an armory. I, for one, would like to know if our adversaries are armed with Narian weapons."

"Agreed. We should head to —"

Lukas suddenly grabbed Breslin's sleeve and tugged backward, bringing him to a stop. "Do you hear that?" The boy looked anxious.

Breslin tossed the power hammer to his left hand while reaching his right arm behind to pull Mythryd free. Seconds later, Venk and Athos were also holding their weapons.

"What is it?" Breslin whispered down to Lukas while straining to hear whatever sound the underling had heard. "What do you hear? Have they returned?"

"I hear…"

"Tapping," Venk finished for his son as he straightened up. He looked around the large chamber and wrung a finger in each ear. "At least I thought I did. I don't anymore."

"It's stopped," Lukas whispered. He pointed back toward

the far wall of the room. Two large, and very open doors were visible, as were several dozen footprints all headed in that direction. "I think it came from that way."

Lukas suddenly jumped up and grabbed his father's hand. "There it is again! Do you hear it?"

A soft, repetitive tapping echoed softly throughout the room.

...*tap-taptaptap-tap-tap-tap-taptap-tap*...

The tapping stopped as abruptly as it had started.

"I heard it that time," Breslin quietly informed his companions. "Young Lukas is right. It came from that way. Follow me and keep quiet. No unnecessary speaking, is that understood? Tristofer, that goes for you, too."

Tristofer nodded and tapped his sealed lips.

The tapping resumed. Breslin motioned for them to follow. As quietly as he dared, Breslin moved toward the source of the noise. They passed through one of the open doors and entered a large, curved hallway that led away from the main hall. Breslin held up a hand and signaled everyone to wait. Within a few minutes, the golden chains present in the hallway began glowing, giving off their welcoming light to the visitors. Once they could see where they were going, they followed the curved hallway until it dead-ended into a smaller chamber with many doors leading off in different directions.

Standing just inside the second room, they waited, motionless, for sufficient illumination. A few moments later they were off again, heading toward a doorway twenty feet away.

...*tap-taptaptap-tap-tap-tap-taptap-tap*...

"That's it," Breslin said in the softest of whispers. "Keep tapping. You're making this too easy for us."

Athos softly grunted in agreement.

The hallway they had just entered had doors on either side of the hall for a stretch of at least two hundred feet. Venk counted nearly twenty-five, a dozen on each side, before they were forced to stop. Another door barred their way, only this one was unlike any they had encountered thus far.

A solid iron door, resting on recently oiled hinges, blocked their way. No fewer than four heavy bars stretched across its length and were anchored into the stone walls on either side. Heavy iron padlocks held each of the bars firmly in place.

"Does that look Narian to you?" Breslin asked, confused. "What's a door like this doing here?"

Athos walked up to the sturdy metal door and peered through the tiny slit at eye-level.

"Looks to be at least a foot thick. The bars are set into the wall on both sides, and each is locked in place. Someone clearly wants to keep people out."

"I'd say it's more likely that they want to keep someone in," Tristofer countered.

Athos, Venk, and Breslin turned to stare at the impressive iron door. One by one, they turned to look down at the power hammer.

"If you use that," Venk cautioned, "then the chances of getting in and out of here unnoticed become very slim."

Breslin hefted the power hammer and eyed the door.

"If there *is* someone on the other side of that door then this is starting to make perfect sense. Whoever it is gave us the hammer. Why? Because he knew that there would be no escape without it. Look at the door! Impenetrable, I'd say."

"Unless you have a hammer that can pulverize rocks with a single blow," Tristofer whispered, understanding.

"Exactly. Stand back. We're going to find out what's on the other side."

Venk steered Lukas away from the door and retreated a safe distance down the hallway. Once he was sure his son was out of danger, he loaded his crossbow and waited to see what the outcome would be. Athos, also armed and ready, joined him. Tristofer appeared moments later, both fingers shoved into his ears. Venk clapped his hands over his son's ears just as Breslin let the first blow fall.

Venk cringed at the sound. The concussive blast echoed noisily down through the hall and, Venk was sure, out into the city. A second blow landed, and now a gritty cloud of dirt and debris appeared. The third blow struck, and despite the heavy ringing in their ears, they could hear a great cracking of stone. The fourth blow punched the steel door right through the wall and sent it toppling over with a loud clang.

Fanning away the heavy dust and pulverized stone now prevalent in the air, Breslin waited patiently for his vision to return. Twenty seconds later, when it finally did, they could see the true power the hammer held, as the door itself was still in one piece but heavily dented. The four bars that had been anchored into the surrounding stone wall had been ripped away, taking huge chunks of stone with them.

They were now in a well-lit chamber that was piled high with books, scrolls, charts, and maps. A lumpy mattress was pushed up into a corner. Several threadbare chairs were scattered about, including a large chair that would be considered over-sized for a dwarf but average for a human. Adjacent to this chair was a rickety shelf full of ancient books. Sitting in the chair, looking as though he wasn't the least bit surprised that someone had just forced their way into his chamber, was the most ancient and wizened dwarf that anyone had ever seen.

A long, dirty, unbraided beard lay unfurled along the ground. Long, thin white hair also came close to brushing the ground, but had been tied up with a simple leather cord. A plain threadbare tunic, long since faded to khaki, and a pair of worn black trousers patched in several places, completed the picture.

Before anyone could ask the elderly dwarf a question, the ancient fellow surprised them with a smile and a bow. He turned to Breslin and shook his head.

"You sure took your time, boy," the ancient fellow accused. His voice was clear, strong, and completely belied his appearance. "I had just about given up hope."

Breslin was flummoxed. He cleared his throat nervously. "Do you know me?"

The little fellow threw his head back and laughed heartily. What came out was a cackle that practically curdled their blood.

"I should say so, boy! Maelnar, is that any way to treat

your father?"

Breslin's eyes opened in shock. No one ever called him by his birth name. In order to prevent confusion, he always asked that people call him by his middle name, Breslin. Who was this person?

"How do you know my name?"

Confused, Lukas looked at the tiny old man. He pointed back at Breslin.

"His name is Breslin, not Maelnar."

"Breslin? Breslin? You're lying. You must be."

"Maelnar Breslin is my given birth name," Breslin explained to his companions. "To make sure the two of us aren't confused, my father goes by Maelnar and I go by Breslin."

"Your father?"

Everyone turned back to the ancient dwarf. He slowly got down from his chair and hobbled over to Breslin to study him closer. The old dwarf's eyes widened with disbelief.

"I can see it now. Dear me, how long have I been gone?"

Breslin stared at the tiny stooped being and dropped down to one knee as he finally realized who he was facing.

"Grandfather."

Chapter 12 — Once Upon A Nar

Grandfather? You're his grandfather?" Venk kept shifting his gaze from the tiny wizened being to his friend kneeling on the ground. His gaze finally settled on Breslin. "You never mentioned your grandfather was also searching for Nar!"

"That's because I didn't know," Breslin clarified, as he slowly regained his feet. He turned to his grandfather and bowed once more, then introduced the others. "My friends, I'd like you to meet my grandfather, Kasnar."

After the introductions were over, Venk approached the old dwarf and bowed.

"Did you send the Questor's Mark?"

Kasnar smiled and nodded.

"Aye. Pleased, I am, to see that you understood it for what it was."

Venk pointed at Tristofer. "Only because of him. I thought it was just a burn on my son's back."

At this, Kasnar cocked his head and stared at Venk.

Slowly, he turned his head so that he was staring straight at Lukas.

"Are you telling me your son bore the Questor's Mark?"

"Bore? You mean bear. Aye. He still has it."

Kasnar shook his head. "Impossible. The mark served only to bring the bearer here."

Venk beckoned Lukas to come over.

"I just looked at it less than an hour ago. Trust me, it's there."

"Indeed? Can you show me?"

Knowing what was coming, Lukas pulled up his shirt and exposed his back to the old man. Kasnar smiled and nodded.

"Just as I thought. There's nothing there."

"What?" Venk sputtered. He spun his son around so that he could see for himself. Sure enough, the mark was gone. Lukas' back was as bare as the day he was born.

"It's gone!"

"Of course, it's gone," Kasnar scolded. "You accomplished your mission, therefore the quest was completed. No more mark."

Smiling profusely, all anger forgotten, Venk stepped back a few steps and pulled his son back with him.

"Argumentative comments withdrawn."

Venk waved an arm, to get everyone's attention.

"Whether he was the intended recipient or not, does it matter? The mark is gone. Our mission is over. I say we get out of here and go home, before whoever created this mess comes back."

"I've waited this long for someone to find me," Kasnar slowly began. "You have no idea how much work it took to bring you all here. I have so many questions. What year is it? Who is on the Council? No, wait. Just answer me this: why did the underling have the mark? How did your father manage to avoid receiving it? I spent years crafting that spell. Years! And now you're telling me that I didn't even get it to the right person?"

Everyone in the room nodded, including Lukas.

"Is that why it took so long for you five to make it here? I activated my spell, what, about six months ago? It's starting to make sense now."

"What does?" Breslin asked.

"To think that I actually second guessed myself," Kasnar angrily exclaimed. He painfully climbed back up into the oversized chair. Sighing heavily, he scooted back so that his aching bones were resting against the hard wood. He eyed Lukas for a few moments before he finally smiled. "How long did it take for you to realize what was on your back, young master ... master ... I apologize lad. What was your name again?"

Lukas nervously cleared his throat. "Lukas."

"Ah, yes. Right. Master Lukas. How long did it take to figure out what was on your back?"

Suddenly shy, Lukas looked to his father for help.

"Months," Venk answered. "It was my fault. I thought it was a burn and it hadn't healed properly. Seeing how Lukas was never in any pain, I never explored further. It was only when Lukas was burned by a drop of molten silver did we learn of its nature. That's when the healer saw his back, asked a few questions, and then let the matter drop."

"Let the matter drop?" Kasnar sharply asked, frowning.

"I wasn't concerned and neither was he. Somehow, and I don't know how, word got to your son, Maelnar, who wanted to see Lukas and ask him why he had a Narian hammer on his back."

"I thought that was the best part," Kasnar confided. "I thought for certain that my son would take one look at the hammer, the only legible part of the mark, and instantly know the message was for him. I never dreamed the mark would be given to another in his stead."

"Maelnar would have known the mark was intended for him?" Tristofer asked. "How?"

"Because he's part Narian, too," Kasnar answered. "Every descendant of Nar has the letters n-a-r somewhere in their name. First name, given name, or sometimes nickname, but almost always in the first name."

Athos gave Breslin a friendly nudge in the ribs. "You knew that, right?"

"I remember my father telling me that at some point, aye."

"How long have you been here?" Venk wanted to know as he glanced around the sparsely furnished room.

"More years than I can count," Kasnar admitted. His eyes had suddenly attached themselves to his grandson's belt.

Breslin, correctly guessing what his grandfather was staring at, eased the power hammer out of the belt loop and held it out, handle first. A gnarled, arthritic hand gently closed upon the handle and gripped it tightly. The ruby on the hammer head glowed brightly, as if sensing the excitement emanating from the elder Narian descendant.

"It's heavy," Venk warned. "Be careful."

Kasnar lifted the hammer high over his head, as though it weighed no more than a feather.

"Not for us, it isn't," Kasnar answered with a coy grin. He tossed the hammer playfully to his left hand, but his heavily arthritic hand was unable to grip the hammer, even as light as it was for him. The hammer spun to the floor and landed with a loud thud.

"I'm not as young as I used to be, I'm afraid."

Having the hammer land closest to him, Athos bent down and clenched his teeth, determined to effortlessly lift the hammer just as Breslin and Kasnar had done.

"You're not fooling anyone, lad," Kasnar merrily informed Athos as the hammer was returned to him. Several veins were bulging on Athos' forehead, while his face had turned beet red. "I appreciate the thought, though."

"Think nothing of it," Athos managed to wheeze out.

Kasnar noticed Breslin staring at him as though his beard had caught fire.

"What is it, boy? Speak your mind."

Breslin was silent for another moment or two before he walked over to the closest chair, plopped it down in front of his grandfather, and heavily sat down.

"Grandfather, what are you doing in Nar? How did you come to be here? Who's been holding you here?"

Kasnar smiled and indicated everyone should take a seat.

"It's a long story, my boy."

"Are we in danger?" Breslin suddenly asked, reaching out to take the hammer that Kasnar had set on the chair besides him. "Obviously someone has held you prisoner. Are they due back?"

"He was just here yesterday," Kasnar answered. "He won't be back for a while."

"Who?" Breslin demanded. "Who isn't due to be back in a while?"

"Patience, lad. Patience. Allow me to tell you my story."

Once upon a time —

Athos snorted in disbelief. Kasnar shot him a glare, cleared his throat, and tried again.

Once upon a time, nearly a full millennia ago, my tale begins. Now that I think about it, it was about the same time the city had finally been found.

Athos whistled. "A thousand years ago? Really?"

Kasnar held up a withered hand and gave him a sweeping gesture. "Think that kind of pillaging out there happened overnight? Now be quiet."

"Sorry."

Now, as I was saying, this tale begins nearly a thousand years ago. I had completed my apprenticeship nearly a century prior, and had become a very gifted toymaker.

Athos snickered. "A toymaker? Hmmmph. Wouldn't have called that one."

Venk elbowed his brother in the gut. Hard.

Ignoring the outburst, Kasnar continued.

I was startled to learn that my skills were becoming well known. Not only was I making toys and trinkets for the children of prominent council members, I found that my services were being requested at other cities. Borahgg was just the beginning. Soon I was filling orders for Graun, Bykram, or any city the six clans laid claim to.

Life was good, lads. My services were in high demand. My toys were selling as fast as I could make them. What everyone really wanted were my dragons. I've been fascinated with dragons for so long, I thought what better tribute could there be than small reproductions that could move around of their own accord? Gold, red, blue, black, if a color combination existed, I've created it. Blue dragons were my favorite.

Tristofer held up a hand. "Really? We saw a blue dragon a few days ago while we were being carried to Bykram. It was from a distance, mind you, but still a very dark shade of blue."

Everyone stared silently at the scholar. Tristofer's cheeks reddened. He closed his mouth and dropped his eyes.

I had just completed a special toy for the daughter of a noble, and was in the process of delivering the gift when —

"What was the gift?" Lukas suddenly asked, breaking Kasnar's concentration once again.

Startled, Kasnar looked at the boy. "What was that?"

"You said a 'special toy'. I was wondering what it was you had made."

"Oh. You're a youngster so I'll humor you. It was a dancing princess, specifically crafted to resemble the girl once she attained a marriageable age."

Lukas nodded and fell silent.

Where was I? Oh, that's right. The human girl. So, I knew the price the girl's father paid easily covered my own costs, plus the time and effort to deliver the finished toy to its owner, and I also thought a change of scenery would do me good, so I paid R'Tal a visit. While the girl fussed over the likeness of herself, her father knew his gold had been well spent, so he drew me aside and wanted to know if I had ever done any commissioned work. He wanted to know if I ever made weapons. Naturally, I had. I mean, who amongst us has never made a hammer? It's the very nature of our kind.

Tristofer's arm rose meekly into the air.

Kasnar shook his head. "Shocking."

"He doesn't even know me and he's already insulting me," Tristofer muttered softly.

Overhearing, Athos grunted, but elected to keep quiet.

The human noble wanted a sword, and a special one at that. Seems he had heard that a few of the dwarves were masters of coloring metal. It's a trick that only a very select few had learned, and how this human knew I was one of them I was not certain. Regardless, he promised me all kinds of riches if I would make a red single-handed blade with a pommel of solid gold. I thought the coloring was odd, but no more so than any of the other unusual requests I had heard in the span of my career.

As I thought back to prior commitments waiting for me back in my workshop, the noble mistook the pause as a sign of refusal, so he began to offer me whatever treasures he thought I might be interested in. After listing jewels, gilded daggers, and even a set of ruby-encrusted tools, if you can believe that, he finally stumbled upon something that piqued my curiosity. He told me that he had a map of Nar.

Naturally I scoffed at this. If you had a map leading to Nar, I argued, why weren't you using it to find the city yourself? He told me that he had tried, but the map was either hiding something or else he had incorrectly interpreted it. Either way you looked at it, I was interested, and he knew it. Said he'd give me the map if I made him his sword.

What could I do? If I didn't agree, then I'd regret it for the rest of my life. I knew this. Sadly, he knew this, too. Therefore, I agreed to the bargain.

After delivering him his sword a month later, he gave me the map. It was an unremarkable thing. Small, even smaller than a standard sheet of parchment. And, I might add, it showed a section of the Bohanis that had already been well mapped. I had been swindled.

Or so I thought.

"The map in father's study?" Breslin interrupted. "That's what you traded for? It's not even accurate!"

"It was drawn by a Narian cartographer, so by definition, it was a Narian map. What the map was used for we'll probably never know."

"But you were swindled! He made you believe it was a map to Nar when it was nothing more than —"

"They told me it was a Narian map. It was. Let it go, lad. May I continue?"

Contrite, Breslin dropped his eyes and waited for his grandfather to resume his story.

Upon closer examination of the map, I found a tiny upside-down hammer in the lower left corner. I believed it was just a mark made by the cartographer and was ready to dismiss it when curiosity got the better of me and I decided, since I was already at a castle, with a well-stocked library, to do some research. Imagine my surprise when I was able to authenticate the map as genuinely Narian.

From the time I could barely walk I have heard stories about the fabled city of Nar. Every child thinks he can find it when he grows to adulthood. Every adult vows if they ever have the resources to properly search for the city, then they will.

I did not have the proper resources to launch a full-scale expedition to Nar, but I also wasn't a pauper. I carefully folded the map and tucked it into my papers. I remember turning around and coming face to face with the little human girl for whom I had just delivered the dancing doll. Standing next to her was a second human child, around the same age and garbed similarly. She introduced her best friend in the world and introduced me as the one who had created her favorite, most bestest toy in the world.

"Bestest?" Breslin smiled, raising an eyebrow.

"I'm paraphrasing," Kasnar explained. "Those were her words not mine. Besides, she was no more than nine years old. Stop making me lose my focus."

"Sorry."

After she introduced her friend, she implored me, even begged me, to make her friend the same type of doll that I had made for her. I told her that this request wasn't an easy one, and perhaps if I were to speak to her father maybe, just maybe, we might be able to work something out. The first girl informed me that her friend's family couldn't afford to purchase pretty things like hers could, and that's why she wanted to deal with me directly.

I found myself between the proverbial rock and a hard place. While I paused to collect my thoughts, the first child grabbed my arm and asked if I would consider doing a trade, as her father had done for me. Not believing this human child could have anything that I would ever want,

I gently asked what she had in mind. She told me to follow her. Turning on her heel, she led me deep into the castle, past several sets of guards, into a large room which I correctly guessed was the nursery set up for all the noble's children. All manner of toys were scattered about. How these children could possibly want more toys was beyond me.

After glancing around the room, I could immediately see that there wasn't anything there that I was remotely interested in. But, not wanting to appear rude, especially to a young daughter of a human noble, I waited to see what the child offered. She and her friend began searching one of three enormous chests, tossing various toys over their shoulders. Moving to the second chest, the first girl gives a shrill shriek and turns around, clutching something to her chest. I couldn't tell what it was. Walking up to me she finally held out this brown stick as though it was made of pure gold.

I took the proffered trade and inspected it. Why would this human child give me a carved stick? Was there something I was missing? Several of the carvings caught my eye. Axes, kytes, and sure enough, even a tiny picture of a hammer, carved into one of the ends.

"You're talking about the power hammer's handle, right?" Tristofer asked. His hand was back in the air.

"Obviously. Be quiet."

"Sorry."

There I was, in possession of two authentic Narian artifacts. Do I agree to create another doll at my own expense? Or, should I ignore my instincts and refuse the trade? What would you have done? The same thing as I, I guarantee it. So I gathered my materials, found a place to work, and created the second doll. I wanted that handle, as you all have clearly deduced the true nature of the trade. How the power hammer's handle came into the little girl's possession I'll never know. I didn't want to know. I still don't.

To be doubly certain that the trade brokered by the girl was sanctioned by her father, I approached the noble and explained what his daughter had done and what she was proposing to do. The human shrugged and waved me off, as though I was a pesky insect. Very well, I thought. If he didn't care if his daughter was trading a Narian artifact for a simple doll, then I wouldn't press the issue. I made the doll, delivered it, and took possession of the handle.

Returning to Borahgg I asked myself what I should do with my new treasures. I probably should have turned both artifacts over to the Council and let it go; however, I was very surprised to learn that I wanted to be the one to find Nar. I wanted to explore, to research, to get my hands dirty, so to speak.

I informed my family that I'd discovered a new lucrative set of customers for my wares, namely the humans. I told them the doll was so well received at the human castle that I had stayed around a little while longer and created a second doll, which was true, and more and more people wanted toys, too.

Back in that time, it was not uncommon for a member of the clan to venture out to either seek his fortune, go on an adventure, or be absent for longer periods of time. Neika, my wife, completely understood and encouraged me to share my 'gift' as she called it, with everyone that I could.

"Didn't you feel bad about lying to grandmother about your intentions?" Breslin demanded, growing angry.

"Aye. I never should have left."

"She thinks you're dead, grandfather. We all did."

Kasnar's hopeful eyes met his grandson's. "She still lives?"

"Aye."

"If only I could gaze upon her beauty once more," Kasnar whispered softly. "I wish to tell her how sorry I am."

"You will," Breslin promised. "Please, continue your tale."

"Right. Let's see…"

I was in such a rush to leave, fearing that the nature of my mission would become known and I would be forcibly detained, that I didn't realize I had left the map until I had made it Topside and was well past the valley. Deciding against returning for the map, as I had committed every detail to memory, I journeyed far and wide, seeking out every clan I could in my quest to learn all there was to know about Nar. Sadly, this part of the tale didn't take long as there wasn't much authentic, documented proof about its existence. Everyone seemed to accept the simple truth that Nar once existed, but no one, and I do mean no one, had any indication where it could be found.

Determination set it. If one human girl could possess two pieces of Narian culture then it was completely feasible to think that other artifacts existed, whether stored in children's toy boxes or perhaps sitting on the shelf of some noble's study. The key to finding Nar, I believed, rested with the people. Somehow, and I didn't have any idea how, I needed to broker more trades like the ones I had done at R'Tal. I needed the people to seek me out just like the human noble from the castle.

Four months of fruitless searching convinced me I had left my home unprepared. I didn't know where else to look, and what's more, I didn't know what I was looking for. I needed more information and it became clear I wasn't going to find it wandering aimlessly Topside. With great reluctance I returned to Borahgg. I told Neika that I had accumulated enough orders to keep me busy for a while so I resumed my duties as a toy maker. Neika was no fool. I knew she suspected I was working on some secret project as I spent countless hours in the Archives when I wasn't in my workshop. I felt horrible for deceiving her. I did everything I could to avoid arousing suspicion. I figured I needed to focus on my work, so I poured every ounce of creativity, every ounce of passion I had into my creations. Beautiful wyverian figurines, capable of flapping wings, walking a few steps, and even breathing fire, began to accumulate on the shelves in my shop. Since I only produced a few a year you can begin to imagine how long I waited.

Days turned into weeks, and weeks turned into months. I fell into a routine. Working tirelessly on my wyverians occupied my time during the day and once a week I'd devote to research in the Archives, looking for everything referencing Nar, no matter how minute. I became a veritable scholar on the subject. Every book, every article, every story that had ever been passed from father to son, I learned. I spent long hours perusing through musty tomes, interviewing various people, and discerning everything I could from my Narian artifacts. What was I able to learn?

Absolutely nothing.

Growing desperate, I came up with a brilliant plan. I started to make more toys. These toys were not as elaborate as my prized wyverians, but they were still quite clever. These were puzzles. The simple metal pieces fit together so precisely that they created shapes. I made griffins, serpents, kytes, and any of a number of other creatures that fit my fancy. The brilliance of my plan, though, was what came next. I made another journey to the human castle in R'Tal and made a gift of a dozen of the puzzles. I also selected several of my wyverians and brought them along, just so they could get a taste of the finer merchandise.

The puzzles were received very well by the children. Never had they seen puzzles like this. They wanted more, always more! I just smiled and said that I was a simple toymaker looking to expand my list of customers. When I was putting a few of the extra puzzles away I let my bag fall open long enough for the king to see one of my wyverians. It was a silver land dragon, with emeralds for its eyes. This model could walk around a few steps and even swish its tail back and forth.

The king fell for it. He said he had to have it. I told him that my wyverians were a passion of mine and that I really wasn't looking to sell them as I didn't need more gold. This story was validated by my refusal to accept payment for the gift of the puzzles. The king began to offer other treasures in lieu of gold. Again, I politely demurred, stating that I had no desire to part with them.

Finally, after the king and I went back and forth for nearly an hour, a silver and gold colored shield was produced. It was Narian, I could see that immediately by the way the Narian blacksmith had masterfully blended the gold and silver together. The king informed me that this was his favorite shield as it had never failed him on the field of battle. He offered it in exchange for my silver wyverian. I meekly accepted. The human king became a valuable ally from that point on.

Returning to Borahgg with my new shield, I…

"Yes? What is it, Breslin?"

"I have that shield. Father gave it to me quite a while ago."

Kasnar smiled. "I'm glad to hear it's still in the family. Now, where was I? Oh, yes."

I returned home with the shield and wondered what my next step should be. Do I try visiting other cities? Perhaps I should venture north into Ylani and try my luck at Zaran, their capital? As it turns out I didn't have long to wait. Word rapidly spread of a dwarf living under the northwestern Bohanis who made wonderfully articulate wyverian figurines. Everyone wanted one. I've never seen demand for a single item so high. I couldn't make them fast enough.

Soon I had the largest private collection of Narian artifacts ever assembled. Mind you, most of the trades were for small, insignificant pieces of armor, or maybe a slip of paper with the Narian seal on it.

However you chose to look at it, I wouldn't refuse a trade if the customer who came asking for a wyverian had a Narian item.

In retrospect that should have been my first warning. I was becoming too careless. It was only a matter of time before I attracted his attention.

"Who's attention?" Breslin demanded, instantly angry.
"Settle down, lad. I'm getting there."

One day I received word that a customer, who wished to remain anonymous, wanted the nicest wyverian I had and was willing to exchange a hammer head for it. I had a handle. I thought this was too good of an opportunity to pass up. I…

"That should have been your second clue something was amiss," Athos remarked.
Kasnar gave him a sour look. "You think? Be silent."
"Sorry."

Against my better judgment, I journeyed to Bykram and met at the agreed upon location which was just outside their main entrance. I waited for two days, and when it was apparent that my mystery customer wasn't going to put in an appearance, I decided that as long as I was there, I should consult with their scholars to see if anything new had been uncovered. However, if you're familiar with Bykram, or any clan city, one does not venture inside without an invitation. Plus, their entrances are hidden. I had been to Bykram the prior year and knew that the only way I'd gain entrance was to be escorted by one of the Kla Rehn. So I waited.

Nearly three days later the door finally opened and a dwarf ventured outside. I introduced myself and indicated my desire to meet with one of their scholars, Zincoff. I was escorted inside and led straight to the library where my story was corroborated. I spent a few extra days there as their library was extensive and I quite honestly lost track of time. Little did I know I was being watched.

I had stumbled across a reference to dendrology, which is the study of…

"Trees!" Tristofer blurted out.
Everyone stared at the scholar. Tristofer mumbled an

apology and went quiet.

Trees. I had found an obscure horticulture manual which had a tiny mention of a practice the Narians used which could modify the behavior of trees. Modify it how? What did it mean? What would the Narians gain by changing how a tree behaves?

"Lower your hand, Master Lukas," Kasnar told him. "We all know where this is going."

Excitement was building again. I was certain I was exploring an angle that no one had ever considered before. What was I looking for? Would I know if I found it? As you can imagine I spent the next several weeks idly roaming about Topside, careful not to venture too far from Bykram as the surrounding forest and mountains were largely unexplored. I had come to the base of one mountain and was gazing up at one of its sides when I spotted a tree. I'm sure you know which one I'm referring to. Anyway, I located a tree that looked as though it had two separate colors on its trunk. Since a closer look was warranted, I climbed up for a better look.

"You climbed all the way up there?" Athos exclaimed. "By hand? That's impressive. I don't care who you are, that's just impressive."

Kasnar nodded. "You make it sound as though it's impossible. Clearly it isn't, as the five of you also made the same journey."

Breslin cleared his throat. "We, uh, were carried up."

Kasnar leaned forward, interested. "Carried? By whom? By what?"

"By Rhamalli!" Lukas piped up.

"What's that?" Kasnar wanted to know.

"It's a who, not a what. He's a dragon," Venk told him.

"You were carried up the mountain by a dragon? You didn't have to climb?"

Venk and his companions shook their heads.

"And the dragon did this willingly? You didn't trick it?"

Everyone nodded their heads affirmatively.

"That is impressive, lads. Allow me to continue."

Once I was standing before the tree I could see right away that this tree had been modified, its behavior changed, as this wasn't just one tree but two. Why these two were growing together meant only one thing to me: concealment. I believed it was hiding something. Getting down on my belly I could see that there was the tiniest of openings in the rock at the base of the two trunks. Applying my eye to the hole revealed an open cavity on the other side!

I spent the next three days painstakingly chipping away at the rock to enlarge the hole. Once it was large enough to pass through, I entered the hole and was about to look around when I heard a commotion outside. Someone was coming up the side of the mountain, and from the sounds of it, it was more than one person. I had been spotted, and more importantly, I had the hammer handle with me. I knew that whoever was approaching was no friend, so I had to find a place to hide the handle. I wrapped it in a piece of cloth that I had and looked up at the junction of the trunks, which was just over my head. I wedged the handle up against the trunks and once I verified that it wouldn't drop back down, I scrambled outside to try and intercept the encroachers before they discovered the cave under the roots. After concealing the hole the best that I could, I headed down the mountain, managing to descend about twenty feet. I stopped, whipped out my hammer and chisel, and pretended I was trying to extricate a stone when they found me.

"Who?" Breslin demanded. "Isn't it time you tell us who your captors are?"

Kasnar nodded. "A Kla Rehn family by the name of Delvehearth."

Breslin blinked a few times with surprise. "You say that name as though we should know it. I've never heard of them."

"Of course you haven't. They're an insignificant moronic bunch of idiots."

Athos and Venk both managed to stifle their laughs, but Lukas let out a loud giggle. Venk silently wagged a finger at his son and then tapped his lips with his fingers. Lukas composed himself and fell silent.

"What can you tell us about this Delvehearth family?" Breslin inquired, already hating the family for their treatment of his elderly grandfather. "What did they want with you?"

"Long story short, they wanted me to unlock the secrets of Narian metallurgy."

"People have been trying to do that for centuries!" Tristofer cried. "No one has had any luck. Wait. Have you?"

"Have I what, Master Tristofer?"

"Had any luck deciphering the mystery of Narian metal?"

Kasnar shook his head. "None whatsoever."

"How long have you been at it?" Athos asked, curious. A quick glance around the area revealed stacks of books and scrolls everywhere. An open notebook lay on the thin mattress. Several scrawls could be seen on its open pages.

"I really can't remember," Kasnar admitted, rubbing his gnarled hands together. "So long that I can't remember doing anything else."

I was escorted back to Bykram in the company of two adult dwarves. I heard the one refer to the other as Bastion, but the identity of the second was never revealed to me. I was quite certain Bastion had plans to eliminate his helper just as soon as I was secured because I never saw Bastion's assistant again after that day. I learned Bastion had been watching me from the time I had arrived at Bykram, as he was the mystery client that was responsible for bringing me to the city.

Bound and concealed by a hooded cloak, I was escorted through the city, unchallenged, as Bastion explained I was a relative who had taken ill. I was taken to his home and locked securely in a cellar. I spent enough time in that house to learn, by keeping my ears tuned to anything happening on the other side of the door, that my captor had made a discovery within the last year or so and it was something large enough that he wanted to keep it secret.

I hadn't learned the nature of this discovery yet, only that somehow he was profiting from it. More expensive furnishings began appearing in the home. They began to take pride in their appearance, as every time I saw Bastion after that he was clothed in his finest attire. The Delvehearths had clearly stumbled onto a fortune, and they were desperate to keep the source of it concealed.

In several years' time I was moved to another location, as I had learned Bastion had accumulated enough wealth to purchase a larger, fancier home as his old home had become too small to contain everything he and his wife had purchased. I also learned that the new home was chosen specifically because of its large storage cellar beneath the residence. Bastion knew there'd be no escape from that cellar without proper tools and he watched me constantly to make sure I never got my hands on any. He wanted all of my knowledge of Nar, and of blacksmithing, and he was prepared to wait as long as necessary to get every last bit of it.

My primary task was to unlock the metallurgical secrets of special pieces of armor I was given. I told them that I couldn't do this without having access to information. Time and time again I was brought more armor, books, and scrolls. It wasn't until Bastion had dropped off the second set of books that I realized just what it was he had found. The imbecilic lout had located Nar, and wherever he had found it, only he knew how to find it again. To make matters worse, I learned that's where the wealth was coming from. He had found the fabled city I had been searching for and was pillaging it, selling whatever valuables he could find. To say that I was angry was a serious understatement.

One thing I will give Bastion, though: he was no fool. He knew that it would only be a matter of time before his supply of armor was depleted. If that ever happened, how would he maintain the lifestyle that he and his family had become so obsessed with? Like so many entrepreneurs before him, he decided if he could learn how to make more armor, he could continue to amass his fortune at an astounding rate. He had found Nar! Surely somewhere in the city some blacksmith had kept detailed notes on the process for creating more. Fortunately for us, Bastion was no blacksmith. He had absolutely no skills with a hammer or chisel. He would be lost if he ever stepped foot in a foundry. He was also no scholar, having only mediocre reading skills.

Bastion realized he needed to find someone who did possess those skills and also was familiar with the deep levels of research necessary to begin to unlock the Narian secrets. How would he go about finding such a person? How could he get them to Bykram? That's unfortunately why I became part of this accursed tale.

"Wait a moment," Tristofer interrupted. "Did Bastion know that he had discovered Nar?"

"I'm coming to that. Be patient."

I believe I was imprisoned in that basement for nearly a century before one night I fell asleep and awoke in this chamber. I can only assume he had drugged my food. Upon awakening, and discovering that

I was here, I began to explore the room. I saw, with dismay, that I was in yet another storage room, but this time all signs indicated that I was in Nar itself. I still couldn't tell you how to get here from Bykram as the way remains concealed from me.

"Don't worry," Tristofer assured him. "We know it. There's no way any of us will ever forget it."

Breslin took a deep breath. "How were you able to create that mark and such a perfect plan to get us the hammer and reveal Nar's location? You're no wizard. None of us ever were."

In the midst of taking a drink of water from a nearby goblet, Kasnar choked.

"Perfect? You think it was a perfect plan? Hardly. You're right, lad, I'm no spellcaster. However, that doesn't mean I didn't have the time to learn."

"How does one learn to cast spells?" Tristofer inquired, insanely curious.

"With time," Kasnar answered, giving the young scholar a patronizing smile. "With lots of time. And it doesn't hurt to have several Narian spell books to guide you along."

"Narian spell books?" Tristofer repeated, shocked. "Narians practiced jhorun?"

Kasnar reached over to the nearest bookshelf and pulled out a dilapidated blue tome from a stack of books in similar condition. He passed it to Tristofer, who was dumbstruck.

"Apparently they dabbled," Kasnar told him. "And fortunately for me, this volume was mixed in with one of the loads of books I was given by Rahygren, Bastion's son."

Tristofer was ecstatic. "The Narians practiced jhorun! I knew it!"

"You did not," Kasnar argued. "You just said so yourself. Now, let me continue."

"Get to the part where Bastion learns he had found Nar," Athos told him impatiently. Although he'd deny it if asked, he had become completely enraptured by Kasnar's tale.

Kasnar sighed. "Fine."

For those of you who are curious how Bastion learned what he had discovered, it was by accident. For that, let me switch briefly to Bastion's routine when his gold ran low.

Eager to hide his new fortune from prying eyes, Bastion only made the journey to Nar once every couple of months. Once there he'd collect some of the smallest trinkets he could find, which usually meant pieces of jewelry, small weapons, and the like. Whatever he chose to bring back had to be small enough to be concealed on his person as he didn't want to be stopped in the streets by anyone.

One day he came back from one of his pillaging trips with his customary load of jewels and artifacts. However, on this trip he had found a set of bejeweled wrist bands, and deciding he wanted to keep them for himself, he chose to wear them back. When he approached his usual contact, an unsavory fellow who stank of rotten fish…

"How would you possibly know this?" Athos demanded. "You said it yourself. You never left this room."

"This was prior to my arrival as a prisoner held in Nar," Kasnar explained. "Rahygren and Krisken, that would be Rahygren's wife, have had numerous heated arguments, many of which I was able to overhear. The two of them were at each other's throats constantly. At any rate, Bastion had brought this character to his house several times, presumably to make riskier and riskier deals. This fellow suspected Bastion was holding out on him and wanted a larger and larger cut of the profits in exchange for his silence."

"I'm surprised Rahygren agreed to that," Venk murmured.

"He didn't want to," Kasnar agreed. "He must have ranted and raved like a lunatic, if one was to believe Krisken. As the number of deals increased, their profits decreased, and soon Bastion was berating his son to look for a way to tie up loose ends."

Venk covered Lukas' ears with both hands.

"I think we all know what that means. There's no need to go into further details."

Kasnar nodded. "As you wish."

When Bastion met with the fellow, like he typically did at whatever tavern the two of them frequented, the man noticed the bands immediately. He demanded to know how Bastion had acquired them.

Thinking quickly, Bastion claimed he had relieved the bands from a drunken traveler. Liking how they had looked, he decided to keep them.

Bastion learned of the nature of the bands and where they hailed from because as soon as he returned, he began searching the blacksmith shops. The search for valuable trinkets was over. He had discovered a much more lucrative commodity. Armor.

The armor was the key, Bastion figured. He had to unlock the secrets of the armor, and in order to do that, he needed a scholar. He began financing excursions to other cities. He hired mercenaries to do his searching for him, thereby leaving him with an irrefutable alibi in case any questionable actions had to be taken. Word trickled back to him of a toymaker who could make wonderful toys and was only interested in exchanging the toys for genuine Narian artifacts. He had one of his men approach me and claim that they wanted to purchase the most expensive figurine I had available and to personally deliver it to Bykram.

I'm ashamed to say that I fell for it.

"That explains how your path and Bastion's crossed," Breslin thoughtfully observed. "But that doesn't explain how jhorun became involved. What happened there? Bastion simply gave you a spell book? Didn't he check the titles before he gave them to you?"

"He couldn't," Kasnar said with a shrug. "He couldn't read Narian. I could. I had been researching it for so long that by then, I had taught it to myself. To this day I don't think he realizes what he's done. May I finish now?"

"Sorry."

As I was perusing through the latest batch of books delivered by my captor, I was startled to find a tome of spells. I was so surprised that I flipped the book over and re-verified it was Narian. It was. It was written in the same fluid language that the rest of the books had been written in, so this was no fluke. Narians had jhorun and they obviously had used it.

I don't think I need to tell you that I read that book from cover to cover. Not only did the Narians practice jhorun, but as with the humans, some had become very adept at it. One such Narian, a skilled spellcaster by the name of Oricfed Galfodin, decided to put his favorite spells to the pen. That book was the result.

Most of Oricfed's spells were useless, as what need have I to turn brown leather boots black? But interspersed throughout the book were much more useful spells, such as how to keep metal as hot as you want without melting it. While it made for some incredibly interesting reading, it still didn't help me out of my present predicament. Nothing in the book was powerful enough to break out of this cell. Perhaps Rahygren had checked the book after all and, since it was harmless, felt he could safely give it to me. I don't know. I was discouraged. I memorized what spells that I deemed useful and returned to my research as I had Bastion checking on my progress every three or four days.

I kept returning to the volume of spells, as I couldn't help but feel there was something I was missing. It was a book of spells! There must be something in there that could help me escape! Two more hours of fruitless searching yielded no extra insight, so in disgust, I threw the book across the room. It hit the back wall and slid down on to the mattress, falling open somewhere around the middle of the book. The scholar in me detested mistreating any type of book, so I bent to retrieve it when I noticed the page it had fallen on. There were two pages that had been stuck together, and the jolt against the wall separated them. While parts of the page had ripped away, as whatever adhesive was holding the two pages together was too strong to break, the note on the page was still legible.

It was simply entitled 'layering.'

"As in the layering of spells?" Tristofer eagerly asked. "Shardwyn started to tell us how complicated a multi-layered spell can be."

"I'm not familiar with that name. I'm assuming he's a wizard?"

Tristofer nodded. "Yes."

The note was only three sentences long, but it was enough to get my hopes soaring again. Oricfed wrote that it was possible to combine two spells together and make them work in tandem with one another. Everyone with me so far?

Breslin, Athos, Venk, Lukas, and Tristofer all nodded excitedly.

Good. I thought back to what this book contained. Spells. Lots and lots of small insignificant spells that individually are inconsequential, but when layered with another, render completely unexpected results. I resolved right then that I had to master each and every spell contained in the book. And, funnily enough, I had to come to terms with the fact that I clearly had some level of jhorun in me as I could perform several of the less complex spells contained in the book and attain successful results.

You can imagine I kept this hidden from Rahygren. Every time he left me alone, I'd retrieve that book and begin to experiment. Let me tell all of you that when it comes to mastering your jhorun, it's not an easy thing to do.

"How did you do it?" Tristofer softly inquired.

"With time," Kasnar answered. "Something that I had lots of."

I began with a spell that would sketch out the dimensions of the room I was in. The spell was designed for cartographers, and I figured if I could make it draw my chambers here, then I could start with that.

It took many attempts to get it right. Jhorun is very fickle. Your mind plays just as an important role as does the spell itself. If you're not thinking clearly about what you want the spell to do then it can easily backfire or give you unexpected results. I won't bore you with the details, but suffice it to say that after much trial and error I could get it to map out not only my room but the existing city of Nar.

I discovered Nar is much larger than I ever dreamt it'd be.

With that spell mastered, I moved on to the others. I learned so many, and could perform them so well, that I then started to experiment with layering. I fetched a fresh sheet of parchment, laid it on the table there, and tried my cartography spell once more, only this time I added in a seeker's spell, specifying I wanted to know where my family was by showing me on the map. At the same time, I imagined holding a map of Lentari, with dots indicating where my family was at that moment.

It didn't go so well. I got my map of Lentari, but it had so many dots all over it that I could barely recognize the map for what it was. I tried again. And again. And again. Each time I got something a little different.

With luck, and a little perseverance, I chanced upon the key to making a multi-layered spell work. You had to have all possible outcomes planned out. Give it a 'if this happens, then do that' clause. I went through every formulation I could think of and asked yet again for the seeker/cartography spell to show me my family. A single dot appeared, and it was right over the Bohanis where Borahgg was.

I was elated! I modified the spell to map out the city of Borahgg and then show me where my family was. I cried right then. There, in the family home that I remembered, was a dot with a tiny label next to it: Neika. Maelnar was nearby, as were several of my siblings and their children. It had worked!

I should also mention that it had taken me several months just to modify my spell from showing my family in Lentari to showing them in Borahgg. It wasn't easy, but it was possible, and that gave me hope.

Now that I knew I could do it, I expanded my experiments and tried to see if I could find inanimate objects. I thought back to my home and knew that Neika would never do anything to the map I had received from the little human girl all those years ago, so I began the painstaking process of modifying the spell to no longer look for my family but instead, display the location of the map in Borahgg.

Sure enough, a tiny dot appeared on my map. It was right where I remembered it being, in my home. I decided to see if anyone else in Borahgg had anything from Nar, so I modified my map again to see if there were other types of Narian artifacts nearby. You can imagine my dismay when after six months of creating my spell, nothing appeared on the paper.

To make sure I had the spell right, I thought about my favorite chisel back in my workshop. I modified the spell, again, to find and display that tool on my map. It worked! It was still in my workshop, provided my workshop was still mine. The map merely displayed the chisel's location; it didn't tell me whether or not the workshop was still mine. I had hoped it was.

"Why not just send a message?" Venk interrupted. "Why go to so much trouble to create a multi-layer spell when a simple plea for help would have sufficed?"

"Rahygren began to suspect I was up to no good," Kasnar answered. "Bastion had passed away years ago, and unfortunately for me, Rahygren took over the family business. He was much smarter than his father ever was. He kept a much closer eye on me. The only way I was allowed to work on the spell was by convincing him that I was attempting to decipher ancient pictographs. I knew he would only believe that story for so long, but I had to try. I needed time. The problem was, I had run out."

"What do you mean?" Venk asked as he nervously looked around, as though Rahygren himself would jump out of the shadows at any moment.

"Suspecting I was plotting something, probably because my attitude had gone through a complete reversal. I was happy, even hopeful. I guess I hadn't ever been like that because Rahygren grew very nervous. A week later he installed that behemoth of a door."

Everyone turned to look at the heavily damaged iron door fifteen feet away.

"I needed a way to defeat the door. Rahygren alone had the key, which he kept on a pendant he wore at all times. There was no way to wrest it away from him as I had become old and feeble. He had me stymied, and he knew it. What he didn't know, though, is that I had a few tricks up my own sleeves. I just needed time. And thankfully, that's what he gave me since he was certain there was no way I was ever going to get through that door without the key.

Confident in my new-found abilities, I began to formulate an escape plan. First, I had to solve the door problem. I remembered reading something about special tools with enhanced power, which the Narians favored. Maybe something like that could break the door down? I had to look and now, thanks to the spell book and my ability to find inanimate objects, I might be able to find something Topside that could be used to free me.

The seeker/cartography spell took close to a year to write. It was my most complex spell ever, but if I wanted to be successful, I knew I had to be as thorough as possible. Any changes once it had been completed would necessitate a year-long wait to plot it all out again. Once I was done, I activated the spell and held my breath. Would there even be anything out there to find, let alone useful enough to help me attain the freedom I so craved?

My map lit up with speckled dots. Turns out remnants of the once mighty Narian people were everywhere. The problem was, however, I didn't know enough about what could be out there to include that in the spell.

"No labels," Breslin guessed.
Kasnar nodded.

There were plenty of things to find, but not enough information to identify. What I needed now was to figure out what I was looking for. What was capable of breaking down that door? Maybe a chisel to cut away the stone from the locking bars? Perhaps a file to cut my way through the door? Perhaps a drill to bore through the locking mechanism?

The answer came when I learned of the existence of the power hammers. There was a tool that was capable of pulverizing the largest boulders with minimal effort. Surely a tool of this magnitude could help me out. However, the more I researched, the more I realized that the hammers were closely guarded secrets. Their construction was passed from father to son by word of mouth only.

My gaze dropped to my map. I had the means to locate one! Surely, I must try! Hopeful again, I returned to my spell book and began crafting an even more complex spell, as this time I needed to narrow my focus. After a year and a half, I was ready. I activated the spell. Much to my chagrin, nothing appeared. There were simply no power hammers left in existence. My hopes fell. Then the tinker in me wondered if the parts to make one still existed. I went back to my books and learned there were four parts comprising a power hammer: handle, head, counterweight, and helix.

"You're talking about the ruby whorl, right?" Tristofer asked.
"To the Narians, it was simply a helix," Kasnar explained.

Two years later I was ready yet again. I activated the spell and waited to see what would happen. Four dots appeared on my map. I held my breath. Since I had specified I wanted one of each component, I knew that I had found what I was looking for. My luck held!

I studied the four areas on the map where the dots were. One was in a tiny lake. Another was in a waterfall on the eastern coast. The third location was in the Selekais.

"And the fourth …" Athos prompted.

Venk sighed. "The fourth is Dual Tree. Pay attention."

Kasnar gingerly picked the hammer up and inspected it. Turning it over and over in his hands, he looked up at his grandson.

"Which location held which component?"

Breslin tapped the hammer's head. "This we found at the waterfall. The weight was at the bottom of the nixie lake, and the gem was in the collection of a zweigelan. The helix was a real pleasure to obtain, let me tell you."

Surprised, Kasnar smoothed down his long thin beard. "Really?"

"No. I was joking."

"Ah."

Kasnar closed his eyes. Breslin eyed the others before subtly clearing his throat. Kasnar's eyes snapped open.

"I'm still alive, lad."

"We thought you had fallen asleep."

"Oh. It's a distinct possibility." Kasnar chuckled. "Will you answer me something?"

Breslin nodded. "Of course."

"Was there an entrance to Nar in the cave under the tree?"

Breslin nodded again. "Aye. That's how we entered the mountain."

The frail old dwarf clapped his hands with glee. "I knew it! If only I had time to look!"

"It's good that you didn't," Breslin pointed out.

Kasnar sat up straighter. "Eh? How so?"

"Had you gone into the mountain, you would have encountered a sealed Narian door. Without a helix, you wouldn't have made it very far."

"And because you had the hammer, you were allowed to pass," Kasnar thoughtfully observed.

"Exactly," Breslin confirmed.

"I think it's high time we got out of here," Venk declared as he rose to his feet. He pulled Lukas up as well. "I don't know about any of you, but I'd like to be long gone from here before our gracious host returns."

Breslin scrambled to his feet. He gently picked up his

grandfather and set him on the ground. Kasnar slapped his hands away.

"I may not be as young as you," the wizened little dwarf snapped as he straightened as much of his three-and-a-half-foot frame as he could, "but I am no invalid. I can walk."

"We may have to run," Athos pointed out as he pulled his large battle axe from his back. He also pulled his smaller close-range axe and began fussing with his two baldrics crisscrossing across his back.

"What are you doing?" Venk wanted to know. He caught his brother's large single-bladed black axe as it was thrown to him.

"Can you carry that for me?"

Comprehension dawned. Venk nodded and fastened the axe to his baldric so that it lay next to his crossbow. Having finished arranging the leather straps, Athos motioned for Breslin to pick his grandfather up and place him in the harness he had created on his back. Nodding gratefully, Breslin moved toward his grandfather.

"Don't even think about it," Kasnar warned. "I'll not be slung over anyone's shoulder like a slab of meat, thank you very much."

Frustration flared.

"Want to see grandmother again?" Breslin snapped.

Kasnar's mouth closed.

"I thought so. This is not ideal, but it'll get us out of here. Master Athos is right. I have a sneaking suspicion we'll need to make a speedy departure. There we go."

Breslin easily lifted his frail grandfather onto Athos' back and strapped him into place. Once he was sure Kasnar was secure, he picked up Athos' smaller axe and added it to his own belt.

"Everyone ready? Let's go."

Tristofer was flabbergasted.

"We can't go! We're in Nar! We have so much to do!"

"What's more important?" Breslin countered back at him. "Stay here longer to look around and run the risk of running into this Rahygren fellow or getting out of here in one piece so you can be the one to announce the discovery of Nar?"

Tristofer hurriedly slung his pack over his shoulder. "It can wait."

Breslin grunted. "I thought as much. Let's go. As soon as we make it outside, Rhamalli can take us back to the valley just as quickly as he can. Rhamalli, is there any chance you can hear us?"

The dragon's voice was silent.

"We're too far inside the mountain. Let's get outside. Everyone stick together."

They followed their own tracks through the dust and emerged back into the large main hall. Every few feet they'd all hear a cry of anguish as Kasnar spotted example after example of Nar's desecration by the Delvehearth family.

"A pox on that accursed family," Kasnar muttered softly to himself. "No amount of punishment is fit for the crimes this city has suffered."

"What about what they did to you?" Lukas asked, looking up at the old man riding on his uncle's back. "They kept you here for so long. Aren't you angry about that?"

"Aye, I am, young master," Kasnar admitted as he smiled down at the underling. "But I forgave the Delvehearths years ago."

"Why?" the underling inquired.

"Because I was raised to see the good in everyone, no matter how foul the person. They imprisoned me, aye. They kept me away from my family, aye. I choose not to dwell on that. Instead, I look forward to seeing my beloved Neika again. I yearn to see my son again, and get to know Breslin here. He was but a very young lad when I left."

"You will, grandfather," Breslin called back from the front of their group. "You will. I promise."

Emerging into the rapidly lightening room, Breslin came to a sudden stop. He held up his arm and signaled the others to stop as well. Standing in front of the main door, blocking any attempts of escape, were five dwarves. All were outfitted in confiscated Narian armor and all had crossbows drawn, loaded, and ready to fire. All five were aimed straight at them.

"That's far enough," a gruff voice barked out at them. "Lay down your arms and surrender before we turn you into pincushions."

Chapter 13 — Just Say No to Bullying

I see you admiring my arrow launcher," the lead dwarf gloated. "It has the capabilities of firing dozens of arrows a minute while you'll be lucky to get off a few shots. Just one of the many lucrative discoveries I've found in here. Now, for the last time, surrender!"

The owner of the gruff voice was wearing a set of Narian armor encrusted with glittering diamonds and sapphires. It had to be the most exquisite suit of armor Venk had ever seen.

The second thing he noticed was a large device set up on a tripod. It was big, bulky, and gave the impression the device had only been created to do dastardly deeds. Its long, cylindrical barrel consisted of straight metal tubes, forming the perimeter of the barrel.

The other two henchmen gripped dense, compact shields a quarter of the size of a normal shield, ugly, tarnished things with many dents and scuffs.

"You must be Rahygren," Breslin spat out, standing up to his full height and pulling the power hammer from his belt. "I hold you and your family responsible for desecrating the lost city of Nar. We will not be the ones surrendering. You will."

Rahygren eyed the power hammer.

"How did-- Where did you ... I don't know how--" he sputtered. "New plan. You give me that hammer and I'll let you choose the manner in which you die. That is my one and only offer to you."

The henchmen's shields pinged sharply and suddenly grew massive in size. Both of the thugs crumpled under the unexpected weight.

Venk eyed Breslin, who returned his puzzled expression. Clearly these foes were unfamiliar with their own equipment.

"What's going on here?" Athos whispered to his brother. "This doesn't make any sense."

Breslin whispered back, "I'm willing to bet they've never stepped foot in Nar before."

"Nonsense," Tristofer argued, as he and Lukas inched closer. "They obviously have."

"Rahygren has, aye, but not them," Breslin argued. "Look at them! They're lost! They're staring at the cavern as though they've never seen it before. And, I'm quite sure they haven't."

Athos nodded. "Hired mercenaries."

Rahygren's annoyed face turned livid with rage. "Enough talk! Kill them! Kill them all! Leave no survivors!"

One of the henchmen took an oblong object the size of a clenched fist from his belt. In a second, it began ticking loudly and the man threw the object directly at Breslin.

The ticking device began expanding in size, turning into a boulder worthy of a trebuchet.

Breslin calmly stood his ground and swung the power hammer as the object neared. There was a loud clang and the boulder reversed directions. It crashed directly onto the henchman who threw it, pinning him beneath his indestructible Narian armor.

"What are you waiting for?" Rahygren demanded as he swung his gaze back to the arrow shooter. "Fire! Kill them!"

Suddenly the air was filled with arrows whooshing by at an alarming rate. Small nuggets of stone flew through the air as dozens of arrows slammed into the rock wall. Breslin stepped in front of the boy and took the full brunt of the relentless attack. Arrow after arrow struck him on his chest, pummeling him so hard that he had to take a few steps backward. However, the numerous arrows bounced harmlessly off his armor.

"So that's why your armor never appears dented," Athos observed, appearing at Breslin's side. "It's Narian!"

Breslin nodded and held a finger to his lips.

Movement in their peripheral vision caught their attention. The shooter was reloading!

"Move, scholar! Find cover! Hurry before that infernal machine starts up again! Venk! Get over here, now!"

Right on cue, the arrows began appearing again, zipping by dangerously close. Athos steered them toward a group of large, crumbling slabs of stone. Athos squatted and hooked his shoulder under the slab; Venk mirrored his actions a few moments later. They both heaved, fully expecting the table to tip onto its side. It didn't budge.

"Breslin!" Venk snapped. "We need to tip this thing over! Hurry!"

Breslin whipped out the power hammer and gave the stone slab a solid thunk, thinking it'd be more than adequate to get the job done. The resulting blow didn't knock the table over, but it did start a series of spidery cracks that crisscrossed across the surface. Moments later the table collapsed into a pile of gravel.

With a curse, Venk pulled his son close and crouched low behind a second table.

"We're not going to last long if we don't do something!" Athos angrily told them. "Think they're going to run out of arrows? Think again."

Breslin tried to peek up and over the lip of their upturned table but had to dart back down again as three arrows were instantly fired his way.

"I'm open for suggestions."

Tristofer pushed his way past Venk and Athos and

grabbed Breslin's arm. Maintaining a surprisingly strong grip on his arm, the scholar yanked him over to where he had been crouched.

"What are you doing? Blast it, Tristofer, I don't have time for this! We must — what is all of this?"

Breslin noticed several rows of mathematical calculations scrawled out on the stone floor. Also visible was a big black X that had been marked on the wall. Curiosity getting the better of him, Breslin turned back to the scholar and noticed that Tristofer's hands were black. In fact, his right hand still clutched a lump of charcoal he must have fished out of one of his pockets. Tristofer pointed at the X.

"Here! Quickly! Hit this spot with your hammer!"

"What? Tristofer, we don't —"

"Stop arguing with me and for once, do as I say! Hit it! Now!!"

Gritting his teeth, Breslin cocked his arm and swung a good, solid blow at the wall, directly on the X. They heard snapping and creaking as a set of cracks snaked up the wall toward the cavern's ceiling.

Rahygren's henchman dove out of the way just as several tons of calcium carbonate crushed the Narian apparatus flat. While Rahygren cursed and swore at his bad luck, Breslin shooed everyone through an open door leading to a small courtyard. Silently they ran, retracing their steps back to the imperial palace.

"We only have a few minutes while Rahygren regroups," Breslin warned, easily matching the sprint that Venk and Athos had set.

With Kasnar still strapped securely to his back, Athos snatched up his nephew and tossed him to his brother. Venk slung Lukas over his shoulder and ran. Not even Kasnar's extra weight, or Lukas', could have slowed the two brothers down as they sprinted through the deserted streets. On and on they ran, stopping only long enough for Breslin to unlock a sealed door. Once they were all through, Tristofer called out to his companions.

"Wait a moment." He was clutching at a painful stitch in his side and couldn't seem to catch his breath. "There weren't any sealed doors on the way to the palace last time. We must have made a wrong turn somewhere."

"Would you like to go back and see whereabouts we went wrong?" Breslin sarcastically asked. He, too, was panting heavily. Dwarves, with their short legs, just weren't meant for running.

"I'm closing this door," Athos declared. He pushed the circular door closed and once he verified it wouldn't open unless one had a ruby helix, like the one on Breslin's hammer, he turned to his companions. "So if we're lost, how do we find the palace?"

"If you had listened to me, this wouldn't have happened."

Athos twisted his head to look over his right shoulder.

"What did you say, old man?"

Kasnar cuffed Athos on the back of his head, knocking his helmet down over his eyes.

"I tried to tell you before we were headed the wrong way but you didn't pay attention."

Athos growled as he tipped his helmet back into place.

"Then speak up. Everyone's running. I'm running. Unless you shout it out, I won't be able to hear you. Do you know which way to the palace or not?"

Kasnar smacked Athos' helmet again, once more.

"There's no need to be rude, Master Athos. Turn left here, then follow the street east. It'll lead straight to the palace."

"How do you know?" Venk asked, careful to stand far enough away from his brother so that he was out of Kasnar's reach.

The frail dwarf pointed at a nearby sign, covered with unfamiliar symbols.

"Because the sign says so."

"It could say anything," Tristofer protested, unhappy he wasn't able to read the Narian script. "You could just be making this up."

Kasnar leaned forward and peered at Tristofer closely.

"Aren't you a scholar? How can you be a professed expert on Narian culture and not be able to read a simple sign that says, 'This way to the palace'? It's the first thing I learned how to do. If you can understand archaic dwarfish, then Narian script should not be that far off."

"Archaic dwarfish? Is that why the script looks familiar?"

Kasnar looked down at Athos and leaned over to whisper in his ear.

"How long have you had to travel with him?"

Athos snorted so loudly that his own exhaled breath shook his mustache, which promptly tickled his nose.

"Gah! Stop that!"

While Athos rubbed his nose to get the prickly sensations to pass, Breslin turned to look back the way they had come. Thankfully no one could hear any signs they were being pursued. However, chances were that Rahygren and his men had probably guessed that they intended to hole up in the palace and more than likely knew the direct route there. Breslin and his companions had unwisely chosen the scenic route.

"Stop dawdling and get moving!" Kasnar scolded him, snapping him out of his reverie. "We'd better get to the palace before they do. Hurry!"

Once more they were running like mad, only this time no one spoke so they could all hear Kasnar's directions.

"Up this street. Turn right once you clear that large pile of rubble."

The group turned right and ran past quiet storefronts.

"Now left here, and then an immediate right."

On and on they ran. Venk thought his lungs were going to burst. Finally, after what felt like hours of running, when in actuality it had only been about ten minutes, they were once more standing in the large courtyard against the eastern wall of the great cavern. There, as before, was the large arched doorway leading into the imperial palace. However, now it was guarded by a lone henchman, standing at alert in front of the slightly ajar palace doors.

"Wizards be damned," Breslin swore. Had Rahygren managed to get here first? If so, where was he?

"I think there's only one," Athos reported as he skimmed the area from the safety of the distant street corner.

"What do we do now?" Tristofer asked. "The longer we wait the more likely it is that our adversaries catch up!"

Venk felt a tap on his shoulder and turned around. Athos was gently lowering his passenger to the ground.

"Take Kasnar. I'll deal with this."

"What do you think you'll be able to do?" Venk asked. He pushed his way over until he was standing directly in his brother's path. "You have no idea what weapons they have, or what they can do. Don't even think about doing something as crazy as this."

Ignoring his brother, Athos looked over at Breslin. "Be ready to run. Venk, damn it, put on the harness and let Kasnar back in."

For once, Venk did as he was told. Once the old man was sitting comfortably on his back, Venk turned to Athos.

"What's your plan?"

Athos pulled out both of his orixes and flicked his wrists, snapping both of them open.

"I'm going to create a distraction."

Giving Lukas a fond pat on his head, Athos quietly snuck off toward the castle, keeping in the darkened shadows of nearby buildings where the illuminated gold chain didn't venture. Getting as close as he dared, Athos lined up the mercenary in his sights and cocked an arm. He'd made more difficult shots than this back home, so getting an orix to buzz directly in front of the unsuspecting guard should be a piece of cake.

Athos hurled his green orix on a perfect elliptical path, startling the guard

The problem was, Athos noted with disgust, the man hadn't abandoned his post. Yet.

Time for another try.

He caught the orix as it returned and threw the weapon again, increasing the spin and changing the angle. The orix spun faster and widened its orbit. Once more the emerald green orix buzzed by the guard, but this time it passed several feet away. Confused, the guard stared at the rapidly moving object. He cocked his head, trying to determine what he was looking at. When two more objects whirled by, he moved from his post.

"He's doing it!" Tristofer whispered excitedly. "The guard

is moving off! We'll be able to sneak back inside the palace in just a few moments!"

Breslin and Venk watched as the unsuspecting guard moved from his position at the palace entrance. Breslin was impressed. Athos was a master with his two orixes. He had the weapons skirting around buildings, darting through open windows, and even brushing by the guard with only inches to spare. They all watched as the guard, wearing a determined expression on his face, ducked into the darkened alley to investigate.

Everyone heard it: the sharp metallic clang. Someone had just taken a blow to the head. Had it been Athos? Should one of them go check to make sure he was alright?

Venk squared his shoulders and was about to run across the open courtyard to see whether or not his brother needed help when Breslin grabbed his arm and pulled him to a stop.

"Our time just ran out. Listen! They approach from the north!"

Everyone listened quietly. Venk cursed to himself. Breslin was right. They were coming, and from the sounds of it, they were approaching fast. Without checking to see what the others were going to do, Venk taxed his tiring lungs to the breaking point by sprinting across the street to the palace door. A quick backward check verified that everyone was easily keeping up.

Breslin reached the palace door first and grabbed Lukas. He tossed him, single-handedly, up and over the crunched chair and through the open door. He looked up in time to see the scholar stare at him in shock.

"Tristofer, get inside! Hurry!"

Venk hurdled the crumpled chair, propping the door open, and turned around in time to see someone dressed in a full suit of golden armor, just like the one Rahygren's man had been wearing, run from one darkened street to another. Was that Athos? It had to be. If it had been one of their adversaries then he would have come straight at them.

Breslin swung the power hammer at the chair in a desperate bid to dislodge the bent metal seat that had been keeping the huge palace door open. However, Kasnar's captor had just appeared from the shadows and was now running all out to get to the door first.

The first blow echoed noisily all throughout the street. The crumpled chair bent inward even farther, but since the chair had been made of the same metal as the famous armor, it refused to break.

Shocked that the chair hadn't been knocked loose by the ferocity of the blow, Breslin hit it again. And again. The only thing he accomplished was to wedge the damaged remains of the chair farther into the wall and the door. There'd be no dislodging that chair now.

Cursing, Breslin gathered up Lukas and ran after Venk and Kasnar. Tristofer barely kept up.

"Through there," Kasnar instructed, pointing to an open doorway on the left. "You'll find a long hallway. Take the second door on your left. Hurry!"

Trusting Kasnar to know what he was doing, Breslin followed the two of them deep into the heart of the palace, ducking through unremarkable doorways and sprinting down endless hallways.

Kasnar suddenly pointed to another arched door, one that had been damaged and was incapable of closing.

"In there. Go!"

"But the door won't close!" Breslin protested, giving the broken door an angry glance.

"Irrelevant. Trust me!"

Once they were inside the room, Tristofer gasped with surprise. The room was almost the size of the entry courtyard. The floors were completely covered with a type of marble that had tiny gold flakes all throughout, causing the entire ground to give off an eerie glow. Hallways and doors were everywhere.

"This is the king and queen's private chambers," Kasnar told them. He pointed at a statue of a stoic dwarf sitting resolutely on a gilded throne. "Just behind the statue is a hidden door. Find it. Open it. Hurry!"

Venk set Kasnar down and joined Breslin inspecting the walls. Smoky gray quartz lined every bit of the walls in the royal chambers, and it appeared to be a single unbroken surface. There was no way a door could be hidden there. Kasnar must have been mistaken.

Breslin gave an exasperated sigh. "There's nothing here, grandfather. No door." He pulled the hammer from his belt. "I can make one, though."

Kasnar irritably pushed by his grandson and ran a withered hand across the smooth quartz. His hand stopped about eye level. A tiny indentation was revealed. Had that always been there? Kasnar pushed. With a loud click, a doorway formed and swung inward.

"Get inside! All of you!"

"But it's dark in there!" Tristofer whined, leaning around their frail guide to peer inside the dark opening.

Venk shoved Lukas through the dark doorway while simultaneously grabbing Tristofer's beard and pulling him forward.

"Ow! How rude! You don't have to —"

Breslin elbowed him in the stomach as he pushed the door closed. A few moments later a three-foot section of golden chain, embedded in the ceiling overhead, began to glow, giving off a welcome, albeit cold light.

Breslin placed his ear to the door. Venk did the same. He looked at his son and held a finger to his lips.

Rahygren had arrived in the outer room.

Tristofer tapped Venk on the shoulder. Venk promptly brushed the annoyance aside. Tristofer tapped again. Venk spun and his mouth fell open. He nudged Breslin, whose own reaction mirrored his.

They were in an armory. Not a large armory designed to equip a battalion of men, but enough to arm several people should the need arise. This was one of the Narian king's four private armories, Kasnar explained. This one had been designed to be used for emergency purposes only.

"How did you know this was here?" Tristofer wanted to know.

"I saw the door here a number of years ago," Kasnar explained, correctly guessing what his companions were thinking. "As you can imagine, I decided to keep the information to myself."

"You clearly had access to the city," Tristofer argued. "Why didn't you just escape?"

"Look at me. Do I look like I could overpower my captor? I had an escort everywhere I went. I think once Rahygren knew I was incapable of escaping he deliberately allowed me out of my room. However, only with an escort."

"That's mean," Lukas softly exclaimed.

"Tell me about it," Kasnar agreed.

Three suits of armor, including one that was practically oozing with jewels, sat somberly on their display stands. Three shields, adorned with the Narian crest, an upside-down hammer amidst a purple backdrop of elegant scrollwork, was visible on each. Half a dozen swords, short swords, axes, and daggers were also sitting neatly on their shelves. All sported a layer of dust several inches thick.

Breslin, Venk, and Tristofer each moved to the suits of armor and began dusting them off, as though seeing the wondrous suits looking anything less than pristine was offensive.

"You already have a set," Venk told Breslin. He reverently picked up a helmet, dusted it off on his trousers, and started to replace his own.

"Leave it," Kasnar whispered. "There are more important things in here to worry about than that infernal armor."

Venk looked longingly back at the glittering pieces of silver and gold. It was genuine Narian armor! It was easily worth a king's fortune!

"I said to let it go, lad," Kasnar softly told him. "It's only a matter of time before we're discovered. Here, take this instead."

Venk looked down at the proffered gift, which turned out to be a dusty, tarnished, metal arm band about three inches wide and half an inch thick.

"What am I supposed to do with this?"

"Put it on. Breslin, you do the same. Even you, Tristofer."

Kasnar handed Breslin and Tristofer identical arm bands and waited.

Breslin stared disbelievingly at the ugly metal band and eyed his grandfather as though he had gone crazy.

"What good is this going to do me?"

"You'll thank me later. Now, do you see that device down on the shelf, next to your left knee?"

"Aye."

"Take that."

"What is it?"

"Something we're going to need. Let's see what else we have in here. Ah. Master Venk, here lad, you take this."

Venk picked up a device loosely resembling a crossbow, but without its limbs. Instead of an arrow track for the bolt to sit in there was another row of metal tubes forming a cylinder. A metal wheel with a small protuberance was situated on the right side. The undersides of the device, directly to the left of where the metal tubes were, had a small rectangular opening with grooves in all four corners.

"What's this?" Venk asked in a hushed tone.

Kasnar wasn't listening. The tiny fellow was down on his knees, searching frantically for something on the lower shelves. He slowly regained his feet and held out an object that was about a foot long by six inches wide.

"Now, turn that there and be ready."

Venk smiled. This was a smaller version of the arrow shooter that Rahygren had used on them.

"Slide that bolt," Kasnar urged his grandson, pointing to the top right corner of the door. "That'll keep the door from opening in case they find the release for it."

"I hear you in there! There's nowhere to hide, fools! Surrender!"

Breslin pushed his way past his companions so that he could talk to his grandfather. He held up a shiny object the size of his water bag.

"So this is a portable arrow shooter? How do I arm it?"

"I'm not sure," Kasnar admitted. "I've only ever read about them. I've never seen them used before."

"What if it doesn't do anything?" Breslin asked. "Why bother taking it?"

"Because you're standing in an *armory*, lad," Kasnar patiently pointed out.

"While I appreciate the thought that you'd want us to be

able to protect ourselves," Tristofer began, holding the small shield as though it belonged to a child, "but I cannot see how this will be that much of a help."

Breslin, holding the power hammer tightly in his hand, made a move to conk Tristofer over his head. The small child-sized shield that he had been given clicked loudly and rapidly expanded its size, becoming a durable, lightweight, full-sized shield.

Tristofer was impressed. "Very well. You talked me into it. I'll keep it."

Kasnar shook his head. "A wise move, lad."

Fifteen minutes later Rahygren's voice called out to them from within the king's private chamber.

"This is your last warning! This is the only deal I'll make with you. Surrender now and give up the hammer! That's the only reason you're still alive."

"How many are out there?" Kasnar suddenly asked.

"Including Rahygren, five. Maybe six, depending on whether or not the guard Athos lured away was with the original group. Why do you want to know?"

"You do realize that as of right now we outnumber them?"

"Aye, we do, grandfather, but in this scenario, we can't count you, Lukas, or Tristofer as being combat ready. Therefore we number three, and at the moment, with Athos out there somewhere, we number two."

"We have the advantage," Kasnar stated.

"In what way?"

"They don't know the true power of the hammer."

Breslin was unimpressed.

"So? Neither do we."

"We show them."

"And risk Lukas?" Breslin shook his head. "I will not involve an underling in any way."

"Lukas is already involved," Kasnar pointed out, "whether you like it or not."

A loud commotion sounded outside the door. Someone pounded on a nearby wall.

"Come out now and I promise to let you live!"

"You promise us?" Breslin barked back. "What does the word of a thief and kidnapper mean to us? Absolutely nothing! This is my final offer. You and your men lay down your arms. If you do that—"

A rumbling began and grew steadily stronger. Everyone clapped their hands over their ears as an earsplitting shriek rent the air. Armor and weapons fell from their shelves as the tremors grew in intensity.

"This is it!" Tristofer wailed. "This is the end! We must surrender! We must…"

Venk snatched a gilded mace from the ground and conked it over Tristofer's head. The scholar collapsed into a heap.

Lukas stared at his father with wide-eyed astonishment.

"Been wanting to do that for quite some time now," Venk muttered angrily to himself.

The deafening wail was so loud now they couldn't hear each other speak. He nervously eyed his son. He had no idea how they were going to get out of this predicament.

* * *

Quietly, Athos crept through the deserted streets, keeping his back to the shadows. He strained his ears to listen for any other sounds in the quiet, tomb-like city; however the only sounds he could hear were the loud wheezes his own breaths were making.

Cursing his foul luck for realizing he was lost, Athos darted across a row of abandoned buildings and knelt down next to a large pile of rubble and listened. Was it his imagination? It sounded like a high-pitched buzzing noise had started, and it was coming from slightly behind him and to the right.

Athos rose cautiously to his feet. He hadn't made it more than three steps when a sharp voice drew him to a stop.

"Oi! Waxrobbe! Where the hell have you been?"

Athos turned to see one of Rahygren's henchman standing at the nearest intersection. He angrily beckoned him over.

"Those bastards have holed up somewhere in the palace. Let's go! Stop dawdling about and move your arse!"

Athos grunted in way of acknowledgement. With the visor on his helmet down, the mercenary had no way of learning his true identity, unless he ventured too close. Athos hesitantly shuffled closer.

The thug in Narian armor cocked his head and put his hands on his hips.

"Dragon got your tongue? Since when are you this quiet?"

Athos cursed silently to himself.

"Say something, old friend."

The goon turned to pull his axe free from its holder on his back, but as luck would have it, the axe snagged on one of the many leather straps holding the Narian armor in place. He took his eyes off of Athos for only a moment to see what his axe had snagged on.

A moment was all Athos needed.

As soon as he was no longer being watched, Athos pulled his green orix from its holder and with a quick flick of his wrist, snapped it open. Athos sighted his target and threw the weapon.

Disentangling the axe from the leather straps holding his stolen armor in place, the mercenary finally turned back around to glare at the impostor. He took a threatening step forward.

"What'd you do to Waxy? Where is he?"

By now the orix had completed its journey around the buildings and was on a return course. The air whistled softly as the orix spun by, causing Rahygren's man to look up in confusion. Athos couldn't have timed it any better. The orix collided with the golden plumed helmet the henchman was wearing and knocked him out. The unconscious dwarf fell forward, landing on his knees. However, he didn't fall forward, as the armor propped the unconscious dwarf up within the suit.

Letting his ears guide him through the city, Athos finally returned to the palace door and noted, with dismay, that the door hadn't been sealed. He jumped over the mangled remains of the chair wedging the huge door open and ventured inside, weapons at the ready. Thanks to the gold chain embedded in the walls, he was able to see the fresh sets of tracks on the dusty floor, and they all led in the same direction: northeast.

Having long forgotten how many hallways and empty chambers he passed through, he continued to follow the loud buzzing. Every step closer seemed to make the buzzing louder, until Athos stopped to tear off a couple of small pieces of his undershirt and stuff them into his ears. He could still hear the buzzing, but at least now it didn't feel like the sounds were trying to implode his skull.

He crept down a long hallway and poked his head through the door. There was Rahygren and two of his henchmen. The three of them were huddled over a strange device sitting in a small cart.

Athos watched as first Rahygren spun a dial on the top of the machine one way, frowned at it, then spun it back the other direction. The mercenary, mimicking his boss, gingerly spun the dial closest to him. Rahygren frowned again and angrily batted the henchman's hand out of the way. In a desperate attempt to appear as though he knew what he was doing, Rahygren touched a small green button to the left of a gray cone. The device responded by vibrating uncontrollably, almost rattling itself right off the cart. The henchman, having witnessed his boss pressing the button, slapped his own hand on the button, silencing the machine instantly.

Rahygren was furious. "I know what I'm doing. Do you not remember me telling you that I've used this before? Don't touch *anything*!"

Seconds later the loud buzzing was back. The two of them both glanced disinterestedly at the raw gouge six feet high and several feet deep left in the wall by the pounding audio waves. Athos grunted. His friends must be hiding within the wall, and thankfully, they hadn't been found. Yet.

Rahygren spun a few more dials and powered the machine down. The level of carnage the disruptor had created was severe and it was only going to be a matter of time before the entire wall was rattled apart. If he was going to do something to save his friends, then now was the time to do it.

From just behind the open doorway, still hidden from sight, Athos removed the heavy ornate helmet from his head and stuck a finger in his ear. His ears were ringing. He eyed the device. It must generate strong audio signals, and thanks to the cone, it could be focused on one spot.

Athos slipped an orix out from its holder under his chest armor. He flicked it open and readied a throw. With his sights set on the back of Rahygren's head, Athos swung his arm back and prepared to strike him down when all hell broke loose. The section of wall just a few feet to the right of where Rahygren's device was targeting exploded outward, but in a geometrically perfect circle. Everything in the circle's path was flung violently backward, and that included Rahygren, his helper, and the device. Athos had barely enough time to duck back through the door when the blast reached him. He was thrown back against the wall and almost knocked out.

Blinking stars out of his vision, Athos rose painfully to his feet and gingerly poked his head back into the room. Rahygren and his follower were sprawled out on the ground, covered with bits of gray quartz and larger chunks of what used to be the wall. Once more the Narian armor kept its wearer safe as it absorbed the full power of the blast. Both were slowly stirring.

Athos quickly scanned the room as he looked for the disruptor. There it was. It was heavily damaged; shattered and several of the metal gears were dented. There was no way this device would be powering back up.

"Hold the hammer next to it again," a familiar voice was saying. "Charge it back up!"

Athos glanced at the circular opening in the wall.

"Tristofer, I'm a little busy here," Breslin snapped and surveyed the room. He clenched his teeth as he spotted Athos, thinking it was another of Rahygren's men.

Athos waved his arms back and forth, giving Breslin a thumbs up. Recognition flashed on Breslin's face as he nodded. Breslin hopped through the perfect circle that had been cut through the solid stone and motioned for the others to follow.

Right about then, one of the mercenaries regained full use of his senses and clambered noisily to his feet. He spotted Breslin and instantly reached for his belt, pulling a small object off in the process. The object was twisted this way and that before it was finally thrown straight at Breslin and his companions.

Breslin, for his part, had spotted the object as it was thrown and correctly guessed that it was another artificial boulder. Sure enough, the boulder rapidly expanded its size in midair as it hurdled toward them. As before, Breslin stood his ground and gripped the power hammer tightly, waiting for the opportune moment to strike at the metal boulder.

There was a loud clang as Breslin's hammer made contact. The synthetic Narian boulder instantly reversed course and flew backward on a direct trajectory back to its original thrower. The shock wave that the impact generated swept through the room, knocking over anyone who wasn't wearing Narian armor. Those that were wearing the special armor were knocked backward a few paces but stayed upright.

The boulder bounced once on the ground and was instantly airborne again, sweeping the henchman along with it. Together they smashed into the back wall, punching a hole straight through to the hallway beyond. Looking through the new doorway they could all see the boulder lodged in the next wall. Below the boulder were two boots sticking out of the rubble. The mercenary was alive, but unable to move as the artificial boulder was pinning his arms to his chest. Not far away was a second pair of boots, also pinned to the ground by several hundred pounds of stone.

Rahygren regained his feet. A frantic look around confirmed his henchmen were gone and he was on his own. Cursing profoundly, he started toward the door when he saw Athos hurrying to intercept him, but thanks to the bulkiness of the armor, wouldn't make it in time. Thinking Athos was Waxrobbe, Rahygren started to smile that smug smile of his when he finally caught sight of his backup's unprotected head. Rahygren's eyes widened with disbelief as he watched the impostor reach up under his breastplate and pull out two long flat metal bars, one green and the other gold. The smile melted right off his face.

Rahygren did the only sensible thing he could think of. He fled.

Tristofer finally appeared in the freshly cut circular

doorway and hopped over.

"We did it! We won!"

"The hell we have!" a shrill voice exclaimed, catching everyone's attention. "Stop him! Catch him! Hurry!"

Everyone turned to stare uncomprehendingly at Kasnar. The tiny little dwarf had a distraught look on his face and looked as though he was going to keel over at any moment. Concerned, Athos approached and laid a hand on Kasnar's shoulder.

"Are you alright? Perhaps you should —"

Athos never had a chance to finish his sentence as Kasnar cocked an arm and smacked him on the back of his head. If Athos had been wearing a helmet, it would have undoubtedly flown off his head. Kasnar climbed up Athos' back to get to his harness. Remembering that Athos had removed it when he had lured the guard away from the palace door, Kasnar abandoned his attempt to climb Athos and instead latched on to Venk and climbed up his back. Once the protective leather straps were once more holding him in place, he gripped Venk's shoulders tightly and gave Venk's shoulders as fierce of a shake as he could muster.

"Hurry! Run! You've got the arrow shooter. If you get the opportunity, *use it!*"

Venk dangerously eyed his brother as Athos began coughing in an attempt to hide his laughter.

"Why do we pursue, grandfather?" Breslin wanted to know. "Now we can leave unhindered. We can go home. You can go home."

"Not yet we can't!" Kasnar insisted. The old man peered intently at the five of them shuffling uneasily from foot to foot. "Do you think small toys are the only weapons to be found down here? Larger, deadlier devices exist that make what you've seen thus far seem like toys. Most importantly, if Rahygren makes it back to Bykram first he'll report us as being the looters responsible for desecrating this city!"

It was suddenly so quiet that a simple chirp from a kyte would have echoed thunderously throughout the room. Breslin and the others nervously eyed each other.

"He wouldn't," Breslin began.

"He can and he will!" Kasnar confirmed. "Now run, boy!"

Breslin took off as though he had been shot out of a trebuchet. The others were right on his heel. Athos had stopped to let Lukas climb up on his back.

"Don't let go, boy," Athos warned as he sprinted after the others.

"Which way would he have gone, grandfather?" Breslin called out from the front of the procession.

Kasnar thunked Venk on his helmet and urged him to run faster.

"Get me up there next to my grandson. I can't hear him. Hurry!"

Venk's curse was lost amidst his wheezes as he doubled his efforts to catch up to Breslin.

"Through there," Kasnar pointed, singling out a long narrow hallway that was heading away from the king's private chambers.

Breslin angled left and ran toward the illuminated hallway, realizing that following Rahygren through this maze of corridors and hallways was much easier than anticipated. Whatever route Rahygren took, the gold chains would light the way.

Following the illuminated corridor led them to a courtyard with doorways in all directions. Quiet and serene, nestled safely within the palace, Venk figured this courtyard must have been used by the king himself. A commotion just ahead snapped his head up and he watched Breslin disappear through the second doorway on the left. Holding his aching side, Venk ran for the door before the crotchety old timer on his back could figure out something else to voice his displeasure.

"What's through here?" Venk wheezed out.

"No idea."

"Wh-what? H-how is it you don't kn-know?"

"You should exercise more. You sound like you're ready to pass out."

"Y-you c-can g-go … g-go …"

"Save your breath, young Venk. You were aware that I was locked up for most of the time?"

Venk nodded. "Y-you saw the h-hidden armory door in the king's r-room. Y-you were l-let out."

When no comment was forthcoming from his rider, Venk turned his head to see for himself what Kasnar was doing. He came to a stop so he could catch his breath.

"You're right, of course," Kasnar admitted. "There were times that I … what are you doing? Don't stop now! Keep going!"

"Ugh."

"As I was saying, there were times when I was allowed out. Rahygren knew that the more knowledge I had at my disposal, the more apt I was to discover the secrets of the armor's impenetrability. I was escorted to the library so many times that I started memorizing the layout of the city every time I left the palace."

"The p-palace," Venk groaned. "Know it w-well?"

"Better than most," Kasnar replied.

"What … is … Rahygren after?"

Kasnar sighed and suppressed a shudder. "If only you knew some of the advances the Narians made. As the value of their armor continued to increase, they were forced to come up with ways to protect themselves. And let me tell you, the Narians were a very creative people. More and more powerful weapons were created. Some could utilize sounds to shatter stone, as you have unfortunately witnessed. Thankfully our own tone disruptor was a newer model than what Rahygren had. Breslin only had to hold his hammer next to it for the helix to power the device."

"How did you know it'd do that?" Venk asked. His lungs felt like they were on fire.

"I didn't. I saw several lights appear on the device whenever Breslin neared. It didn't take a genius to figure out the disruptor needed a power source. The power hammer had a helix; therefore, it had a power source."

They rounded a corner and came to a halt when they saw Breslin squatting next to an open doorway. He held up his hand then put a finger to his lips. He silently pointed through the door and mouthed 'Rahygren'.

Venk nodded. He automatically reached behind his head to grab his crossbow but instead punched Kasnar in the eye. Venk sighed and waited for the inevitable. Three seconds later, after the shock had worn off, Kasnar pulled himself halfway out of the harness and leaned forward to better glare at his steed. Giving Venk a look which clearly said they would be revisiting this particular argument in the not-so-distant future, he lowered himself back into his harness and waited.

Breslin motioned Venk over and kept a finger to his lips. He forked his fingers at his eyes and then pointed into the room. Venk slowly leaned forward to look in. It was another of the security checkpoints, and this door wasn't closed, it was open. More specifically, it was wedged open much the same as the palace door had been. Rahygren was doing his best to dislodge whatever he had used to prop the door open, and just like they had experienced earlier, the crumpled object refused to cooperate. Breslin gripped the power hammer in his right hand and held his red axe with his left.

"We end this," Breslin softly told Venk. His eyes widened as he saw that the two of them were alone. "Where's Athos and Lukas? Where's Tristofer?"

"Athos tripped while carrying Lukas and went down, taking Tristofer with them. I saw them. They're fine. They should be here at any minute."

Breslin tiptoed into the room while Venk and Kasnar watched quietly from the doorway. This was too easy. Rahygren was so busy trying to pull whatever it was he had crammed in between the door and frame that he never noticed Breslin silently approaching from behind. Just in case things went wrong, Venk pulled the handheld arrow shooter from his belt and held it tightly in both hands.

Unfortunately, this was the time that his brother and his son arrived, followed closely by the scholar. Wheezing loudly, Tristofer coughed noisily. Rahygren, alerted to their presence, spun around and reacted instantly. Their adversary unclipped something from his right forearm and pointed it straight at Breslin.

The device belched out a large, gray mass and as it flew toward Breslin it rapidly spread out. It was a net! Breslin had seen Rahygren fire the weapon and had instantly dropped to the ground. Unfortunately for Venk and Kasnar, they were directly in the line of fire.

The net hit them square on, and before Venk could let a choice profanity fly, or fire a shot from his arrow shooter, he and Kasnar found themselves completely immobilized as the ends of the net burrowed deep into the surrounding stone and held them tight.

"Is it me or is this net getting tighter?" Kasnar suddenly asked, worry was evident in his tone. The wizened little fellow had crouched down in his harness, which brought his head down below Venk's shoulders. The two of them were pressed tightly against one another, and with the net continuing to constrict around them, found themselves being forcibly flattened against the wall.

"Quick, cut them loose!" Athos snapped to Tristofer as he whipped out a dagger. He grabbed one of the strands and swiped his knife across it, expecting the net to part right down the middle. It didn't.

"My dagger is ineffective!" Tristofer cried. He was raking his dagger against the strands and might as well have been trying to cut through solid steel.

Breslin regained his feet and turned to look back through the doorway at his companions. He saw Athos frantically sawing away at the net while Tristofer searched through his possessions for something that would be successful in freeing his friends. A commotion started just to the left, causing Breslin to look back at Venk. The metal wrist band, given to them by Kasnar, had activated. Miniature metal squares unfolded from the metal bracelet and snapped into position, forming the large metal square he had seen earlier during the demonstration with Tristofer. Thankfully the net's constrictions were thwarted by the large plate of Narian metal which bowed down the middle but refused to break. The net ground to a halt and held them helplessly against the wall.

By this time Rahygren had managed to dislodge whatever it was that had prevented the door from closing and hurried through.

"We're fine!" Venk called out to Breslin. "Get after him! Athos, go with him."

"I have to look after Lukas," Athos protested, casting a worried glance at his nephew. "I cannot leave an underling alone in the —"

"I'll look after him," Tristofer calmly told him. "Leave this net to me. Go help Breslin."

With a final look at his immobilized brother, Athos ran toward the sealed door just as Breslin held the hammer up to the jewel. The door creaked open.

"Stop him at all costs!" Kasnar shouted to them.

Both of them nodded and disappeared through the door.

"Another hallway," Breslin muttered crossly. "Who would have imagined it?"

"Where do you think we are?" Athos whispered.

"Maybe a barracks of some sort?" Breslin suggested. He peered closely at the large hall and looked worriedly at his companion. With a hall such as this, and since it was already illuminated, there was no telling which door Rahygren might be hiding behind.

"What now?" Athos wanted to know. "There are doors everywhere. He could be hiding in any of those rooms. How do we know where to look?"

Breslin pointed up at the ceiling. "See the chains up there? They're already lit. That would indicate Rahygren has passed by. As long as the hallway is lit, we move forward."

Athos grunted in acknowledgement.

Breslin counted sixty doors, thirty on each side, before they finally rounded a corner and saw that the lights in the hall had faded to darkness in the distance.

"He's nearby," Breslin whispered. "Be ready."

"What do you think?" Athos asked. "Does he flee or is he trying to find a way to fight?"

Breslin thought for a moment. "Personally, I think he's looking for a weapon. The sensible thing to do is to flee, seeing how he knows he's now outnumbered. The problem is I can't imagine him wanting to give up the location of the city, not after all these years of taking what he wants and selling it to whomever will buy it. But what if there's a third option? What if one of these rooms has a secret passageway that leads out? If anyone would know of such a passage, it'd be him."

Athos shrugged. "What if there's a Narian princess behind one of those doors? What does it matter? Whether he fights or flees, we must find him. Period."

Inching forward, stopping only to cautiously poke their heads into each room, they worked their way toward the dark end of the hallway. As they were checking another one of the featureless square rooms, they both paused and looked at each other.

"Do you hear that, too?" Athos asked. He pointed toward the door. "It's coming from out there. What is it?"

Breslin's face had gone pale. He'd heard that noise before. It was one of the audio disruptors, like the one which had been used against them in the Narian king's private chambers! They had to get out of there! Breslin spun on his heel, grabbed Athos by his arm, and pulled him out of the room.

"What are you doing? We don't want to be out in the open like this! We should get back in…"

Athos trailed off as Rahygren appeared in a doorway about twenty feet away. He was holding another device, one that Breslin had instantly recognized. It was just like the device he had used to blast their way out of the hidden armory, and what was worse was the fact that this one was bigger. How had he powered it? Did he have one of the ruby whorls? He couldn't have or else he could have made it through the doors without worrying about propping them open. Maybe this one still had a charge?

Athos' speculation was cut short as Rahygren made a few adjustments on the machine, pointed it in his direction, and grinned maliciously at the two of them. The whine the device was emitting increased in volume and began rising in pitch. Breslin was mesmerized as waves of distorted air began to appear over the machine, much like the distortion one would see from heat waves over a fire.

Rahygren smiled evilly as he held out his index finger, pointed it down, and jabbed the machine with it, presumably over that which triggers the device. At the same time, both arm bands being worn by Breslin and Athos activated, and less than a second later had expanded to its full size. Holding his left arm up to receive the brunt of the audio waves, Breslin stepped in front of Athos and braced his left arm with his right. Wave after wave of tonal distortions slammed into him, shoving him backward along the stony floor.

Much to Rahygren's chagrin, the Narian shield refused to buckle under the brutal assault. Such was the power of the device that it shoved Breslin backward, into Athos, and then pushed the two of them into the closest room.

Once the concentrated sound waves hit the tiny confines of the small square room, the walls began to crumble. Huge chunks of stone broke free from the walls and crashed to the ground, narrowly missing Breslin and Athos, who were still crouching behind their protective metal shields. Breslin was trying to brace the shield with his body to free up his right hand to get to his hammer when Rahygren suddenly aimed the device at the ceiling.

The ceiling, already weakened by the destruction of several load bearing walls, broke apart and collapsed, burying Breslin and Athos under tons of rubble. Rahygren screamed with triumph and shut the machine off, pulling a set of earplugs out of his ears in the process. When the whine finally died down and the air cleared, Rahygren surveyed his handiwork.

"To think you actually had me worried." Rahygren carelessly let the device fall to the ground. "Good thing I still had a few of these tonal disruptors, as our friend Kasnar calls them."

Rahygren climbed to the top of a particularly large boulder and sat down on it as though he didn't have a care in the world.

"Every hundred or so years someone manages to find my city. I guess I was due. Your little group are the first visitors I've had in about one hundred fifty years. I was starting to think people had given up trying to find Nar. Well, one can hope, can't they?"

Rahygren looked down at the large pile of rubble and kicked a small stone away from the rock he was sitting on.

"I wonder how you people managed to find your way here. How did you get through the sealed doors? It must have something to do with that hammer. To think you made it all the way here only to fail now. I pity you. So let's talk about that hammer. How in the world did you find an intact power hammer? Pah. It matters not. The hammer belongs to me now."

"Can you move?" Athos whispered to Breslin.

"No," Breslin whispered back. "I can barely breathe."

Athos tried to shift his weight to his hip so that he could free up his arm, but couldn't move an inch.

"Good thing you put that armor on," Breslin whispered. "You'd be flatter than a piece of parchment right now if you hadn't."

Above them, barely distinguishable through the broken rocks piled over them, they could hear Rahygren prattle on and on about how he was going to claim the hammer as his own, how he now had access to every part of the city and the palace thanks to the power of the helix embedded in the hammer. All thanks to their wonderful gift of the power hammer.

"How do we get out of here?" Athos growled. "I need to personally shut him up."

"I can't feel the hammer anymore," Breslin realized. "It's not there! Of all the infernal luck!"

Athos grunted from somewhere on his left.

"I have more leverage than you, I think."

Breslin heard a slight scraping sound.

"I can move my right arm," Athos told him in hushed tones. "Not far, but I can feel around a bit."

Breslin heard more shuffling and scrapes as Athos forced his right arm to slide underneath a giant boulder that was sitting partially on his legs. Thanks to the armor, the massive stone wasn't quite sitting flat upon the ground. A little more questing with his arm revealed a very welcoming touch. He could feel the tip of a wooden handle. It was the hammer!

"I can feel it!" Athos whispered excitedly. "I don't know how that's going to help us as I lack the leverage to move it. Maybe if I…"

Athos again tried to turn on his hip. This time he was partially successful as he was able to bring his right knee up closer to his chest. The rock pile shuffled noisily.

"Quiet, you fool!" Breslin hissed. But it was too late.

"You can't possibly still be alive under all of that," they heard Rahygren's voice say. "You should be crushed flat with all that tonnage on you."

Ignoring Rahygren, Athos shifted his knee again. This time the tip of his boot came into contact with the hammer's handle. Inexplicably, it slid along the ground as though it weighed no more than a normal tool.

"The hammer moved!" Athos all but shouted. "How? Why?"

"Do you think you can get it to me?"

"Let me try."

Athos gently straightened his leg and felt along the floor to see if he could feel it again. Ah. There it was, almost out of reach.

"You'd better hurry."

Athos hesitated. "Why?"

"He knows we're alive. I believe he's digging like mad to get to the hammer first."

Athos cursed and doubled his efforts. He managed to get his boot just under the head of the it.

"Ready? I'm going to try and kick it over to you."

"I'm ready. Do it!"

Athos kicked out as hard as he could, smashing his knee. All he managed to do was give the hammer the gentlest of nudges. Thankfully, that was all that it took. The handle was now resting just inside Breslin's left hand.

Breslin's fingers closed about the handle. He had just enough room to tap the underside of the huge rock. Dust and debris filtered down through the rock pile and into their eyes and mouths as the rock began to split. It was time to go all out. Breslin began hitting the rocks as hard as he could with his limited leverage. Soon, he could move both arms.

Finally, the great boulder shattered into a thousand smaller pieces. A stream of rocks, large and small, cascaded down the pile. Breslin finally stood. A single smash from the hammer pulverized the rest of the rocks and Athos was free.

Rahygren let out a string of profanities as he saw Breslin wielding the power hammer. He dove toward the door to scoop up his tonal disruptor. Before he could activate the device, though, Breslin threw the hammer straight at it and watched with satisfaction as the hammer smashed the device out of Rahygren's hands and sailed through the open doorway. Rahygren screamed with triumph as he saw the power hammer resting up against the wall amidst pieces of his disruptor.

"You stupid fools! Now you're finished!"

Rahygren tried to scoop the hammer up, startled to discover he could barely lift it. The red helix was no longer glowing. The clunky hammer felt as though it wanted to be on the ground. Rahygren bared his teeth as he fought to raise it into a defensive pose.

"Hey!"

The voice brought him back to reality. Rahygren snapped his gaze up to discover Athos standing directly before him, arm cocked. A split second later Athos' gauntleted fist smashed into his face, breaking Rahygren's nose and sending him straight into unconsciousness.

Athos smirked. "Easiest punch I've ever thrown."

Breslin pulled the hammer from Rahygren's limp grasp. Sliding it back into place on his belt, he looked over at his companion and smiled.

"Got any rope?"

Chapter 14 — Joyful Homecomings

Can you believe it? It's simply incredible! Not only have I been welcomed back with open arms, but they want me to lead the team that'll properly excavate the city!"

Breslin gave the scholar a friendly smile.

"Does that mean you're staying in Bykram now? You're not returning with us?"

Tristofer gave Breslin an incredulous look. "What, and leave all this behind? Let someone else explore the city? Absolutely not. This is my home. Besides, they *need* me."

Father and son approached. Lukas smiled up at Tristofer.

"You're staying here?"

Tristofer nodded.

"I am. This is the biggest discovery in the history of our people. Someone has to oversee everything and who better than me?"

"Who indeed," Athos muttered with a chuckle.

Tristofer slapped a friendly hand on Athos' shoulder. When no crass remarks were forthcoming, Athos grinned and returned the gesture.

"What do you think will happen to the Delvehearths?" Venk asked Tristofer. "He needs to be held accountable for what he's done."

"He will be," a new voice chimed in.

Everyone turned to see Prixus, prominent council elder from Bykram, step through the doorway in the heart of the huge stump and out into the daylight. A long, steady stream of Kla Rehn poured out of their Topside entrance and gathered around their departing guests.

"Rahygren and his family have disgraced the Delvehearth name. All their misbegotten wealth has been confiscated. Their belongings will be auctioned off, with the proceeds going to the newly created Nar Restoration Committee, which Tristofer here will lead."

"I want to apologize," Breslin began, bowing his head. "I deceived you into thinking we were looking for something besides Nar. I, we, figured you had deduced we were looking for the city and that's why you led us astray."

Prixus nodded. He patted his chest to quiet the clanking adornments on his robe.

"Think nothing of it, Master Breslin. As soon as I heard rumors that the map we gave you was incorrect, an investigation was launched. A woman by the name of Krisken was responsible for the false map. It is I who should be apologizing."

"Why would this Krisken person want to deceive us?" Breslin asked. "We don't even know her."

"Krisken Delvehearth," Prixus clarified. "Rahygren's wife. She is an assistant cartographer."

Breslin nodded. "She must have known what we were looking for and made certain we wouldn't find it."

"Aye. Therefore, she and her husband have been assigned to the Narian Restoration Committee and will be repairing the damage to the city. Half their wages will be channeled directly back to the NRC."

"Does that mean Tristofer will be their master?" Lukas

asked, raising a hand.

"It does, young lad," Prixus confirmed, an evil smile appearing on his face a moment later. Tristofer mirrored the smile.

Kasnar appeared, walking slowly toward them. Flanking him on either side were two orderlies wearing a healer's blue arm band. Breslin bowed his head.

"Grandfather, have you been cleared to travel?"

Kasnar's snow white head nodded.

"They tell me I'm strong enough to make the journey home. Where's my steed?"

Athos snorted with disgust. "I know you're not talking about me, old man."

Laughter echoed across the open glade. Everyone within earshot waited to see how Kasnar would respond.

"You're saying you'd force an old man to walk all the way back to Borahgg?"

Athos quickly turned to his brother. "He's not serious, is he?"

Venk shrugged. "Sounds like it."

"There's no way."

"Then you tell him," his brother told him, nodding in Kasnar's direction.

Athos looked at the frail wrinkled dwarf's face and swallowed nervously. Kasnar burst out laughing.

"Fear not, Master Athos. I do believe another mode of transportation is at our disposal."

"You mean you're not riding on my back? Thank the maker."

"Are you quite finished with your complaining?" a loud, deep voice asked.

Everyone jumped to attention and automatically looked around. A huge shadow was cast over the area as a giant red dragon, concealed behind a row of trees, rose to his feet and spread his wings. Several of the more cautious dwarves started inching back toward Bykram's subterranean entrance.

Rhamalli set something down onto the soft grass before them. Something big. It was the basket. Athos let out an uncharacteristic whoop of excitement. Puzzled, Venk turned to his brother.

"You hate to fly. Why in the world would you be excited about experiencing that terror again?"

"Are you daft, brother? It means we won't be walking!"

Venk silenced his objections as he thought about being carried all the way back to Lake Raehón and its valley. That would save them days of travelling on foot! Suddenly his feet and his back were feeling much better. It was a shame that his stomach wasn't.

Waving goodbye to their friends, Breslin and his companions sat down on the floor of the basket and screwed their eyes shut again. Lukas and Kasnar were the only two who not only kept their eyes open for the duration of the flight, but also seemed to be unaffected by the basket's nausea-inducing swaying. On and on they chatted, covering subjects as diverse as jewel cutting and how to best scare one's sibling.

Five hours later Rhamalli informed them that he was approaching the valley. Descending through the clouds, they each gasped with shock as the cool mists coated them with dew. Breslin and the others still refused to open their eyes.

Once they were finally standing back on terra firma, they bade the dragon farewell and made for the closest entrance, one of the large boulders scattered across the valley floor. Activating the hidden switch, the boulder opened to reveal a long, dark staircase leading down. Whistling merrily, they descended the stairs, with Breslin leading, followed by Lukas, Venk, Kasnar, and Athos.

"Do we let them know we're back?" Venk asked Breslin as soon as they emerged into Borahgg's cavern.

Breslin looked down at the glowing circular plate and briefly contemplated dropping his axe handle on the plate so that they could let everyone know they had visitors. But, since he was quite certain his father had no idea that *his* father was still alive, he opted for silence.

"Looking to surprise Maelnar, eh?" Athos correctly guessed. "Excellent!"

Breslin grinned back at him. "My father is going to go into hysterics. That is something I just *have* to see!"

"What do you think he'll do?" Kasnar worriedly asked.

"It's been so long since I've seen him."

"Fear not, grandfather," Breslin assured him. "I know he'll be at a loss for words!"

Breslin led them through the city, pausing only long enough to answer questions his grandfather asked. Not seeing his home city for more than eight centuries was bound to generate a question or two. Kasnar wanted to know about everything. Who was on the Council? How large had Borahgg grown? What types of trade existed between the other cities? Or the humans?

Kasnar was rendered speechless when he learned that the newest allies to his people were the dragons. How long ago had that happened? What must have transpired to bring about an allegiance with the wyverians? He had missed so much he could only hope he'd live long enough to get caught up.

They approached the center of the city and headed straight toward the largest building, one with a white domed room spanning the entire structure. Both of the guards at the main double doors recognized Breslin and leapt to attention. They hurriedly opened the doors and waved the group through. Pushing by curious onlookers, Breslin headed straight toward the large auditorium reserved for Council use. Hearing a disturbance behind him, he glanced backward and saw a large procession was now trailing his own, all curious to see what was going on.

There, sitting in the front row before the black dais typically reserved for the current speaker, was his father, chatting with the elder to his right. As soon as Breslin brought the procession to a stop, he watched his father look up and make eye contact. Maelnar rose to his feet.

"My son, you're back! I had no idea you had returned! Were you successful?"

Breslin pulled the power hammer from his belt and set it down on the closest table, directly on its head in the traditional Narian upside down manner. He rotated the hammer so that his father could see the helix glowing brightly on the side.

Maelnar's eyes widened. There was a collective gasp of astonishment as the elders spotted the magical piece.

"A Narian power hammer. Wizards be damned! Did you

find Nar?"

Breslin nodded. "We found more than that, father. There's someone here you need to see."

The four dwarves stepped aside to reveal Kasnar. The ancient fellow had his hands clasped behind his back, a huge smile on his face.

Maelnar seemed puzzled. Then recognition dawned. "Father?"

Kasnar held out his arms. "Hello, boy. It's been a long time."

"Father? I don't understand. Where have you … why are you…"

"Still alive?" Kasnar chuckled, finishing his son's sentence. "It's easy. I had to see you again. And your mother. I'm told she's still alive."

Maelnar slowly nodded.

"Aye, mother is alive. She thinks … father, she thinks you're dead. I thought you were dead!"

"I know this is a lot to take in, my boy, and I'll be more than happy to explain. All in good time. Please, I must see your mother. Can you tell me how I can find her?"

Breslin eyed his father. Maelnar's mouth was open, but nothing came out.

"He's done nothing but speak of how he wished to see the two of you again," Breslin softly told his father. "Is grandmother home?"

"She's here," Maelnar whispered.

Breslin leaned forward. "Sorry? What was that?"

"Mother is here today. Neika is the guest of honor for the annual convention of educators. She's been a teacher ever since father vanished."

"She always did enjoy working with children," Kasnar noted with a smile.

"Father, this is incredible! She's not going to believe this. Mother is going to —"

"Have conniptions?" Breslin asked, smiling.

Maelnar nodded. "Undoubtedly."

"That's what I said about you," his son informed him. "Where is she? Can you send for her?"

"She's across the hall. Just a moment."

Maelnar beckoned to one of his underling assistants. He scribbled a note and handed it to the young boy.

"Give this to Neika. Do you know who that is?"

The boy nodded eagerly.

"Excellent."

Maelnar handed the underling the folded message. The boy instantly darted off through the open doors. He turned back to his father and shook his head in disbelief.

"I have so many questions, Father."

"I know you do, boy, and now I have nothing but time to answer anything you want to know."

"Have you been in Nar?"

"For almost the entire time I was gone, aye."

"Were you there willingly?"

Kasnar shook his head. "No."

"Prisoner?"

"Aye."

Maelnar's face darkened. "Who held you against your will?"

Breslin placed his hand on his father's shoulder. "He's already been dealt with."

The underling ran back into the room and sheepishly handed Maelnar another note. Maelnar looked around.

"Where is she?"

"She's not coming," the boy all but whispered.

Baffled, Maelnar opened the note to read his mother's response.

I am preoccupied. I will be there when I can.

For the first time Maelnar noticed that the entire auditorium was on its feet and was watching intently. He faced the other members of the Council and bowed.

"Fellow Elders, I'm sorry, but I have to go."

"No explanations necessary," one elder told him, waving him off. "Your family needs you. Go."

Maelnar nodded appreciatively and hurried to his father's side. Kasnar gratefully took his son's arm and left the way they had come.

"Someone want to take this thing?" Athos called out, pointing at the power hammer.

"Grab it for me, will you?" Breslin called back.

"Grab it for me, will you?" Athos mocked, in a falsetto. "He knows I have no Narian blood in me."

Gritting his teeth, Athos picked the hammer up and struggled to catch up to his brother. Venk was kind enough to take a turn at lugging the heavy tool along while they all headed toward the second auditorium where the conference of educators was in full swing. Venk and Athos both noticed that the entire Council had abandoned their session and had elected to follow Maelnar and his father. Evidently, word of Kasnar's return was spreading like wildfire.

The procession came to a halt as a woman's stern voice could be heard.

"I told you that I'd be there just as soon as I could."

"Mother, I have some news that all of you may want to hear."

The auditorium went silent.

"Nar has been found."

Cries of astonishment sounded immediately. A dozen different conversations erupted. His mother, as frail and wrinkled as his father, smiled tenderly at him.

"I know you've had an interest in Nar for quite some time," his mother began.

"Mother, I hate to interrupt you," Maelnar began, "but…"

"You've already interrupted me," Neika told him, interrupting her own son. "Twice now."

Maelnar swallowed. "Mother, there's someone here that's been waiting a long time to see you again."

Neika's wrinkled hand touched a young female underling's arm to get her attention.

"Do I have any more appointments today?"

"No, my lady," her personal assistant told her.

"Have I missed any appointments today?"

"No, my lady."

His mother tilted her head and looked up at her son. "Are

you sure? Who?"

"Me."

Kasnar stepped out from behind his son and approached his wife. To Kasnar, she looked as though she hadn't aged a day. Neika gasped with shock as she instantly recognized her dear husband.

"Kasnar! Dear me, Kasnar! Can it be you? This is not a ruse?"

"It is I, my beloved. I've waited so long to see you!"

Neika slowly rose to her feet and embraced her husband. All conversation died off as everyone got to their feet and silently filed out of the meeting hall.

"Where have you been?" Neika managed to ask between her sobs.

"Nar."

The sobs stopped instantly and Neika pulled out of the hug. She looked at her husband and put her hands on her hips.

"Nar? Really? Is that the best story you can come up with?"

Breslin reached over to Athos to reclaim the power hammer. Once he had it, he plunked it down on the table next to his grandparents. Two women, waiting to leave the room, glanced backward at the loud noise. Both reacted with surprise as each recognized the significance of the tool.

"It's a power hammer!" one excitedly told the other.

"I'm sure they know, Trinidra," the woman's companion told her. "Let's leave them be."

"What's a power hammer?" Neika asked as her untrained eyes studied the strange hammer.

"It's what enabled me to rescue grandfather," Breslin told her.

Satisfied with her grandson's explanation, Neika returned to her husband's arms. Deciding his grandparents needed some alone time, Breslin turned toward the door and motioned for the others to follow suit. Maelnar turned to follow them as well.

"I'm surprised they let you keep the hammer," Athos told him once they made it outside.

"I have to make it available for study should someone want to see it," Breslin told him, "but otherwise, the hammer is mine."

"Just like your father's map," Venk said, remembering the tiny framed map in Maelnar's study.

"Aye."

A hand suddenly clasped Venk's shoulder. He looked over to see Maelnar standing beside him.

"Did you mean what you said on the way over here, lad?"

Venk nodded.

Athos looked at his brother, confusion evident on his face. "What did you say to him?"

"Then you'd better take your leave," Maelnar quietly told him. "There's much to be done, wouldn't you agree?"

Venk let out the breath he had been holding. He grinned. "I would."

"What needs to be done?" Athos asked, growing irritated for being ignored.

"Graun's loss is Borahgg's gain," came Maelnar's cryptic answer. "Welcome to the Kla Guur, lad."

"What did I miss here?" Athos asked, turning to stare at his brother.

"Master Venk has become the first apprentice I've had in many years," Maelnar answered. "I make the same offer to you, Master Athos, if you're willing."

Athos shook his head. "An apprentice. That's why he's so excited. I appreciate the offer, Master Maelnar, but I'm comfortable where I am. You have yourself a fine new apprentice. Just do me a favor and go easy on him. He can be a little slow at times."

Venk's smile vanished and he glared at his brother.

"You can go shove your …" Venk trailed off as he noticed his son watching him intently. "I mean, we'll miss you, too. Graun isn't that far from Borahgg. Besides, we'll always be Chanus, except now we'll have dual residency!"

"I'll see you in my workshop in a fortnight, Master Venk. Your training will begin once you and your family are settled."

Venk bowed low. "Thank you for everything."

Maelnar returned the bow. "My pleasure. Oh! Bring

Lukas. He might enjoy this, too."

Venk stared incredulously at his son. Lukas, who had overheard, stood there with his mouth hanging open.

As Maelnar turned around to watch his parents chatting like two lovesick teenagers, he heard Lukas tell his father that the house they were going to move into had to be large enough for two foundries: one for his father and one for his own.

Keep reading for a sneak peek of *Something Wyverian This Way Comes (Tales of Lentari #2)*! Now available!

Author's Note

Here we are again! I knew I was going to write a fourth book, but I wouldn't have imagined it would be set in Lentari. I can thank you, the fans, for that. If not for your encouragement, and your dedicated loyalty, *Lost City* would be, well, it would have remained lost. J

Lost City is the first story set in my new Tales of Lentari series. I've tried to write each of the Tales of Lentari books in such a way where they could be read out of turn, if you so choose. Yes, it is helpful to read them in order, but not necessary.

One of my favorite things to do is to chat with the fans. I absolutely love the fact that I can pose a question to the fans and within minutes, MINUTES, I have a response on Facebook, or I can pose questions on the blog and I'll get people giving me their opinions. I love knowing that if I ever get stumped for character names, or if I need some ideas for jhorun, or even dragon colors, I can ask and get a dozen different ideas in less than ten minutes.

So, the question I'm often asked now is, what's next? What's next for Lentari? Well, I can safely tell you guys that I've already started on the next story. The plot has already been mapped out and I've already broken it into chapters. I'll even tell you that the writing has begun. Want to know what it's about? Well, I won't give any spoilers away, but what I will tell you is that my favorite mythological creatures are going to be prominently featured. In fact, they will be protagonists in the next book. Dragons! This story is going to feature the dragons and our favorite wyverian couple, Pryllan and Kahvel!

I've only barely started working on this one but I can tell you that I'm enjoying it immensely so far. Dragons are huge. Dragons are powerful. The all-powerful Dragon Lord, Rinbok Intherer, is going to have to ask for help. Mwahahaha… LOL!

As I've said many times before, and will say again, I encourage any reader of my stories to leave reviews wherever they purchased the book(s). Good review, bad review, it doesn't matter. I know not everyone will enjoy the stories, but if you do like the book, please help me out and leave a review and let others know what you liked, or didn't like, if it comes to that. You won't ever hurt my feelings. I can take critique, both good and bad. How are you expected to grow, as a writer, if you ignore advice that your readers give you? So don't worry about what I think. The fact that you took a chance on this book speaks volumes!

Care to follow me online? This is where you can find me!

Official website/blog: www.AuthorJMPoole.com
Facebook: /BakkianChronicles

Feel free to stop by the blog and say hello!

If you'd like to follow the progress on the latest book I'm working on then I would encourage you to sign up for my newsletter so you'll never miss another book release, or contest, or any other bit of news that I pass along to the readers.

Thank you again for reading my book. Stay tuned! More adventures are on the way!

Jeffrey M. Poole

Fan Submissions

Thanks to all of you who submitted your suggestions when naming a fictional character. I had way more submissions than I did the first time I asked for help, so for that, thank you very much! Not all made it into the book, but I did use quite a few of them. Here are the ones I used:

Rhamalli — April Enos
Trindolyn, Jocastin, Rohath — TinaSings
Kovabel, Plukren — Scott Poe
Alpin, Kemxandra, Tristofer — Charlotte Dixon
Creedyn — Sallrw
Cantreya, Jurin, Prixus — Clawra
Samara, Timeki — Debbie Poole
Sabriella — Liz Moss
Bykram — Mark Berry
Elva — Christina P.
Rahygren, Krisken — Raymond Baker
Graemlin — Andrew Dyer
Zincoff, Neika — Nicki Jones
Oricfed Galfodin — Freddy Gandolfi
Bastion Delvehearth — Laura Matthews
Waxrobbe — Bob Terry
Trinidra — Brett Gable

For those who submitted some names which weren't used, rest assured they are still on my list of possible names which may show up in a future story! Thanks again for all the submissions!!

Continue the Tales of Lentari.
Here's your free sneak peek at Book 2
Turn the page!

Something Wyverian This Way Comes

Prologue

How many have fallen now, beloved? How many more must fall before he will do something? Surely he will seek help from our allies, or perhaps —"

"He will not seek help. You know him as well as I."

"What are we to do? We must do something. There is too much at stake!"

The huge golden dragon angled his long serpentine neck to look back at their nest. After a few moments, his mate came up next to him and gently twined her green neck with his. Together, they gazed into the dark recess of their cave.

"I cannot believe Rinbok will sit idly by while the rest of us suffer."

"Rinbok has become stricken."

Pryllan's eyes widened with surprise. This was not news she wanted to hear. She clicked her fangs together, worried.

"How long has he had it?"

"At least a month," her mate told her.

"We have allies! Why will he not prevail upon them for help? They will come to our aid. I know it!"

"He believes the time of the wyverian is over," Kahvel said softly.

Anger flared. Pryllan bared her fangs and growled. "Do you believe that?"

Kahvel's neck untwined itself from hers. His large golden head turned to regard her. "I want to believe he's wrong. So many of our brethren have succumbed, my love. So many! I begin to wonder if perhaps he's right."

Pryllan wrapped her long tail around her mate's body and shook him. "You cannot think like that. I do not agree with Rinbok Intherer about this. Neither should you."

Kahvel was silent for a few minutes before he responded. "No. For Pravara's sake, I refuse to."

"How strong is your resolve?"

"Why do you ask that?"

Pryllan's green slitted eyes narrowed. "Would you disobey

Rinbok's orders?"

Kahvel looked back at the dark opening of their cave and sighed.

"Aye, I would. Now explain yourself."

"We must consult the humans. They have a wizard. A wizard and his jhorun could help us."

Kahvel shook his head. "There's no way we can ask the human wizard for advice without word reaching their king. The human king would have to inform Rinbok for fear of jeopardizing the wyverian-human pact."

"What about Steve?"

Her mate's surprise was evident by the way his body gave a slight jerk and then froze. Slowly Kahvel's head turned to face her.

"That human is in another world. Besides, he is but one human man. What could he possibly do?"

"Whether he would be able to help us remains to be seen. However, if there is a chance that he might be able to do something, do you not want to try?"

Kahvel was silent for a full five minutes before answering.

"Very well, I am tired. I will stand watch. I know not how to initiate contact with a being in another world so I cannot offer any guidance on how to proceed."

Pryllan unfolded her wings from her back and stretched them out to their fullest potential. "Perhaps a dwarf would know. I remember hearing somewhere that one of the dwarves has contacted him before. I must find out which one."

"Be discreet," Kahvel warned. "Remember, we must not arouse Rinbok Intherer's suspicions. Confide in only those that you trust."

Pryllan nodded. Beating her wings, she lifted off the ground and ascended into the air. Gaining altitude, she dipped her right wing and started to turn east. Looking down at the rapidly passing grasslands of the valley, she briefly wondered how she should make contact with the dwarves. She knew of five entrances scattered throughout the valley. She knew there were more subterranean entrances hidden within the forest, but since she could not reasonably move her bulk in such close proximity to the heavy concentration of trees, she ignored them and instead focused on those that were more readily accessible.

As a member of the largest species of winged creatures that called Lentari home, she was more at peace in the wide-open skies with the wind under her wings than being stuck on the ground for an indeterminable amount of time. She couldn't imagine a worse fate for a dragon, than being grounded. That was why she must prevail. That was why she had to find the only human she had ever allowed to ride on her back. The problem was this particular human was in another world.

She knew of the portals, which, if the right portal key were used, would create a doorway to allow travel between the two worlds. She knew that the key to activate Steve's portal was kept in his world and since he and his mate had been responsible for the well-being of the young human prince, contact between the worlds was strictly monitored. Any contact with the other foreign world would have to be from their end, not from Lentari. Now with the threat to the human prince neutralized, both the human king and Steve kept keys so either side could initiate contact with the other. The problem with the portals, unfortunately, was that only a human would be able to fit through. There was no way a creature her size would be able to use it.

There was that instance last year when Sarah, Steve's wife, had accidentally teleported her, and her rider, back to his world. She had seen firsthand what Steve's home world looked like and quite frankly, he could have it. There were small metallic bugs scooting along the ground and loud speeding monsters flying through the air faster than she could go; none of it appealed to her. But, it was Steve's world, and he was her friend. She knew if she could just make contact with him, he'd be willing to help.

Choosing the most frequently used dwarven entrance, Pryllan landed quietly beside the large boulders and camouflaged herself. The last thing she needed was to have it look as though she was lying in ambush for a dwarf to go in or out of the hidden tunnel. Her mate had said she'd need to be discreet, so discreet she'd be.

Invoking her species natural ability to protect itself, her skin took on the coloring of the surrounding environment. In this manner, she could choose to look like either an enormous mound of grass, or she could become a group of the huge stones. She opted for the latter. Now, all an outsider would see would be a large jumble of stones sitting near the individual rock that hid the door leading down. All she had to do now was to wait.

Nearly an hour later she felt several tremors in the earth. Cracking open an eye to investigate her surroundings, she saw that the dwarf door was opening. The large boulder lifted easily off the ground and swung up into the air. A group of three dwarves, chatting merrily, emerged from the depths of the earth and started north while the door noiselessly swung back down and clicked into place.

"Pardon me."

All three dwarves whirled around and stared, disbelievingly, as a pile of nearby boulders sprouted eyes. Two green reptilian eyes blinked a few times as if they had just awoken after a long nap. Both eyes swiveled as they locked onto the dwarf that was nervously edging out in front.

"Who are you, dragon?" the lead dwarf exclaimed. "Why do you lie in wait for us? I thought there was a pact in place which prevented such atrocities from happening again."

"Be at ease," Pryllan told the dwarf as gently as she could. She let her camouflage drop and presented herself before the dwarf in her true form. "I come in peace. I'm looking for a dwarf."

Relaxing somewhat, the lead dwarf narrowed his eyes as he stared at the enormous green dragon.

"Who is it then? Who are you searching for?"

"I'm looking for, er, for…"

Pryllan hesitated as she realized she had completely forgotten the dwarf's name. Suddenly, and without explanation, it came to her.

"Breslin. I'm searching for Breslin. Do you know where I can find him?"

"How do you know Breslin?" one of the other two

dwarves suspiciously asked.

Facts started falling into place. Pryllan smiled. "We fought together during the battle with the human sorceress."

The dwarves' demeanor instantly reversed. Gone were the skeptical frowns and scowls.

"Why the ruddy hell didn't you say so before? Any friend of Breslin is a friend of ours! I am Loken. That's Argus on my left and on my right is Xaj."

"I am Pryllan."

"I thought as much," Loken nodded. "You're looking for Breslin? Well, if you're willing to wait, he's due Topside in just a few hours."

"That is acceptable," Pryllan told them.

Several hours later Pryllan was flying back to their nest. The news Breslin had given her hadn't been very encouraging. Apparently, there was a way to communicate with Steve in his home world, but that would work only if Steve was holding a special sword, while Breslin maintained physical contact with his own weapon. Holders of the Mythra weapons could then communicate telepathically; otherwise, someone would have to journey to Steve's world and ask him directly. Since she couldn't fit through the portal and didn't know who to trust when it came to her family, she hesitated in confiding with the dwarf. She liked Breslin well enough, but not enough to relay her concerns about her fellow dragons.

Returning to her nest, she approached Kahvel, who had encircled the nest with his body and had clamped his tail with his teeth. With as much stealth as she could afford, she crept over Kahvel's resting body and carefully curled up in their nest. She thought again of the importance of protecting those she cared about. Pryllan vowed to find a cure for whatever was plaguing her fellow dragons. She would not allow those under her care to come to harm.

Snuggling up next to Kahvel, basking in the warmth his body was generating, she fell asleep, pondering how to best contact her human friend.

ABOUT THE AUTHOR

Jeffrey M. Poole is a professional writer who writes in both the fantasy and mystery genres. His series are listed below. Jeffrey lives in picturesque Southern Oregon, with his wife, Giliane, and their Welsh Corgi, Kinsey. His interests include archery, astronomy, archaeology, scuba diving, collecting movies, collecting swords, and tinkering with any electronic gadget he can get his hands on.

In March, 2015, Jeffrey became a proud member of SFWA, the Science Fiction & Fantasy Writers of America! Jeffrey encourages readers to connect with him on Facebook (facebook.com/bakkianchronicles). Fans can also follow him online and sign up for his newsletter at: AuthorJMPoole.com.

BOOKS BY JEFFREY POOLE

Epic Fantasy
BAKKIAN CHRONICLES

The Prophecy

Insurrection

Amulet of Aria

Disneyland Debacle (short story)

Winter Wonderland (short story)

Epic Fantasy
TALES OF LENTARI

Lost City

Something Wyverian This Way Comes

A Portal for Your Thoughts

Thoughts for a Portal

Wizard in the Woods

Close Encounters of the Magical Kind

The Hunt for Red Oskorlisk (short story)

May the Fang be With You (Pirates trilogy #1)

The Hammer is Strong with This One (Pirates #2)

These are Not the Stones You're Looking For (Pirates #3)

Blast from the Past

DRAGONS OF ANDELA

Harness the Fire

Strike the Spark

Clear the Water*

Mystery
CORGI CASE FILES
Case of the One-Eyed Tiger
Case of the Fleet-Footed Mummy
Case of the Holiday Hijinks
Case of the Pilfered Pooches
Case of the Muffin Murders
Case of the Chatty Roadrunner
Case of the Highland House Haunting
Case of the Ostentatious Otters
Case of the Dysfunctional Daredevils
Case of the Abandoned Bones
Case of the Great Cranberry Caper
Case of the Shady Shamrock
Case of the Ragin' Cajun
Case of the Missing Marine
Case of the Stuttering Parrot
Case of the Rusty Sword
Case of the Secret Staircase (short story)
Case of the Unlucky Emperor
Case of the Ice Cream Crime